IN VITRO

M.J. KUHAR

Helping talented writers publish exceptional books

This is a work of fiction. References to real people, events, establishments, organizations, or locales are intended only to provide a sense of authenticity and are used fictitiously. All other characters, and all incidents and dialogue are drawn from the author's imagination and are not to be construed as real.

In Vitro
Copyright © 2026 M.J. Kuhar

Printed in the United States of America.
For information, address
Acorn Publishing, LLC
3943 Irvine Blvd. Ste. 218, Irvine, CA 92602

www.acornpublishingllc.com

Interior design by Kat Ross
Cover design by Damonza

ISBN-13: 979-8-88528-146-1 (paperback)
Library of Congress Control Number: 2025918909

DISCLAIMER

This story is a work of fiction. Names, characters, institutions, events, and incidents in this book are either the product of the author's imagination or used in a fictitious manner. Any resemblance to a person living or deceased is purely coincidental. This book is not intended to give medical advice or describe the process of in vitro fertilization in a comprehensive manner.

This book is dedicated to children who've come into the world through the miracle of in vitro fertilization. You are a blessing.

PROLOGUE

December 13, 2010: Breaking headline on the website of KTXR, Richmond, Virginia.

PREMIER FERTILITY CENTER SHUT DOWN AMID RUMORS INVOLVING POSSIBLE ILLEGAL USE OF DONOR SPERM

McArthur Fertility Institute, located in Richmond, Virginia, has been ordered to cease all operations by the Virginia Department of Health. Dr. Owen Hicks, the Institute's director, had his medical license suspended pending an investigation into the Institute's possible use of donor sperm without patient consent.

Earlier this morning, the university released a statement saying, "All fertility services, including in vitro fertilization, are temporarily suspended pending an investigation into possible inconsistencies regarding use of donor sperm. We continue to have our patients' safety and well-being as our primary focus." Additionally, KTXR learned that more than one hundred patients who became pregnant during the previous year simultaneously received registered letters referencing "possible inconsistencies" and were directed to call and arrange counseling and/or genetic testing as appropriate.

McArthur University recruited Dr. Hicks and his partner, Dr. Ajay

Kumar, to start the Institute twelve years ago. Boasting a pregnancy rate 30 percent higher than the industry norm, it has become a premier center in the field of infertility treatment and cutting-edge technologies.

Calls to McArthur were referred to their legal representative, Kirsten Clarke, of Powell, Siegel and Hill, LLC.

Tune into the ten o'clock news as KTXR interviews two couples who received treatment at McArthur and are currently pregnant and facing some tough decisions.

CHAPTER 1

TWO MONTHS EARLIER

The first time Evie and Leon Coleman entered the luxurious lobby of the McArthur Fertility Institute, she'd gone right to the fountain and gazed at the glittering coins littering the bottom. Beside her, Leon fished a shiny penny from his pocket and held it out to her. She'd tossed it toward the far side and watched her reflection in the disturbed water. Her large brown eyes stared back at her, shimmering with so much hope.

Now they'd been coming here for months in an increasingly desperate attempt to have a baby. They'd spent most of their meager savings on one IVF cycle. If this didn't work, they'd have to find another way. The procedure two weeks ago had been technically successful, and today they'd learn if they would finally become parents.

A solemn hush surrounded them. The outside noise became a mere whisper. Leon turned her toward him, smoothed her curly black hair with his big hands, and then enveloped her in his strong arms.

Standing outside the clinic's door, she drew in a breath,

momentarily closed her eyes for a quick prayer, and took Leon's hand. As she moved to open the door, he tugged her to a stop.

His tone was soft but urgent when he whispered, "Evie, I love you. No matter what."

Dr. Joyce Porter was running late. As she strode down the hall toward the conference room, her high heels clicked a nervous beat. She smiled, remembering how thrilled the young couple had been, plying her with questions about their barely begun pregnancy.

Evie and Leon Coleman were one of her favorite couples. The whole process had been hard for them, both financially and emotionally. She'd taken her time answering their questions until her assistant knocked on the door to let her know the four o'clock meeting was about to begin.

As she rushed along, she reminded herself why she loved her job.

She'd been with the Institute for two years, following ten long years of medical school, residency, and fellowship training. She'd turned down two offers from other university programs and accepted the clinical director position at McArthur because of its outstanding reputation as a place of cutting-edge research and treatment. It also offered her the most generous salary and benefit package, which was important given her $150,000 student debt.

Joyce would never admit it, except to her husband, but she often felt overwhelmed by the responsibilities and fast pace of the Institute. Some might call it imposter syndrome. At thirty-four years of age, she wondered if she would ever feel entirely comfortable in a place like McArthur, which pushed the boundaries of science in the service of advancing the field of reproductive medicine.

During medical school, she'd fallen in love with Obstetrics

and Gynecology, and chose to work in the evolving field of in vitro fertilization. Her mother, a staunch Roman Catholic, worried that most of what Joyce did each day was immoral. She told Joyce almost every time they spoke that her work was "definitely against the Church's teaching." But Joyce found great personal satisfaction in helping couples like Evie and Leon become parents.

Her heel skidded on the polished floor.

"Nice shoes, Dr. Porter," said one of the OB residents who was hurrying in the opposite direction.

She was embarrassed to admit, even to herself, that she wore high-heeled shoes to shore up her confidence. She was the youngest staff member, and at five foot two inches, she was also the shortest.

Inhaling a deep breath, she pushed quietly into the room and took a seat at the far end of the long conference table. Dr. Owen Hicks was a stickler for starting meetings on time, and he never missed an opportunity to chide a tardy team member. Along with often being rude and arrogant, he was particularly hard on female staff, so it was no surprise to Joyce when he paused mid-sentence and fixed her with a steely-eyed glare.

"You're late, Dr. Porter," he growled.

"Sorry, sir. I got behind in the clinic and—"

He waved a hand and cut her off. "I don't care. You should manage your time better, so you aren't always late."

Heat rose to Joyce's cheeks, and the rest of her colleagues averted their eyes. Only her friend Sally Cohen dared to look at her.

Hicks wore expensive tailored suits and striped ties, and always combed his thick gray hair back from his forehead. He wasn't a particularly tall man, and Joyce sometimes wondered if his aggressive manner was a result of insecurity about his height.

Over the next thirty minutes, he grilled each of the staff members. He was headed to a conference and was always testy when he had to be off site for any length of time. He refused to accept that the staff was capable. They resented his micro-managing but put up with his behavior to remain part of the prestigious institute.

Joyce caught Sally's glance as Hicks droned on, and they both did a slight eye roll. Despite being good friends and colleagues, they were polar opposites in many ways. Sally was outgoing and gregarious, always the life of the party. Joyce tended to be quieter and more introspective. Sally came from a big loud New York family, while Joyce and her younger brother had grown up in a small rural town in Maryland. Sally had warm brown eyes and a mane of luscious chestnut-brown hair. Joyce's eyes were a sapphire blue, and she wore her blond hair in a short messy bob.

After the stuffy new-faculty reception during Joyce's first week at McArthur, Sally had invited her for a drink. They'd bonded over gin and tonics, and since then, they'd made it a point to eat lunch together once a week and enjoy a glass of wine a few times a month.

One evening, after a second glass of wine, Sally told Joyce that no one at McArthur really liked Owen Hicks. They admired his work and the fact that his department was one of the highest revenue generators at the university but found him to be pompous and cold. The McArthur Fertility Institute had one of the highest pregnancy rates per cycle in the country, a fact he never failed to work into most conversations. His patented technique for embryo culture and ongoing research into cryopreservation of sperm and embryos made him famous internationally, and researchers from all over the world flocked to collaborate with his team.

Joyce squirmed in her seat and surreptitiously slipped off her shoe. Her feet were killing her. While massaging the ball of her sore foot, she thought about the research she would present next month in New Orleans. Although not nearly as prestigious as the Paris conference Hicks was attending, she was thrilled to have her article accepted for presentation and looked forward to participating on the speaker's panel. She had ambitions to someday become a famous speaker who was invited to travel the world.

Her daydreaming about New Orleans was interrupted when Hicks announced, "That's it. We're done. Dismissed."

The staff gathered their papers and swarmed toward the door.

"Dr. Porter," Hicks called before Joyce could follow her coworkers. "I need a word with you. Walk with me to my office."

In the small park across from the McArthur Institute, the bright afternoon sun illuminated cheerful rust and gold chrysanthemums in well-tended flower beds. Evie and Leon sat together on the ornamental bench, too excited to drive home. They couldn't stop smiling and exclaiming, "We're pregnant! We're going to have a baby!"

"Let's go out to dinner and celebrate," he suggested.

"Leon, we can't. We need to save our money for the next ultrasound. Dr. Porter said we'll be able to see the heartbeat in a few weeks." Evie impatiently pushed an errant strand of hair behind her ear. "Our health insurance didn't cover any of the IVF treatment. Without that grant program Dr. Porter suggested, I don't know how we could've afforded it. And don't forget we have a $2,000 deductible for the prenatal care and delivery."

"You worry too much." He sighed, but she could see in his face that he was worried too. Leon worked as a mechanic at their town's Ford dealership, and Evie was a receptionist for small family-owned insurance agency. Money was tight, and Leon hoped to keep their medical expenses to a minimum before the baby was born. As it was, they'd had to borrow from his parents and her sister.

"Maybe we'll have twins," she mused. "A boy and a girl."

Leon shook his head. "I want one healthy baby. That's all. And I don't care if it's a girl or a boy."

"Should we tell anyone?"

He grasped her hand in his large calloused one and kissed her palm. "Not today. Let's keep it quiet for now. You heard Dr. Porter. It's still really early."

"But she also said my hormone levels are excellent."

"I know, Evie, but I don't want to jinx it." He pointed to her abdomen. "How do you feel? Can you tell?"

She rubbed the area with slow circles. "Not really. I feel the same as before, a little bloated and sore." She turned to him beaming. "Oh Leon, I can't wait to feel the baby move."

"But she said that's months away."

"I know. But it's all I can think about."

Leon put his arm around Evie's waist and pulled her close. "You're going to be a great mom."

"And you're going to be a great dad," she said, hugging him back. "Now, I'm hungry. Let's get ice cream before that long drive home. Calcium is good for the baby, right?"

As they stood up, a tired-looking woman pushing a twin baby stroller walked by. Inside the stroller were two sleeping infants, each wearing identical pink hats.

Evie looked at Leon and grinned. "Maybe two scoops—in a waffle cone."

Joyce walked through the reception area and waved at Esmeralda. The administrative assistant offered an encouraging smile. As Joyce entered Hicks's private office, the heavy oak door swung closed, and a twinge of anxiety rolled through her. She looked through the tall, mullioned windows at the late afternoon sky before taking in the spacious interior. The room was large for a faculty office, reflecting the place of privilege its owner held in the university hierarchy. It was meant to be intimidating, and she had to admit the old-fashioned grandeur was quite effective.

Multiple diplomas lined the walls, along with awards for scientific achievements. Several pictures of Hicks and well-known scientists were prominently displayed. There was even a photo of two famous political figures with a smiling toddler. According to watercooler rumors, Hicks had helped them become pregnant.

Flashing back to her first time in this office, she realized she'd never felt comfortable with Hicks. At the time, she'd attributed her discomfort to the normal awe at meeting someone of his stature for the first time. While the reverence was long gone, the discomfort remained, and if anything, the feeling had intensified. At staff meetings, his gaze often lingered on her in an appraising manner, one which always made her look away. She tried not to be overly sensitive, but she suspected he singled her out more than others for daily criticism. She momentarily tightened her lips as she remembered his earlier cutting remark.

How unfair for him to call me out, she thought. *I'm only late when it's something important!*

Hicks settled into a leather wingback chair in the corner of the room like it was a throne and motioned for Joyce to sit on the adjacent couch. He looked her over with a gaze that felt predatory and sinister. For a moment, she imagined Hicks trying to kiss her and felt slightly sick.

Sinking onto the luxurious couch, she took a deep breath and told herself to stop being dramatic. But, unbidden, she remembered a previous late afternoon meeting. At the end of that meeting, Hicks had followed her to the door and his hand had brushed her hip. She'd been embarrassed and confused but had ignored the gesture and exited in a hurry.

Today, this sitting arrangement felt too intimate, their knees almost touching. She would have preferred it if he'd been seated behind his ostentatious desk, giving her plenty of distance.

"So, Dr. Porter," Hicks's gravelly voice cut into her thoughts.

"I understand you're not planning to attend the Paris conference."

"That's right. My paper was accepted for the Society of Reproductive Medicine conference in New Orleans next month. I don't want to be away too much while our patient load is so heavy. We have over thirty couples scheduled to begin IVF in the next four weeks, and you know—"

"Yes, I know," he interrupted. "But you have to understand that if your career is to advance, then you must make it a priority to attend these important meetings. I was looking forward to showing you Paris and introducing you to my esteemed colleagues. Who, by the way, will all be there." This last comment was emphasized with raised eyebrows and a stern look. "My wife doesn't enjoy these meetings anymore, so she stays home with our daughters. Since you won't be in Paris, I expect you to attend several events in New Orleans with me." As he spoke, his gaze traveled from her mouth to her breasts, then down her body. Finally, it rested on her legs which were crossed at the ankles. Joyce met his piercing hawk-like gaze and squeezed her knees closer together, wishing her pencil skirt was a little longer and a little less fitted. "Yes, well, I already have plans to attend the meeting with Dr. Cohen."

At this, Hicks's expression turned glacial. "Dr. Porter, I don't think you comprehend the importance of my continued support for your nascent academic career. I expect you to arrange your schedule to accompany me. Do you understand?"

Her face warmed and she looked away. She took a deep breath before answering, "Yes, sir, I'll do my best."

Rising from his chair, he held out his hand to her. She hesitantly gave him her own, and he squeezed it painfully. After holding it a moment too long, he commented, "See that you do."

As she rushed toward the exit, Hicks's hand again casually brushed along her lower back and then down to her hip. She flushed and refused to look at him as she strode away.

As Joyce left the office, she noticed Esmeralda was already

gone for the day. Looking outside at the lowering angle of the sun, she realized it must be close to 6:30. She pushed Owen Hicks from her mind and remembered her tai chi class started in a half hour, and she'd have to hustle to not be late. *Oh geez. Late again. Maybe Hicks is right. But there's always so much to do and not enough time in the day.*

Briefly, she wondered if she should skip class and head home. She was tired and her feet hurt from the killer heels. A glass of wine and some leftover take-out while catching up on her journal reading sounded like a better plan. But she reminded herself, she always felt calm and focused after class. Deciding it was absolutely worth it, she race-walked to her office to change into her uniform. If the traffic was light, she'd be right on time.

CHAPTER 2

Dr. Ajay Kumar, Director of the McArthur Institute's Reproductive Endocrine Lab, met up with Hicks while he was preparing to lock his office door.

"We have to talk," Kumar whispered as he pushed the door open and stepped inside.

Hicks looked at him with a curious gaze before following. "Go on," he said, noting that Kumar looked uncharacteristically agitated.

Kumar shut the outer office door. "Something is wrong with our sperm preservation process. You know how we always freeze some in case the husband can't provide a sample on the day of the retrieval? The last few vials of several different husbands' sperm have all been non-motile. Not one swimmer— just dead or quivering."

Hicks snorted dismissively. "Ajay, it isn't like we haven't had issues before. Figure out what's going on and fix it."

"I've been trying, but we have a substantial number of couples in cycle right now. I'm not sure what's going to happen in the next few weeks. And we're also having some problems with the embryos not properly developing after fertilization, so you can see that it's not one simple problem or fix. And we're almost out of the frozen samples we've banked for emergencies." Kumar paused, taking a nervous breath. "And of course, you're going out of town next week, again." This last statement ended in a long-suffering whine.

"Oh, for God's sake, Ajay! Stop complaining. You know what to do until the problem is fixed. Stay the course and keep those pregnancy rates up." With that admonition, Hicks pushed Kumar back into the hallway, slammed the heavy door, and marched off.

Joyce entered her office and changed into loose-fitting black tai chi pants and a long-sleeved tee emblazoned with the martial arts logo, taking care not to bang her elbow or knee in the cramped space. Unlike Hicks's office, hers was barely big enough for a desk, coat rack, and bookshelf. Her gaze rested on a picture of her husband, Bill, taken years ago when they'd been on their honeymoon in Hilton Head, South Carolina. He was wearing his favorite Pittsburgh Pirates ball cap. He looked tanned and fit and gazed at the camera with a confident smile.

Looking past the picture on her desk, she noticed the African violet that was growing lopsided toward the small window, seeking light. She shrugged into her coat and grabbed her tote, both recent brand-name finds at her favorite discount store. Stuffing the new tote with the monthly financial reports for the clinic and the latest *Journal of Reproductive Endocrinology*, she headed out the side door to the staff parking lot.

She waved at Dr. Ajay Kumar as he exited from the opposite side of the clinic, and he nodded distractedly as he opened the door of his older model sedan. She wondered about his late departure but figured his workload must be as overwhelming as hers.

Kumar was an enigma. After two years, she barely knew him. As the director of the Reproductive Endocrine Lab, he was tasked with overseeing all technical aspects of the in vitro process, which were vital to the program's success. Professionally, they got along, and Joyce found him pleasant but distant. He was a small man, dark and compact, who moved energetically and always seemed to be in a hurry.

Sally had told her he emigrated from India as a teen with his parents, both university professors, and attended college and graduate school in the United States. Kumar and Hicks had gone to the same medical school and had been recruited together to start the Institute. The Institute's success was attributed to the dedication and brilliance of their team, as well as the novel techniques they perfected for processing sperm and storing embryos.

She wondered if Kumar ever felt jealous, forever lost in the shadow of Hicks's oversize personality and success. After all, Hicks was the one who was asked to speak at international conferences, who wrote the oft-cited textbook, and who had the biggest office at the university, after the president.

Not my problem, she thought, as she threw her purse in the backseat, climbed into her well-loved Honda, and sped away.

Driving home after tai chi class, Joyce mentally reviewed her day. She savored the image of delight tinged with fragile hope in the faces of Leon and Evie. They had borrowed money to afford their IVF cycle despite the assistance they received from the university. The grant program, designed to help financially challenged patients, was something Joyce had proposed and fought for when she'd first arrived at McArthur. Hicks had been firmly against it, but with unexpected support from the university's president, who liked the optics of helping the needy, the McArthur Foundation agreed to fund the program for three years. She was thrilled Evie and Leon had applied. And then Hicks intruded into her thoughts.

She grudgingly admitted to herself that he was right about

her career. His support and introductions to important people in the field could indeed help her advance. She dreamed of becoming part of the "elite" inner academic circle, the ones who were invited to write articles and received plum speaker invitations.

But the man gave her the creeps. She needed to find a way to let him know that his insinuations and casual touches were unwelcome. Maybe she'd talk about it with Sally at their next lunch.

She wondered who else in the department might be able to help advance her career and thought about approaching Ajay Kumar. She considered Kumar and his team the magicians behind the curtain who deftly utilized modern technology that was merely dreamed about decades earlier.

If I can shadow him for a few days while Hicks is away, she thought, *maybe I'll have a better understanding about what actually happens in that lab.*

Ajay motored through the sluggish evening traffic with a scowl on his face. His meeting with Hicks had gone as expected, but he was tired of the stress and the expectation that they maintain their unusually high pregnancy rate. From the time they'd met in medical school, Hicks had been driven to exceed expectations, and he felt completely justified in using any means to achieve his ends.

Hicks was at the top of his game and had it all, power, prestige, and fame. Ajay realized he too enjoyed a measure of recognition from the success of the clinic, but the lion's share went to Owen Hicks.

And it always has, he thought resentfully. Once again, Hicks was traveling, all expenses paid, to an international conference, and Ajay was left behind, expected to solve all problems with quick discretion.

As he maneuvered through the evening traffic, Ajay ruminated about his own career. He had turned down several offers from other universities and even briefly considered returning to India with his family. However, he felt compelled to stay at McArthur because of his daughter. Riya was only five and had cerebral palsy. Her associated medical conditions required nearly constant care on the part of Nita, his wife.

Riya had a team of doctors, therapists, and caregivers who knew her. Overall, she was doing remarkably well. Last week, she'd contracted pneumonia and landed in the ICU, but the pediatric team quickly recognized the problem, and she was now back home.

I can't leave anytime soon. he thought. *It would be too hard on my family.*

Pulling into the driveway, Ajay realized he needed to watch his back. Hicks didn't understand that the current problems weren't going to be easily solved, and what they were doing to cover it up wasn't exactly ethical or legal. As the past had demonstrated, when anything went awry, Hicks had a way of pushing the responsibility off on others and emerging as the hero rather than the villain.

Turning off the car, Ajay gathered his thoughts while listening to the ticking of the cooling engine. Before opening the kitchen door, he pasted a smile on his face and pushed aside all nagging thoughts of work.

After entering with a confident stride, he leaned over to kiss his daughter, who was sitting at the table in her custom-made wheelchair. His wife, standing at the stove, was stirring a fragrant pot of vegetable curry. He gazed into her tired, loving eyes and enveloped her in a warm hug.

After finishing her leftover mandarin chicken, Joyce settled down in her small living room with a glass of wine. Her fat tabby, Mittens, vaulted into her lap. She called Bill, and he answered on the second ring. "Hi, it's me."

"Hey, sweetie, what's up?"

"Nothing much. I was late for my tai chi class. I really hate that! You know me, I'm the person who arrives three hours early at the airport, but today I couldn't keep up. Hicks even made a snide remark about it at our staff meeting."

"Hmm, sounds like there was a lot going on. But I do remember you being late for our first date," he teased.

"I wasn't late! You were early. Anyway, we're learning a new style. It even has some kicks and spins. Oh, and my favorite couple—the really cute ones who always have lots of questions —is pregnant. How about you?"

"Pretty routine day. I'm almost done with my Advanced Statistics class, thank goodness, and I met with my advisor. She has some good ideas for how I can establish a control group for my study."

As they chatted about the details of their days, Joyce realized how much she needed these phone calls. Although they'd made the decision together to live apart for a few years so each could pursue their dream career, she really missed him.

He'd been fortunate to land a spot in the Public Health and Policy doctoral program at Johns Hopkins. She counted the days until they would live together again in the same city and worried that he kept mentioning the possibility of a post-doc fellowship at the Center for Disease Control. Atlanta was a lot farther away from Richmond than Baltimore.

Talking to Bill daily kept her grounded, even though some evenings they only spoke for a few moments, each of them too exhausted from the stress of work or classes. Their nightly phone calls showed commitment to their marriage. They prioritized seeing each other every weekend, but that didn't always happen, especially if she was on call or Bill was on a research deadline.

"I'm really looking forward to this weekend," she said. "I've made reservations at our favorite bed and breakfast in Williamsburg. When do you think you can get there?"

"Well, I'll try to leave a little early, but you know the Friday traffic around DC can be a bear."

She pictured the new sexy silk pajamas she'd found on sale at Victoria's Secret. She really hoped Bill would leave his books and papers behind so they could sleep late, take long walks, and have plenty of sex. They hadn't been together in almost two weeks, and she wondered if he missed their physical intimacy as much as she did. She pictured them making love in a large four-poster bed in a candlelit room and felt a tingle of anticipation. The weekend couldn't come soon enough.

"So, what does the rest of your week look like?" he asked.

"Not too bad. I see patients in the afternoons, and Hicks leaves next week for Paris. He'll be gone for two weeks. Thank God!"

"Good news. That guy sounds like a jerk. I'm glad you won't have to put up with his nasty remarks for a while."

If only it was just nasty remarks, Joyce thought, but instead she said, "Everyone is looking forward to a little break. We are still crazy busy, but we all work better when he's not peering over our shoulders. I'm thinking of asking our IVF lab director if I can spend a few days with him learning the technical protocols."

"Sounds like a great idea. Okay, gotta run. Early seminar tomorrow morning, and I'm presenting."

"Good luck. Love you."

"Love you too. Bye."

Evie and Leon stood next to each other in their tiny bathroom, brushing their teeth over the single bowl sink. Earlier in the evening, they'd gone to the library and checked out several books on pregnancy and newborn care. Evie planned to stock up on yogurt, raisins, and lots of fiber-containing fruits and vegetables because she'd read that pregnant women sometimes got constipated. She wished she could afford organic, but produce was expensive.

She'd make an appointment with her local OB the next morning and transfer care in a couple of months. As much as she liked Dr. Porter, she was ready to go back to her doctor and feel like a "normal" expectant mother.

As they prepared for bed, their black-and-white rescue cat, Daisy, jumped on the comforter and prepared to settle in. Leon shooed her away.

"What are you doing?" Evie asked.

"Getting Daisy off the bed. Now that you're pregnant, she can't sleep up here."

"What do you mean? Why not?"

"Didn't you read that cats can carry some kind of germ that is bad for pregnancies—toxo something."

"Toxoplasmosis. Yes, I know about it. But, Leon, I won't get it from Daisy sleeping on the bed."

"I don't want to take any chances," he insisted.

She patted him on the arm before sitting down on the bed. "Great. That means *you'll* change the litter box every day, right?"

With a dramatic groan as he climbed in on the other side, he retorted, "Well, if I have to." He turned out the light and they snuggled together with Daisy at their feet. "Love you, Evie," he said, caressing her still flat abdomen, "and love you, baby boy or girl."

She sighed contentedly. "We love you too, Leon."

CHAPTER 3

Monday morning was dark and chilly, and Joyce moaned when the alarm buzzed at 5:35, hitting the snooze button for the second time. She nudged the cat off her feet and burrowed into the pillow for a few more moments of slumber.

With Hicks in Paris, she hoped the week would be more relaxed. Standing under a blistering hot shower, Joyce closed her eyes and let the water sluice over her shoulders, back, and pubis. She was a little sore from the weekend, and she smiled thinking about her time with Bill.

Maybe absence does make the heart grow fonder, she mused, happy the weekend getaway in Williamsburg had been everything she'd hoped. Their time together had felt like a second honeymoon. In between taking long walks to enjoy the fall sunshine and perusing the charming shops, much of the time had been spent in bed "making up for lost time," as Bill put it.

Joyce had arrived first at their bed and breakfast on Friday evening and spent an hour soaking in a bubble bath. After putting on her new lingerie and the luxurious robe she found hanging in the closet, she lit the scented candles thoughtfully provided by the innkeeper. They gave the room an intimate glow. The eiderdown comforter on the antique canopy bed was turned down and the pillows were fluffed. A bottle of their favorite cabernet was breathing, and she thought it all looked very romantic. She'd even sprinkled a few pink rose petals on the pillow, their floral scent reminding her of her wedding bouquet.

When Bill arrived much later, things got off to a rocky start. He was tired and irritable after battling the Friday evening rush-hour traffic, prolonged by a fender bender on the interstate. However, after emerging from the bathroom and finding Joyce in her red silk pajamas, her smile sultry and warm, his mood quickly improved.

As their lips crushed together, they reached out hungrily and immediately moved to the plush bed where their lovemaking was quick and urgent, sans tender caresses or romantic murmurings. Afterward, they shared the wine and devoured the gourmet cheeses, crackers, and olives Joyce had purchased from a nearby upscale epicurean shop.

"God, I've missed you," he murmured.

"Me too," she agreed. "How much longer do you think you'll have to stay in Baltimore?"

"Not too long. Maybe a year, year and a half at most."

Gently swirling the wine and admiring its legs, Joyce set the glass down before snuggling closer to Bill. "Any chance you could move to Richmond sooner to do the writing and commute weekly for your seminar?"

Looking annoyed, his eyebrows drawing together in a scowl, Bill jerked away and retorted, "Well, maybe. But Joyce, we've talked about this. I've explained I need to have all my data collected before I start writing. And that will take at least another year. Why do you keep bringing this up?"

"I know," she sighed, sorry she'd mentioned it and worried it might ruin their weekend. "But I really miss you, and so does the cat."

"Well, then," he teased, his mood improving. "I'll see if I can put a rush on things." With their previous loving intimacy restored, Bill pulled Joyce into his lap and began kissing her neck while his hands caressed her breasts. She leaned into him and stroked his cheek, then her lips found his, their conversation clearly over.

Joyce was jerked out of her romantic weekend reverie when the shower water began to cool. She turned the faucet off and reached for an oversized towel. While drying herself, her phone buzzed.

Oh no, she thought. *Too early. Not good.* Just as it was about to switch to voicemail, she answered breathlessly.

It was Dr. Ajay Kumar. "Dr. Porter, I have some bad news." After a long pause, he added in his soft lilting voice, "There are no viable embryos to transfer this morning."

"No!" Joyce exclaimed, closing her eyes and feeling slightly sick. "That can't be right. Everything was fine yesterday. You told me so last night. What happened?"

"I'm not sure," Kumar said, "but I was hoping you would notify the Goldschmidts and cancel the transfer. Maybe they won't want to make a long trip in for nothing."

"I'm sure they'll still want to come, and they'll have questions about what happened. And so do I! I'll need some kind of explanation by the time I see them later this morning."

"I'll get back to you after I check a few more things," Kumar promised.

Another thought struck Joyce, "Do we have to worry about the other procedures scheduled for later this week?"

"No, those should be fine."

"Good. I'd like to go over all the lab procedures with you as soon as possible. How about today after the staff meeting?"

Kumar hesitated. "All right," he finally said. "I'll get back to you once I've spoken with the weekend technician."

They hung up and Joyce dressed, choosing a comfortable corduroy skirt, a cozy cowl-neck sweater, and well-worn Frye boots. The cream-colored sweater and chocolate brown skirt complimented her fair skin. She smiled at herself in the mirror as she added whimsical ceramic cat earrings she'd purchased at a craft fair the previous autumn.

Sitting in the small apartment kitchen, a relic from the '70s with its ancient avocado- colored appliances, Joyce munched on a piece of toast and drank her French roast coffee. Even though money was tight, gourmet coffee was one small luxury she allowed herself. She figured she'd earned it, especially since she was driving an old Honda and shopping at discount clothing stores. She dreamed of the day when their student-loan debt was erased, and she and Bill were finally living in their first real home.

Sipping the fragrant coffee, Joyce considered how devastating Kumar's news would be to the Goldschmidts. She dreaded speaking with them. She struggled with this part of her job, but the emotional highs and lows were as much a part of the daily routine as were the patient consultations, ultrasounds, and surgeries. Sally often warned her about becoming too emotionally involved, and Joyce knew she was right. Still, it was hard not to become attached to couples during their treatment.

Gulping the last dregs of her coffee, Joyce donned her raincoat, shouldered her oversized tote stuffed with work, and headed off.

In Paris, Dr. Hicks was finishing an excellent lunch. He always enjoyed attending conferences in France, as the French considered the two-hour midday repast a mandatory part of conference events. While they weren't much on breakfast—a stale croissant and a miniature cup of coffee, lunch was always a memorable meal and included wine selected to complement each course. He had dined on an entrée of smoked herring with potatoes and roasted almonds, followed by *Le Plat Principal* burgundy beef Bourguignon with mashed potatoes and petite green beans. The *fromage,* featuring a selection of ripe local cheeses, was followed by the most exquisite crème brulé he'd ever tasted.

How civilized, he thought. *Wine with lunch.*

He wished Joyce Porter had come. Thinking about her made him pause and consider their last conversation. He'd thought she was ambitious and driven to move up in the academic world, and yet she didn't seem to understand how the game was played. He hoped she wouldn't continue to be so prudish.

He indulged in a quick but vivid fantasy of unbuttoning her blouse, unhooking her brassiere, and grasping her full breasts. Then he would bury his face in her cleavage before taking a firm nipple into his mouth and giving it a quick bite. She would perhaps struggle a bit, but that would make it even more satisfying. He thought she might be married, but since her husband lived in another city, he dismissed any concern.

Sipping the last of a fine dessert sauternes while barely listening to a colleague bloviate about his latest research, Hicks checked his phone when it chimed with a message. He scowled at the text from Kumar. He was sick and tired of Ajay's whining.

Hicks debated when to return the call, but with the time difference, it was better to call now and get it over with. Excusing himself to his colleagues, he headed toward a secluded hallway niche. He thumbed in the number and tapped his fingers on the table while the trans-Atlantic call connected.

Finally, he heard the accented voice of Dr. Ajay Kumar, "Hello."

"Ajay, what in the hell is going on? What do you mean there were no viable embryos for transfer this morning? That's unacceptable." After a few more moments of ranting, Hicks paused for a breath and Kumar began to speak.

"I told you last week I was concerned about the new sperm processing, and now it appears it may not be producing embryos that grow into viable blastocysts. If we continue with this, the whole next cycle of patients may fail. I think we have to stop and go back to our old process."

"Nonsense," Hicks whispered, not wanting to be overheard by the conference attendees milling in the hall. "That would mean going back to dismal results for those couples who have male-factor infertility, which is half our patients. More than half. They come from all over the world because we get them pregnant when no one else can. I want you to continue using the new method but do a backup for each couple with donor sperm. Use donor B-007, like we do for the charity cases funded by Porter's stupid grant so we don't have to fund more than one free IVF cycle."

After a long silence, Kumar spoke, "I'll talk with Dr. Porter and let her know our concerns and the backup plan. Then she can get the patient's consent at the time of egg retrieval and—"

"Are you crazy?" he hissed. "Don't tell her *anything*! With her holier-than-thou attitude, it would be a disaster."

"I don't know how I can keep it from her. She's coming by today to go over all our procedures, and she plans to spend time working with me this week. She said she wants to be more hands on for the laboratory part of things."

"Well, think of something to keep her hands off. She can't know. Now, I must go. I'm introducing the next speaker." With that, Hicks disconnected and stormed down the hall toward *Une Grande Salle.*

"Are you ready, Dr. Porter?" asked Selena in her musical Jamaican accent. "Mr. and Mrs. Goldschmidt are in the first conference room. She's crying and he looks like he wants to punch something. I gave them some water and a box of tissues."

Joyce glanced into Selena's sympathetic brown eyes. Selena's calm demeanor and warm compassion made her a favorite with patients and staff. She'd been a nurse with the Institute since its opening day, and Joyce felt Selena was what made the place tick.

"I know," Joyce said. "That was how they sounded on the

phone. This is their third cycle, and they were so hopeful." Shaking her head slowly, she continued, "Sometimes I don't know how our patients manage to keep going. Their disappointment after a failed cycle is crushing."

Looking serious, Selena said, "Good luck, Dr. Porter. I know you'll say the right thing." With a wink, she added, "And I'll have an ice pack waiting in case Mr. Goldschmidt connects with your nose."

Joyce walked down the hallway. The walls were painted a muted sage green, its soothing color intended to help patients feel calm and relaxed. She glanced at the abstract art, which vaguely reminded her of a Georgia O'Keefe painting with its squiggling figures that looked like sperm swimming toward a vagina. It was a suitable theme, she supposed, for a fertility clinic. Except here, the sperm swam in a dish and the whole act of procreation was sterile and devoid of loving intimacy.

She appreciated Selena's encouragement and humor. It meant a lot that the nursing staff liked and trusted her. But every time one of her couples failed to conceive, Joyce felt like a failure. She needed to get a grip or risk professional burnout. Having to talk with disappointed couples who asked pointed questions about the hard science of IVF reinforced her feelings of inadequacy. She looked forward to spending time with Dr. Kumar and hoped it would silence her nagging doubts.

After inhaling a deep breath and mumbling a quick prayer, Joyce squared her shoulders and entered the sunlit conference room where the couple sat at a small round table. They were professional people: he, a successful financial analyst, and she, the owner of a well-known event-planning firm.

Neil, clothed in a charcoal-gray suit, starched white shirt, and conservative red-striped tie, had probably come from work. His hair was cut short with a bit of gray at the temples. Joyce thought he'd developed more gray over the last few months.

His wife, who'd taken the day off expecting to have an embryo transfer, was dressed casually in black leggings, Vans slip-ons, and a mauve knit tunic top. Her wavy blond hair was pulled back in a loose ponytail, and she wore no makeup. Her eyes were puffy and red. Immediately, they both looked up as she entered.

"Hello, Cassidy. Hello, Neil. Thank you for coming," she greeted them. "I know you have a lot of questions, but first let me say how sorry I am about this cycle. Please understand, it's not your fault. You didn't do anything wrong. It's just that sometimes the whole process of fertilization and early embryo development doesn't go smoothly. There are a lot of possible reasons. Something might have been wrong with the embryos. Or it might have to do with the eggs or the sperm or something else. There's still a lot we don't understand."

Cassidy continued to weep quietly, while Neil gently rubbed her back. Several emotions flitted across his face, which finally settled into an unnatural calm.

After a moment, he looked directly at Joyce and challenged, "Are you sure there hasn't been some mistake? This is our third cycle, and this is the first time there have been no embryos to transfer. The only time." Neil's face flushed as he raised his voice. "Our first cycle, we had two good ones. The second, there was one, and we really had our hopes up when the pregnancy test came back positive. Then Cassi had the early miscarriage. This time, you told us there were four viable embryos. You even talked about freezing a couple for a future cycle." With a flash of anger, he continued more loudly, "Maybe there's something wrong with you and your lab!"

Choosing to ignore the last comment, Joyce calmly replied, "You're right. We did talk about freezing embryos for a future cycle. I wish I could tell you exactly what went wrong. I spoke earlier with our embryologist, Dr. Kumar. Two of the embryos stopped dividing, and the other two completely disintegrated. I can't explain it—Cassidy's hormone levels were good, and the fertilization and initial embryo growth were all fine. All our lab processes are carefully monitored, and we have stringent quality control measures. Dr. Kumar and his team are very experienced, and McArthur prides itself on excellent care and high pregnancy rates."

She paused to give the couple time to process this news.

Neil turned to his wife. "Cassi," he said gently. "I'm so sorry. I know it's my fault. My sperm aren't strong enough."

"Neil," Joyce said with a reassuring tone, "many men have male-factor infertility, and we've seen many successful pregnancies at McArthur. Your sperm have successfully fertilized your wife's eggs in the past. You shouldn't assume this is your fault."

Neil's anger returned. "I can't take it anymore! I'm a failure! I have three brothers, and they all have kids. Lots of kids. In fact, my brother Jacob said he smiles at his wife, and she gets pregnant." He shook his head as the anger drained away and the grief set in. "It isn't fair."

He blew out a breath and asked hesitantly. "So, what's next? Is there anything else, or does this mean we'll never have a baby?"

For the first time, Cassidy spoke softly, "Dr. Porter, what about donor sperm? Is that something we should try?"

Almost before she completed the sentence, Neil burst out, "Never, no way!" His eyes blazed. "Cassidy, we've talked about this. You know how I feel. I don't like it." Standing up so quickly that the chair crashed sideways to the floor, he raked his fingers through his short hair. Turning to face his wife, he continued, "I won't agree to it! I'd rather adopt than have some unknown college kid donor."

Absently rubbing the wedding band on her fourth finger, Cassidy raised tearful eyes. "And I'd like to have the joy of carrying our child and giving birth. It would still be our baby, Neil. Don't you want that for us?"

Joyce took a deep breath as Cassidy reached for another Kleenex to dab her moist eyes and Neil righted the chair. He sat down, his shoulders slumped and his head in his hands.

Looking at the grieving couple, Joyce felt completely inadequate. She hated this part of her job, especially when she had no good explanation or advice. This couple had already spent almost $60,000 and had nothing to show for it. Their marriage was strained, and they both looked like they couldn't bear much more.

The conversation lasted another thirty minutes as Joyce tried to help them process their anger and grief and move toward options. They were conflicted, so she recommended taking a few months off and seeing a counselor who specialized in supporting couples undergoing infertility treatment. Both worried that by waiting, their chances decreased even further. Cassidy was thirty-eight years old, and Neil would turn fifty soon.

As Joyce rose to end the meeting, she said, "Let's make an appointment for you in two months. That will give Cassidy's body time to recover from the strain of these cycles and give you time to discuss how you would like to proceed. We can also repeat the blood work testing her ovarian reserve. Many couples move toward adoption at this point, but we can certainly consider one more cycle if that's what you want."

She watched the couple make their way toward the reception area, stopping off to hug Selena as they said good-bye. The other clients in the waiting room looked uneasily at their sorrowful expressions and then glanced away, as if the couple's failure to conceive might be contagious.

Joyce took her time walking back to her office, her hands in the pockets of her white lab coat. Although she had remained calm and professional while speaking with the Goldschmidts, she felt physically and emotionally drained after witnessing their raw grief. She wondered if there were any chocolate-chip cookies left in the staff lounge. She knew better than to deal with stress by eating, but chocolate-chip cookies were the perfect combination of fat, sugar and salt, and they always made her feel better. Her stomach growled, and she realized she hadn't really had lunch, just a container of low-fat yogurt eaten at her desk while catching up.

Neil's comment really bothered her. It had been personal and accusatory. "What if there's something wrong with *you* and *your* lab?" She understood his emotions—anger and grief lashing out at the only person in the room who had any power, but it still hurt. And oddly, his remark mirrored her own thoughts. What if something was wrong in the lab? How would she even know?

Selena moved toward Joyce. "Are you okay?" she asked with concern. Pointing to her face, she joked, "It doesn't look like you need an ice pack. Maybe some chocolate?"

Joyce tried to smile. "I'm okay. But that was rough. Cassidy is devastated, and Neil is angry because he feels so helpless, like it's his fault. They're going to take a few months off, and I suggested they see our counselor."

"Are you ready for your next patient, or do you need a few minutes?" Selena asked. "They're in Consult Room 2. It's a new couple, the Millers. They came all the way from Cedar Rapids, Iowa. Have you ever been to Iowa? I hear they have a great state fair."

"You know, I think I will take a few minutes. Are there any cookies left?"

Selena smiled and said, "No chocolate-chip, but we do have those peanut butter ones with the chocolate kiss on top. And there's fresh coffee. Take your time, honey. The Millers have family in the area who told them about McArthur. They've already been to one other IVF clinic for a consult, and they have *lots* of questions. Maybe you should have two cookies."

Joyce slipped into the staff lounge and poured a cup of coffee into her favorite blue mug. Selena's coffee, thick and dark, was almost like espresso. Sitting at the round table, she sipped the rejuvenating beverage while munching on a cookie, eating the chocolate kiss first. She perused the couple's medical record on her laptop as Selena entered the room.

"I'm almost ready. I reviewed their history this weekend, and it looks like their evaluation is complete. IVF is the next step for them. Did you give them our brochure and the protocol handout?"

"Just the brochure. The handout is in the folder on the desk. They're nice folks. You'll like them."

After Selena's coffee and the rich cookie, she felt ready to continue. Carrying the laptop and an "old school" legal pad and pen, she knocked gently on the door of Consult Room 2 and stepped inside. The room was almost identical to the one where she'd met with the Goldschmidts.

She glanced through the partially open blinds and saw the sun-dappled park opposite the Institute. The couple was seated at the table, just as the Goldschmidts had been, and they looked up as Joyce gently closed the door. But the atmosphere felt completely different. This room was filled with hope and possibility, not anger and despair.

Joyce smiled as she looked into the expectant eyes of the couple from Iowa and extended her hand in greeting.

"Good afternoon. I'm Dr. Joyce Porter. Welcome to McArthur Institute. How can we help you?"

———

The staff meeting that afternoon was mercifully short, and everyone seemed more relaxed with Hicks away. After the meeting, Joyce walked to the Embryology lab with Kumar. He moved a few steps ahead of her and seemed lost in thought.

Kumar paused to let Joyce enter the lab in front of him. A pungent medicinal smell greeted them. The technicians were wiping the counters and preparing to leave for the evening. They nodded to her as she and Kumar entered his small windowless office. Leaving the door ajar, he gestured to a chair and asked, "Where would you like to begin?"

"As you know," Joyce said, settling onto the chair, "I met

with the Goldschmidts today, and you can imagine how extremely upset they were. Neil asked a lot of very specific questions, especially about our lab procedures. Why don't you begin by explaining what types of testing you did to determine what might have gone wrong?"

Kumar's gaze drifted to the picture of his daughter while drumming his fingers on the desk. He let the silence stretch, then finally said, "Well, we have a standard process for inseminating the ova with the sperm. As you are aware, we've had good success with pretreating the eggs to facilitate greater sperm penetration, particularly when dealing with male factor infertility. Following any pre-treatment, we culture them overnight in a special solution that is pH balanced and contains specific nutrients that sustain the dividing embryo. The first thing I did was look at the log from yesterday to determine which batch of culture solution was used, and then I spoke with the technician to confirm that it was properly prepared."

"What were you looking for?"

"I wanted to verify that he used the proper filtered water, tested the pH accurately, and maintained sterile technique. One of our most experienced technicians, Richard Carnegie, was on call this weekend, and I am confident in his work."

"Then what?" Joyce asked.

"I checked the incubator to make sure the temperature and humidity were constant. And all that checked out."

"Okay. Anything else?"

"I retested the culture solution myself, and it was completely normal. All the parameters were completely within normal limits."

"Can I look at the culture plates?"

Kumar's mouth tightened and he exhaled sharply. "Well, there isn't anything to see. The embryos in those plates disintegrated. As for the other two, they arrested their development at the two-cell stage."

"Didn't you keep them? Why didn't you allow them to incubate for another twenty-four hours? Haven't we sometimes had embryos that divide more slowly?"

"Yes, that's true. But these had already been at that stage for twice the normal time. I'm sorry, but they've been disposed of."

She leaned forward. "Dr. Kumar, we have three more egg retrievals this week. I need you to assure me there are no problems in the lab. These patients are depending on us, and I'm depending on you and your team."

He glanced down at the floor before looking her in the eye. "Everything is fine. It is very sad for the Goldschmidts, but in my opinion, it is bad luck and not anyone's fault."

"All right," she answered. "I'll have Dr. Cohen do the egg retrievals later this week, so I can be with you in the lab and watch the whole process from start to finish."

"As you wish. Now, do you have any other questions?"

"I would like to review all current lab protocols."

"Of course. Shall I email them, or do you want hard copies?"

"Email is fine. Thank you, Dr. Kumar. I know you and your team are doing their best. It's so hard when we must give patients unexpected bad news."

She rose and left the office.

Once she was gone, Kumar slowly exhaled. He wasn't sure how he was going to deal with her dogging his every step this week. He turned off his computer and prepared to leave for the day. As it powered down, he hoped between now and the next egg retrieval, he could devise a way to keep her out of the lab.

Joyce and Sally sat in Joyce's office eating a hasty lunch. Every Tuesday, they ordered Greek salads from the local deli and caught up on each other's lives and the latest university gossip.

"Did you see today's email from Hicks?" asked Sally, as she stabbed a piece of cucumber. "It said we have a visiting professor coming next month."

"I read that. Some guy from France named Dominique DuPage."

Sally cocked her head. "Maybe it's a woman. Hard to tell with a name like Dominique."

Joyce made a non-committal sound. After forking a piece of juicy tomato glistening with Greek dressing, she continued, "Did you have a chance to look at the attached resume? Pretty impressive."

"I agree," Sally said. "He—I really hope it's a he—is currently working at St. Roche IVF Center in Montpellier. I think that's in southern France." Waving her hands, she continued. "Maybe this is the man of my dreams! He'll sweep me off my feet and take me back to Montpellier where we'll have a chic apartment in town. On weekends in the summer, we'll visit his family's chateau which will, of course, be in the middle of a vineyard. And during the winter, we'll ski in the Alps."

"Sounds like you have it all worked out." Joyce laughed.

Sally continued spinning her fantasy. "I can see him now. Dark wavy hair, a little long so it brushes his collar. Dreamy brown eyes with thick lashes, a deep dimple in his left cheek, and a smile that shows a slightly crooked front tooth."

"Why a slightly crooked front tooth?" Joyce asked, caught up for the moment in Sally's make-believe doctor.

"So he's not too perfect."

They munched on their salads and pondered this mystery man.

Finally, Sally broke the silence. "Well, enough of that. How was your weekend with Bill?"

"Wonderful, once we got past the initial awkward phase. This long-distance marriage thing is really tough. We're both so caught up in our work during the week that it's hard to unwind and just be together on the weekends. By Friday, we're both really beat."

"Tell me again how you ended up in two different places."

"We got married the summer before our third year of

medical school. After graduation, we were lucky and both landed positions in Pittsburgh. I knew I wanted Ob/Gyn and Bill was set on Internal Medicine. After our internships, we both stayed on for residency. He finished the year before me and then worked a year at the VA until I was done. By then, we realized we both wanted academic careers, so that meant more training."

She nibbled a black olive. "Bill was very lucky he was accepted into the Public Health Program at Johns Hopkins, and I applied for Reproductive Endocrine fellowships in Maryland, Virginia, and DC so I could be close. But once I finished, I had to get a job. We both have student loans, and McArthur was the best offer. So now we take turns commuting on the weekends."

"Well, I'm glad you're here. It's nice to have a friend in the department. What do you think you'll do once Bill finishes?"

"I'm not sure. We talked about it some this weekend. I really want him to move here while he finishes his dissertation, but he says that's at least a year off. To be honest, this is a sore spot for us right now. And I'm worried because he's talking about applying for a fellowship at the CDC in Atlanta once he finishes his Ph.D. He's really into this epidemiology stuff and wants to be at the center of the big policy discussions."

Sally looked sympathetic when Joyce added, "Bill thinks I'm pushing him too hard to finish his research and move to Richmond while he writes his dissertation. He gets angry every time I bring it up. But I really miss him, and the drive every weekend is such a pain. I can't imagine what we'll do if he goes to Atlanta."

"Yeah, I guess I can see that. Don't you think you'd move with him and find a job there?"

Joyce nodded. "Yeah, probably."

"Well, at least you have your weekends to look forward to. Some of us spend them alone doing laundry, going shopping, or reading journals."

"Hey, I thought you were seeing that guy from the business

office—you know, the one who helped change your flat tire last month."

"You mean Doug Westover? We are, sort of. But he has a three-year-old son from his first marriage, so he's tied up some weekends."

Selena appeared and their conversation stopped.

"Okay, ladies," she said. "Lunch break is over. You have patients to see, and the daily test results are ready for review." They both nodded, and she withdrew.

"Sally, before we go, would you do me a favor."

"Sure."

"I want to spend some time in the lab this week with Kumar —you know, really get some hands-on experience with the lab techniques. Would you be willing to staff the egg retrievals for the rest of the week?"

"Okay, but I'm also back-up for the residents. It should be fine unless there's an emergency."

"Great. Thanks," Joyce said as they gathered their salad containers and headed down the hall toward the staff fridge with their leftovers. "See you later."

Selena handed Joyce a list of patient test results, and she was pleased to see three patients were having very good responses to hormone stimulation and would likely be ready for egg retrieval soon. The others were still early in their cycle. At the bottom of the stack, there was an interoffice mail envelope addressed to Joyce.

"What's this?" she asked Selena.

"I'm not sure. I didn't open it because it looks sort of official."

Joyce unfurled the red twine and opened the top flap. Inside was a sealed envelope with the university logo embossed in the left upper corner. After slitting the envelope with her finger, Joyce unfolded a letter printed on thick university stationery. It was from Vice President of Patient Quality, Mary Francis Welch.

Joyce had met Mary Francis once about a year ago when she hosted a new faculty gathering. She was a former Army nurse who'd been with the university for twenty years and was well respected. She was tough but kind and had a reputation for standing up to the other administrators when she felt they were heading in the wrong direction. Under her leadership, the university hospital and outpatient clinics had established a comprehensive quality assurance program that garnered accolades from patients and regulatory agencies. The letter from Mary Francis commended Joyce on the excellent patient satisfaction scores, which she noted were in the ninetieth percentile. Joyce finished the short letter and decided it was nice to get a compliment from an administrator. It stood in contrast to her recent interactions with Hicks.

Joyce turned back to Selena. "The letter was from VP Welch. She's pleased with our clinic scores. I'm glad someone in administration notices how hard we work."

Looking up from the stack of phone messages, Selena said, "I called the lab about the pregnancy tests, and they said we'd have them within the hour." Then she grinned and added, "Brooke Petro and Kaitlyn DeFranco have both called already—twice!"

Joyce smiled. "Selena, you have the patience of a saint. Those two have been making me crazy." She eyed the row of closed exam room doors, "What's next?"

"An ultrasound. Sue Li is right at six weeks, and she's so excited to see the heartbeat."

"Did her husband come with her?"

"No, he's away this week on a business trip to China, but her mother is with her."

"Oh no, not the dragon lady."

"The very one. But she's mellowed a lot since they found out Sue Li is pregnant. And she likes you. She only gives Dr. Cohen a hard time. Do you want me to come in with you?"

"No, thanks. I've got it. I'll let you know if I need anything."

Joyce tapped on the door and entered. In the semi-darkness, the ultrasound machine gave off a pearly gray light. Sue Li smiled shyly in greeting.

As Joyce's eyes adjusted to the decreased light, she checked the patient information listed in the ultrasound record. Turning to Sue Li, she inquired, "How are you feeling?"

Beaming, the patient's mother proudly informed Joyce that Sue Li had gained two pounds and only had "a little bit" of morning sickness. Joyce looked questioningly at Sue Li who nodded her head in agreement.

As Joyce applied warmed gel to the ultrasound wand, she explained, "I'm going to do the same kind of transvaginal ultrasound that you had when we monitored your ovaries during the IFV cycle. This allows us to see the early development of the baby in the uterus. By six weeks, we can get a very accurate measurement of growth and see the fetal heartbeat. Are you ready?"

Sue Li nodded, and her mother almost bounced off her chair with anticipation. Joyce gently placed the probe into Sue Li's vagina and maneuvered it until the uterus was in the center of the screen. Everyone in the room held their breath until a definite flutter came into view. Joyce adjusted the volume, and Sue Li heard her baby's heartbeat for the first time. "Is that it—the baby?" she asked.

"Yes," Joyce said. "The heartbeat is nice and strong and regular."

Then Sue Li began to laugh, reaching out to her mother. Grasping her daughter's hand, the "dragon lady" began to cry. Honored to share their joy, Joyce savored the moment.

CHAPTER 4

It was late Monday afternoon when Joyce opened the rear door of her trusty Honda, throwing her oversized handbag and raincoat into the back seat, happy to be at end of the workday. One of the things she most enjoyed about her job at McArthur was not having night call. While she still took occasional phone calls from the clinic's IVF patients, she didn't have to come in at night to deliver babies or do emergency surgeries. Every evening, as she left the university, she said a quiet prayer of gratitude that she was going home to sleep in her own bed.

As an intern, she had often put in eighty-hour weeks. It had been the same for her husband, although she teased him that his call nights were easier because he sometimes got a few hours of sleep if the ER was quiet. She rarely slept, always up with deliveries, ER visits, or emergency surgeries. The worst part had been when they had opposite schedules, when there were weeks they hardly saw one another.

Kind of like now, she mused.

Joyce paused next to her car, momentarily caught up in the past. Unwillingly, memories flooded back as she remembered one of her worst call nights. It had been a Wednesday, and a patient had died. She'd come straight from the OB clinic and found Labor and Delivery buzzing with controlled chaos. A harried nurse informed her that a transport from an outlying hospital had just arrived, a seriously ill pregnant woman with dangerously high blood pressure and a bleeding disorder.

Preliminary evaluation showed the baby was in distress, and the OB team moved into high gear as they prepared for an emergency Cesarean delivery. The patient lay on the bed, freckles standing out in a pale swollen face framed by a surgical cap that barely contained a cloud of curly red hair. Tears ran down her face as she struggled to raise a hand encumbered by an IV to wipe them away.

"Don't let me die," the woman whispered urgently to Joyce as they entered the operating room. "And don't let my baby die." Her swollen hand grasped Joyce's, and her edematous eyelids opened wide in fear.

A short time later, after delivery of a healthy five-pound girl, the new mother developed massive hemorrhaging. Her chart adamantly stated that she and her husband refused to allow the transfusion of any blood products due to their religious beliefs. The medical team agreed that without blood, the patient might die, and Joyce offered to leave the operating room and talk to the husband.

"Without a blood transfusion, your wife may die," she'd said. But the new father had been firm in his resolve, his religious beliefs unyielding. A short time later, the patient died.

During the following weeks, Joyce had nightmares. In her dreams, she saw the massive amount of blood and heard the OR team's frantic voices. But worst of all, again and again, she saw the woman's last gaze, felt her hand, and heard her plea, "Don't let me die."

Joyce suppressed a shiver as she tried to shake free of the gripping memory. Breathing deeply, she refocused her eyes and came back to the present. The cool fall air tickled the bare skin at the back of her neck as she stood under the darkening sky. With a final full diaphragmatic breath, she released a silent prayer of gratitude. Thankfully, she no longer had to cover OB call. Taking care of infertility patients had its challenges, but at least no one died.

Her heartbeat still elevated, she again took deep breaths, trying to break free of the awful memory that still felt so real. Snapping her seatbelt buckle and hoping to put herself in a better mood, she turned on the stereo and cranked up an eclectic '80s mix of her favorite driving tunes. But that didn't suit her mood, so she tuned into NPR's Evening Edition and turned the volume to low.

As she headed out of the faculty lot, her cell phone buzzed. Looking at the screen, she saw it was her mother.

Oh no, she thought. *Not now. I don't want to talk to her. Not after the day I've had.*

Feeling guilty, she turned up the radio and let the call go to voicemail. A few minutes later, she turned into a small bumpy driveway and entered the parking lot beside her apartment building. She wished it had covered spaces, but she guessed she should be happy she didn't have to hunt for a spot on the street.

She climbed the inside stairs of the ivy-covered brick building, turned left at the top, and unlocked Apartment 3-B. Snapping on lights as she walked down the narrow hall, she entered the kitchen and tossed the mail onto the stained laminate counter with its ghostly pale gray comma-shaped pattern.

She opened the door of the ancient refrigerator and surveyed its meager contents, consisting of a half bottle of wine, a container of orange juice, and a few breakfast items. Staring into the freezer, she was again surprised to find almost no food. A lonely bag of peas, a small carton of double-fudge ice cream, and a single Lean Cuisine macaroni-and-cheese dinner were its only contents. She placed the frozen entrée in the microwave and poured a glass of pinot grigio. She settled onto the kitchen chair and reached for the mail. Mittens wound himself around her leg, plaintively meowing.

"Oh, so you want dinner too?" She got up from her chair and headed to the cabinet next to the stove. Thankfully, it contained a better selection of feline food offerings than her freezer.

As the cat daintily nibbled the food, Joyce headed toward the bedroom and changed into a comfy pair of sweatpants and an oversized Pitt sweatshirt that was so old the cuffs were frayed. She debated between thick wool socks or pink Ugg slippers and decided on the slippers.

The bedroom was small but neat. When she'd moved into the apartment almost a year and a half ago, Joyce decided to exert some effort to make it a comfortable oasis. The walls were a butter yellow with white crown molding. A brass double bed, covered with a cheerful, blue-patterned quilt and piled high with colorful pillows, took up most of the space. A bedside table held a reading lamp and a copy of a "bodice ripper" romance novel obtained from the used bookstore. She preferred "real" books to e-books when she wanted to relax and escape.

An antique chest of drawers with an attached mirror, glass wavy with age, stood in the corner. Joyce remembered purchasing it with Bill at a flea market. On its top rested a blue-and-white Chinese bottle lamp, a wedding picture of Joyce and Bill holding hands and smiling as they ran down the church steps, and a decoupaged jewelry box. The box was a gift from her Aunt Celia and housed her sparse jewelry collection. Her mother and father's fortieth wedding anniversary photo stood slightly off to the side in a silver filigree frame.

In the corner, a small gingham covered bench sat next to a miniature Norfolk pine. The floor was covered with an ancient mustard yellow shag carpet, the same vintage as the avocado kitchen appliances. Joyce had mostly hidden it with a newer cream-colored area rug.

A professionally framed watercolor of a seaside ocean scene hung above the bed. It was her one good piece of artwork, purchased last year when she inherited a small amount of money after her godfather passed away.

Wiggling her toes into fuzzy pink slippers, Joyce headed back to the kitchen. As the microwave dinged, the cell phone buzzed again—her mother calling back. Joyce sighed and poured a splash more wine before hitting the answer button on the phone. Breathing in through her nose and out through her mouth, she thought to herself, *Be strong, Porter. You've saved people's lives. You can do this.*

"Hello, Mother."

"Joyce, how are you? It's been weeks since we talked."

Her mother had a way of getting right to the point. No opening banter or chit-chat. No easing into the conversation with mindless pleasantries. Before her retirement last year, her mother had been an executive assistant to the CEO of a medium-sized manufacturing plant. She'd held that position for twenty years and knew how to zero in on any task. Before that, she'd taught business classes at their local high school. Marilyn Bauer often said that compared to teaching, working for a CEO was a breeze.

"I know, Mother. I'm sorry. Bill and I were away last weekend. Remember, I told you we were going to Williamsburg."

"Oh, that's right. And how is Bill? Is he still living in Baltimore? When are you two going to be in the same place? I worry about you living there in Richmond all by yourself. You should get a different job, one where you can live in the same city with your husband."

"Bill's fine, and we had a great weekend together. Thanks for asking," she said with a hint of sarcasm. "Williamsburg was charming. All the shops were decked out for Halloween. You and Dad should go sometime. And I told you before, I like Richmond, and I like working at McArthur."

"You know how I feel about that job," her mother cut in. "You shouldn't be working at that clinic. It's immoral—test tube babies, lesbian couples having babies, women getting pregnant with sperm that isn't from their husbands . . ."

Joyce sat down, closed her eyes and tried to tune out her mother, who unfortunately was just hitting her stride. She took a sip of wine, and then another bigger gulp as her mother ramped up the diatribe. It followed a familiar theme.

"Joyce, you're on a dangerous path. You know this because I've told you. Just about everything you do every single day is against the Catholic Church's teaching. I talked to Father Daniel about it, and he gave me a book explaining the Church's doctrines. I've read most of it, and it's pretty clear that conception is supposed to happen *in the woman's body through the act of intercourse with her husband.*" The last phrase was uttered with great emphasis.

Joyce held the phone slightly away from her head and prayed for her mother to take a breath. She felt guilty about not keeping in closer touch, but she dreaded the lectures about her "immoral career." Talking with her mother made her feel defensive and resentful, like she had to constantly justify her career. She was an adult, yet her mother often made her feel like a willful teenager—one who'd been caught after the midnight curfew making out with her boyfriend on the front porch, guilty and ashamed. She still blushed when she remembered that long-ago night.

"Mother, we've talked about this. I love what I do. Don't you think it's God's work, helping to bring children into loving families?"

Before her mother could begin another riff on the evils of IVF, Joyce quickly steered the conversation in a different direction. "How's Aunt Celia? The last time we talked, she and Uncle Bernie were heading to New England to see the leaves." As her mother switched gears, Joyce exhaled in relief. Half an hour later, she finally ended the call, saying it was time for her to watch reruns of *Lost.*

Joyce strode back into her '70s kitchen to reheat the

microwave entree. As the steam rose from the macaroni and cheese, almost burning her hand, she realized the wine glass was empty. Although tonight's phone call with her mother hadn't been quite as stressful as her earlier conversation with the Goldschmidts, Joyce decided she'd earned a refill.

CHAPTER 5

Joyce was still tying the drawstring of her blue scrub pants as she hurried down the hall from the staff locker room to the IVF pre-op holding room. The female changing room was a small compact area with lockers for stashing street clothes, a wooden bench, and a lavatory. Before McArthur Institute opened, Dr. Hicks insisted the university provide a dedicated day-surgery unit so that McArthur patients would not have to go to the hospital's main surgery suite for their procedures. Although she hadn't been on staff at that time, Joyce appreciated the care taken by the architects in designing the unit. She also appreciated that it was an easy walk from the clinic, because most days she was running late. Just too much to do. Today was no exception.

The renovated university building's state-of-the-art day-surgery suite boasted a pre-operative area, two procedure rooms, and a separate post-op recovery area. It was not designed to do major surgical cases but functioned very well for the egg retrievals and embryo transfers that happened three or four times per week. Additionally, the suite contained something not found in most standard operating rooms, an ancillary IVF lab located between the two procedure rooms with glass pass-through windows into each room. Joyce remembered how impressed she'd been with the set-up the first time she'd toured the facility.

The IVF lab was the domain of Dr. Kumar and his two assistants, Richard Carnegie and Chandra Singh. Both Carnegie and Singh were graduate students. Kumar or one of the assistants was present at every egg retrieval or embryo transfer procedure.

Joyce felt a growing frustration that she'd missed the opportunity to shadow Dr. Kumar during the past week because something had always come up. As a medical student, Joyce had done a specialty rotation in her senior year and spent time in an IVF lab. She assumed much at McArthur was similar, yet McArthur had pioneered several new processes that were cutting edge.

What happened in the lab had always seemed mysterious, almost magical. Once the pale straw-colored fluid from each ovarian follicle was suctioned and collected in a trap, it was handed off to the embryologist. The fluid was carefully examined under a low-power dissecting microscope until the egg, sometimes referred to as an oocyte, was isolated. If the fluid failed to yield an egg, the embryologist relayed this information back to the physician doing the procedure, and they flushed the follicle with additional media solution until the oocyte was retrieved.

The identification of each egg was celebrated as a success, with the goal to retrieve as many as possible. The more eggs retrieved, the better the chance for successful fertilization. And the more fertilized eggs, the better the chance for healthy embryos, called blastocytes in the early stages of development, to implant and result in pregnancy. This was the reason the whole process existed, and why people were willing to pay tens of thousands of dollars for the privilege of being treated at McArthur.

After identification, each individual egg was placed in a labeled container with special media. These containers were transported back to the main lab in a warming unit and eventually combined with sperm, either from the husband or a preselected donor. Sometimes the eggs were pretreated or manipulated to allow for easier sperm penetration. And finally, the eggs were incubated overnight and examined the following day for fertilization. This was the part of the process that particularly interested Joyce because of the recent spate of problems. Usually, when all went as planned, couples returned three to five days after the initial procedure to have one or two embryos transferred back to the woman's uterus. The rest were frozen to be used in a future cycle.

Nearing the pre-op area, Joyce took a few breaths and attempted to shed her irritation. It was Friday, and Hicks returned in a week. The previous day, she'd been set to shadow Kumar, but then she was tapped to give an "emergency" lecture to the medical students. Dr. Hicks, the designated speaker, had neglected to inform her before he left for Paris that he'd scheduled her to cover for him. In typical fashion, he'd waited until the last minute and then texted her that morning, leaving her a mere two hours to prepare.

A nurse emerged from the OR and interrupted Joyce's internal tirade.

"Dr. Porter. I'm glad to see you. Just after we prepped the patient and were ready to move to the OR, Dr. Cohen got called away. Apparently, a patient rolled into Emergency with extremely low blood pressure. Dr. Cohen felt it was probably due to a ruptured tubal pregnancy, and she was afraid to take a chance on waiting until after this procedure."

Joyce nodded briskly to the nurse. Placing a paper mask over her nose and mouth, she ducked into the pre-op area to greet the patient and her husband. She didn't know them well since they were Sally's patients, but they were quite understanding about the last-minute switch.

Moving through the short hall to the sink located outside the procedure room, she watched the anesthetist and nurse roll the patient through the wide door, her husband trailing behind. Unfortunately, as often happened when she was annoyed,

Joyce's mind returned to yesterday's medical student lecture and her wrath toward Hicks. Thinking about him made her blood pressure rise.

How typical, she thought disgustedly as she waved her hands under the scrub sink faucet to start the water flowing and opened a scrub brush soaked in pink topical antiseptic. *The man is such an inconsiderate jerk.*

Fortunately, the class was for first year students, and the topic was the physiology of conception and pregnancy, a subject she knew backward and forward. Still, she would have liked more time to polish her presentation to make the overwhelming amount of information relevant and engaging. She always tried to include interesting patient stories because she remembered that was what had made her early med school years tolerable.

Scrubbing her hands for the required five minutes to completely remove all infectious particles provided plenty of time to ruminate. She knew it was simply unfortunate timing, but she really wanted to get into that lab and see for herself what was happening before Hicks returned. He was due back in a week, so she supposed she still had a chance.

While cleaning carefully under each fingernail with the plastic pick, Joyce considered two additional instances this week where the patient's eggs had fertilized only to have the embryos arrest their development in the same manner as the Goldschmidts. There had also been one heartbreaking case where no fertilization occurred at all. She quizzed Kumar extensively after each event, but he continued to assure her that everything was fine. She wished she could believe him, but something felt off. Four episodes in one week didn't seem like coincidence.

One of the couples had a single frozen embryo in storage, so their second cycle had not been completely lost.

Holding her dripping sanitized hands aloft, Joyce backed into the OR and greeted the patient and staff. The surgical technician handed her a sterile towel, and she thoroughly dried each hand. Sidestepping the ultrasound machine, Joyce carefully stepped into the sterile paper gown held aloft by the technician, and the circulating nurse cinched it around her waist. Finally, she shoved her hands into the size six surgical gloves, handed the scrub tech the other half of the waist tie, and twirled to wrap the sterile gown around her middle.

The ritual of sterile gowning for any surgical procedure was soothing, and it allowed Joyce to clear her mind of other details and focus on the immediate job at hand. She always felt calm tempered with anticipation descend when she completed the ritual and stepped up to the operating field.

The patient snored softly under light sedation, the anesthetic block already in effect. After cleaning and draping the operative field, Joyce positioned herself on the stool at the end of the table, ultrasound wand in hand. The wand, sterilely draped and outfitted with a specific needle and guide, allowed for visualization and aspiration of each mature ovarian follicle.

Carefully inserting the wand into the patient's vagina, Joyce studied the image on the screen and visualized both ovaries. She noted seven mature follicles on the left and five on the right. Holding the wand steady against the largest follicle, Joyce advanced the needle, pierced the follicular wall, and applied gentle suction to drain the contents into a small sterile trap. She carefully removed the trap and handed it to the nurse who passed it through the window to Dr. Kumar in the adjoining lab. The follicle was then flushed with additional sterile media which was collected in a second trap and passed to the lab.

"We have an egg," Dr. Kumar announced through the small cutout window, and Joyce visualized the next follicle and repeated the process.

Thirty minutes later, all mature follicles had been aspirated and a total of twelve oocytes retrieved. Joyce thanked the OR staff and stripped off her gown and gloves. She then assisted with moving the patient to recovery and wrote brief post-op orders. Returning to the bedside, she discussed the procedure with the couple.

"Everything went very well, and I'm so pleased we have twelve healthy eggs to inseminate. Amber, you may feel a little cramping when the anesthesia wears off completely. Take some Tylenol tonight if you need it."

"Oh, Dr. Porter. That's great news," the patient's husband said, his face splitting into a grin as he squeezed his wife's hand. "Thank you for everything. And please thank Dr. Cohen for us. How many embryos do you think we'll have?"

"Well, it could be as many as twelve! But that's very unlikely. I'm hoping for at least five or six, so there'll be some to freeze for a future cycle. Have you considered how many you want transferred? Did Dr. Cohen talk with you about the increased risks with multiple pregnancies, like twins or triplets?"

The couple nodded, and Amber spoke. "But she also told us that the success rate increases if more than one embryo is transferred."

"Well, yes. So, there is a balance, a type of tradeoff. I recommend transferring one and not more than two. But you think about it. You don't have to decide until the day of transfer."

The couple continued to express how thrilled they were with the number of eggs and their hope for a successful cycle. Needing to get back to the clinic, Joyce wrapped up the conversation by reminding them the nurse would be in touch the next day for a post-op check-in. Since she was on call for the weekend, there was a chance she might see them again. As she left, she heard them whispering about how wonderful it would be in nine months to finally cuddle a baby of their own.

It was late Friday afternoon, and Evie couldn't wait for the weekend. As the receptionist at the Horner Insurance Agency, she was tasked with opening and closing the office. The boss, Fred Horner, was usually at his desk by eight a.m., so Evie only had to unlock the front door and turn on the reception area lights when she arrived. Mr. Horner's wife was an attorney, so he often left mid-afternoon to pick up their children, leaving Evie as the only person until the official closing time of five p.m. Sometimes, one or two of the agents stayed if they had a late client meeting.

Friday afternoons were usually slow, and today everyone but Evie had departed early. As she closed and double-locked the outer door, she realized she was exhausted. Despite only working part time, she still felt worn out. The initial weeks of pregnancy stimulated massive hormone production, which caused fatigue. But knowing the reason did not lessen her lethargy.

To keep awake, she took frequent walks to the bathroom, not only to relieve her bladder, which seemed to have shrunk to half capacity, but also to shake off the somnolence. On her day off, she found herself craving an afternoon nap. She often awoke to find Daisy curled up at her back. She did not tell Leon that she let the cat sleep next to her. He was such a worrywart. She wondered if he would be one of those fathers-to-be who gained "sympathy" weight as the pregnancy progressed. Two nights ago, she'd caught him eating Rocky Road ice cream before he went to bed.

Evie experienced mild morning sickness most days, but instead of dreading the sensation, she reveled in the slight nausea and sensitivity to food odors. She felt reassured by the sensation, a sign that the baby was doing well. So far, she had not vomited, but she kept a supply of saltine crackers at the ready to ward off the metallic taste that sometimes accompanied the nausea. She missed drinking coffee in the morning, but the aroma of freshly brewed coffee roiled her stomach. In a show of solidarity, Leon declared he wouldn't drink coffee in the morning until he got to work, and on weekends, he abstained altogether. She smiled. He was such a loving and attentive man and so excited about the pregnancy.

As she headed down the stairs and onto the sidewalk, the

extreme exhaustion of early pregnancy slammed her. She hoped it wouldn't continue for the remaining eight months. Her sister-in-law suffered dreadfully during her first trimester, and then miraculously awakened one day feeling marvelous. Evie hoped to feel marvelous soon.

During the six-block walk to their apartment, she moved along at a leisurely pace, enjoying the sensation of the late afternoon sun caressing her face. She loved the contrast between the brilliant blue sky and the white puffy clouds. The slight breeze felt delightfully cool in contrast to the sun's warmth. She was fortunate she could walk to work since they only had one car. She wondered if they would need a second vehicle once the baby was born. Or maybe Leon would hitch a ride with one of his work buddies.

They hadn't really talked about whether she would continue working. She believed her sister might be willing to watch the baby a few days a week since she was already staying at home with her toddler, but she hadn't asked. They had not told any of their family members or friends about the pregnancy. It felt too early to announce. And, they reasoned, if something happened, they didn't want to relive the disappointment each time someone inquired how she was feeling. Waiting until the end of the first trimester when the risk of miscarriage all but disappeared seemed prudent. That meant five more long weeks before they could share the news.

She turned onto the sidewalk leading to the front door of the townhouse apartment they'd moved into three years ago, shortly after they'd married. The first floor of their townhome, one of the more modest units, contained a living room, eat-in kitchen, and telephone booth-sized powder room. Two small bedrooms, a medium-sized linen closet, and a bath comprised the upper floor. Right now, the second bedroom was mostly used for storage, but she could hardly wait to clean it out and set up a nursery.

Evie mounted the two small stairs and unlocked the front door. Daisy leapt off the couch and padded toward her. Bending down to give the cat a quick head rub, she glanced at her watch and wondered when Leon would get home. Some Fridays he stayed late performing the end-of-week deep clean. She guessed this was a small price to pay because he had most Saturdays free. She shrugged out of her jacket and hung it on the coat rack beside the front door. Entering the kitchen, she removed a foil-covered glass baking dish from the refrigerator and set it on the counter. Tonight, they were having lasagna, courtesy of Leon's mother, and a big green salad. It was Leon's favorite meal, and Evie appreciated her mother-in-law's thoughtfulness.

As the oven preheated, she kicked off her shoes and poured a glass of lemonade. Her stomach rumbled with hunger and she snacked on cheese and crackers.

The oven beeped to let her know it was ready, and Evie opened the door and slid the lasagna onto the top rack. Then she set the small table and added some candles. Why not have a bit of romance?

While assembling the salad items, she felt a small twinge followed by an ache in her lower abdomen, right above her pubic bone. She had experienced this pulling sensation before and been reassured it was a normal feeling in the early stages of pregnancy. Dr. Porter told her it was from the uterus stretching and growing, but this felt a bit more intense, like menstrual cramps. She sat down on one of the kitchen chairs, and the feeling immediately subsided. She decided to remain sitting while she tore lettuce and chopped vegetables for the salad.

Maybe I'll talk to Leon about driving to work next week, she thought. *It might not be good for me to be walking so much.*

At that precise moment, the front door opened, and Leon bounded in. "Hi honey," he said, leaning in for a quick kiss. "How are you feeling?"

She smiled in welcome and stood to give him a hug. "You say the same thing every night."

"Well, I want to know every night because it's been a whole nine hours since I've seen you. A lot can happen."

"True. So far so good, but I'm still super tired." She thought about mentioning the ache in her lower abdomen but decided against it. She didn't want to worry him. When she stood, the cramping sensation returned.

"What's for dinner?"

"That lasagna your mom brought over yesterday. It's in the oven and will be ready in an hour. And I'm making a salad."

"Yum," Leon replied enthusiastically as he headed up the stairs to wash and change out of his grease-stained work clothes. "My favorite meal! I bet this baby is gonna love lasagna."

Evie finished the salad, covered the bowl with plastic wrap, and set it back inside the refrigerator. The cramping continued, and she headed to the powder room, thinking the sensation might be from a full bladder. After all, she'd just finished a whole glass of lemonade.

Arising from the toilet, she glanced down at the toilet paper in her hand, preparing to toss it into the bowl. Wide-eyed, she stared in disbelief at the bright red stain. Her heart began to race as she considered the quarter sized spot on the tissue. Surely this was not normal. She should not be bleeding! Turning around, she investigated the water in the toilet bowl. It was pink tinged. Taking deep breaths, she tried to stay calm. She flushed the toilet, found a sanitary pad in the cabinet under the sink, and slowly dressed.

She heard Leon pounding down the stairs as she gingerly stepped from the powder room.

Seeing her face, he stopped cold. "What's wrong? Are you okay?"

She shook her head slowly and carefully sat down on the couch. Daisy jumped up next to her and tried to climb into her lap, but Evie gently pushed her away.

"Leon, we have to call the doctor. I went to the bathroom, and I'm bleeding."

CHAPTER 6

Joyce turned off the computer and straightened the files on her desk. It was after six p.m. on Friday, and she had one more thing to do, water the plants. The African violet was doing better since she'd placed it closer to the window facing the sun and the peace lily, a gift from her Aunt Celia her first day at McArthur, was thriving.

She remembered reading somewhere that the peace lily was designated by NASA as one of the top ten household air-cleaning plants, which was fitting since Aunt Celia's husband, Uncle Bernie, had been a NASA scientist. Joyce envisioned all that clean well-oxygenated air entering her lungs every time she took a relaxing breath.

Carrying a copper watering can, Joyce entered the empty staff kitchen. She enjoyed working after hours when it was calm. It gave her time to organize her thoughts and plan for the next day. Back in her office, she drenched the base of the African violet, taking care not to moisten the furry leaves.

Her cell phone chimed with an incoming text. Setting the can on the floor, she swiped open the message. It was from the answering service regarding a patient with some bleeding.

Scrolling through the message, she was surprised to see the caller was Leon Coleman.

"Oh no," she murmured to herself. "Not Evie."

Noticing her battery was low, Joyce plugged the phone into the charger and dialed the number from the office phone. She visualized the couple and sought to remember when Evie was due for her first ultrasound. She recalled that her initial human chorionic gonadotropin (HCG) and progesterone hormone levels had both been good, with repeat levels showing appropriate increases.

"Hello," a deep male voice answered on the first ring.

"Hello. This is Dr. Porter. The answering service said you called and left a message that Evie's having some bleeding. May I speak with her please?"

"Sure. I'll put you on speaker."

After a brief pause, Joyce heard Evie's voice. It was distant and trembled slightly. "Hello, Dr. Porter. Thank you for calling back. We're so sorry to bother you on a Friday night."

"It's okay. That's why we have an answering service, so you can get through to us if you're having a problem. What's happening?"

"Well, I was really tired today, and while I was making dinner, I had that pulling sensation again in my lower abdomen. But I sat down, and it went away."

Joyce murmured encouragingly, and Evie continued.

"Right after Leon got home, it came back again, and I went to the bathroom thinking it might be because my bladder was full. When I got up, I noticed there was blood on the toilet paper, and the water in the toilet was pink."

At this point, her voice broke, and there was a long pause before she resumed speaking, this time in a barely audible voice. "Dr. Porter, I'm really scared."

With the phone in one hand, Joyce reached down to restart her office computer and waited for it to boot so she could access Evie's medical record.

"Evie, remind me again. When did you have the embryo transfer?"

Leon answered, "About three weeks ago."

The computer was taking forever to boot, so Joyce continued questioning the couple.

"When did you have your last hormone levels drawn?"

This time Evie replied, "This past Tuesday."

"And when are you scheduled to come in for your ultrasound?"

After a brief silence, Evie said, "I'm not sure of the date, but I think in about a week."

There was another silence, and then Leon spoke. "I looked at the calendar, and we're scheduled to come in next Thursday. We were supposed to come in on Tuesday, but one of the guys at work is on vacation, and I have to cover that day."

Joyce glanced at the computer screen, where the icon had finally stopped swirling and the log-in screen for the electronic health record had appeared. Trying to hold the phone to her ear with her shoulder, she awkwardly typed in her username and password and waited again for the prompt to enter the patient's name. All the security features meant that it took forever for the patient's records to finally appear and required multiple clicks through many menus until Joyce could finally view Evie's chart.

Joyce moved the phone to her other ear to alleviate the cramp in her neck.

"I'm still at work, so while I'm bringing up your chart, tell me how you feel right now."

"I'm laying down on our couch, and I still feel a few cramps, but I don't think I've had any more bleeding."

"Okay, that's good. And how much bleeding did you have? Was it like the start of a period?"

"Oh no. It was only on the toilet paper when I wiped."

"How big was the spot?"

"About the size of a quarter, but it was bright red. And that's what scared me, and why I told Leon to call."

Joyce hummed sympathetically before asking, "And did you actually see any blood in the toilet?"

"Not really, just a pink stain."

Joyce quickly clicked through Evie's chart, before continuing. "I'm looking at your chart now, and so far, everything has been going well. You know, sometimes patients have a bit of spotting right when the pregnancy is burrowing into the lining of the uterus. We call that 'implantation bleeding.' And even a little bit of blood can irritate the uterus and make you have some cramps."

Now Leon asked, "Can we come in tomorrow for an ultrasound?"

"I think it's too soon. If we don't see anything, it wouldn't necessarily mean there was a problem. But I know how frightening it is to have bleeding, so let's have you come to the clinic tomorrow for a blood test. We'll make sure Evie's hormone levels are still okay. In the meantime, Evie, you should take it easy. No scrubbing floors or taking long bike rides. I'd like you to stay home this weekend and off your feet as much as possible."

"We can do that," Leon said before Evie could reply. "I won't let her do any work."

"And one more thing," Joyce added. "Don't put anything in your vagina. No tampons, no douching, and no intercourse."

"All right," Evie answered. "What time do you want us there tomorrow?"

"How about eleven?"

"That's fine," Leon said.

"Good. I'm on call this weekend, so I'll see you both tomorrow. And call back tonight if the cramps become more severe or you have bleeding that's more than a pad an hour."

Evie's voice sounded stronger now and less frightened. "Will do. And thanks, Dr. Porter, I feel better. See you tomorrow."

For the second time that evening, Joyce turned off her

computer. As the screen went dark, her cell phone chimed again. This time it was a text from her friend Sally.

Hey. Meet @ Zelda's for a drink?

Joyce thumbed in a response. *Not Zelda's. Too noisy. Sacco's?*

K. See u there @ 730

Walking toward her favorite wine bar, Joyce questioned the wisdom of meeting Sally downtown on a Friday night. The streets were packed, and parking had been a bear. A group of boisterous college students jostled her as they passed, no doubt getting psyched for college football the next day.

Zipping her coat against the cool night air, she rounded the corner and Sacco's Café came into view. The rustic sign glowed, illuminating the line of patrons waiting outside. She wondered if Sally had scored a table. She was having doubts about accepting the invite since she was on call, and she made a habit of not drinking when on call. But it was Friday night, and she looked forward to seeing her friend.

The wooden-plank door swung open as she reached for the handle, and she was immediately wrapped in raucous chatter and the smell of garlic and freshly baked pizza. A glow emanated from the wood-fired brick oven. It backlit a dark-haired man in a chef's hat deftly removing a pizza from the oven's depths. She heard her name and turned to see Sally waving from one of the side booths.

Threading her way toward the table, Joyce barely missed colliding with a harried waitress carrying a large pizza and a handful of napkins. Sally stood and greeted Joyce with a broad smile. She wore an oversized rust-colored cowl-neck tunic, black leggings, and ankle boots, and she smelled like her favorite Bvlgari perfume.

After giving Joyce a hug, she gestured enthusiastically toward the opposite bench. "Have a seat. I already ordered us some wine."

Joyce noticed two Bordeaux glasses and an open bottle of L'Ecole on the table.

Removing her coat and sliding onto the upholstered banquette, she raised her voice to be heard over the din. "It's busy here tonight. Lots of students and families. Is it a football weekend?"

"I think so. I saw a lot of black and gold scarves and hats. Maybe it's Homecoming or something."

Sally reached for the bottle of wine and skillfully poured a generous amount into the nearest glass.

Joyce put her hand over top of the other wine glass. "None for me. I'm having water tonight."

"No way! Why only water?"

"I'm on call, and I don't like to drink when I'm on call."

"Joyce, be serious. When was the last time you got called in at night? That's why we work at a university that has residents, so we don't have to go in at night."

"I know, but it still doesn't feel right. Did I ever tell you about the attending physician we had in my residency program who used to come into the OB call rooms to sleep it off after he'd been on a bender? We could always tell. His eyes would glitter, and he'd leer at the female staff. One time, he even made a pass at me."

"Oh God. What did you do?"

"I locked myself in the staff lavatory until he stumbled off to bed."

"Did you tell anyone?"

"I told Bill, and he encouraged me to report it. A few days later I told my chief resident, but he just shrugged it off and told me to stay out of his way. Apparently, everyone knew about his 'problem' and they all ignored it as best they could."

"That's outrageous." Sally huffed indignantly.

"That's what I thought, but there's more. About six months after he made a pass at me, there were two more incidents."

Sally leaned in toward Joyce. "But didn't you say the drinking had been a well-known problem?"

"Yup. But there was a powerful wall of silence surrounding

this guy. He belonged to one of the biggest physician groups in the city, and he was the president of the local medical society. No one wanted to cross him. He had a reputation for being vindictive and mean, even when he wasn't drunk. If you spoke out against him, you were likely to incur his wrath."

"I hope this has a good ending. What finally happened?"

"The last straw came when he showed up drunk one night to a delivery. The nurses complained and so did the on-call resident. Hard to ignore, even for our reluctant chief. The next day, he and another senior resident bypassed the hospital administration where our drunk doc had a lot of friends and went to the department chair, Dr. Bromsgrove."

She took a sip of water. "Bromsgrove was a good old boy who tried to give them the brush-off and defend his 'esteemed' colleague, but they stood firm. They told him if he didn't get this guy into rehab, they were going to file a complaint with the state medical board."

Sally shook her head incredulously. "What took them so long?"

"Fear, I think. I didn't know it at the time, but they'd tried to blow the whistle a year before and nothing happened. They both knew how vengeful this guy could be."

Sally sat back in her seat and took a sip of wine. "That's some tale. Did the lush go to rehab?"

Joyce picked up the water glass, swirling the liquid until the ice cubes clinked together before setting it down again. "I don't actually know what happened. He sort of disappeared. We were told he was 'on leave.' But I don't think he ever had his hospital privileges revoked or his license suspended. He came back halfway through my last year, and I didn't see much of him. Two years later, I heard he died unexpectedly from pneumonia. I didn't even send a card."

Sally unfolded her napkin and carefully placed the fork to the side. Then she leaned in. "I had a similar experience during medical school with a resident coming onto me. He didn't have a drinking problem, but he got handsy one night in the call room. I had to be careful after that to never be alone with him. I tried talking to my attending, but he gave me the same 'stay out of his way' advice you got."

"Sometimes life isn't fair," Joyce stated cynically.

"Well, I don't think that experience should keep you from having one glass of this outstanding wine on a Friday night. Hydrate and eat something. You'll be fine. You know, they have excellent pizza here."

"Well, maybe I'll have a sip, and then it's back to water. Since you mentioned it, I am hungry. Pizza sounds great. What type do you like?"

"How about their house special white pizza—I think they call it the 'Marilyn Monroe.'"

Joyce raised her eyebrows doubtfully and studied the menu. "Hmm, that might be a little adventuresome for me. How about The Garden of Eden? It has mushrooms, onions, green and red bell peppers, and black olives."

"That sounds good too. And what a fun name! Do you think they had pizza in the Garden of Eden?"

"Not sure. But I bet they had wine." As the waitress approached, Joyce inhaled the wine's bouquet before taking a small sip. "This is delicious. We'll have to order it again some night when I'm off duty."

Turning to the waitress, they placed their order for one medium-sized Garden of Eden pizza and two small salads, and Joyce asked for some sparkling water with a twist of lime.

After the waitress left, they leaned toward each other, struggling to be heard over the Friday night babble.

"Where's Bill this weekend?"

"He's not coming. And I don't want to talk about it. It's a sore spot right now."

"C'mon. I'm your best friend. What's going on?"

"He says he's behind in his thesis research."

"Okay. That's nothing new."

"He said he doesn't want to spend five hours in the car when we'll only have a few hours together on Saturday night. I get it, but I spend the same amount of time in the car when I drive to Baltimore. We made a commitment to be together on weekends, and he's not holding up his end. And I'm annoyed that he doesn't think it's worth it, even if we only see each other for dinner on Saturday." Joyce's normally calm demeanor suddenly disappeared. Her cheeks flushed and her eyes flashed. "And now that we're talking about it, I'm starting to get mad!"

Sally searched her friend's face before replying. "I know you're hurt and frustrated, but I kinda get Bill's point. That trip on I-95 is a bear, and you know you won't have much free time. My last call weekend, I was in the office eight hours on both days. And when I got home, I was beat." She patted Joyce's hand. "I understand why you're miffed, and I'm sorry Bill decided to stay in Richmond." She was saved further explanation when the waitress returned with the sparkling water. As she was leaving, Joyce's cell phone buzzed with an incoming text message. She apologized to Sally, who waved her off. "Go. Take care of it. Being on call is a drag. But if you don't come back, I'll have to bring your pizza to work on Monday."

Joyce glanced down and saw the message was from Leon Coleman.

"Not good," she said. Scooting out from the booth, she headed toward the quiet back hallway to return the call.

CHAPTER 7

Driving to work early on Saturday was a mixed blessing. Traffic was light, and Joyce sailed through four green lights before finally hitting a red. Determined to keep a positive outlook in spite of her frustration with Bill and her worry about the Colemans, she decided to treat herself to some Starbucks. Sitting in the drive-thru after placing her order, she glanced out the window. It was going to be a sunny fall day, perfect for a football game. She loved fall, which she always associated with new beginnings. It was an intoxicating feeling, like anything was possible.

After generously tipping the cheerful college student with the butterfly tattoo on her wrist, Joyce tucked the waxed bag containing the oversized muffin into her tote bag. Balancing the coffee cup on the console, she maneuvered her trusty Civic back onto the street. Two blocks later, she pulled into the faculty lot, locked the door and headed for the clinic's back entrance.

The hallway was dark, and she switched on the lights before turning off the alarm system. She turned left and headed to her office to eat her breakfast in peace. She figured she had a good fifteen minutes before Selena and the medical assistant showed up. They had ten patients scheduled for bloodwork and ultrasounds.

Plopping down in her desk chair, Joyce took a sip of the steaming latte, broke the muffin in half, and then opened the local newspaper. She flipped to the crossword puzzle and began filling in answers.

A few minutes later, Selena stepped in. "Did you unlock the clinic front door when you came in this morning?"

"No. I came in through the back. Why?"

"I found it unlocked this morning. The lock was flipped, but somehow, the mechanism hadn't engaged."

"Hmm. Maybe it's broken," Joyce said, glancing up from her puzzle.

"Maybe. One of the other nurses found the same thing last week. She thought the night custodian hadn't properly closed it when he finished cleaning."

"Please put in a work order on Monday for someone to fix it. The last thing we need is someone wandering around the clinic after hours."

The morning passed swiftly, and Joyce was surprised to see it was almost eleven. There were two more patients before Evie and Leon. She performed the routine ultrasounds and gave both couples instructions for the upcoming week.

Before heading into Evie's exam room, she found Selena at her workstation. "How're they doing? They called twice last night and were in a panic after Evie passed a small clot."

A small furrow creased Selena's smooth umber forehead, a sure sign she was concerned. "They both look terrible, like they didn't get much sleep."

"Is she still bleeding?"

"Only some brown spotting. But poor girl. She told me she was afraid to shower this morning."

"Oh goodness. She must really be terrified."

"I'd say. They really want an ultrasound."

"I know, but it's too soon to see anything helpful. I thought

I'd do a quick cervical check, draw some blood, then send her home to bed rest for the weekend."

Selena gazed down at her paperwork.

After a short pause, Joyce continued, "You know, there isn't really anything I can do at this point. Whatever will be, will be."

Selena looked up. "I know that. Seeing you today will make them feel better. They know you care." She shifted her weight on the high-backed stool. "They're both so sweet. I really want things to work out for them. I know we don't have favorites, but if we did, they'd be on my list." Selena smiled as she shooed Joyce down the hall. "So, go in there and work your magic."

Joyce knocked twice and entered the room. Evie was seated on the edge of the exam table wearing an oversized powder-blue sweater and jeans. Her hair was a riot of tightly sprung curls pulled back in a clip. Her face looked puffy. In the unforgiving light of the exam room, her light-brown skin was sallow. Selena was right. She looked terrible.

Leon, sitting in the chair next to his wife, looked only slightly better. His dark brown eyes were bloodshot, and he hadn't shaved. The buttons on his flannel shirt were mismatched, like he'd dressed too quickly. Both tried to smile when she greeted them, but it was half-hearted at best.

"Hello. I'm glad you were able to come today," Joyce said. Hoping to put them at ease, she pulled out the rolling stool and sat down, then looked directly at Evie. "What's happened since I talked to you last night?"

Leon started to answer, but at a look from Evie, he closed his mouth and slouched back in his chair.

"I haven't had any more bright red bleeding. Just some old brown stuff." She pointed to her lower abdomen and added, "My stomach still feels a little heavy."

"Any more cramps?"

"No, not really. But I've been scared to move around too much." Looking a bit ashamed, she looked away before adding,

"I'm sorry, but I didn't even shower this morning. I was too afraid."

"It's okay. I understand. Are you still having morning sickness?"

"Yes, a little. But not too bad. I didn't eat much for breakfast today, just a piece of dry toast and some tea."

Joyce repositioned the stool so she could make eye contact with both of them as she spoke. "It's very frightening to have any kind of bleeding when you're pregnant. It's a good sign that it hasn't continued and that you're still having some morning sickness. Did you get any sleep?"

Evie's gaze shifted toward Leon and then back at Joyce. "No. Neither of us did. We've both been so worried." Evie stopped, took a shaky breath, and then asked quietly, "Am I going to lose the baby?"

Joyce tried to speak reassuringly. This was always difficult, being optimistic but not raising false hope. "I don't think so, but we'll know more after your blood work comes back."

Leon sat forward, his hands balled into fists. He spoke urgently. "Isn't there anything you can do? There must be something!"

Joyce stood up from her chair and handed Evie an exam drape. "Let's have you get undressed from the waist down. I'll be back shortly to do a quick exam." Then looking at Leon, she added, "We'll talk after that."

Standing in the hallway waiting for Evie to disrobe, Joyce found herself thinking about Bill. She wondered what he was doing. He'd told her he was planning to spend most of the day in the library. Wandering to the end of the hallway, she noticed the gorgeous fall day. If the weather was the same in Baltimore, she doubted he'd remain inside all day. She sighed because she still faced several hours of work.

She tapped twice and re-entered the exam room. She gently guided Evie through the abdominal and pelvic exams and then helped her sit up.

"I have good news. I don't see any new bleeding, and only a small amount of old brown discharge coming from your cervix. So far, it doesn't look like you miscarried."

"But is everything okay?" Leon persisted.

"For now, yes. But we're still not out of the woods." Joyce washed her hands at the small corner sink and then pivoted to face Evie. "What I'd like is for you to go home and take it easy. Hang out on the couch and watch old movies. Take a nap. Read a magazine." Joyce pointed at Leon and grinned. "Let him do all the cooking and the housework. It'll be good practice for after you have the baby."

For the first time, Leon and Evie smiled. Their shoulders seemed to relax. They no longer appeared as frightened.

"I can do that," Leon said, "But is it okay for me to leave Evie for an hour so I can go to the store? We're almost out of food. We usually go shopping together on Saturdays. And lately, she's been craving popsicles, those bright green ones."

Joyce scrunched her nose and frowned dramatically. "Lime green! Hmm. Maybe it's a boy." Then she nodded at Leon. "It's fine for you to shop as long as there's a way for her to call you in case something changes."

"No problem."

"I'll call you with those test results later today. Take care."

Back at the nurse's station, Joyce told Selena and the medical assistant they could take off once the Colemans left. She figured she had enough time to head to the cafeteria for a quick bite before the two afternoon procedures, an egg retrieval and an embryo transfer. Then there would be the afternoon patient phone calls once the lab results were in. She pulled out her phone, texted Bill that she missed him, then grabbed her wallet and headed to the cafeteria.

By early Sunday evening, Joyce's neck and back ached, and she was exhausted. She'd worked a solid ten hours both days and had one more call to make.

Leon answered and reported Evie was doing better. She'd spent the weekend resting on the couch, eating popsicles and watching reruns of *Buffy the Vampire Slayer*. When Evie got on the phone, she sounded more cheerful. The cramping and bleeding were completely gone. Despite the couple's fears, she hadn't lost the pregnancy. Joyce assured her again that her hormone levels were good. There were several possible causes for the bleeding, but the most likely explanation was that it was the embryo implanting. Joyce didn't mention the possibility of a twin pregnancy, but she wondered about it, particularly given the high hormone levels along with the slight bleeding. Everyone, Joyce included, was eager for their upcoming ultrasound. Evie asked if she could return on Monday to her desk job at the insurance company, and Joyce said yes.

Pushing open the apartment door, Joyce felt around for the foyer light before stepping into the lonely darkness. As if to dispute her assessment, Mittens strutted into the hallway, tail held high in a proud salute. He voiced a feline greeting and wrapped himself around her legs. She bent down to scratch him between his ears and then ran her hand down his back. She ended with a gentle tug on his fluffy tail.

"Hey you. I'm glad you're happy to see me. I suppose you're hungry too. Let's see what exciting entrée we have in store for you tonight."

After feeding the cat, she debated whether to eat or take a shower. She decided the shower was more important and headed off to the bathroom. Emerging thirty minutes later in gray fleece lounge pants and a long-sleeved hoodie, she noticed a missed call from Bill. She wasn't ready to call him back. They'd briefly spoken this afternoon while she was still at work, but it hadn't gone well.

Picking up the TV remote, she pushed the power button and

plopped down heavily on the old couch. It was slightly lumpy, so it took a minute to settle in and find the most comfortable position. Dinner tonight was a bowl of popcorn and a diet soda, and she was looking forward to the next episode of Masterpiece Theater's *Downton Abbey*. She decided to watch her show before returning Bill's call.

While the lavish opening theme swelled, a wave of resentment began to build as she replayed their afternoon conversation in her head. She'd had some down time waiting for the lab results, so she'd phoned Bill. Their discussion had been surprisingly bland, no more than a polite exchange of mundane details about the weather and their weekend activities. Because she'd been at McArthur for ten hours both days, she'd been too tired to exercise or shop for groceries.

By contrast, Bill had taken a five-mile run on Saturday afternoon and then gone out to the pub with his friends. On Sunday morning, he did his laundry then played soccer with an adult rec league. In between bouts of athleticism, he focused on his thesis project and was quite pleased with its progress. He'd finished most of the background research, and he was back on track with the writing. For him, the weekend had been both relaxing and productive.

Reflecting on Bill's apparent contentment with his solo weekend made Joyce feel even more lonely. They didn't seem to be on the same page anymore, and she wondered if he'd even noticed. He'd sounded energized and happy while describing his weekend, and she realized she hadn't said much during their brief exchange. Even more worrisome, he didn't seem to notice her ennui. Uncomfortable questions without answers tormented her. Was it possible he was seeing someone else? Joyce immediately felt disloyal for even considering the idea. But really, was it possible there was some reason he hadn't come other than his dislike of weekend traffic? She hated the distance, which lately felt emotional as well as physical. Slowly, her anger was replaced by fear, and she was plagued with unanswerable questions.

Mittens jumped onto the couch beside Joyce and carefully stepped into her lap. With his feline ESP, he seemed to know she needed comfort. She stroked his silky fur and switched her focus back to the television. At least the weekend was over. She was grateful that Monday at seven a.m. sharp, the on-call responsibilities would pass to Sally. She promised herself that she'd find time to exercise, shop for groceries, and do her laundry during the upcoming week.

Her mind drifted back to work. The fourteen active IVF patients had kept her occupied all weekend with ultrasounds, egg retrievals, and medication adjustments. Next week looked to be equally busy. She sincerely hoped the black cloud hovering over the lab would lift and their fertilization rates return to normal. Kumar kept assuring her everything was fine, but she struggled to believe him.

The pristine English countryside flickered across the screen, and Joyce's mind shifted from the responsibilities of a 21st-century infertility practice to turn-of-the-century British nobility. Mittens purred contentedly while Joyce covered them both with an afghan and settled in.

CHAPTER 8

Ajay Kumar arrived at the lab early Monday morning. He flipped on the lights and set his thermal travel mug on the desk next to the picture of his daughter taken on her last birthday. She had birthday cake on her face and was wearing a big smile. While waiting for his computer to chug through its start-up sequence, he hung his jacket on a hook and stowed his lunch in the small office refrigerator. He reviewed the logged entries from the weekend egg retrievals, which had been staffed by his lab assistant Dr. Chandra Singh. Dr. Singh, a postgraduate Embryology and Anatomy fellow, was always thorough in his documentation.

Scrolling quickly through the entries, Kumar saw several of the eggs had been fertilized with "augmented" sperm. An "A" placed next to the entry was the lab's shorthand for the practice of mixing donor sperm with the husband's sperm. While this was ethically permissible and sometimes medically appropriate, it required detailed informed consent from both the patient and her partner. When Hicks had first suggested this "backup" plan, Kumar had been appalled and vehemently opposed. While there was no doubt that it boosted the pregnancy rate, particularly in couples with male-factor infertility, it completely side-stepped the informed-consent process, a gross ethical and legal violation. While this plan had been used infrequently in the past, mainly for couples like the Colemans who had received a Foundation grant to help them afford IVF, recently Hicks had ordered that it be used for all couples until the fertilization and pregnancy rates improved.

Kumar squirmed in his chair, thinking Hicks was really over the edge this time. He'd never been comfortable with this practice, but he had long ago learned to keep his mouth closed. Both lab technicians were familiar with the practice, but they had been kept in the dark about the fact that not all couples formally consented. From Hicks's point of view, they were giving the patients what they paid for, a better-than-average chance at a healthy pregnancy. And so far, no one had caught on.

What would happen if someone did?

He pushed the terrifying thought aside. He determined he would work unceasingly to identify the problem so no more entries would show the "A" notation unless it was at the patient's request.

He clicked on the email icon and watched several messages download. One was from Hicks, so he opened it first. He sighed as he read the text.

Ajay, what the hell is happening? You told me you fixed the problem. Have you managed to keep Porter's nose out of the lab? I'll be back in a week, so just keep a lid on things. BTW, the visiting professor from France is interested in our clinical protocols. He's especially interested in our hormonal treatment of women with premature ovarian failure. I don't think he'll spend much time in the lab. Look for him sometime next week.

Stepping back into the main lab, Kumar approached the incubator and prepared to transport the dishes containing the eggs and sperm to the enclosed sterile area. As he readied the microscope located in the negative pressure hood, he offered a quick prayer they would show evidence of fertilization and not need the "A" intervention. If that were the case, he would take it as confirmation that the problems of the past two weeks were behind them. He wasn't thrilled about that Frenchman coming to visit either. He had enough to worry about. One more person poking about and asking questions was one more thing to contend with.

Taking a deep breath, he placed the glass dish on the microscope stage and adjusted the binocular lens to peer at the egg and murmured, "Ah yes, this one looks fine."

After examining a few more samples, he let out his breath and felt his heart rate calm. *Disaster averted, at least for today.*

"Good morning, Dr. Porter." Selena looked up from her hallway desk. "My, my, we were busy this weekend."

Joyce stopped to pick up the stack of mail from the nurse's station inbox. "We certainly were. Have you heard from Dr. Kumar? How many embryos do we have?"

"He said all the couples have viable ones, and we should schedule two transfers for tomorrow. You can call him for the details. Will you be doing them or should I talk to Dr. Cohen?"

Joyce glanced up from the pile of junk mail. The topmost flyer, a picture of a serene beach and azure ocean, was for a conference scheduled in February at the Maui Ritz Carlton. She gazed at it longingly before replying, "Talk to Sally. She's covering procedures this week. I can help in a jam, but I really need some catch-up time. I have that conference in a few weeks, and my talk still isn't finished."

Selena looked interested. "The one in New Orleans? Who else is going?"

"Sally. And Dr. Hicks. Jim Torrey agreed to stay behind and man the fort. It should be a good meeting."

Joyce threw away all the junk mail except for the Maui brochure, picked up her shoulder bag and headed toward her office.

Selena spoke to her retreating back. "Dr. Porter, there's one more thing."

Joyce turned. "Yes?"

"There's a man waiting in your office. He's a bit hard to understand, but I think he said his name is Dominic something. He told me he's a visiting professor from France and that you're expecting him."

Joyce abruptly stopped, pivoted, and hurried back to Selena's station. Bending over, she whispered, "Good grief! He wasn't supposed to be here until next week! What's he like? Young, old? Tall, short?"

Selena smiled as Joyce finger-combed her short blond hair and bit her lips to add some color. "He's average height and easy on the eyes. Go on, you look fine for someone who worked a busy weekend."

Joyce raised her eyebrows. "That bad?"

"No, really. You look fine. Better get a move on. Your first patient is in the waiting room filling out paperwork. She's an attorney and is already tapping her foot impatiently. You know what that means."

"Hmm. Do you think she'll send us a bill for her time like the last one did?"

"Anything is possible, but I wouldn't keep her waiting too long."

As Joyce walked down the hall, she wondered about the man in her office. She wished she'd taken more care with dressing this morning instead of putting on the first clean thing she found, a plain black pencil skirt and simple white blouse. At least the blouse was trimmed with pearl buttons, and she was wearing low heels instead of her normal flats. They added a few inches to her otherwise petite stature and always made her feel a little more in control. She looked down to assure herself that the shoes matched, remembering the time she'd come in wearing one black and one dark blue. Then she touched her ears to make sure her earrings were in place. The small pearl studs had been a gift from her parents when she'd graduated from college.

She shook her head, silently laughing at herself. Why was she suddenly so concerned about her appearance before meeting the mysterious Frenchman? Would he turn out to be the tall, dark, and handsome man of Sally's dreams, or someone with a flat nasal accent and a condescending attitude? At least now she knew Dominique was a man. And given that he was French, he was bound to be interesting.

When she entered her office, a man with dark wavy hair and a dimple in his chin rose, extended his hand, and smiled. He wore a starched blue collared shirt that matched his eyes, a maroon patterned tie and navy pleated dress slacks. On his feet were polished black loafers with tassels, and a tan trench coat was slung over the back of the chair.

Good God, she thought. *Not too tall, but dark and handsome for sure. He even has a slightly crooked front tooth. And wait 'til I tell Sally—the dimple is in his chin!*

She shook herself back to reality in time to hear his low cultured voice. "Good morning, Dr. Porter. My name is Dominique DuPage. I am visiting from Montpellier, France. Your Dr. Hicks instructed me to report to you upon my arrival." His spoken English was excellent, with a slight but utterly entrancing accent.

Joyce nodded, put down her shoulder bag, and extended her own hand in greeting. Grasping his, she felt a warm flush stain her cheeks. She hoped he didn't notice. "Hello. It's good to meet you Dr. DuPage. Forgive me if I seem a bit flustered, but we didn't expect you until next week. Please sit down."

Joyce stepped around the desk and carefully placed the Maui brochure in her filing tray. Then she removed her coat, maneuvering around him on her way to the coat rack. The small office felt even smaller with him sitting and quietly observing her. She thought she smelled a faint whiff of spicy cologne.

"First of all, welcome to McArthur. How long will you be with us?"

He spoke somewhat shyly. "It is a great honor, Dr. Porter, to be invited to your prestigious institute. Dr. Hicks has graciously extended the invitation for one year, but I find I will only be able to stay for about six months. That is as long as I can reasonably expect my colleagues at St. Roche to do without me. Our facility does not see as many patients as yours, but it is still a strain when one of us is away."

Joyce glanced away while her thoughts whirled. Six months! Hicks hadn't said a thing about six months. What were they going to do with the charming Frenchman for six months? He couldn't follow her around for the entire time, but he couldn't see patients either without a Virginia medical license, hospital privileges, and malpractice insurance. It didn't matter how well trained he was, these types of things were complicated and took time.

Pondering this latest development, Joyce felt the familiar frustration sweep over her. Hicks was such a pain in the ass, always making promises and then letting everyone else do the work. He hadn't even bothered to send her a note letting her know DuPage's arrival day.

"Dr. DuPage," she started. But he interrupted her.

"Please call me Dominique."

"Okay. Then please call me Joyce." She paused and took a breath, biting her lower lip as she gathered her thoughts. She walked around the desk and slowly lowered herself into the chair. She tugged her skirt into place, carefully folded her hands, then looked up at the handsome Frenchman sitting patiently across from her.

"Dr. DuPage, ahh, Dominique." She paused, trying not to look as flustered as she felt. "As I mentioned, we didn't know you were coming this week, so we aren't as prepared as I'd like. I have a full schedule of patients today, and I'm not certain what you can and can't do with visiting professor status. Have you filled out any paperwork yet with the university?"

"Oh yes, months ago. And with your state of Virginia as well."

She relaxed. "That's great. Then the first step is probably to have you go to our Human Resources Department. They'll get you a staff ID badge and make sure everything is in order. I'll ask Selena, the nurse you already met, to walk you over. Why don't you plan to come back here to the clinic once you are done in HR?"

Dominique stood up and gathered his coat and briefcase. He flashed his crooked smile and the dimple in his chin deepened. He bowed slightly. "Thank you, Dr. Porter, ah, I mean Joyce. I apologize that my arrival was such a surprise. Perhaps we can have lunch together and speak a bit more when you are not so rushed."

"Sure. Sorry to rush, but I have a patient waiting. Please follow me to the clinic, and Selena will take you to HR."

As they rounded the corner leading back to the clinic, Sally Cohen entered from the main hallway. Seeing DuPage, her eyebrows shot up and she looked questioningly at Joyce. Joyce placed a hand on his arm and asked him to pause. She gestured toward Sally.

"Dr. DuPage, this is Dr. Sally Cohen, one of my colleagues. And, Sally, I'd like you to meet Dr. Dominique DuPage. He just arrived from France and will be working with us for the next six months."

Dr. DuPage looked at Sally and smiled his endearing smile, chin dimple in full view. He took her hand and Joyce wondered if Sally expected him to raise it to his lips for a formal kiss. After a quick handshake, they both spoke in unison, "I'm very pleased to meet you."

Laughing, Sally continued, "Where are you headed?"

He looked at Joyce, and she answered, "I thought I'd have

Selena walk Dr. DuPage over to HR. They can get him squared away."

"I was just heading over to the Admin building myself. I'm happy to walk with you and show you around a bit."

Joyce nodded as they turned and walked toward the main lobby. "Thanks, Sally." To Dominique she said, "See you at lunch."

Selena bustled over. "Okay. Time to get to work. I've put Madame *L'Avocate* in Consult Room *Un*. She's tapping her foot again and reminded me she must leave in minutes thirty for another *importante* appointment."

Joyce chuckled at Selena's attempted French and then listened as she continued the update. "The patient after her needs an ultrasound. She arrived fifteen minutes early and is in the restroom. We'd best shake a leg if you want to finish in time for lunch with Monsieur Doctor DuPage."

"Oh. My. God," Sally gushed to Joyce later that afternoon. "He's *gorgeous*! And on top of that, he seems nice, and maybe even a little shy. And that accent!" She did her best Southern belle swoon and fanned her face. "Why, honey, I could listen to him all day."

Still going with the Southern belle theme, Sally sashayed into Joyce's office and perched on the same chair that Dominique had occupied earlier. She fluffed her hair and pretended to arrange an imaginary hoop skirt. "See, I told you he would be wonderful. So what do you think about the man of my dreams?"

Joyce looked up from the computer screen where she was working on the conference presentation. She saved her work and then turned her attention to Sally. "Mmm. Yes, he is charming. Thanks for taking him to lunch. I'm sorry I missed it, but I got too bogged down with patients."

"No problem. My patient cancelled her surgery at the last

minute. I think she told the nurse she was coming down with a cold and didn't want to have anesthesia. Anyway, I had some unexpected free time, so it all worked out perfectly."

Joyce leaned toward Sally. "I'm all ears. What did you learn about him?"

"For starters, he's divorced. He has a twelve-year-old daughter named Juliette. She lives with her mother in Paris, but Dominique is already looking into ways she can visit him while he's here. It sounds like he is quite devoted to his daughter, and that he has an amicable relationship with his ex-wife."

"Good to know. Anything else? Did you talk at all about his professional practice or their IVF clinic?"

"Absolutely not! I figure there'll be plenty of time for the work-related stuff. I was on a mission to learn all about him as a person. I also found out he likes to ski, and he has been to the United States once for a conference in Orlando. He's hoping to take Juliette to Disney World while he's here."

"Did you tell him about Busch Gardens in Williamsburg? That's a lot closer, and they have really cool events around Halloween and Christmas. I bet a twelve-year-old would love it."

"I'll pass that along."

"Does it really sound like he's going to be around for six months?"

Sally popped a mint in her mouth from the small tin she kept in her white coat and offered one to Joyce. She declined, and Sally replaced the tin. "Yeah, I really think he is. He sublet a condominium from some Humanities professor who's going to Oxford for six months to study Shakespeare. Dominique says the two-bedroom condo is in a lovely restored building in the Museum District with good access to public transportation. It doesn't sound like he has a car or plans to buy one while he's here."

"That's not too far from where you live."

"I know!" Sally grinned. "Isn't it great? In fact, I offered to pick him up tomorrow and bring him to work with me."

Joyce laughed out loud at Sally's enthusiasm. It was hard not to respond to her friend's excitement. "We sound like two high school girls giggling over the new boy. When you got back from lunch, where did Dominique spend the rest of the afternoon?"

"I took him over to Dr. Kumar for a tour of the lab. I'm not sure where he went after that."

"I should probably try to find him some office space, or at least a desk and a computer. What do you think about putting him in the empty space where the medical students sometimes hang out? We don't have any students scheduled for the next few weeks, and there's already a desk and computer in there. It's one hallway over, but at least he'll have somewhere to stash his trench coat."

Sally glanced at her watch and quickly stood up. "Oops, gotta run. I need to pick up my dry cleaning before the place closes. See you tomorrow."

Joyce let the early evening quiet settle around her. She reflected on how different the room felt once Sally left. She was such a bundle of raw energy that sometimes Joyce felt positively bland standing next to her. Dominique would have his hands full if Sally decided to set her sights on him. Joyce looked at tomorrow's to-do list and added "Dom office."

She was an unapologetic list-maker, and nothing gave her greater satisfaction than scanning the list at day's end with its string of checked-off items. The longer the list, the better. Sometimes she included routine items like mailing a birthday card, so she could feel the satisfaction of checking it off. On a really bad day, she sometimes added things she had already done, like "empty the trash can" just so she had something to check off. Each check mark was a minor victory, and the list helped her stay focused and feel productive.

Today's list reminded her to "Finish presentation," and she turned her attention back to that task. She was reporting the first years' experience from the McArthur Foundation's financial assistance program for patients like Evie and Leon Coleman. The numbers were small, but overall, quite encouraging in terms of successful pregnancies. She was happy to add Evie's pregnancy to the list of successes. She studied the data tables. The pilot group of patients showed statistically significantly higher pregnancy rates than their general clinic population. Joyce suspected it was because they were on average 3.2 years younger, and most of them had Fallopian tube blockage as the main cause of their infertility. She glanced at the presentation outlined on a legal pad and estimated she'd completed about half the slide deck.

She rubbed her forehead, trying to massage away a mild headache. Editing the charts and graphs was slow going. Deciding what to highlight and what to leave out was always the question. Statistical data was the bedrock of all scientific presentations, and presenting it in a way that was interesting and engaging was an art.

Being asked to participate in a national symposium was a huge honor, and Joyce was eager to make a good impression. Establishing a strong professional network was important for her career. That way, no matter where Bill ended up, she would have contacts that could help her land a position. With a guilty start, she realized she hadn't thought about him all day.

Her stomach suddenly growled, and Joyce decided to call it a day. She still needed to buy groceries and pick up something from the deli for dinner. Cooking for herself seemed like too much trouble. By the time she was done, she was usually too tired to eat. She'd call Bill early and then take a relaxing bath. It would be wonderful to turn in early and get more than six hours of sleep.

As the computer powered down, she reached into the bottom desk drawer where she stored her purse and heard a soft knock. Popping up too quickly, she bumped her head on the underside of the desk and stifled a groan. Rubbing the side of her head, she gingerly stood up. Dominique watched from the doorway, an expression of regret and embarrassment on his face.

"Are you all right? I'm so sorry. I didn't mean to startle you."

"I'm fine. Just a bump. I do that at least once a week."

Dominique backed away. "I've come at a bad time. It looks like you're leaving."

"I am. I was on call this past weekend, and I'm exhausted. Do you need something?"

"No. I just stopped in to say good night, and to let you know how grateful I am to be here. I'm sorry you weren't able to join us for lunch."

"Me too. I skipped lunch today, too many patients. Tomorrow should be better. I have the morning free. Do you want to stop by around nine? We can have coffee and talk about what you'd like to do during the next six months."

He smiled. "Very well. I'll see you then." Before departing, he made a slight bow and murmured, *"Bonne soirée."*

His retreating footsteps echoed in the hall, and Joyce admitted to herself she found him charming and attractive. Not only was he handsome in a Gallic sort of way, he also exuded French chic. No wonder Sally was smitten. She had to agree that his personality was quite pleasant, and he had impeccable manners. During their brief conversations, she'd noticed his gaze was direct, and he listened intently. She put on her coat and stepped into the quiet hall, devoid this evening of the cleaning crew. Placing her key into the lock and hearing it click, she found herself thinking about tomorrow and realized she was looking forward to seeing Dr. Dominique DuPage again.

CHAPTER 9

Balancing her shoulder bag and two sacks of groceries, Joyce struggled up the staircase. She sat one of the bags on the landing, dug into her pocket for her key ring, and then wrestled open the apartment door. Mittens strolled out from the bedroom, hunched upward in a graceful stretch, and opened his mouth wide in a big yawn. With a haughty stare, he strutted over to his food dish and looked up expectantly.

Joyce stowed the frozen items, fed the cat, then put away the other groceries. As she put away the last item, her cell phone chirped. Caller ID showed a smiling photo of Bill. For a minute she considered letting it go to voicemail. She was exhausted and wanted to relax in peace. Reluctantly, she pushed *Answer*.

"Hello."

"Hi sweetie, it's me. I figured I'd call early tonight since you just got off weekend call. You sounded wiped yesterday. I bet you're planning a long hot bath and then off to bed."

She put the phone on speaker, sat it on the counter, and began setting the table for one. "You got that right. I just got home from the store, and I haven't eaten yet. Can I call you back in a few?"

"Well sure," he said, sounding slightly hurt. "But why don't we talk while you make dinner? That's what we did when we were living together."

What he said made perfect sense, but she didn't want to talk yet. She needed some decompression time. She wanted to sip wine and enjoy her curried chicken salad while scrolling through the daily news on her iPad. Maybe there'd be a juicy celebrity scandal or some major weather event to read about. She always skipped the political stuff or anything that seemed too contentious. On nights she felt more mentally alert, she did the *New York Times* crossword puzzle.

"You're right, but I'd rather have dinner and a little alone time before we talk. You know I'm grumpy when I haven't eaten, and today I missed lunch."

There was a long silence before Bill cleared his throat. When he spoke, his voice was tight, and he sounded annoyed. "All right. Call when you're done." Then he hung up.

Joyce tapped the key to close the phone line, feeling guilty. It wasn't Bill's fault that she'd missed lunch and was feeling hypoglycemic and bitchy. He'd been perfectly reasonable, and she gave him credit for understanding she'd want to take a bath and head off to bed early.

As she spooned the salad from the deli container over fresh romaine, she thought again about their current living situation. The first year they'd been apart had gone by quickly as she adjusted to her new job and Bill settled into his graduate program. During that year, he took a full load of courses and acted as a teaching assistant. But even with their crazy schedules, they'd managed to talk every night and see each other on weekends.

For some reason, maintaining their connection this year was a bigger challenge. Bill had happily settled into his academic life and was thriving. He loved his graduate program and genuinely respected his boss, Dr. Smythe, a trim no-nonsense fifty-something public health nurse who'd spent eighteen years working for an NGO in Africa doing HIV prevention and outreach. But instead of being happy for him, she felt jealous and resentful. He seemed to effortlessly handle the stress of new situations and was adept at adapting. He talked about his "lunch bunch," a group of simpatico grad students from his department that he often hung out with.

The chicken salad, flavored with turmeric and a hint of curry, was delicious. As she chewed, she realized missing lunch had become the norm and not the exception. She had no "lunch bunch." She also had no social life while Bill regularly played tennis and soccer and met up with his pals at the pub. She admitted to herself that other than twice weekly tai chi classes and an occasional night out with Sally, she did nothing outside of work.

Thinking about Hicks dampened her appetite. The episode in his office before he left for Paris had been unsettling. She wasn't naïve, but she'd assumed the old quid pro quo between senior faculty and new hires was a thing of the past.

Does he expect me to have sex with him? The very thought was nauseating.

Hicks knew a lot of important people who could be immensely useful to her in furthering her career, but what would she do if he demanded a physical relationship as the price for his mentorship? She took a sip of wine.

She felt conflicted. She loved Bill and would never consider cheating on him, but what would happen if Hicks continued pressuring her? She wouldn't sleep with him, of course, but she worried about outright rejecting him. Shoving the unanswered questions aside, she settled back to enjoy her quiet dinner.

The candle flickered while a Pink Martini CD played in the background. She knew most folks kept a curated playlist on their phone, but she preferred listening to music the old-fashioned way. As she finished her salad, she wondered where Dominique DuPage was eating tonight. Would he have stopped at a store to stock his kitchen, or was he one of those bachelor types who never cooked for himself? Maybe she should have offered to take him out to breakfast tomorrow. Frowning, she asked herself why she was so concerned about the eating habits of the Frenchman she'd just met. And why did thinking about him fill her with a pleasant sizzle of anticipation?

A quick look at the clock showed an hour had passed. Determined to stick to her plan of making it an early night, she stacked the few dishes in the dishwasher and stowed the leftovers in the refrigerator. She headed to the living room, wine glass in hand. Settling on the sofa, she dialed Bill. He answered on the second ring.

He still sounded annoyed. "Hello."

"Hi, honey. I've had some dinner and some wine, and I'm feeling a whole lot better. I'm sorry I snarled at you earlier."

There was a short pause before he replied in a neutral way, "It's okay. I get it, and I'm glad you're feeling better. How was your day?"

"Pretty busy but tomorrow looks better. I don't have any patients or surgeries scheduled, so I'll have time to finish my conference presentation."

"That's great. Is that the one in New Orleans?"

"Uh huh."

"Any other big news? How many people did you get pregnant today?"

"We had two positive pregnancy tests, which was great because last week we only had two the whole week. We were all getting a little worried."

"Oh yeah, I remember that. Did you ever figure out what the problem was?"

"Not really. It seemed to be in the lab, but Kumar insisted everything was fine. I'm never quite sure what to make of him. He's extremely polite but never very forthcoming. I always feel like I'm dragging things out of him. Sometimes, he seems evasive, like he's keeping some kind of secret."

"You mentioned spending some time in his lab. Did you learn anything new?"

"It turned out I was only able to grab two hours one day. Jim Torrey was out with a bad back for a couple of days, and I had to cover. And then there was the medical student lecture Hicks stuck me with at the last minute."

"That guy is complete scumbag. I can't imagine Dr. Smythe pulling a stunt like that."

"Well, you're lucky. Maybe public health professors are more considerate than reproductive endocrinologists. We could do a collaborative study on personality types and see who scores higher on the congeniality scale."

They both chuckled at the thought and then spent the next few minutes trying to one up each other with outlandish questions and humorous categories.

A few minutes later, Joyce switched to a new topic. "A visiting professor from France arrived today, Dr. Dominique DuPage."

"*Oui, oui.* Is Dr. DuPage a monsieur or a mademoiselle?"

Remembering her first impression, Joyce smiled and replied, "Very much a monsieur. Sally is smitten. At lunch, she grilled him on his personal life. He's divorced and has a twelve-year-old daughter who lives in Paris with her mother. He's subletting an apartment in the Museum District and staying for six months."

"Do you know why he's come to McArthur?"

"Not really. We didn't expect him to arrive until next week. He's another one of Hicks's little surprises. I didn't really get a chance to talk much with him today. He works at St. Roche, which I think is a pretty well-known IVF clinic in France. I'll meet with him tomorrow and find out what he wants to accomplish in his six months."

Bill's voice sounded puzzled. "Why is he working with you? I thought you said Hicks invited him."

"Well, he did, but like everything else, all Hicks's work goes to the rest of us. Why would this be any different? He isn't even back from Paris yet."

"I'd say Hicks has some nerve, telling the guy to show up when he isn't even in town."

"Well, he's the boss. And he's due back in a few days. We swallow our objections and soldier on. But on the bright side, I don't think it's going to be so bad. Sally said he's a nice guy, and it sounds like he's willing to help out in the clinic. We can use an extra pair of hands. I realized tonight that he needs some type of office, or at least a desk, so I'm going to appropriate the student lounge until we find something more suitable."

Their conversation flowed smoothly and easily, and Joyce was grateful that he didn't seem to hold a grudge regarding her earlier testiness.

Later, soaking in a lavender-scented bath, she resolved to plan something fun for their next weekend. Maybe they could spend the day at one of the nearby farms sipping cider and going through the corn maze. Afterward, they could enjoy a romantic dinner and maybe a movie or dancing. She made a mental note to look at the list of weekend events. Thinking about their upcoming weekend together filled her with optimism.

Maybe things will turn out okay for us, she thought as she drifted off.

Evie couldn't sleep. The mild cramping sensation in her lower abdomen came and went, and she'd gone to the bathroom twice to check for bleeding. Beside her, Leon slept soundly, his chest rising and falling. She debated whether to wake him but finally decided to wait unless something changed. His work at the auto shop was physically demanding, and Mondays were always busy. Since neither of them had gotten much rest over the weekend, he'd been especially tired today.

The moon cast pale cool light across the room, illuminating the chair in the corner where Leon's work clothes lay ready for the next day. He had draped the gray work shirt with the shop's logo over its back, and neatly stacked his folded navy work pants, belt, underwear, and socks on the seat. His boots were lined up beneath the chair. His wallet, spare change, and watch sat in a bowl on their dresser. Early in their marriage, she'd teased him about this habit, which he said went back to the first grade when his mother made him lay out his school clothing the night before so he wouldn't miss the bus while hunting for his socks or shoes. She hoped they had a little boy like Leon so she could help him lay out his clothes each night before school.

Even though they were barely pregnant, Evie already thought about the life growing in her womb as a son or daughter with a personality all their own. If the baby was a boy, she hoped he would love fixing things like his dad. She could almost see him, dark eyes glowing with excitement, as he pulled on his kid-sized tool belt and helped his dad. He would probably love lasagna and hate peas. And as he got older, he might play baseball every spring and soccer every fall. Or maybe basketball in the winter. Another thought flitted across her consciousness.

What if their son hated sports? She decided it would be okay. Maybe he'd love reading, or chess, or making chalk drawings on the driveway.

If the baby was a girl, she imagined detangling her dark curls after an evening bath and putting her hair into pigtails tied with pink ribbons before she left for school. Their daughter would also be highly organized when it came to getting dressed and would never miss the bus because she couldn't find her socks or shoes. She would come home each afternoon and do her homework right away at the kitchen table before heading to her room to play with her dolls. Maybe she would create fingerpaint masterpieces or stage a puppet show. She might be a tomboy who was always outside running and jumping with her friends, a girl who came home needing a bath to wash off the outside dirt.

Evie smiled, thinking about her unformed child. She couldn't wait to meet him or her. What would their name be? Asha Rose if it was a girl, after her aunt and Leon's grandmother. And Avery if it was a boy, because she'd always liked that name. It was too soon to even think about names, but she thought about it daily. The presence of a baby inside her, however miniscule, already felt so real. She wondered if Leon had ideas for baby names. The one time she'd brought it up, he'd refused to discuss it. He was superstitious and felt they shouldn't talk about it until the pregnancy began to show.

She got up quietly and went to the kitchen for a drink of water. While Leon slumbered, she read an article in a parenting magazine about breastfeeding, then flipped to another about the pros and cons of allowing the baby to have a pacifier. Putting the empty glass in the sink, she ambled back to bed and climbed in. Curling up next to his warm body, she felt a rush of love and contentment. She realized with relief she hadn't felt any lower abdominal discomfort for the past half hour and was finally able to drift into a restful sleep. She dreamed about a small boy wearing a Spider-Man Halloween costume drawing a green dinosaur on the driveway, while a little girl in a pink unicorn bicycle helmet stood next to him blowing bubbles. She stirred, suddenly wide awake.

"Oh my God," she whispered. "What if we have twins?"

***

Dominique looked around the unfamiliar apartment. It was comfortable in a shabby chic sort of way. The sofa, covered by a beige muslin slipcover and adorned with brightly patterned throw pillows, was slightly overstuffed and wonderfully comfortable. The walls were covered with ornately framed medieval etchings of all sizes and shapes, likely from old English churches. They were illuminated by strategically placed accent lights. An antique brass plant stand containing an oversized fern stood in the corner. A small sign stood next to it that said, *Please water me weekly*. He hoped he could keep it alive for the next six months.

Although it was after midnight, he didn't feel tired. He realized he still wasn't acclimated to the time change. Ruminating on his first day at McArthur, he felt hugely uncomfortable with the realization that no one had been expecting him. He wondered where the breakdown in communication had occurred.

The clinic staff had been welcoming, especially Sally Cohen. In contrast, he found Joyce Porter friendly but reserved. He hadn't learned much about her, other than that she'd been at McArthur for two years.

Before leaving France, he'd broken off a two-year relationship with a surgical nurse at St. Roche. While they'd enjoyed each other's company, their interests had begun to diverge. Toward the end, he began feeling pressured because it was clear Amelie wanted to marry and start a family.

He thought he should try to sleep. After brushing his teeth, he punched the pillow and attempted to get comfortable on the overly soft mattress. As his mind quieted and sleep began to cloud his thoughts, he found himself remembering Joyce's surprised look this afternoon when he'd stopped by her office. He also remembered the warmth of her gaze and the feel of her handshake when they'd first met. But unlike Sally, she'd worn a thin gold band and a small diamond on her left hand. He wondered about her husband. For some reason, he'd had the impression she was living alone. Sensing there was more to learn, he smiled in anticipation of their morning meeting.

CHAPTER 10

"Good morning, Dr. Porter."

Joyce looked up from her desk and smiled at Dominique. Today he was wearing a starched shirt with a small blue pinstripe and a gold-patterned tie. His wavy brown hair was a bit windblown, and her grin widened when she noticed the chin dimple peeking out.

He's gorgeous, she thought before saying, "Dominique, hello. Please come in." She gestured toward the office chair. "Would you like some coffee or tea?"

"Coffee, please. I'm not yet acclimated to the time change. Perhaps coffee will clear my head."

"Cream or sugar?"

"Both if it's not too much trouble."

"No trouble. Make yourself comfortable and I'll be back shortly."

She grabbed her empty mug and gave a friendly nod to one of the nurses as she walked to the staff lounge. After selecting a clean mug decorated with the university's logo, she filled both mugs then added a generous dollop of half and half to Dominique's. She stuffed a packet of sugar, a plastic spoon, and a paper napkin into her coat pocket before heading out. She found herself wishing she'd suggested a breakfast meeting, but her office was more private, so perhaps it was better. They'd likely have multiple interruptions in a public space.

Dominique stood up as Joyce entered the room, and she wondered if all European men were so polite. She cautiously placed the steaming mug on the desk and fished the other accoutrements from her pocket.

"Don't worry," she joked. "My lab coat is clean. I just put it on this morning, and I haven't had time to fill the pockets with candy wrappers or notes to myself."

He chuckled and accepted the items. He added the entire packet of sugar to the fragrant liquid, stirred twice, then carefully set the spoon and empty packet on the napkin. He raised the mug to his lips, took a slow sip, and murmured his approval.

"This is very good hospital coffee."

"That's because it isn't hospital coffee. One of our patients owns a string of coffee shops in Virginia. She got pregnant last month, and a week later, twenty pounds of their house blend arrived. It's enough to last until Valentine's Day."

They settled into their chairs, quietly sipping the premium brew before Joyce asked, "What did you and Dr. Hicks discuss about your visit? What do you hope to learn at McArthur?"

He took another sip before answering. "I've been reading about your extraordinary rates of pregnancy. I would like to study your stimulation protocols and use that information to increase our clinic's rates. Right now, they are quite average, so we have room to improve." He shifted in the chair and leaned forward. "I'm also interested in your laboratory set up—insemination techniques, culture protocols, things like that. I heard you even have a robot in your lab. And I have a special interest in male infertility. I oversee our clinic's donor sperm program. I hope I will have an opportunity to work with Dr. Kumar."

"I can orient you to the clinic this week, but Dr. Kumar's in charge of the lab. After we confirm your privileges, you can see patients on your own if you like. We have stand up meetings in the conference room at 4:30 p.m. most days to discuss our patients, and you're welcome to attend. We'd love to have your help with the daily ultrasounds and cycle monitoring. I'm sure we can learn a lot from you."

Once more, Dominique sipped his coffee before replying, "I'm eager to be helpful. On the drive this morning, Dr. Cohen informed me she's the IVF lead this week. She invited me to scrub in with her this afternoon."

Unexpectedly, Joyce felt annoyed. *I'll bet she did,* she thought. This was followed by another, what her mother would call an 'uncharitable' thought, *That girl doesn't waste any time.*

Out loud she commented, "That's a good way to begin. Let's plan to have you work in the clinic this month. As for spending time in the lab, you'll have to arrange that directly with Dr. Kumar. He's quite good at his job, but he doesn't often welcome guests." She smiled. "I don't think I've seen a robot in there—just several very busy technicians."

"I understand. His job is critical. Perhaps he finds observers disruptive."

She considered his comment. With his experience and interest in the lab, she wondered if he'd be helpful in addressing some of her own questions. However, she wasn't ready to air her concerns or suspicions with a newcomer. She switched to a new topic. "Dr. Hicks would like to meet with you. I received an email from him this morning. He's back on Thursday. I suggest you speak with his secretary and make an appointment. After we finish, I'll show you to his office. It's located in one of the original university buildings and is quite grand."

"Thank you. Everyone so far has been very gracious."

"Dr. Hicks likes to show off McArthur's program. We often host distinguished visitors."

He gave an embarrassed laugh. "I don't really think of myself as a distinguished visitor."

"Oh, I assure you, you are, or he wouldn't have extended the offer."

"Well, I am most grateful. I heard him speak at a conference last year. Your program is quite remarkable. You are most fortunate to work with him."

Joyce's eyes narrowed slightly. "Indeed. He's a popular speaker," she replied in a neutral voice. "He travels a lot." Then with more enthusiasm she continued, "Our patient results speak for themselves. That's the reason I came to McArthur. Much like you, I wanted to learn from the best. I also find great satisfaction in helping these patients become parents."

She picked up a lanyard sporting university colors from her desk. A standard metal key and an electronic keycard dangled from the swivel hook. As he accepted the lanyard, she explained, "Here's a key to an office you can use while you're here. You might have to share when we have medical students, but at least you'll have a place to stash your coat and briefcase. It's equipped with three desks. They all have phones and computers. Pick one and let our office manager Kayla know. She'll arrange with IT for you to have an email account and phone number."

He turned the key card over in his hand.

"I'm sorry I can't offer you a private space."

"It's fine," he said. "I doubt I'll spend much time there. I appreciate you finding a place for me to store my things. I didn't bring much, so sharing is fine." He motioned toward her blooming plants. "Perhaps I'll get a plant."

She smiled. "We don't have students for the next several weeks. If I were you, I'd claim the most comfortable chair too." Then she pointed to the card key. "This also allows you access to the clinic, including the back entrance off the parking lot. It's very convenient, especially in bad weather."

"Does it access the laboratory and outpatient surgical suite?"

"Yes, but only the lab that's within that area. It doesn't work for the main lab on the other side of the building."

Seeing the puzzled look on his face, she inquired, "Does that seem odd to you?"

"No, of course not. I'm a visitor, so it makes perfect sense. I'm here primarily to work in the clinic with you and your colleagues. Do you have a key for the main lab?"

"No."

"I hope I'm not out of line, but may I ask why not? What happens if you need something from the lab and it's after hours or on the weekend? At my clinic, all permanent staff, both clinical and laboratory, have complete access to all aspects of our facility."

She looked thoughtful. "I guess I never really thought about it."

"What if you need to do an unexpected insemination on the weekend? How do you access the sperm bank or process a sample?"

"Well, that doesn't happen often. Our patients are very compulsive about communicating with us when they're in cycle. It's a rare weekend when we don't have a lab tech here both days. If I need something and they've gone home, I text or call and they come back. That's only happened once. The techs who work on the weekends are graduate students, and they always check in before they leave."

"I understand. It sounds like your system works for you."

There was silence, and Joyce considered asking him about his family. She hesitated, wondering if he would feel it was too personal.

While she debated with herself, Dominique spoke. "I have a twelve-year-old daughter, Juliette. I'm hoping her mother will allow her to come for a visit while I'm here. I think she's old enough to travel alone. And they have a direct flight from Paris."

"That sounds like fun. I hope she'll be able to visit during the Christmas break. You should think about taking her to Busch Gardens in Williamsburg. They have a lot of special events during Halloween and Christmas."

"I don't know much about Halloween. Most French people don't celebrate it, but the first of November, All Saint's Day, is a national holiday. Do I have to go to Williamsburg to experience the American Halloween?"

"Oh no. You'll see lots of decorations on people's homes all around the city. Halloween evening, kids dress up in costumes and masks and go door to door. They say, 'Trick or treat!' and then you give them candy. I live in an apartment and last year there were about twenty kids from our complex who came around. I always enjoy seeing those little ghosts and goblins, and last year there were a lot of superheroes and cartoon characters too."

"You said you and your husband live in an apartment in Richmond. Is he also a physician?"

Joyce hesitated. "Well, it's complicated. Bill, that's my husband, is a physician. We met in medical school." She picked up a framed picture sitting on the desk next to a round container holding pens and handed it to him. "This is a picture we took on our honeymoon."

"You both look very happy," he said, briefly studying the picture then handing it back.

"We were." Joyce took the picture and set it back down on the edge of the desk. She continued. "Bill lives in Baltimore right now. He's in a Public Health Ph.D. program at Johns Hopkins. He likes big picture policy work more than seeing patients. His dream job would be working at the Centers for Disease Control in Atlanta as an epidemiologist heading up his own research team. His current mentor used to work in Africa doing AIDS prevention research."

"That must be hard for you," he said, his blue eyes sympathetic. "How often do you see him?"

"It's a challenge, but we try to see each other on the weekends. It doesn't always work out, especially if I have to work or Bill has some type of paper due." A wistful feeling washed over her. "This past weekend I was on call and Bill stayed in Baltimore to work on his thesis. We both agreed it was best. The drive is stressful, and we would only have had a few hours together on Saturday."

"That makes sense, but you look like you miss him."

Joyce felt increasingly uncomfortable with the conversation. It was one thing to talk about her long-distance marriage disappointments with her friend Sally, but quite another to share her feelings with this man she didn't know. His expression conveyed genuine warmth and empathy, and she realized again how appealing he was. Immediately, she felt guilty. Some consternation must have shown on her face because he responded.

"I'm sorry if I've upset you. It is none of my business. Please forgive me."

"No problem." Determined to veer away from the personal, she stood up. "Let's take a walk and I'll show you your new office. Then we'll head over to Administration, and you can meet Dr. Hicks' secretary. Her name is Esmeralda, and she's been here forever."

As he rose to join her, his hand accidentally upset the empty coffee mug which in turn knocked over the honeymoon picture of Joyce and Bill. His face flushed as he quickly mopped up a few drops of coffee with his napkin. "I apologize. I'm quite clumsy this morning. I think I'm still jet-lagged."

Righting the picture, she observed, "It's okay. Nothing broke. This is a small office. I knock things over all the time." She pointed toward the door, motioning for him to exit first. "Let's go check out your new digs."

CHAPTER 11

Joyce scanned the Thursday afternoon schedule where Selena had highlighted Evie Coleman's name with a yellow marker. She hadn't heard from either Evie or her husband and hoped that meant everything was okay. She felt a personal connection to this couple who she thought would be wonderful parents. Because of their financial situation, they only had one shot at IVF.

She was perched on a stool in the nurse's station waiting for Dominique DuPage. She peered down the hall toward the back entrance of the clinic and saw no sign of him. He was shadowing her this afternoon before seeing patients on his own. He'd spent the morning assisting Sally with egg retrievals and embryo transfers, and she wondered what had delayed him. She decided to begin without him because she hated getting behind schedule.

As she hopped down from the stool, Dominique rushed through the clinic's back door, pulling on his white coat. A slight frown marred his face. "I'm late. I apologize. Our last procedure was delayed because of something in the lab. Dr. Kumar was a little vague, but it sounded like it had to do with the sperm processing."

She stepped back into the hall to brief him out of earshot of the patient. "I'm just getting started. We'll be meeting with

Samantha and Josh Gibbons. During their first IVF cycle she experienced moderate OHSS, and they're here to discuss a possible second cycle."

For a moment, Dominique looked puzzled at the acronym, then recognition dawned. "Ah yes, ovarian hyperstimulation syndrome. Very challenging. I find it interesting that some women have ovaries that respond so vigorously to the medications that they leak fluid into the abdomen, or even the chest. Thank goodness the condition is much less common than in the early days of IVF. Does she have polycystic ovary disease?"

"Yes, so we were watching her pretty closely."

"Did she require hospitalization?"

"No, fortunately not. But she did gain an impressive amount of weight after the hCG injection. We'd already planned to freeze the embryos, so other than having her monitor her weight and abdominal circumference, she didn't need any other treatment. We all breathed a sigh of relief when she got her period."

"I took care of a patient once who had severe hyperstimulation. Her nausea and vomiting caused dehydration, and she required hospitalization. Then she developed shortness of breath and was diagnosed with a blood clot in her lungs. After all that, we thought she'd give up on IVF, but she insisted on another cycle. We gave her much lower doses of the hormones the second time and used a different medication to trigger ovulation. It took a lot longer, but that cycle was successful, and she had a beautiful baby girl."

"That's wonderful. I like stories with happy endings." Pointing toward the Consult Room, she said, "Shall we?"

Upon entering the room, Joyce introduced Dominique to the couple. During the past week, she had observed that his ready smile and gentle manner were well received by patients. Their partners also seemed to like him. She had no reservations about him stepping into the clinic rotation and looked forward to working with him as a colleague. The couple asked several thoughtful questions, especially about the likelihood of recurring

OHSS, and Joyce walked them through the options and risks. After thirty minutes, they seemed satisfied and confirmed they were ready for a second cycle.

After the visit, Joyce spent time acquainting Dominique with the clinic's electronic medical record system. He had just received his login name and password from IT, and she was impressed at how quickly he picked up the nuances of the system. His written English was excellent, and he had no trouble documenting today's visit.

The afternoon passed swiftly as they worked companionably through the appointments. They established a routine where Dominique documented the completed visit while Joyce reviewed the chart for the next patient. Once he was finished, she gave him a quick synopsis, and they entered the room together. Now, only one patient remained, Evie Coleman. She wanted to see this couple without an observer and wondered at her feeling of protectiveness. This didn't happen very often, but there was something special about them, their obvious devotion to each other and their eagerness to have a baby.

As he tapped the computer keys, she spoke hesitantly. "Dominique, I have a request. This last couple has had some challenges, and I would like to see them alone if you don't mind."

He looked up from his typing. "I understand," he said. "We all have certain patients who are special. Once I finish this record, I'll go back to my office and do some reading. I'll see you later."

She was relieved. "Thank you for understanding. This has nothing to do with you. You're doing a great job with the patients. They all like you."

He waved her off. "It's fine. I'll see you at the afternoon meeting."

She took a breath. Evie and Leon either had a viable pregnancy or they didn't. The situation was out of her hands. As she mentally prepared, she whispered a quick prayer. Her mother thought she'd lost her faith, but that wasn't true. She prayed every day, for her patients and herself. She prayed the infertility treatments would be successful and that her patients would have blissfully uneventful pregnancies and healthy babies. She prayed that she would be compassionate and competent. She also prayed that when there were challenges, she would find the right words to convey both hope and realistic expectations.

Joyce rapped softly on the door and stepped into the hushed gloom of the ultrasound room. Evie sat on the table, a drape over her legs. Leon sat next to her, holding her hand. They looked at her anxiously.

"Hello, Evie. Hello, Leon."

They both murmured a greeting.

"How are you feeling?"

Evie looked at Leon before speaking. "Fine, Dr. Porter. I haven't had any more cramps or bleeding. I still have morning sickness. In fact, I threw up twice this week. The strangest things make me nauseous, like the smell of coffee and my favorite bath gel."

"That's great," she said, and the couple stared back at her doubtfully. "Morning sickness is miserable for the mother, but it usually means the pregnancy is healthy. Are you ready to take a look?"

Evie and Leon nodded.

She helped Evie slide down the table and readied the ultrasound machine. After gently inserting the probe, she centered it on the uterus and took a moment to get her bearings. She quickly identified a gestational sac and carefully manipulated the image. She was thrilled to see a fetal pole with cardiac activity. She turned up the audio, and a reassuring swish of fetal heart tones registered 160 beats per minute.

The couple stared back at her, eyes wide with expectation. Leon spoke first, quietly, like he was afraid that if he said the wrong thing the ultrasound picture would go blank. "Is that . . ."

"Yes!" she responded. "That's the sound of your baby's heart beating. It's nice and strong and healthy. I'll take a few measurements and then print a picture for you."

The couple looked stunned. For a moment, neither of them said a word. Then Leon's eyebrows shot up and Evie covered her mouth with her hand before they both began to giggle. Leon jumped up from his seat, pumped his fist twice, and shouted, "*Yes!*"

Joyce smiled and continued the scan. She measured the crown rump length, froze the image, and snapped a picture. She maneuvered the wand to a different angle and smiled even wider.

"Oh my, look at this. Your baby has a twin."

"What!" Leon exclaimed, his voice cracking. He sat down so fast he almost missed the chair. "There's more than one?"

"Yes, I'm definitely seeing a second gestational sac! See that small grapelike structure. It's filled with fluid that nurtures the brand-new pregnancy. And I see another strong heartbeat. This one is slightly faster than the first. Listen."

The couple clutched each other's hands and gazed at the screen in awe while listening to the gentle swishing of Baby #2's heartbeat. A small tear slid down Evie's cheek, and Leon leaned over and gently wiped it away.

"Congratulations, you have twins! Let me take some additional measurements. We measure both the size of the sac of fluid around the babies and from the top of what will be their head to the base of what will be their buttocks. It's called a 'crown rump' and is very accurate in early pregnancy. Then I'll see if I can get a picture showing them both together."

"Can you tell if they are boys or girls?" Leon wanted to know.

Joyce shook her head and grinned at his enthusiasm. "Way too early for that. We usually look for that somewhere during the second trimester, around the fourth month."

She continued the examination, documenting measurements and taking pictures. Leon kept up a steady stream of comments, while Evie closed her eyes, a slight smile playing on her lips. She gently tapped Leon's arm. He stopped talking and leaned in.

She whispered, "I had a dream the other night about a little girl in a pink unicorn bike helmet and a little boy dressed like Spider-Man. They were playing in front of our house."

Joyce concluded the exam and helped Evie sit up. "Go ahead and get dressed, then I'll come back. I'm sure you have lots of questions." She printed a series of images, handed two grainy pictures to Leon, and left the room.

Stepping into the hall, Joyce viewed the images of the twin gestation and felt a quiet satisfaction. This was definitely the best part of the job, and she felt buoyed by the couple's joy. Although it was still the first trimester, she believed their chances were good. There were always risks, and twin pregnancies were riskier than singletons, but Evie was young and healthy.

Selena was speaking on the phone when Joyce emerged from the room a second time. She gazed questioningly at Joyce. Wrapping up her conversation, she replaced the phone in the cradle and said, "Your face says it's good news."

"That's right. Twins!"

"Oh my. That's wonderful. They're going to be such great parents."

"I agree. Can you imagine Leon getting up at night to change diapers?"

"Well, he'd better be ready to help. Twins are a lot of work. My sister had twins, and she didn't sleep for a year!"

Joyce nodded while typing in the chart.

"Are you going to the team meeting?" she asked Selena.

"I may skip today. I still have a few more calls. And I forgot to tell you earlier, but Dr. Hicks's assistant called. The doctor wants you to stop by his office after the meeting."

"Did she say what for?"

"No, just that he was eager to speak with you today."

"Okay. Thanks for letting me know. See you tomorrow."

Joyce fixated on Hicks's request as she strode toward the

conference room. She'd known it was coming since getting his email earlier in the week. While the summons wasn't unexpected, it was decidedly unwelcome. She'd hoped for a reprieve while he caught up after a two-week absence, but no such luck. She figured their meeting would only run half an hour, so that meant she could get there before Esmeralda went home for the evening. She always felt better meeting him when someone was around.

She assumed he'd quiz her on her conference presentation. It was almost complete, but she had yet to send it for his review. Frown lines appeared between her eyebrows as she unconsciously raked her hand through her hair in irritation. She was a full-fledged tenure-track faculty member, and she resented his interference. She didn't need his approval. He'd had nothing to do with the pilot program. In fact, he'd made it abundantly clear from the start that he didn't approve of a special assistance fund for IVF clients. If the university president hadn't been supportive, the Foundation would never have allocated two years' worth of resources.

When Joyce entered the conference room, staff members seated around the rectangular table were chatting quietly among themselves. As the physician covering the IVF Clinic for the next two weeks, it fell to Sally to run the daily meeting. Dominique caught Joyce's eye, and she moved to sit next to him. She glanced at the familiar names written on the whiteboard while Sally shuffled through a stack of charts.

"Let's start with some good news. We have a new colleague joining us today." With a big smile, Sally gestured toward Dominique. "Dr. DuPage comes to us from the St. Roche IVF Clinic in Montpellier, France. He'll be with us for the next six months. We look forward to working with him and learning from his experience across the pond. So let's take a moment and briefly introduce ourselves."

Each member of the team announced their name and described their role at McArthur. Dominique listened carefully and jotted down each name on a small pad he carried in his pocket. After the introductions, he spoke in the same self-deprecating manner Joyce had previously observed. "Thank you. It is a great privilege for me to join you here at McArthur. I expect to learn much from you and hope you might learn some small things from me as well."

Around the table, heads nodded appreciatively.

Sally smiled at Dominique and glanced at the clock. "Thank you, Dr. DuPage. Now, let's continue our meeting with more good news. We had three positive pregnancy tests today, and two were from patients using donor sperm. Dr. Kumar, would you like to comment?"

Kumar looked uncomfortable. He shifted in his seat before quietly answering. "We have an excellent group of donor men, mostly from the university's graduate school. As you know, we are experimenting with a process of pre-treating the donor semen sample with magnetic nanobeads to eliminate poor-quality sperm. This improves the selection of a high- quality spermatozoa. Once we perfect our process, we plan to use it for intracytoplasmic sperm injection with the husband's sperm. It looks quite promising."

Sally nodded appreciatively. "Thanks, Dr. Kumar. We appreciate you and your team's good work. Now, let's talk about the six-week ultrasounds. I did one today for the McCauleys—there's a gestational sac, but no fetal pole, so probably nonviable. Follow-up blood work is still pending. Joyce, how about the Colemans?"

Joyce grinned. "I'm pleased to report they have twins! Everything looks good so far. Normal growth and positive fetal heart tones."

Several team members nodded enthusiastically and returned her smile.

"Didn't she have some earlier bleeding?" one of the nurses asked.

"Yes, probably implantation bleeding. It looks like it's

resolved. I didn't see anything that looked like residual blood today on the scan."

"Did they use some of Dr. Kumar's super awesome donor sperm or magic nanobeads?" Rob Torrey asked.

"Nope, no need. They sought IVF for tubal occlusion."

As she said this, Joyce glanced at Kumar and saw he was staring down at his legal pad and drawing a series of intricate doodles. She wondered if it was her imagination, but he seemed more reticent than usual. As if he felt her gaze, he looked up briefly, then resumed his sketching.

The meeting continued uneventfully until Sally wrapped it up with a final announcement.

"When you lock up the clinic in the evening, pay attention to the front door. It hasn't been locking properly. Maintenance says they can replace the mechanism, but it's on back order for at least a month."

The staff took their time getting up, chatting and jostling each other as they filed out. Sally erased the whiteboard while Joyce dawdled, pretending to be arranging her notes until the room was empty. She walked over and closed the door.

Hearing the soft thud of the door, Sally momentarily stopped the back-and-forth motion of the eraser. "What's up?"

"I've been 'summoned' to see Hicks today. I think it's about my conference presentation."

"What? That's crazy. You've done lots of presentations. You're a great speaker."

"That's what I think, but you know how he is. Always wants the last say on everything. He also said something about me accompanying him to some conference events. He promised to introduce me to important colleagues."

Sally finished cleaning the board and put down the dry eraser. After several seconds, she replied, "Be careful, Joyce. I speak from experience. Hicks is a known skirt-chaser. Keep an arm's length away, and you should be fine." She picked up her stack of folders and moved toward the door, then stopped again.

"One last thing. Don't agree to go anywhere with him that isn't a public event."

Now it was Joyce's turn to look thoughtful. "What do you know?" she asked.

Sally shook her head and remained silent, motioning for Joyce to exit the room. She followed her out, pausing to lock the door.

Joyce sighed in frustration. "Okay, you don't want to elaborate. I get it. Thanks for the advice. Good meeting today. See you tomorrow."

CHAPTER 12

Joyce stepped into the anteroom of Hicks's office. "Hi, Esmeralda," she said with a warm greeting. The vivacious Latina woman smiled from behind her desk. She was in her mid-forties with jet-black hair arranged in a tight bun and large gold hoop earrings. She was a petite dynamo who always wore impossibly high-heeled shoes and multiple bracelets that jangled when she moved her arms.

"Well, hello, Dr. Porter. Dr. Hicks just stepped out. He'll be right back."

"How've you been?"

"Oh, pretty good. Yannely got engaged last weekend. She and her fiancé are planning a Valentine's Day wedding."

"That's great. Do you like her fiancé?"

"Yes, I do. Javier is very polite, and he has a good job with the Richmond Police. He'll take good care of her."

Before they could speak any further, Hicks swept into the room. He inclined his leonine head toward Joyce and motioned toward the inner office door. "Come in."

Esmeralda stood up behind her desk. "Dr. Hicks, do you need anything else today?"

"No."

"Is it okay if I leave a few minutes early? I have some personal errands."

Hicks nodded brusquely then disappeared into his office. Joyce's heart sank. So much for her safety plan of having someone within shouting distance. Onto Plan B, remaining at arm's length.

She lingered in the outer office while Esmeralda put on her coat and gathered her things. "Good night, Esmeralda. Maybe next time you'll show me some pictures of your grandchildren."

Before she could reply, Hicks barked, "Dr. Porter, are you lost?"

Joyce gave a small wave and entered the office.

"Shut the door."

The door felt heavy as Joyce carefully closed it. She turned back toward the imposing desk where Hicks was backlit by the setting sun. She was relieved when he gestured to one of the heavy wooden chairs facing it rather than the couch. Slowly she sank down onto the cushy leather seat, carefully smoothing her skirt as she planted both feet on the floor and nervously gripped the arms of the chair. She took a deep breath, in through her nose and out through her mouth, and told herself to relax.

Hicks absently twirled a pen in his left hand. "Dr. Porter, I've yet to receive a draft of your conference presentation."

"Yes, sir, I know. It's almost complete, but I'm waiting for one more piece of data. We've had several pregnancies this month, including two of our couples from the Foundation Assistance program, and I want to include them in the final statistics."

Hicks set down the pen, rolled his chair back slightly, and steepled his fingers. "Yes, Kumar told me there have been several pregnancies after that short dry spell. What do you think was the problem?"

How odd he's asking me, she thought, before saying, "I'm not sure. Our clinical protocols haven't changed, so I wondered about the lab. While you were away, I spent some time with him going over their procedures. We couldn't identify any problem, and things seemed to improve. I'm not aware that any particular cause was identified."

"What did you and Kumar review?"

"We went over everything step by step, from the time the ova are handed off after the retrieval to when the embryos are ready for transfer. Some failed to fertilize and others disintegrated shortly thereafter."

"Did you notice anything special about the couples who had failed cycles?"

She paused, a slight wrinkle creasing her brow, then slowly shook her head. "Not really, other than they were clustered in the same week."

Hicks nodded, then abruptly changed topics. "Are you staying at the hotel across from the convention center?"

She shifted in the chair while processing this new question. "Do you mean for the conference?"

"Of course I mean for the conference."

"Sally and I booked a room at the conference hotel. Is that the one you mean?"

He bobbed his head. "When do you arrive?"

"Sunday evening."

He nodded again. "Fine. A medical supply company is hosting a breakfast first thing Monday morning. Plan on attending it with me. We can meet in the lobby and walk over together. There's also a cocktail reception on Tuesday. I expect you to accompany me to these functions. I'll have Esmeralda send you the details."

"What time will breakfast end? Dr. Georgia Browne is the opening session keynote speaker."

Hicks laughed dismissively. "Don't worry. You'll have plenty of time to get to the session. The first fifteen minutes are all introductions and other logistical bullshit anyway. You could show up half an hour late and still catch most of the talk."

Joyce looked down at her hands before commenting, "I don't like to walk in late."

He gave another snide laugh. "You've got to be kidding." He leaned forward and propped his elbows on the desk. He fixed his eyes on her. "Listen to me. Most people don't care about those plenary sessions. Working here at McArthur, you already know all that stuff because we're on the bleeding edge of the field. That keynote talk by Georgia Browne is a dog-and-pony show. The real action is at the small breakouts and the informal hallway conversations. That's where you suss out the true game-changing innovations."

"What about Dr. Cohen? Will she be joining us?"

"Sally's a big girl. She can fend for herself. I'm sure she has other friends or colleagues she can hook up with."

Joyce looked away. When she finally raised her eyes, Hicks was staring at her. His gaze rested first on her breasts, outlined in her form-fitting sweater, and then on her mouth. She wet her lips nervously and felt a flush creep up her neck and burn her cheeks. Then came a rushing sound in her ears. As if from far away, she heard him continue, "And that's why it's important you stick with me. It's very convenient we're at the same hotel. Do you understand?"

Joyce clumsily pushed the heavy visitor's chair away from the desk, fighting the plush carpet's drag, and rose from the seat. "I understand. Now I have to go. I just remembered something in the clinic that I didn't finish, a patient I promised to call. I'll have a draft of my talk to you by the end of tomorrow." She threw open the heavy door and hustled out.

Rushing headlong down the hallway, Joyce rounded a corner and collided with Dominique. His arm shot out and he quickly steadied her. Stepping back, he noticed her rapid breathing and scarlet cheeks. His handsome face radiated concern. "Are you all right? Your face is flushed. Are you ill?"

Without answering, Joyce shoved him aside and speed-walked in the direction of the clinic and the safety of her office.

Dominique doggedly followed. "What's wrong?" he persisted. "Please tell me."

She pushed open the exterior door of the administration building as he caught up with her. The cool fall air felt good on her overheated skin. The further away she got from Hicks, the better she felt. She slowed her pace and allowed him to catch up. "I'm okay. I just had a meeting with Dr. Hicks."

He raised one eyebrow in a silent question.

"He's been after me to send him a copy of my conference talk, and he's angry with me because I haven't."

"But why? You're a faculty member, not some medical student."

"I'm not sure. Lately, he seems to have it out for me. He's always criticizing my work."

"That isn't true. When I spoke with him last spring about coming to McArthur, he specifically mentioned you and praised your management of the IVF program. He was quite complimentary."

Now it was Joyce's turn to look puzzled. She shook her head. "That seems hard to believe."

"Is the talk for the New Orleans conference?"

"Yes. Are you going?"

"I'm looking forward to it. It's a lot closer to fly from Virginia than France. Who else is going?"

"Just Sally and me. And Dr. Hicks, of course. Are you registered? Where are you staying?"

"I sent in my registration a month ago, but I don't have a hotel reservation. Do you have any recommendations?"

"Sally and I are staying at the hotel across the street from the convention center. We're flying in on Sunday. Let us know your plans. Maybe we can meet up."

As they approached the back entrance, Dominique hastened to open the door and waited for Joyce to enter. She considered his courtly manners, European charm, and appealing accent. All things considered, he was a very attractive package. She thanked him and stepped inside. They stood facing each other.

"You don't have to walk me home," she joked.

The edges of his mouth turned up in a grin and the dimple appeared. "I'm glad you're feeling better. I'll go make that hotel reservation right away. *Bonne soiree.*" He did a quick heel turn then strolled in the opposite direction toward his temporary office.

Joyce watched him for a moment, a small smile playing on her lips. As she entered her office, she realized she felt strangely flattered by Dominique's attention. While retrieving her purse from the lower desk drawer, she was careful not to bang her head. She smiled again remembering his concern for her when she bumped her head his first day at McArthur.

She was glad he was going to the conference. It would be fun getting to know him in an environment other than the clinic, and perhaps he could add a layer of safety. She hoped by hanging out with him and Sally, she could minimize her alone time with Hicks. She'd finish the presentation this evening and send it off first thing in the morning. Maybe then he'd leave her alone.

As she walked to her car, she wondered why Hicks was so insistent she accompany him? Maybe she was imagining it, but his gaze today had felt particularly invasive and inappropriate. She needed someone to talk to. Sally had cautioned her but then clammed up. She wondered anew what that meant and decided to broach the subject with her again at their next girls' night out.

She pondered the odd line of questioning about their diminished fertilization rates a few weeks ago. Not only was it strange that Hicks brought it up, but it was peculiar that after a few questions, he abruptly changed topics. That, combined with Kumar's behavior at today's meeting, made her wonder again if there really had been a problem and not just a set of "unfortunate" events as Kumar alleged. She shook her head and decided there was nothing to gain by giving it any more thought. As she entered her car, she caught sight of Kumar walking to his car. Striding next to him, gesticulating angrily, was Hicks.

Joyce's cell phone vibrated and chirped. "Hello."

"Hi, sweetie," Bill said. "Happy Thursday. How was your day?"

She considered the mundane question, but she reasoned it would be the same greeting even if they were living together in the same city. It was probably the same welcome that thousands, maybe millions, of married couples voiced each night when they reconnected after work. There was comfort in their ritual of evening calls, but it wasn't like living together.

"Fine. It was pretty routine." She considered whether she should mention the uncomfortable meeting with Hicks.

As if reading her mind, Bill queried, "Did you see Hicks? I remember you said he was coming back today."

"Unfortunately, yes. He called me into his office this afternoon and berated me for not sending him my presentation."

"That's ridiculous. Since when does he critique your talks?"

"Since he became overly interested in this presentation. I think it's crazy too. I finished updating the data this afternoon, so I'll email it first thing tomorrow. He also informed me that I'm attending a sponsored breakfast and cocktail reception with him."

"That sounds interesting. It's always great to have someone introduce you as an up-and-coming star to the doyennes of the academy. Conferences are excellent opportunities to expand your academic network, so it's great Hicks is willing to do that for you."

Joyce hesitated before responding with minimal enthusiasm. "Yeah, I guess."

"What's wrong? You don't sound very happy about it."

She debated how much to share. "I get a weird vibe from him."

"How so?"

"It's hard to explain. One minute he's being really tough on me and criticizing my work. The next minute, he's asking me to accompany him to invitation-only events." She decided against mentioning the leering gazes and suggestive comments. That wasn't something to discuss on the phone.

"Maybe he's trying to push you so you improve—a tough love kind of thing. Or maybe he doesn't want it to seem like he's showing favoritism. Take advantage of the doors he can open for you and go along."

She felt fairly certain it wasn't either of those motivations and wondered again why she was hesitating to confide in him. "You're probably right."

"I can't talk too long tonight. We can catch up tomorrow. I'm doing laundry and packing. Do I need to bring anything special —you know, like my snorkeling gear or cross-country skis?"

She laughed. "No. It's a little cool for snorkeling and not quite cross-country ski season yet. I was thinking, would you like to go to Busch Gardens this weekend? They have it decorated for Halloween. And on Saturday night, they're having a Monster Mash parade."

"Sounds fun. Do I need a scary mask?"

"I think you can skip the mask."

"Any chance you might get home early on Friday?"

"Not much of one. Why?"

"I realized last weekend that I made a huge mistake. I missed you. A lot. I should have driven down to see you, be with you, even if it was only for a few hours. I promise to do better, starting this weekend."

"Well, that sounds encouraging. We have afternoon sign-out at four. I'll try to wrap up things and be home by five. Does this mean you might get here at a decent hour?"

"That's the plan. And don't worry about dinner. I'm cooking."

"Yum. What are you making?"

"It's a secret, but I think you'll like it."

"I can't wait to see you."

"Me too. Love you."

"Love you back. Now go finish packing. See you tomorrow."

CHAPTER 13

Bill struggled up the stairs to Joyce's apartment carrying an overstuffed grocery bag in one hand and a large bouquet of flowers in the other. He paused at the door, stooped to set the bag on the concrete landing, and fished out the key from the depths of his pocket. A light rain was falling and blowing into the stairwell, spraying a fine mist on everything. He hoped the paper grocery sack would hold together at least until he got to the kitchen.

When the door swung open, he stepped inside. The apartment's faint floral scent greeted him. It smelled like Joyce, he thought with a smile. The cat strolled out and eyed him suspiciously before giving a dignified sniff and strutting off. He didn't bump against his leg or make any other friendly gestures. It always took a while for him to warm up after a long absence. *Kind of like Joyce*, he thought wryly.

He dropped the keys on the kitchen counter and placed the bag atop the table. The kitchen was still as cramped and ugly as he remembered it. Although his kitchen space was smaller, at least it didn't sport unsightly avocado green appliances. He shook his head. Who would have predicted they would still be living in genteel poverty eight years after finishing school? But that's exactly where they were, since only Joyce was working full time and they both had hefty student loans. On top of that, they were paying for two separate residences, albeit modest ones.

On his second trip to the car, he shouldered his backpack, then hoisted the duffel bag and the other bag of groceries. The raindrops were bigger now and coming down at a steady pace. He wondered if their weekend plans would be rained out.

Back in the kitchen, he switched on the radio and tuned to a station playing oldies. He and Joyce had similar taste in music, preferring classic rock and tunes from the '80s and'90s. He quickly unpacked the groceries, then rooted under the sink for a flower vase. He found one stuffed behind the cleaning supplies and filled it with water. He remembered to clip the stems before arranging the yellow button mums, burnt-orange alstroemeria, peach colored fall roses and burgundy spider mums. He eyed it critically, decided it looked pretty good, and placed it on the coffee table so she would see it when she came in the front door. He opened the wine, poured himself a glass, and began preparing their feast.

Joyce hustled back to her office. It was a little after five, and she was determined to make good on her promise to be home at a reasonable hour. She'd emailed the completed presentation to Hicks that morning but had heard nothing. Her patient load had been light, and there hadn't been any unexpected emergencies. The last appointment had cancelled when they'd unexpectedly become pregnant without any medical intervention. All in all, a great way to start the weekend.

She texted Bill, *Almost done. Home in 30.*

A short time later, he replied, *Starting dinner see u soon.*

She gazed out the window and noticed it was splattered with raindrops. They might need different weekend plans if it continued. She'd investigate indoor options tonight after dinner. But then again, it might be nice to have a cozy weekend in. Moving toward the exit, she was joined by Sally.

"Hey there. TGIF. When does Bill get in?"

"He's already here."

"Wow, that's a change. I didn't think graduate students got days off."

"I don't think they do, but he managed to leave right after lunch. He's at the apartment now cooking dinner."

"Outstanding! I hope it's something good."

"Well, he said it's a surprise, but I suspect it's shrimp scampi over linguini. That's his favorite go-to meal."

"Yum. You're lucky to have a man that can cook."

"Well, only when the spirit moves him. I think he feels guilty because he didn't come last weekend, so he's pulling out all the stops."

"Nothing like a little old-fashioned guilt to motivate."

Joyce chuckled. "How about you? What are your plans?"

"I'm meeting Dominique for brunch on Saturday, and we'll probably go to Agecroft Hall in the afternoon. He's interested in seeing some of the sights in Richmond. Plus, it's a good rainy-day activity."

Joyce raised her eyebrows. "So you and Dominique are spending Saturday together. What about Dylan in the business office?"

"His name is Doug, and we're friends who occasionally go out. We aren't exclusive or anything."

"I see. But aren't you on call?"

"I was, but at the last minute, Jim asked if we could switch. His wife wants him to go to her cousin's fortieth birthday party next weekend. It's some big shindig at a fancy hotel in Arlington."

Stepping outside, Joyce opened her umbrella while Sally flipped up the hood of her raincoat. Turning slightly, Joyce said, "Well, have fun. It sounds like we'll have lots to talk about on Monday."

Sally winked and grinned. "I sure hope so."

The first thing Joyce saw when she entered the apartment was the huge colorful bouquet. It was quite magnificent. *He really is pulling out all the stops,* she thought. "Hello," she called, raising her voice slightly to be heard over the music blaring from the kitchen.

The music stopped suddenly, and Bill appeared from the kitchen wearing a navy blue-and-white striped apron. He strode to her and enveloped her in a bear hug, pressing her wet coat against his chest. He nuzzled her neck, her faint lily of the valley and vanilla scent tickling his nose, before bussing her thoroughly on the lips.

"I missed you," he murmured, ending the kiss.

"I missed you too. I'm so glad you're here." She pushed him away slightly and gazed at his face. Then she threaded her hands through his thick hair and pulled him to her for a second, even longer, kiss. Finally, they stepped back.

"How long 'til dinner?" she asked.

"I thought we'd eat sometime around seven."

"Okay. I might need a snack since I only had a cup of yogurt for lunch."

"No problem. Go change into your weekend duds. I've made an antipasti plate. We can enjoy that with our wine."

"What are you making for our 'surprise' dinner?" Joyce asked as she sniffed the air. "It smells like garlic."

"Shrimp scampi over linguini and a Caesar salad minus the anchovies."

Joyce smiled, remembering her earlier conversation with Sally. "Excellent! One of my favorites."

She shrugged off the damp raincoat and hung it on the coat rack. She nearly tripped over Bill's duffel bag when she entered the bedroom. He'd set it inside the door, along with his bulging backpack. She picked up both items and moved them under the window, opposite the bed. It wasn't a big room, and it always felt cramped when Bill spent the weekend. But being with him was worth the small annoyance of tripping over his luggage. Quickly shedding her skirt and blouse, she donned a marled gray sweater tunic, black leggings, and her favorite fuzzy pink slippers.

With her work clothes removed, she felt the tension of the week slip away and tingled in anticipation of the upcoming weekend with Bill. She didn't even mind if it rained and they had to change their plans. She thought about Sally spending the weekend with Dominique. Well, maybe not the whole weekend, but it sure sounded like they'd be together for most of Saturday.

Well, good for her, she mused and then wondered why she felt irritated with her friend. Pushing the confusing thought aside, she moved to join Bill in the kitchen.

He had set out a platter of pickled vegetables, sliced meats and small rounds of a freshly sliced baguette. An open bottle of an excellent soave stood next to it, chilling in a makeshift ice bucket. He looked up from the bowl of shrimp he'd finished peeling and deveining. "I know you like reds, but the wine steward told me this pairs well with the scampi. I did buy a bottle of red if you prefer that."

"No, this is great. What a beautiful antipasti plate. Should I take a picture and post it to Instagram?" she asked with a smile.

"Probably not. I'm almost done, and the salad is in the fridge. It'll take me about a half hour to put it all together. Why don't you carry the antipasti and your wine into the living room? I'll join you shortly. We can sip wine and talk about our day, like normal married people do."

"I can stay here and nibble while you cook. I think normal married people probably talk in the kitchen while cooking dinner."

"Your choice. The living room is a nicer space, don't you think? This kitchen feels like it could be a TV set for *That '70s*

Show. Promise me when we finally buy a house, it will have a kitchen from the past decade."

She giggled. "I wasn't aware that you're so sensitive to avocado green." She picked up the wine and antipasti plate. "I'll meet you in the living room. Do you mind if I start snacking? I'm famished."

"Go right ahead. I'll just be a minute."

She settled herself on the couch and speared a pickled artichoke heart. She decided they needed music and chose a playlist of mellow pop tunes. Back on the couch, she lazily turned the pages of Bill's *National Geographic*. She couldn't even remember the last time she'd sat and leafed through a magazine. She thought she could become accustomed to letting him cook every evening. But that wouldn't be fair. Perhaps they could take turns. Her go-to meal was peppercorn pork with wine sauce, mashed potatoes, and roasted asparagus.

Bill entered the room with a wine glass in hand. He sat down and helped himself to bread and salami.

"Nice music. Now, tell me about your day. What did Dr. Bad-tempered have to say about your presentation?"

"Nothing. I emailed it this morning but didn't hear a thing. That's so typical. He'll make a big deal and then drop it."

"How are your patients?"

"Fine. I have three couples in cycle. Jim Torrey's on call this weekend."

"I thought you told me Sally was working."

"She was, but she switched with Jim at the last minute. Something about his wife's cousin's birthday party next weekend. Even though it was last minute, Sally sounded like she had a full weekend planned. She's meeting our new doctor for brunch on Saturday and then taking him to Agecroft Hall for some local history."

He shook his head admiringly. "She doesn't waste any time, does she?"

"Nope. Sally goes after whatever she wants at warp speed.

It's a little odd because she's been seeing this guy from the business office for the last three months, Derek or maybe Don." She shook her head as if it might jiggle the name loose. "I can't remember his name. Anyway, she says they aren't exclusive, but I wonder if he knows that." She bent forward and skewered another artichoke heart. "How about you? Anything exciting happen at your meeting?"

"Not really. There's an outbreak of a new coronavirus in Nigeria and Hopkins is sending a team to assist the CDC. They're asking for volunteers."

She tried to read his face. Could he possibly be thinking about volunteering? The thought filled her with dread. She tried to keep her anxiety in check before commenting, "Yikes, that sounds dangerous." She paused before asking quietly, "Are you thinking of volunteering?"

"No, not this time. I'm beginning the data collection for my own project and being gone four to six months would set me back. Besides, I didn't think you'd want me to be 8,000 miles away. We're having enough trouble as it is."

Joyce turned toward him, frowning. "What do you mean? That we're having trouble?"

"Joyce, relax. I didn't mean it like that. Bad word choice. I meant living in two separate cities and only seeing each other on weekends has been hard on us. It's frustrating when our schedules don't match, like last weekend. I'm looking forward, as much as you, to being done with my Ph.D. so we can live in the same place."

"And where do you think that might be?"

Now Bill frowned. "I'm not sure, probably in a city somewhere on the East Coast. I want to work with a large public health program, and you need an IVF clinic."

Joyce chewed on a pickled carrot as she formed her next comment. "Let's do a better job planning our next move," she said carefully. "I know we both signed onto our current positions because they're so good for our careers, but I don't think we really considered the stress of living in two places. At least I know I didn't. Now we're paying for two shabby apartments on top of our loans. I'm tired of having no money, driving an antique Honda, and buying my clothes at discount shops."

"Yeah, me too."

"And what about starting a family? I'm surrounded every day by couples who waited until everything was 'perfect' and now they can't conceive. That might be us if we put it off too long."

He looked troubled. "Joyce, where's this coming from? I remember how upset you were when we found out you were pregnant in med school. You said you didn't want to have a baby, that it would be too hard to raise a child and finish your training."

She stood up and crossed the room to turn down the music. "Yes, but that was almost ten years ago. And since I had that miscarriage, we haven't tried again. We're both in our mid-thirties and no one knows better than me that it only gets harder, especially for me. I have aging ovaries!"

Bill lips curved into a grin before realizing she was dead serious.

"I'm thinking about stopping the pill."

"Whoa. I don't think we should discuss this tonight," he said, standing up and heading for the kitchen. "We've both had a long week, and it's time to relax and enjoy my delicious home cooking. Speaking of which, I'm going to put on the pasta and make the scampi. We'll eat in about twenty minutes."

"Okay, but promise me we'll find time to finish this discussion. I've been thinking I'd like at least two kids. Growing up, one of my best friends was an only child, and she always said she wished she'd had a brother or sister."

"Fine. But only if you agree that for tonight, we're done."

Joyce heard Bill running water into the pasta pot and setting it down on the cook top with a thud. She wasn't sure why she'd broached the subject of starting a family, other than it had been quite a while since they'd talked about it. Maybe it was because her thirty-fifth birthday was in two months. By the time her mother had turned thirty-five, Joyce and her brother had been in grade school. Her mom had resumed working, part-time at first, and then full-time once they'd both entered middle school.

A couple of Joyce's friends from med school had just had babies and posted cute pictures of their smiling cherubs on Facebook. It sounded like they were making it work, although most of them had full-time nannies.

Bill's right, she thought. *We shouldn't talk about this when we're both tired.* She hoped when they finally got around to discussing it, they'd find some common ground rather than conflict.

CHAPTER 14

Evie and Leon snuggled together on the couch. She rested her head on Leon's shoulder while he gently stroked her hair. They'd returned from dinner with his parents. Leon's mom always made pot roast with carrots and potatoes on Sunday. Among her many domestic talents, she was also an excellent baker, and they'd enjoyed homemade yeast rolls and fresh apple pie with vanilla ice cream.

Evie let out a contented sigh. "Mmm, I ate too much. Your mom makes the best rolls. And I wish I could learn to make apple pie like that. Her crust is to die for."

"Well, you are eating for two, no make that three," he said smiling. "So you can probably have three rolls, one for you and one for each of the babies."

"No way," Evie laughed. "I would be the size of a small house by the time the babies were born!"

He glanced at her curiously. "What did you and my mom talk about when you were in the kitchen? It looked serious."

She moved away slightly and made a wry face. "She talked about wanting to be a grandmother—again. Then she asked when we're going to have children."

He shook his head. "I'm sorry she's putting pressure on you.

She means well, but she can be *so* annoying. She finally stopped asking me because every time she did, I told her it wasn't any of her business. That we'd start our family when we were ready."

"I didn't really know what to say, and you know I'm not a good liar. I finally told her we both wanted a family and were hoping to be pregnant by Christmas. And then I asked her to please not bring it up again."

He looked relieved. "Good response. What did she say?"

"I think she knew something was up because she gave me a funny look. Then she completely changed the subject and started talking about Thanksgiving. She's already planning a big meal and wants me to make the cranberry relish and a side dish."

Leon considered this before replying, "I thought we were spending this Thanksgiving with your family."

"Well, we are. But your mom has it all figured out. She's already invited my parents *and* my sister and her family."

"Wow, that's a crowd! With my two brothers and their families, we might have to eat in shifts. Or maybe she'll put a big tent up in the backyard. That would be a first!"

They both grinned at this idea, and then Evie's expression became serious. "Maybe by then things will be far enough along and we can tell everyone about the twins. Have you been thinking about what we'll say? My sister Joan knows we had IVF because of the money we borrowed. I don't think she'll say anything, but you never know what might come up."

"Have you told her yet?"

"Not yet, but I'd like to tell her soon. And we probably should tell our parents. I'm a little worried about that. You know how negative my parents were about IVF. They think it's against God's plan and that babies should only be conceived through 'natural' processes. I'm not sure why our minister brought it up in his sermon a few weeks ago, but that only reinforced their opinions."

Leon cleared his throat. "Yeah, that was bad timing. Let's wait until after the checkup with your regular doctor. I think our parents are going to be so excited we're finally pregnant that it won't even come up. And when you talk to Joan, ask her to keep the other stuff a secret. Are you going to tell her right off about the twins?"

Evie shifted, trying for a more comfortable position. "I'm not sure. I still worry a little about the bleeding."

"You aren't having any, are you?" he asked, his face creased with concern.

"No, not for at least a week. When I talk to Joan, I need to ask if I can borrow some of her maternity clothes. I can hardly button my jeans!"

He patted her tummy and leaned over to plant a gentle kiss on her cheek. "You look wonderful. And I can't wait to see you with a baby bump."

She covered his hand with hers and smiled. "I expect it will be a lot more than a bump. I remember my Aunt Sadie having twins. Toward the end, she couldn't even drive because if she put the seat back far enough to make room for her belly, then she couldn't reach the pedals!"

They both laughed. "Aunt Sadie is a lot shorter than you, so you'll probably be okay. But I'll be happy to drive you to work if you can't reach the pedals."

She turned to face him. "Leon, we need to talk about that. I'm not sure how long I'll be able to work. I've been reading about twin pregnancies, and most women end up on some type of bedrest. The article I read said having twins makes the pregnancy 'high risk.' I may need to stop working a few weeks or even a few months early."

"It's going to be fine. Don't worry about that yet."

"But we need that money . . ." She stopped speaking when he leaned over and kissed her gently on the lips.

He looked at her tenderly. "I can work an extra Saturday or two if we need some cash. Don't worry. It's not good to be stressed when you're pregnant."

She sighed, then settled back against his shoulder. He put his arm around her and pulled her close. "You're right," she said. "You know what would make me feel even more relaxed?"

Leon looked at her expectantly, then he looked shocked. "Evie, we can't. We can't. It's only been a week since the bleeding stopped—"

She grinned and put her hand to his lips to silence him. "Yes, that would make me feel relaxed, but that wasn't what I was thinking."

"Then what?"

"A bowl of chocolate ice cream and a foot rub."

"I thought you said you were stuffed."

"I was, but now I really want some ice cream. With chocolate syrup. And maybe a cherry."

He stood up. "Absolutely. You're the boss. One bowl of double-chocolate delight coming right up." He wagged his finger at her. "But no cherry. They have some kind of red dye, and that can't be good for you or our babies."

———

Bill finished packing his duffle bag, shoved his shaving kit beside his running shoes, and then zipped the flap.

Joyce watched morosely, leaning her hip against the bedroom door jam. "I hate this part."

"What part?"

"The part where you leave. The apartment always feels so quiet and lonely after you're gone. Even Mittens notices. He wanders around sniffing and looking under things. Once you left a sock behind, and he dragged it over to me with an accusing look."

"Yeah, I know. I feel the same way when you leave Baltimore."

"We never did have that conversation about starting a family."

"Joyce, give it a rest. That type of discussion deserves our full attention. We shouldn't start it now when I'm heading out." He glanced at his watch. "Look, it's already past four. I probably should've been on the road an hour ago to avoid the worst traffic. I really need to get going."

"I know. Can we agree to spend time discussing it next week?"

"Okay, but not on the phone. We should do this face to face, after a good night's sleep." He shrugged into his jacket before picking up the duffel and laptop bag. Then he followed her into the small foyer. Setting down both bags, he pulled her into his arms.

She tucked her head under his chin, inhaled deeply his unique clean scent, then wrapped her arms tightly around his waist. "I wish you didn't have to go," she whispered.

He moved his arms up and down her back in a soothing gesture. "I love you. And I know this is hard, but it isn't forever. Maybe another year or so. I promise we'll talk about starting our family soon, but I don't think you should get pregnant until we're both settled and in the same place. I wouldn't want to miss the chance to rub your sore feet or take a midnight run to the store to buy pickles!"

"Well, the foot rub sounds good, but I don't even like pickles."

"Who knows what you'll like when your hormones are raging?" He kissed her once hard on the lips, pushed her gently away, then turned and picked up his gear. "I'll text you when I get home."

She sighed. "Okay. Be safe." As he headed down the stairs, she called after him, "I love you," then gently closed the door.

A lonely Sunday evening loomed ahead as Joyce stood at the window watching Bill's car turn the corner and disappear. She already missed him with a physical ache. She thought about their intense lovemaking and the wonderfully languorous feeling that always enfolded her when she lay snuggled against his chest listening to the soft thud of his heart. Almost as wonderful was waking up next to him with the sunlight softly streaming through the window, feeling cherished and content.

Often, she'd find him gazing at her with desire and they'd enjoy a passionate reprise before rolling out of bed and racing each other to the shower. The "loser" had to make breakfast. She sighed, already dreading the next week of cold lonely nights without his warm body curled around hers.

It wasn't often she felt at loose ends. She should relish the free time, but instead she felt empty and unfocused. She supposed she could catch up on her reading, but she didn't think she could concentrate on the technical jargon of a journal article, and it was too late to go to the gym since it closed early on Sundays.

She decided to do laundry and figured she'd get her exercise running up and down the stairs to the building's laundry room. She hated the fact there was no interior staircase. As she lugged a basket filled with almost two weeks' worth of clothes down the two flights, she mused, *I can't wait 'til we have a house with a shiny new washer and dryer, one of those energy-efficient stacking combos. The spacious laundry room will be next to our oversized garage containing a used but still in good condition European sedan and a mid-sized SUV with two kids' car seats.*

This was one of Joyce's favorite daydreams, imagining what their house would look like someday. She figured it would be a traditional brick two-story with upper dormer- style windows. Two mature oak trees on the front lawn would shed copious colorful leaves in the fall and be home to several bushy tailed squirrels who would grow fat on their acorns. Twin flower urns would flank the front steps, overflowing with pink and white petunias in the summer, yellow mums in the fall, and Christmas topiaries with white lights in December.

She smiled as she visualized a swing set with a slide, a tire swing, and a mini fort with a bright green roof. She mentally stepped onto a deck through patio doors at the rear of the house and noted that the well-appointed space contained a gas grill and teak patio furniture with colorful striped teal and coral cushions and a large matching umbrella. But then reality intruded as she remembered their student loan debt.

They each had borrowed about $150,000, which was much less than some of their med-school classmates. Bill had been able to pay off some of his debt while working at the VA, but even with reasonable interest rates, their current combined loan payments were over $3,000 each month, almost a third of her paycheck.

It made saving for a down payment on a house difficult. It was also the reason why they both drove used cars and lived in apartments that were not much better than they'd been able to afford while in school.

She shook off her money woes to focus on the upcoming weeks. The conference was only two weeks away, and she had a long to-do list. Tomorrow she'd ask her next-door neighbor, a single woman who worked at the public library, to watch Mittens and bring in the mail. Then she'd call Sally to see if she wanted to share a ride to the airport. It seemed silly to take separate cars and pay double for long-term parking. She didn't mind traveling by herself, but it was always nicer to travel with a companion.

She piled the clothes in the washer, added soap, and started the cycle. She climbed back to her apartment and set the timer for thirty minutes to remind her to take them out and put them in the dryer. Then she cleaned the apartment. It didn't take much time to dust and vacuum the compact space, and she was finished when the timer dinged.

She bounded down the stairs, tossed the clothes into the dryer, and then headed upstairs to hang the "delicates" over the bathroom tub. As she hung the last camisole, her cell phone vibrated with a call from an unknown number.

"Hello."

"Joyce, this is Owen Hicks." There was a pause, and she could hear a slight buzz from the connection.

"Yes, Dr. Hicks. Sorry, I didn't recognize your number."

"I'm calling from my office line. I finished reviewing your presentation, and I'd like to propose some changes. Nothing too big, just a few minor details that I think will strengthen your final conclusions."

There was another pause before she slowly answered, "Okay. When do you want to meet?"

"Well, now, of course."

She experienced a flash of dismay, followed by a burst of anxiety. She was momentarily tongue-tied, trying to decide how to reject his unwelcome request.

"Uh, I'm busy. It's the weekend, and I have a lot to do. I need to get my cleaning and laundry done, and I still have to grocery shop and pay bills. And besides, my husband is here." As her frustration rose, so did her tendency to babble. She hoped the white lie about Bill would signal Hicks to back off.

"Doesn't he live somewhere else?"

"Well, yes, but he's here this weekend. He goes back tomorrow morning." This was a bigger lie, but she didn't care. Hicks was really creeping her out. She felt her gut tighten with foreboding.

"Well, bring him along. I'd like to meet him. What's his name?"

What the hell? It was one thing to have Hicks harass her with inuendo at work, but something entirely different to have him call her at home on a Sunday. She finally managed to respond weakly, "That won't be possible. We're on our way out for an early dinner."

"I see," he drawled, and Joyce thought it sounded like he didn't believe a word she'd said. She'd had enough. Her anxiety was replaced by a burst of anger that spurred her to action. How dare he call her on a Sunday afternoon with such an inappropriate request?

"Dr. Hicks, I'm very sorry, but I have to go," she said in a firm tone. "Thank you for looking over my presentation. I appreciate it and look forward to hearing your suggestions. Tomorrow I'll call Esmeralda and get on your schedule. And now, I really *must* go. Have a good night." And before he could reply, she hung up.

She held the phone gingerly, like it was going to explode at any moment. Then she shoved it into her back pocket. The anger receded, and she was plagued by self-doubt. There was no way she was going to meet Hicks in his office after hours on a Sunday. His bizarre request juiced her anxiety level, and she wondered if she was safe. Mentally she gave herself a shake.

Buck up, Porter. The man is a jerk, but he isn't stupid. He's not going to show up tonight on your doorstep. Take it easy, and tomorrow, just smile and pretend that you're grateful for his interest in your work.

She took some deep breaths and felt calmer. She slowly walked through the apartment and into the kitchen. Maybe some nice chamomile tea would help her relax. She wondered if she should block his number. She relocked the apartment door before remembering her laundry downstairs. Well, it could wait. She sat down at the small table and placed her phone on its smooth surface. While waiting for the kettle to boil, she pulled up Sally's number and hit *Call.* Sally answered on the fourth ring, "Hey girlfriend, what's up?"

Joyce felt relieved to hear her cheerful voice. "Hi, Sally. Listen, do you have a moment to talk? I just had a bizarre phone call from Dr. Hicks."

"You've *got* to be kidding. He called you on a Sunday evening! Why?"

"I'm not really sure. He said it was to talk about my research presentation." Joyce hesitated before adding, "He's at the office now and asked me to meet him there."

For a long moment, Sally said nothing. Then she stated firmly, "You aren't going."

"Of course not! But what do you think's going on?"

Sally ignored the question. "What else did he say?"

"Oh, he said he had some suggestions that would strengthen my conclusion."

"What did you tell him?"

"That I was busy, and that Bill was here and we're going out to dinner."

"Is Bill still there?"

"No, I lied. He's on his way back to Baltimore."

Again, there was a pause, and Joyce spoke into the silence. "Look, Bill left a couple of hours ago and I'm feeling lonely. And now I'm freaked out about that phone call. Could you come over? We can drink wine, eat crackers and cheese, and talk about our weekends. And maybe you can tell me what to do about Hicks."

Sally's voice was filled with regret. "As much as I'd like to, I can't. I've got too much to do."

Joyce changed the subject. "Can you at least tell me how things went with Dominique on Saturday?"

Sally chuckled. "It went well. Really well. We had a nice day seeing some of the Richmond sites, and he even took me out to dinner."

"Lucky you. Where'd you go?"

"HogsHead Café. He wanted to try southern-style barbeque."

"Well, that's a good place to go. What'd he think?"

"I think he enjoyed it, but I doubt it's going to be a steady favorite given his European palate."

Even though Sally couldn't see her, Joyce nodded vigorously. "I have to agree. I don't mind barbeque occasionally, but for me, a little goes a long way. Now, on a different topic, do you want to share a ride to the airport? I think we're on the same late-afternoon flight to New Orleans."

"Sure, that works. Why don't you drive over and leave your car here? My landlady won't mind as long as it's on my side of the driveway. Do you want to take my car or an Uber?"

"Either is fine."

"Okay, we can decide later. I'm really looking forward to this meeting. New Orleans is my kind of happening town. I love how there's music everywhere and lots of good jazz clubs. Let's plan a girl's night out on the town! Bring something sexy to wear."

"Sure, that sounds fun. But I may have a few events to attend with Dr. Hicks. He promised to introduce me to some of his colleagues. He said it will be good for my career, but after tonight's conversation with him, I really don't want to go."

Another long silence followed this remark, and Joyce wondered if they'd lost the connection. "Hello? Are you still there?"

"I'm still here," Sally replied. Then she asked in an odd voice, "Joyce, what kind of events?"

"Some kind of networking breakfast and an evening cocktail reception."

"I see."

"Sally, what's going on? You sound like you think I shouldn't go, but I feel sort of trapped. It's not like I can say 'no' to the boss."

"Just be careful. Breakfast should be fine but watch out at that reception. With enough free alcohol, things can sometimes get out of hand."

"Are you speaking from experience?"

"Sort of. Anyway, I've heard things. We can talk about it sometime, but not tonight. I've gotta go," she said, wrapping up the conversation. "My sheets are in the dryer, and they're prob-ably fried to a crisp. I'll see you tomorrow. Bye."

"Okay. Good-bye." Joyce considered the abrupt sign-off and her friend's strange reaction. Now her alarm meter was really buzzing. She'd thought by confiding in Sally she'd get some perspective and much-needed advice, but the bubble of anxiety returned, and she wondered who she could trust.

CHAPTER 15

Monday morning, Joyce headed to work feeling irritable and tense. At three a.m., she'd jerked awake thinking she'd heard a knock on the front door, but after listening to a full five minutes of silence, she'd convinced herself she'd been dreaming and eventually fell back into a fitful sleep. Thoughts of her conversation with Hicks circled in her head like an annoying advertisement jingle. She remembered Sally's odd evasiveness and wondered what else she knew but wasn't sharing.

She sat listlessly at her desk, catching up on emails and paperwork, when the desk phone rang. It was Esmeralda. "Hello, Dr. Porter. Dr. Hicks would like to see you today to go over your presentation. He's free at eleven."

She glanced at her schedule. Since she was free, she decided it was probably best to get the dreaded discussion over with. She wasn't scheduled to see patients, and her committee meeting ended a few minutes before eleven. "Okay. I'll come by then. Thanks, Esmeralda." Slowly replacing the receiver, she thought about texting Bill for moral support. She decided against it since she hadn't shared the previous day's weird phone call with him.

She accomplished little over the next hour. Finally, she

printed a copy of the PowerPoint slides for her presentation and slipped them into a folder. She knew Hicks wouldn't ignore her abrupt termination of yesterday's call. Like many powerful and egotistical men, he preferred having the last .word. She wondered if anyone had ever hung up on him.

With a sigh of relief, she headed to the committee meeting. At least she would have something else to think about for a while. She tried to concentrate on the presentation about eliminating institutional practices that fostered racism, but she couldn't ignore the dull gnawing sensation in her gut. Her foot bounced, and she compulsively clicked her pen. No more coffee, she decided as she put the pen away.

Esmeralda was on the phone when Joyce entered the ante-room of Hicks's office. She nodded her head as she jotted notes on a yellow legal pad. She mouthed a silent "Hello" and gestured for her to sit. Joyce sank down on the scratchy brown wool sofa and opened her folder, trying to look nonchalant.

Precisely at eleven, the inner door swung open, and Hicks appeared. Esmeralda was still on the phone, and he looked at her with an annoyed expression. Glancing up, she saw his scowl and quickly ended the call. In rapid staccato sentences, he dictated a list of tasks, then gestured brusquely to Joyce. She rose to her feet, accidentally spilling the contents of the folder, which spread out like a fan on the beige carpet. Embarrassed by her clumsiness, she bent to retrieve them. As she stood up, she noticed the top button of her blue silk blouse had worked itself open, showing a hint of cleavage, and found Hicks staring at the top of her breasts. She reflexively grasped the folder to her chest and followed him into his office. He closed the door with a deci-sive *thunk*.

Hicks waved Joyce toward a chair and parked himself on the throne-like chair behind the desk. It was a seating arrangement that emphasized his power and authority. Normally, this would have exasperated her, but today she welcomed the arrangement.

With the large desk between them, she felt safe from his "accidental" touches.

Hicks fixed Joyce with an unwavering stare, then spoke in a grave tone. "I'm disappointed we weren't able to meet yesterday. It would have been more convenient for both of us."

She forced herself to look him in the eye, uncertain how to respond. She held his gaze and cleared her throat, which had suddenly become very dry. "Ah, w-w-well," she stammered. "Sundays are usually busy for me. They're the one day I have to catch up."

He leaned back and steepled his fingers. "I see." Then he sat up abruptly and queued her presentation on his computer screen. He clicked through a few slides.

"What made you decide to submit a proposal discussing the Foundation IVF grant program?"

"Because it's a unique type of program, and we're having excellent results. Over 50% of our couples are successful during their first cycle. With two cycles, it's almost 90%. I think it's important that access to reproductive technologies isn't just available to those with discretionary income to spend or generous health insurance, and this pilot program shows it can be done in a fiscally responsible way. Each couple's situation is evaluated on a case-by-case basis, and they receive a grant that supplements their contribution. It's a win-win for the university and our patients."

He looked at her condescendingly before asking, "Did you ever consider that perhaps some couples shouldn't have children?"

She shot him a look of disbelief. She couldn't believe he was saying this—the man who traveled the world touting groundbreaking assistive reproductive technologies. Out loud, she said, "But that's why clinics like ours exist—to help couples who want children but can't conceive. We have a mission to *all* patients—to help them by offering whatever technologies are most appropriate for their situation. We don't judge their reasons for wanting a family, and we shouldn't withhold care purely because they can't afford expensive treatments." She tried to keep her voice calm and measured, but she heard the stridency in her tone.

Sure enough, Hicks blustered back. "I wasn't a fan of this idea of yours when it first came up, and I'm still not. But once President Cobain got behind it, I had to back off. But when you present it next week in New Orleans, you'd better be prepared for questions and comments from folks whose opinions coincide with mine. The 'right' to have a baby isn't an essential healthcare mandate."

Joyce had to concede he had a point. Not everyone felt the substantial costs of reproductive technologies should be borne by the public. She softened her tone. "I understand. And you're probably right. My presentation isn't aimed at the politics of health care. I'm simply outlining a way that clinics might consider funding IVF for community members who are deserving but lack deep financial resources."

Hicks nodded. "Fine. Now, let's talk about these graphs. I find them confusing. I think you can do a better job."

Over the next fifteen minutes, he grilled her, and she took detailed notes. She barely had time to ponder her resentment regarding his arrogance. She inwardly sighed with relief when they finished. Much as she hated to admit it, his changes were on point and improved the presentation.

"When does your flight get in?" Hicks asked, changing subjects once again.

Oh no, she thought. *Not this again.* She considered stalling and saying she didn't remember, but she figured he'd keep asking until she gave up the information. "We leave Richmond around 3:30 p.m. and have a short stopover in Atlanta. We'll probably get to the hotel around nine. I think the airport is only about twenty minutes away."

"Call me when you get in, and we'll have dinner."

Joyce felt her stomach clench. She sat up straighter. "Sir, I appreciate the invitation, but I don't think that will work. I'm traveling with Sally, and we'll probably grab something to eat when we stop over in Atlanta. Let's meet in the lobby on Monday morning like we discussed. What time is that breakfast again?"

"Seven." Hicks looked displeased, but he didn't belabor the point. "Fine. I'll see you then."

He stood up and opened the door, angling himself so she had to brush by him. At the last minute, she did a quick sidestep and managed to avoid direct contact. Her heels tapped urgently on the polished marble floor of the hallway as she beat a retreat to the safety of her office. She felt like she was being stalked, then wondered if she was overreacting. Although he hadn't specifically made any quid pro quo type comments, his unwelcome touches and dinner invitations were sending up red flags. She'd been looking forward to the chance to present her work and network with colleagues in The Big Easy. Now she felt apprehensive and ambivalent.

Back in her office, Joyce bent to retrieve her wallet from the lower desk drawer when Dominique knocked. This time she avoided hitting her head as she straightened up.

"*Bonjour*. I'm headed to the university café for lunch. Would you care to join me?"

"Sure. I was getting ready to walk over and pick up a salad."

"How was your weekend?" he inquired conversationally as they meandered through the flaming fall landscape enroute to the lunchroom.

"It was fine. How about yours?"

"Very informative. Sally gave me a tour of Richmond, and I got to taste barbeque for the first time."

"What did you think?"

He turned to her with an amused expression, "Honestly, I

didn't love it." He smiled. "Sally suggested I try the special or the baby-backed ribs. While we were waiting to order, the guy eating the ribs next to me had something called a Pickle Back. He drank a shot of the American Jack Daniels whiskey and then a shot of pickle juice."

Joyce puckered her lips. "Yuck! That sounds horrible. You must think Americans have no taste. But not to worry. I don't think our university café will have any drinks that need a pickle juice chaser. Just boring coffee and soft drinks."

They stepped into the large airy cafeteria that was already bustling with the lunch crowd and joined the salad station line. "I'm going to ask Dr. Kumar if I can spend some time in the lab," Dominique commented.

"Good luck. He's not really the accommodating type. I've been here over two years, and only recently did he agree to let me spend a few hours shadowing him. We had a week with unusually low fertilization rates, and I was worried."

"What did you learn?"

"That the whole process happening behind the scenes is nothing short of miraculous. The scientific knowledge and technical skills required are significant. Kumar runs a tight ship. And since our rates improved the next week, it seemed like everything was okay."

"I'd expect nothing less," he replied. "Kumar and Hicks are responsible for some of the biggest breakthroughs in IVF technology. While I'm here, I don't want to miss an opportunity to observe this firsthand. I'm especially interested in the excellent pregnancy rates for couples with male-factor infertility." They shuffled forward in the line as he continued, "Why do you think he's so reluctant to show off his lab?"

"I'm not really sure. Since I first met him, he's always seemed like he's holding something back. Almost secretive. And I've noticed at department meetings, if someone asks him a question, he always squirms a little before answering."

"Maybe he's shy and doesn't like being in the spotlight."

Joyce thought a moment, then said, "You might have more luck talking with one of the assistants. Try Richard Carnegie. He's very smart and quite personable. He recently finished his master's degree in Embryology, and I heard he's applying to medical school."

"How long has he worked with Kumar?"

"I'm not sure, but it seems like it must be at least four or five years. I asked Sally about him once. She said he was here when she arrived, and she's been here almost five years."

Just as they mentioned her name, Sally bounced into the crowded cafeteria and quickly scanned the crowd. When she looked in their direction, Dominique and Joyce waved. She smiled and hustled toward them. "Hi there," she said in a cheerful voice. "I've only got a few moments to grab something for lunch and this line looks awfully long."

"Do you want us to pick up something for you?" Joyce volunteered. "I can drop it by your office."

"Yes, thanks, that would be great! I'd like a Caesar salad with chicken and one of those yummy rolls."

"How about a drink?"

Sally pressed ten dollars into Joyce's hand before rushing off. "Don't bother. I'll have water. Thanks again," she called over her shoulder, swimming upstream into the swarm of hungry staffers.

Joyce and Dominique watched her speed away. His dimple flashed and Dominique remarked, "She has a lot of energy. Does she ever stop moving?"

"Nope. She's like the Energizer Bunny."

He looked puzzled. "What is an Energizer Bunny?"

Joyce laughed. "I'm sorry. You probably wouldn't know. It's a toy in a TV advertisement for a long-lasting battery. It refers to someone who never seems to get tired or run out of energy."

"That seems like a good description of Sally. Are you two close friends?"

"My first week at McArthur, we met at a new faculty reception and hit it off. Since then, we try to meet for lunch at least once a week. Sometimes we get together after work for a drink or dinner. So, I'd say we're good work friends."

They reached the front of the line and ordered their salads. Once they settled at a window table looking out at a walled garden, Dominique resumed their conversation. "Is it considered acceptable for colleagues to have, how should I say it, a personal relationship?" A faint blush stained his cheeks.

"Do you mean a friendship or a romantic relationship?"

He pulled slightly at his collar, as if it were suddenly too tight and refused to meet her eyes. "I guess I mean a friendship that might become romantic."

Joyce felt herself begin to blush and wondered at her response. "Well, it depends. Friendships outside of work are quite common, and two colleagues might have a romantic relationship, but it gets complicated if one of them is a student. And even more complicated if one of them is a supervisor. Those are really frowned on because of what HR calls an 'imbalance of power.' One person can claim he or she was coerced and felt they had to go along." She toyed with her salad before asking, "What are the rules at your clinic in France?"

"Pretty much the same, but sometimes they happen anyway, the romances I mean. Like your American poet Emily Dickenson says, 'The heart wants what it wants.'"

Joyce couldn't help but remember the morning meeting with Hicks. She didn't think his heart had anything to do with it. In her mind's eye, she felt him looking at her breasts and angling to brush against her when she was leaving. It made her feel dirty. After an uncomfortable moment of silence while they focused on their food, Joyce pointed through the window to the lovely fall day and changed the topic to a much safer one—the weather.

Joyce dropped by Sally's office before heading home that evening. "I hope you enjoyed your salad." Setting two dollar bills and some coins on Sally's desk, she added, "And here's your change."

Sally looked up from sorting papers into colorful folders. "Thanks. I wish I could have joined you, but you know what Mondays are like."

Joyce nodded, then pivoted toward her real reason for stopping by. "Can I ask you something?"

"Sure."

"Did Hicks ever come on to you?"

Sally froze, her hand resting on a stack of papers. She asked in a cool voice, "Where did that come from? Why would you even ask that?"

"Because of what happened to me last night, and then again this morning."

"What do you mean?"

Joyce eased herself into the chair facing the desk so she could look her in the eye. "I've been feeling really uncomfortable around Hicks for a while now. When I'm in his office, he always stands or sits too close, and it's hard to walk by without him brushing against me. And once or twice, he put his hand on my butt. He made it seem casual, like an accident, but it wasn't."

Sally remained silent, and Joyce pushed on. "And then there are his comments. At first, he acted all friendly, very complimentary and flattering. But lately, he keeps wanting to see me outside of work and is irritated by my refusals. That phone call last night really shook me, which is why I called you. I felt so anxious that I hardly slept. And today, he asked me to have dinner with him when we arrive in New Orleans."

Sally's poker face remained. "What did you say?"

"I told him you and I were traveling together, and we'd get something to eat on our layover in Atlanta. I don't expect we'll get to the hotel until after nine." With a quick explosion of emotion, she whispered, "And I don't want to have dinner with him alone!"

Sally frowned slightly but remained close-mouthed.

"Why won't you say something?" Joyce said, her voice rising in frustration. "You're my friend. But the few times I've talked to you about Hicks, you've just told me to be careful and left it at that. Please talk to me! What do you know?"

Sally stood up and closed the door. Then she sat down again behind her desk, head bowed and fingers interlaced like she was praying. Finally, she spoke in a low voice. "You've got to promise to keep this between us. *Forever*. Because if you tell anyone, I'll deny it."

"Okay."

"Six months after I arrived at McArthur, Hicks began showing up at my office in the late afternoon or calling me and asking me to come to his office when Esmeralda had left for the day. He was always complimenting me, on my clothes, my hair, my clinical skills. I was flattered he was interested. He also seemed concerned about how I was settling in. One evening, he invited me out for a drink. He said his wife was out of town visiting her sister. I declined and he didn't ask again."

She picked up a pen, clicked it a few times, then set it down. "That year, the ASRM meeting was in San Diego, and he asked me to attend some functions with him. He promised to introduce me to his colleagues and help me build my own professional network."

Joyce shifted uncomfortably as Sally continued.

"I agreed, since the offer seemed genuine. Hicks is so well known and respected, and I thought it would really help me establish my reputation if he introduced me." She closed her eyes and took a deep breath. "This is really hard to talk about."

Inside, Joyce was screaming for Sally to continue, and she sat on her hands to quell her impatience. Maintaining a façade of placidity, she gently encouraged, "Go on."

"At one of the receptions, I don't remember which one, the

booze was really flowing. I hadn't eaten much all day, and I was jet-lagged and exhausted. After two really strong gin and tonics, I was buzzed. The place was so noisy and crowded that I just wanted to leave. You know, go back to my room, take a shower, and order room service. But Hicks pressed me to stay and kept introducing me to people. Somehow, I ended up drinking one more G and T." She lowered her head, as if too ashamed to continue.

Joyce held her breath. She could see how hard this was on her friend, and she didn't want to rush her.

Sally stared at the desk and continued. "I told Hicks I wasn't feeling well and needed to leave. He made excuses to his colleagues and offered to walk me back to my room. I was feeling a little unsteady and allowed him to take my arm. When the elevator got to my floor, I thanked him and tried to leave, but he held onto my arm and insisted on staying with me. When we got to my room, I tried to say good night, but he pushed his way in, and then . . ."

Joyce watched as Sally held her head in her hands and slowly massaged her temples. She continued in a muffled voice, "And then he pushed me back onto the bed. I struggled some, but the alcohol and the jetlag made me weak. I remember saying 'No' a few times and asking him to stop, but he tore my panties off and . . . he forced himself into me." This last was uttered in a whisper. And then she put her head on the desk and burrowed her face in her arms.

"Oh God, Sally. No." Joyce didn't know how to comfort her friend. "I'm sorry. I'm so sorry. What a horrible thing he did! It's not your fault. It's *not* your fault. He's a monster!"

A heavy silence descended. The air whooshed through the overhead vent, and a small clock ticked. The information seemed totally unbelievable yet completely plausible. She simultaneously felt shocked and unsurprised.

Sally finally lifted her head. "I imagine you're going to ask me if I told anyone, but before you do, the answer is no."

Joyce started to speak, but Sally held up her hand.

In a stronger voice she said, *"Don't* say anything. Don't. Judge. Me. And don't ask me why not."

"Okay. I won't. But what did you do? How did you handle it?"

"The rest of the conference, I tried to ignore him and forget what had happened. I connected with some friends and hung out with them the rest of the week. I chalked the whole thing up to too much booze and not enough food or sleep. I was on the pill, so I wasn't worried about pregnancy. My biggest concern was some type of STD—so I had that checked out when I got back. I didn't want anyone at the university to know, so I made an appointment at the County Health Department. Everything came back negative."

"Thank God." The room was again hushed. Somewhere down the hall, a door slammed. Joyce finally broke the silence. "How could you continue working at McArthur?"

"When I got back, I asked myself that very question, but I decided I wanted to stay. I didn't want what happened with Hicks to force me to leave a top-notch program. For a time, I considered going to HR, but then I realized it would be my word against his. And because of his status at the university, it was unlikely anything would come of it. And I worried he might retaliate and ruin my career."

"Did he try anything again?"

"Unfortunately, yes. The next time he asked me to come to his office, I told him I would only come during the day when Esmeralda was around. So, he had her call me the next day and ask me to come to his office on my lunch break."

"Did you go?" Joyce asked quietly.

For a moment, Sally's face looked frozen, then she continued wearily. "I went. And as soon as Esmeralda escorted me in and closed his office door, he launched into a long- winded diatribe. He implied that what happened at the conference was no big deal and, in fact, *I'd come on to him.* Then he had the nerve to say he hoped I didn't expect any special favors for sleeping with him."

Joyce gasped. She forced herself to be patient and allow her friend to continue at her own pace.

After an interminable silence, Sally sat up straight and said grimly, "I was so mad. I picked up the picture of his wife and two daughters, you know, the one that sits on his desk."

Joyce nodded.

"And then I shook it at him. I told him if it ever happened again, I'd call his wife."

"So has it—happened again?"

"No, but given his fixation on you, I suspect his pattern hasn't changed. Right before you started, we had a female graduate student in Kumar's lab, young, pretty, *naïve*, who abruptly left after six months. I always wondered if Hicks had anything to do with her rapid departure."

"Sally, I am so sorry. I hardly know what to say. That should *never* have happened to you, or to anyone. Thank you for trusting me enough to tell me. Forewarned is forearmed. I'll make sure to not be alone with Hicks in New Orleans. And I know you said you didn't go to HR, but maybe you should reconsider."

"It's been over three years." Sally waved her hand dismissively. "What's the point?"

"The point is he's doing it to other women, and someone at the university needs to know. This kind of harassment is illegal. He's a predator who should be stopped!"

Sally stood up, leaned over, and placed her hands on the desk. Her dark brown eyes flashed. "Joyce, you listen to me," she hissed. "Drop it. Like it or not, it's a man's world, and stuff like this goes on all the time. There's nothing you or I can do or say to get Hicks ousted. The best we can do is stay out of his way and use his influence to move our careers up the ladder. Better to have him as a 'friend' than an enemy."

For the second time that day, Joyce felt stunned. Dr. Sally

Cohen, her admired colleague and friend, had just told her to accept that harassment was part of academia. She felt slightly nauseous, and her right eyelid began to twitch. She needed to get out and process the feelings Sally's revelations had provoked. Suddenly, the office seemed too small and the air too thick to breathe.

She couldn't look her friend in the eye as she deliberately arose and, without another word, slipped out of the room.

CHAPTER 16

The rest of the week, Joyce was distracted by worries about her lecherous boss and the pending trip. Whereas before she'd thought there *might* be a problem, now she knew she was facing a showdown sometime in the future. Sally had begged off their usual lunch date, and she wasn't sure where things stood with their friendship.

At least she could look forward to getting out of town. She was driving to Baltimore to spend the weekend with Bill. She had one more patient to see before she hit the road.

As she perused the chart, she noted that Karin McCabe had spontaneously conceived eighteen months ago, but the pregnancy ended in a miscarriage. After an infertility workup, which was normal except for a mildly depressed sperm count, they underwent six unsuccessful cycles of ovarian stimulation with a timed intrauterine insemination (IUI). Both husband and wife were in their early thirties and otherwise in good health. They were here to discuss further treatment options.

She finished reading the referral letter and thought about her own miscarriage years before. She'd been a third-year medical student when she'd unexpectedly become pregnant a week before their first wedding anniversary. Although she'd been on the pill, she occasionally forgot a dose when she was on call. After two skipped periods, she'd purchased a home pregnancy test. Both she and Bill had been ambivalent when the cobalt-blue plus sign emerged, and they'd even discussed the possibility of her obtaining an abortion. She estimated she was about two months along, but she'd known from the start she'd never be able to go through with a termination.

Seven days later, they'd been on a weekend ski trip with friends when Joyce awakened shortly after midnight with severe cramps and bleeding. She'd finally roused Bill, and he'd driven her to the nearest hospital. Although it was a small rural facility, they had a well-staffed emergency department, and the place was hopping. After a half-hour wait, she'd been seen by a harried young doctor in between his triage of four teenagers involved in a multicar pile-up due to icy roads and underage drinking.

While waiting for test results, she'd had a massive gush of blood followed by the passage of several large clots and a small grape-like sac. The cramps had immediately lessened, and both she and the ER doc concluded she'd miscarried. He'd looked at her sympathetically and asked if she wanted to wait until morning to be evaluated by the on-call Ob/Gyn, but she declined. Because her blood type was Rh negative, she'd received a shot of RhoGAM to prevent her from developing antibodies that could cause problems with a future pregnancy. Then she and Bill trudged out of the hospital as the first hint of daylight appeared over the snowy mountains, giving them a distinctive pink glow.

The calm beauty of the winter morning had contrasted with Joyce's emotional upheaval. On the drive back to their friend's cabin, she'd shed a few tears of sadness but mostly she'd felt relieved at no longer being pregnant. Bill's emotions had been less complex. He'd been thankful Joyce was okay and grateful they didn't have to figure out how to deal with a new baby on top of medical school.

They hadn't talked about it the rest of the weekend. Bill ended up skiing that afternoon, while Joyce stayed home napping and watching TV. They didn't tell their friends about the trip to the ER, making excuses that Joyce was feeling a little under the weather. The following Monday, after minimal discussion about the weekend's events, they'd reported to their hospital assignments. And that was the end of it.

A nearby phone chiming brought Joyce out of her reverie. She quickly refocused, walked the few steps down the hall, and rapped on the exam room door. As she entered, a medium-height man with distinctive auburn-colored hair stood up and extended his hand in greeting. "Hello, Dr. Porter. I'm Jim McCabe and this is my wife, Karin."

Joyce returned his firm handshake and extended her hand to his wife. Like her husband, she had red hair, although it was her cat-like green eyes that were her most arresting feature. "I'm pleased to meet both of you. I've gone over the information your doctor provided. You've received excellent care. I'm sure he told you that miscarriages are very common, especially during the first three months. That by itself doesn't mean you have an infertility problem, but it's concerning that you haven't conceived again in over a year, even with the ovarian stimulation and IUI."

After completing the history and physical exam, she ushered the couple to the separate consult room and explained the basic IVF process. "Do you have any other questions?"

Karin gazed intently at her husband, then turned her luminescent green eyes directly at Joyce. "Here's the thing, Dr. Porter. Since we're going to have IVF, we want to be assured that we will have a *normal* baby, one without any type of birth defect or disability. We'd like to have all the testing that's available to make sure our embryos are completely normal before they are transferred to my uterus. My sister has two children with special needs. Both kids require lots of special care, and it's been really tough on their family."

Jim chimed in, "The kids are very sweet, and their parents

are great with them, but Karin's sister spends all her time taking care of the kids and arranging their services and treatment. She had to quit her job as a social worker. I'm not sure we could handle it—a child with physical or mental disabilities."

Karin added, "I can't imagine going through IVF, getting pregnant, and then finding out our baby isn't normal."

Joyce nodded sympathetically. "I understand. Many genetic conditions can be diagnosed prenatally, but others only manifest as the child grows older. I'll arrange for you to meet with a genetics counselor who can identify any specific testing that should be done given your family history."

"But we've already had one miscarriage!" Karin protested.

"Yes, but that doesn't mean you won't have a healthy pregnancy. In a way, a miscarriage is nature's way of making sure you have the best chance for a normal baby. There's a good chance something wasn't quite right with that pregnancy, and your body recognized it."

The couple looked at each other in silent communication. Joyce was anxious to wrap up and resisted the urge to look at her watch. After a short silence, Karin sighed and said, "We appreciate your time. It sounds like an appointment with a genetics counselor is our next step."

Joyce nodded. She tapped on her laptop screen and selected a tab. "I'll make the referral right now, and you can pick up the number to schedule an appointment on your way out. I expect you'll feel better once you have a more complete understanding of your situation. I recommend you do that first, before making a final decision about IVF. Let's see you back in a month or so after you've had the consult."

The couple thanked her again and headed down the hall toward the reception desk. She was surprised to find Dominique perched on a stool at the nurse's station. He nodded toward the McCabes. "Last patient?"

"Yes. An anxious couple with mostly unexplained infertility

who want a guarantee their IVF baby will be completely healthy."

Dominique gazed at her sympathetically. "That's always a tough conversation. Does McArthur have some special way of providing that assurance?"

"I wish we did."

"What did you tell them?"

"The usual. How 97 percent of babies are normal, and then I referred them for genetic counseling."

Dominique looked intrigued. "Do you send all your patients for genetic counseling?"

"No, but this couple has a niece and nephew with problems."

"Do you think your genetics folks will be able to reassure them?"

"Maybe, but I think they'll have a better understanding of the types of testing we can do both pre-implantation and prenatally. And then hopefully, they'll be able to make an informed decision about IVF. It might not be for them."

Dominique fell into step with Joyce as she headed out.

"I'm trying to get out a little early tonight," she said. "I'm driving to Baltimore to spend the weekend with Bill. How about you? Any plans?"

"Not really. Sally is on call, so I may stop in on Saturday to see how things run on the weekend. Maybe I'll spend time in the lab. I took your suggestion and spoke with Richard Carnegie. There's a retrieval tomorrow, and possibly one on Sunday."

"Well, don't work too hard. Any news about when your daughter can join you for a visit?"

"She probably won't make it until the winter break, and that's fine with me. I don't want her to miss school. I'm sure we'll find plenty to do whenever she comes."

"I understand there's a sculpture of George Washington by a famous French artist, I've forgotten his name, in the Virginia capital building."

"So I've heard. I'm not sure my daughter will be interested in a statue, but I might check it out this weekend."

She unlocked her office door. "I've got to get on the road. Enjoy your weekend. I look forward to hearing about your adventures on Monday."

He gave her a slight bow and smiled, his dimple giving him a roguish look. "Good night, Joyce. Safe travels."

Saturday evening, Joyce and Bill settled into Bill's small living room. Joyce looked around at the drab mustard walls and coffee-colored curtains. They'd finished Indian takeout from a local restaurant and the scent of coriander, turmeric and garlic lingered. Bill reached for the TV remote and asked, "Do you want to watch a movie?"

She looked up from her iPad where she was skimming news reports and said, "Maybe later. Let's talk first."

"About what? We've been talking all day."

She cocked her head to the side and said patiently, "Yes, we have, but only about unimportant stuff. I want to continue our conversation about starting a family."

He groaned. "You've got to be kidding. It's Saturday night and we're both tired. I think we should postpone it. Let's kick back and relax."

"That's what you said last week—that we should put it off until we'd both had a good night's sleep. Well, I slept pretty well last night, and if we wait until tomorrow, you'll want to postpone again."

"Look, we had a great day," Bill said with an exasperated sigh. "And now, I'd like to veg out in front of the TV. Can't it wait until next weekend?"

"Not really. I leave for New Orleans on Sunday, so I'll be packing and practicing my presentation on Saturday."

"Is it even worth it—me driving to Richmond next weekend?"

The minute the words left his mouth, Bill knew he'd made a big mistake. Joyce faced him, her lips forming a tight line of frustration. "I guess that's up to you," she said sarcastically. "Do *you* think it's worth it?"

He immediately looked contrite. "Joyce, I'm sorry. I didn't mean it that way."

"Then how did you mean it?"

"Look, I don't like living in two places any more than you, but for now, it's our life. We have to make the best of it. What I meant was that you'll be busy, and it's a long drive to spend only one day together."

She looked at him with a mixture of anger and hurt. "And you're saying you don't think it's worth it. That *I'm* not worth it. That *we're* not worth it."

He raked his hands through his hair in frustration and tried again. "I didn't say that. I only meant that it might be easier for you if all you had to do was focus on packing and finishing your presentation."

"Well, I can focus just fine with you around. We did it during all those years of med school and residency."

Bill threw up his hands in surrender, "Okay. Fine. I'll drive down on Friday as usual, but it might be late. I don't think I'll be able to leave early again. On Saturday, I can always hang at the coffee shop and do some writing while you pack." He clicked the *On* button of the remote, and the TV screen flickered to life. "Now, do you want to watch a movie?"

"No," she said, reaching for the remote and turning it off. "I want to talk about having a baby. I'm still on the pill, and, ideally, I should be off for a few months before we try to conceive. I'm thinking about stopping in December."

"Geez Joyce, why now?" he said with annoyance, finally turning to face her. "What's the hurry? You're getting settled into your job at McArthur, and I have at least another year at Hopkins. I think we should wait until we're living in the same city. It's tough enough managing our lives right now. I can't imagine having a baby on top of everything else. And then there's our finances. We aren't exactly flush with cash. We'd have to find daycare and—"

"As the one with a real *job*, I know all about our finances!"

Bill flushed. "Joyce, that's hardly fair—"

"Listen, I'm around couples all day, every day, who put off starting their family until the 'perfect' time, only to discover that they can't conceive. I'm almost thirty-five. If we end up, God help us, as infertility patients, I'd rather go through it sooner than later. That way, if it doesn't work, we'll still have options."

"Good God, Joyce," he said in a voice dangerously close to a shout. "What makes you think we'll have an infertility problem? As I recall, the first time you got pregnant, it was because you missed one pill."

"Well, it might have been more than one pill," she said, trying to sound reasonable. "And I was a lot younger. And because we were living together, we had a lot more sex."

"So how does this work exactly? You're going to call me up and tell me to drop everything and head to Richmond so we can have sex?" He shook his head in amazement. "Do you know how crazy that sounds?"

"It's not crazy," she insisted. "And I did think about that. I understand that you might not always be available during my fertile time. We might need to freeze your sperm so I can be inseminated if you aren't around when I'm ovulating."

Bill stared at her in wide-eyed disbelief, then his expression became pained before his eyes flashed with anger. Slowly he hefted himself out of the lumpy chair.

"Where are you going?" she asked in a rush.

"Out."

"Why? We aren't done talking."

"We *are* done talking. And I need to take a walk."

"You can't walk around Baltimore by yourself on a Saturday night. It's not safe!"

"I'll be fine. This neighborhood is well lit and as safe as anywhere. It's mostly students. I'll be back in an hour."

"Please don't go," she begged, reaching out to stop him. "Look, I'm sorry. This past week, I saw a string of couples all in their mid-thirties who waited to get pregnant, and every single one of them reminded me of us."

He waved her off, grabbed his jacket, and then disappeared.

She watched the door slam shut and stood there in stunned silence. They hadn't had a fight like this in years. In fact, she couldn't remember their last major disagreement. She felt a pang of guilt followed by remorse. She wished she hadn't pushed so hard. But then again, she'd been thinking about it a lot lately. The voice in the back of her head reminded her with annoying regularity that her biological clock was ticking.

She'd always thought that was a dumb way to phrase it, but in some ways, it accurately portrayed her recent surge of temporal anxiety. It was probably because her birthday was approaching. Or maybe it was all those Facebook college and med-school friends who posted cute pictures of their smiling kids.

An hour later, almost to the minute, he returned. He entered as quietly as their cat and didn't speak as he removed his jacket and hung it in the closet. She was the first to speak. "How was your walk?"

"Fine." There was another awkward silence and then he added, "It feels like rain, and the wind is chilly."

She arose from her chair and tried to hug him, but he stepped back from the embrace.

"Not now, Joyce. I'm still angry, and I don't want to say something I'll regret."

She struggled to hide her hurt expression. After a moment she said, "Okay, but when do you think—"

"I'll let you know." Then he went to a small liquor cabinet, pulled out a bottle of Maker's Mark, and poured himself two fingers. She gazed mutely at him for a moment, then turned and headed toward the bedroom.

CHAPTER 17

The windshield wipers slapped relentlessly against the glass, barely able to keep up with the biblical downpour. Joyce struggled to see the roadway through the wall of water. Each passing car generated a miniature tsunami, and the eighteen-wheelers caused waves big enough to rock her small Honda. It was Sunday afternoon, and she was tired and hungry. She didn't usually mind the drive from Baltimore to Richmond. Once out of city traffic, she generally settled into her "driving zone" and listened to music or a podcast while the miles rolled by, but today, the percussive rain made listening to a podcast difficult, and she wasn't in the mood for music. That left her brooding about the weekend, her thoughts as drab as the pewter-colored sky.

Following their argument the previous evening, she'd gone to bed and read for a while, hoping that sooner or later Bill would join her. Eventually, she'd fallen asleep with the bedside lamp on. It was still on when she'd awakened at four a.m., alone in their bed. She'd gotten up and discovered him asleep in his clothes on the couch, TV remote in hand, the sound on mute. She'd gotten a drink of water, covered him with the handmade afghan his grandmother had given them as a wedding gift, and slid back into bed.

The next morning had been strained and filled with uneasy silences. They'd walked to a local bakery and purchased croissants and coffee, then buried themselves in the Sunday paper. Conversation had been infrequent and banal, with neither of them addressing the elephant in the room. Shortly before noon, Joyce packed up. After a quick good-bye, she'd headed out. Bill hadn't walked her to the car.

Slogging along the rain-drenched highway, she was filled with regrets that she'd pushed so hard. Replaying the scene in her mind, some of that regret metamorphosized into a slow burn of anger. She admitted to herself she'd become a little obsessed with the idea of starting their family, but seeing infertile couples week after week served as a constant reminder of her declining fecundity. She grudgingly conceded that Bill had a point with his concern about their finances, and she felt embarrassed she'd been so snarky about her "real job." Their educational loan payments were substantial, but they couldn't wait another ten years until they were debt-free. In her mind, the biggest obstacle was their current living arrangement. McArthur had onsite daycare that took babies as young as eight weeks old, and she was sure her mother would come occasionally if she needed overnight help. But being a single parent until she and Bill were in the same city would be hard.

Chewing on her lower lip, she realized most of her anger stemmed from her husband's ongoing refusal to even have a discussion. He'd done what he'd always done, clammed up and walked out. All morning he'd maintained an emotional distance, and he'd barely hugged her good-bye. Before leaving, she'd tried once again to apologize and clear the air, but he'd clung to his chilly demeanor, professing once more that he "wasn't ready to talk about it."

Her cell phone buzzed. Wondering if it might be Bill calling to apologize, she quickly glanced at the screen. When she didn't recognize the number, she felt a momentary stab of dread that it might be Hicks. Then she rationalized that since he hadn't bothered her for almost a week, it was doubtful he'd repeat a Sunday afternoon call given her previous reaction. A melodious *ding* indicated the caller had left a voicemail. Now she felt confident the caller wasn't Hicks. He was much too arrogant to leave a voicemail. Because driving conditions were poor, she decided to wait until she was safely in her apartment before listening to the message. As a passing car sent a sheet of water cascading down her windshield, she wondered who'd call her on a Sunday afternoon, and more importantly, what they might want.

Leon knocked briefly on the front door festooned with a wreath of silk flowers and miniature gourds, then let himself into his childhood home. The smell of roast beef and freshly baked biscuits tickled his nose and made his mouth water. He was carrying the chocolate cake Evie had baked that morning, and she trailed behind clutching a festive *Happy Birthday!* mylar balloon and a foil-wrapped pot of golden mums. His mother, Delores, wearing a hot-pink apron proclaiming she was the *Birthday Girl*, bustled into the foyer. Her curly gray hair was gathered into a bun, and large brown eyes and generous smiling lips radiated welcome. She threw open her arms and enfolded him with a long hug. He thought it funny that his mom always greeted him like he'd been gone for a year instead of a week. He carefully set the cake on the hall credenza, then returned the hug.

"Leon and Evie!" she exclaimed. "So good to see you. Come in quickly and shut the door. I don't want the cold and rain blowing in."

"Happy birthday, Mom," they said in unison, and Evie stepped forward to give her mother-in-law the balloon and flowers, receiving a hug in return.

"Oh, they're beautiful. Such a wonderful color. You know mums are my favorite, and these look like they'll last a good long time. And a birthday balloon too! I haven't had one of those in . . . Well, I can't remember when." She turned and called out, "Howard, Leon and Evie are here. Come help with their coats."

Leon's father, wearing a heather-blue sweater and tasseled loafers, appeared in the doorway. He was a distinguished-looking man, tall and thin, with slightly stooped shoulders. He smiled broadly at Evie. "How's my favorite daughter-in-law? Here, let me help you out of that wet coat."

Having disposed of their moist outer garments, they all traipsed through the dining room enroute to the kitchen. The dining room table was set with the "good china" in honor of Delores's birthday. They'd offered to take her out to celebrate, but she'd insisted she'd rather cook and enjoy their company at home. She set the flowers and the balloon on the round breakfast table before turning to them and saying, "Dinner is almost ready."

She pointed to a spot on the counter in front of the toaster oven. "Howard, please carve the roast. The platter and knife are over there."

She turned to her son. "Leon, put that delicious cake on the table next to those lovely flowers, and then please pour the iced tea."

Moving with the grace of a ballet dancer half her age, she deftly removed a pan of buttermilk biscuits from the oven and set them on the top of the stove. "Evie, would you turn out the biscuits? Be careful you don't burn yourself. The breadbasket is next to Howard."

Under his breath, Leon's dad muttered, "She would have made an excellent drill sergeant."

"I heard that," Delores said, but her face broke into a contented smile as she stirred the gravy before pouring it into a small pitcher. When the last-minute preparations were completed to her satisfaction, the family sat down together, bowed their heads, and joined hands for grace.

Leon's father closed his eyes. "Heavenly Father, we thank you for this family, and for our ability to be together today. And we thank you for blessing us with this food and with so many gifts. We pray for all our brothers and sisters who aren't with us today. And lastly, we thank you for the many wonderful years you've given my beautiful wife, Delores, who as you know, is the best cook in Virginia. Ahh-*men*."

"Amen," they echoed, grinning at Howard's last remark.

The platter of roast beef and two bowls, one filled with mashed potatoes and the other with peas, were passed. Next came the breadbasket filled with fragrant biscuits followed by the gravy pitcher. Leon was savoring his first mouthful of hot buttered biscuit when he felt Evie grip his thigh under the table.

He turned to look at her and noticed she was pale.

She hastily rose from the table, napkin to her mouth, saying, "Excuse me, I'm not feeling well," then bolted toward the downstairs bathroom.

Leon shoved back his chair and quickly followed, pausing a moment before the closed door, then gently pushing it open. He found her kneeling on the floor next to the toilet, her head propped in her hands.

"What's wrong? It is the babies?"

"No, they're fine," she replied faintly. "I think it was the smell of all that rich food that got to me. I didn't want to puke all over your mother's fine linen."

"Did you throw up?"

"No, but I felt like I wanted to."

He took a paper cup from the dispenser next to the bathroom sink and filled it with cool water. He handed it to her, and she took several small sips before giving it back to him. A minute later, she slowly pushed off the side of the toilet and got to her feet. Leon lowered the lid so she could sit down and crouched beside her, a worried look on his face.

"How are you now?"

"Better. The nausea is mostly gone. That's the problem with this darn morning sickness. It comes without warning then goes away just as fast. And it doesn't just come in the mornings."

A sharp knock sounded on the door.

"Rats, it's my mother," he whispered. "And she'll have *a ton* of questions. We might have to tell her."

Before she could reply, Delores' muffled voice came through the door, "Evie? Leon? Are you all right?" She sounded concerned. "Do you need anything? What can I do to help?"

Leon silently mouthed to Evie, "What should I say?"

She made a weak thumbs up gesture.

"Everything's okay, Mom," he said. "Evie felt a bit dizzy. We'll be out in a minute."

"Oh dear. Stay put. I'll bring a cold compress." They listened as her footsteps retreated down the hallway.

"I feel terrible," Evie said mournfully. "I've ruined your mom's birthday dinner."

Leon took both her hands into his. They were cold and clammy. "It's okay," he said in a comforting manner. "She'll understand. Do you want to go home?"

"Not unless you do. I'm feeling almost normal, and I don't want you to miss out on your mom's home-cooked meal."

"I'm sure she'd pack it up for me."

They heard footsteps and then another rap on the door. Leon opened it slowly and his mother's anxious face peered in. She handed him the damp washcloth which he placed on Evie's forehead.

"Thank you," she said softly. "I'm feeling better now."

"Have you been sick?" Delores asked curiously.

Now Evie looked uncomfortable. She stared questioningly at Leon, who gave a slight shrug.

A short silence followed before she replied, "Yes. The last few weeks. I've had a few similar episodes. They usually go away pretty quickly."

Leon's mother, trying not to look too hopeful, finally asked, "Do you think you might be pregnant?"

Once again, Evie turned to Leon with a wordless plea. He finally spoke up, "Let's go sit back down. We have something to tell you and Dad."

Delores clapped her hands to her mouth in the universal gesture of delighted surprise. "I knew it," she said before rushing down the hall. "This is the *best* birthday gift ever!"

Evie and Leon followed slowly, his hand at the small of her back. He spoke in a low tone, "We don't have to tell them everything if you don't want to. We can tell them you're pregnant, but not about the IVF or the twins."

"I can't imagine your mother settling for that."

"I think we can trust them to keep the news quiet until we're ready."

She sighed and unconsciously rubbed her tummy. "I guess, but I worry that something might slip."

"It's only another month until Thanksgiving. We can tell them we're planning a general family announcement then."

"Okay. You're right. It's just that everything still feels shaky. And if, God forbid, something happens, we'll have to tell them, and it will break their hearts."

He chuckled and gave her a reassuring hug. "You worry too much. Let's tell them we're pregnant and you're due sometime in June. That should be enough for now."

When they entered the dining room, Delores and Howard looked at them expectantly. Standing in the doorway, Leon took a deep breath and announced, "Mom, Dad, we're pregnant."

Both parents jumped up and rushed to enfold them in a group hug. Congratulations were given and happy tears shed.

Finally, Delores shooed them back to their seats.

"Now, tell us everything. How long have you known?" she asked.

Leon cleared his throat, then began, "We've only known for a few weeks. Evie isn't due until sometime in June. We wanted to wait until we had an ultrasound at the end of the first three months and knew everything was okay before we told anyone."

"Can I tell my church group? You know, we've all been praying for you. And your third-grade Sunday school teacher Mrs. Davidson will be so excited."

Evie squeezed Leon's thigh so tightly he thought it might leave a bruise.

"Well, Mom, here's the thing. We hadn't planned to tell anyone yet. And we really don't want to answer a lot of questions until we know everything is fine." He pivoted in his seat and shot his dad a "Help me out here" kind of look, then refocused on his mother. "We're planning on telling everyone at Thanksgiving, so please don't say anything to your church group, or *anyone* else, until then."

Delores looked disappointed and started to protest, but Howard silenced her with a warning look before turning to them and saying, "Of course. Of course. We understand. That makes perfect sense. Thank you for sharing this joyful news with your mother and me. We respect that it's your news, and that you don't want to talk about it yet." Once again, he looked at his wife with a serious expression before adding, "And you can count on us to keep your secret. *Both* of us," he emphasized.

Delores gave a brief nod and said in a resigned tone. "Okay. Mum's the word until Thanksgiving. But can I at least ask . . ."

"Now, no more questions," Howard said emphatically before she could resume her third degree. "Let's eat. This wonderful food is getting cold, and we have birthday cake to look forward to."

With that pronouncement, the family resumed their Sunday supper, and Delores, true to her word, remained mute about Evie's pregnancy.

Dominique hit the *Call end* button on his phone. He was disappointed he hadn't reached Joyce, but then he remembered she was away for the weekend. He hoped she wasn't having problems driving back in the ferocious rainstorm.

He'd spent most of the weekend at McArthur, helping Sally with egg retrievals and embryo transfers. He'd also managed to devote a few hours each afternoon to shadowing Kumar's assistant.

Joyce had been right to suggest he connect with him. Richard Carnegie was a pleasant fellow, full of information. He had a blond buzz cut and looked like the movie stereotype of the American "boy next door." He radiated enthusiasm and seemed eager to talk about his work. This was a marked contrast to the taciturn and almost secretive attitude of his boss. In their short time working together, Richard had shared that he played football in high school, went to the University of Virginia for undergraduate studies in Biology, and got engaged to his high school sweetheart on Valentine's Day. He also mentioned he'd finished his master's degree in Embryology in June and was in the process of applying to medical schools. While he found the whole science of IVF fascinating, what he really wanted was to be a trauma surgeon.

After observing Richard for several hours, Dominique concluded that the basic lab techniques of washing and preparing the sperm and inseminating the eggs were almost identical to those of his home clinic in France. The nutrient media used and the preservation process for non-transferred embryos were also quite similar. However, one glaring difference stood out: the frequent use of donor sperm. In some cases, the donor was mixed directly with the husband's sample, and in other cases, the eggs were separated into two groups. One group was inseminated with only the husband's sperm and the other with only the donor's. He'd questioned Richard about this, asking about the informed consent process, but Richard hadn't known details about the specific patients. He said he received a weekly list of upcoming retrievals from Kumar, and if there was an "A" next to the patient's name, he used donor mixed with husband's sperm to inseminate all eggs. If an "A+" notation appeared next to a name, then he separated the eggs and inseminated half with husband's sperm and half with donor. Dominique was intrigued by the frequency with which augmentation was utilized. Of the five procedures that had occurred over the busy weekend, all but one had been on what he termed the "A list."

Dominique was eager to speak to Joyce about this practice. He knew that McArthur was famous for its success in treating male factor infertility, and he wondered if this was their "secret." He remembered the first staff conference he'd attended when Kumar had been asked about his "super" donor sperm and "magic nanobeads." At the time, he recalled Kumar had looked uncomfortable and hadn't really spoken about the process in any detail.

During some down time in the lab, he'd also questioned Richard about the nanobead processing technique. Richard said it was mostly experimental, and they used it very rarely. He vowed to ask Kumar for more information on Monday. He wondered if Kumar would agree to let him observe this process when it was next utilized. Maybe he could schedule some additional time in the lab before going to the conference. If not, it seemed unlikely he would have another opportunity until mid-November.

Mulling it over, he began formulating questions. Grabbing a notepad, he jotted them down.

1. What percentage of couples use donor sperm?

2. Why did they mix the sperm for some couples but separated the eggs inseminated by donor sperm for others?

3. What type of patient consent was required?

4. How were the donors chosen? By the couples or by the lab?

Satisfied he'd captured his thoughts, he opened his computer and began reading an online journal. That seemed a fitting activity for a rainy Sunday afternoon. Two hours later, his phone buzzed. It was Joyce, returning his call.

"Hello."

"Hi, this is Joyce. I got your voicemail."

"Good afternoon, or maybe it's almost good evening. How was your weekend?"

There was silence, and he wondered if they'd been cut off. "Hello? Joyce?"

"I'm here," she eventually replied. "Fine. My weekend was fine." Another pause, then, "The drive back today was a little scary. The heavy rain made it hard to see."

"I'm sorry to hear that. I'm glad you made it safely."

There was another brief pause, "So, you said you spent some time in the lab this weekend and have questions. I don't really know if I'll have any answers. I haven't spent much time in the lab. That's Dr. Kumar's domain."

"Yes, I know, but these are clinical questions."

"Go on."

"What do you know about the A list?"

"The what?" Joyce's voice sounded puzzled.

"The A list."

"I've never heard of it."

CHAPTER 18

The following Wednesday, when Joyce and Dominique stopped by the lab to talk to Dr. Kumar, he'd been out sick. Richard Carnegie had also been away. The on-duty technician, a young woman with straight blond hair pulled into a ponytail, said Richard was taking a week's vacation for medical school interviews. When questioned, she'd never heard of an "A" list. The current weekly schedule showed a couple who had requested donor insemination for half their eggs. They were Dr. Torrey's patients, and she didn't know anything about consent forms.

Later that day when Joyce reviewed their chart, their consent was well documented. The chart contained signed forms from both husband and wife as well as a detailed note from Dr. Torrey. The couple had chosen Donor Z021 from McArthur's sperm bank.

Joyce felt they were at a dead end, so she suggested they put their questions on hold until after the conference, when they could speak directly with Kumar. Dominique looked mildly disappointed but readily agreed.

On Friday afternoon, she headed toward her car. Planning to stop at the market to pick up cat food and a few fresh food items, she thought about dinner, a simple stir fry whenever Bill arrived.

In order to keep the peace, she'd decided to back off the baby campaign.

Pulling into evening traffic, her thoughts switched to the New Orleans conference. She barely noticed the steady stream of cars that flowed like lemmings toward unknown destinations. Driving on autopilot, she felt her anxiety level rise. She was nervous about her presentation as well as attending social events with Hicks.

Another worry was her strained relationship with Sally since the revelation of her sexual encounter with Hicks. She'd been adamant that the single occurrence was firmly in the past. Darting around a lumbering bus, Joyce's thoughts swirled like a kitchen blender. How could Sally so casually dismiss the incident? She seemed to view it as part of the academic game, a mildly regrettable interlude, something one simply did to keep moving ahead. Joyce strongly rejected that premise.

As the Friday traffic inched along, she contemplated their friendship. They were good travel companions, and going anywhere with Sally was always a fun-filled adventure. But right now, there was tension. When they'd met in the hallway at the clinic, they'd exchanged brief pleasantries and quickly averted their eyes. At the last minute, Sally had begged off their usual weekly lunch, saying she had errands to run. Their longest conversation had been this morning, when they confirmed details for sharing a ride to the airport on Sunday afternoon.

Joyce groaned in frustration as a Lexus SUV with a California license plate cut her off right when the light turned red. As she drummed her fingers on the steering wheel, her cell phone buzzed. The screen flashed a picture of Bill in a Big Foot suit he'd worn for a Halloween costume party while they'd still been in medical school. She pushed *Answer* and put the phone on speaker. "Hello," she said.

"Hello," he echoed.

"What's up? Have you left yet?"

"Not yet. That's why I'm calling. I'm running late."

"You're still planning to come, aren't you?" Her voice sounded strained.

"Yes, but don't wait on me for dinner. I'll grab something and eat on the way down."

"Okay. When do you think you'll get in?"

"Probably not 'til after ten."

Her reply dripped with hurt and disappointment. "Fine. Thanks for calling. Drive carefully."

They said a curt good-bye and ended the call. *Not a great way to begin,* she thought glumly.

The next morning, Bill finished his breakfast, closed the sports section of the *Richmond Times Dispatch,* and quietly sipped his coffee. Joyce sat across the small table in her pink chenille robe. It was ragged and worn around the sleeves and not at all sexy, but she loved its cozy feel.

He gazed at her expectantly. "So, what's our agenda for the day?"

"I have to pack, but otherwise, the day is open."

"What would you like to do?"

She wondered if this was a trick question. What she really wanted was to talk about the cloud that had settled over their relationship and his unwillingness to discuss having a baby, but she remembered her previous resolve to back off. Stalling for time, she stood up, walked a few steps to the kitchen counter, and poured herself another cup of coffee. She looked inquiringly at Bill and gestured toward the pot. He shook his head and waited. She added some milk then returned to the table.

"I'd like to talk to you about a situation at work," she finally said. "I'd like your opinion on something."

"Okay. Shoot." He closed his iPad and gazed at her intently, his blue eyes alert.

"Remember when I told you my boss invited me to attend a reception with him?"

He nodded. "Sure. You said it was a chance to meet some influential people, 'giants in the field' I think you called them. You thought it would help you expand your professional network."

"Right. Well, it isn't just a reception. He also wants me to attend a breakfast on the opening morning."

"Okay. Is this a problem?"

She shrugged. "I didn't think so, but now I'm not sure."

"I'm not following. First you were glad to have an opportunity to network, and now you sound like you think there's a problem. What changed?"

Joyce hesitated, then surprised herself by blurting out, "He's been coming onto me for the last few months."

Bill's face registered disbelief then quickly turned to shock. "Good God, Joyce. That's a helluva thing to say about your boss. Are you sure?"

"Yes. I'm sure," she retorted, slapping the table with the palm of her hand for emphasis.

"Okay, okay." He took her hand. "Calm down. I believe you. Now, start at the beginning." He squeezed her hand gently and then released it.

She took a deep breath and began. "First, it was little things."

"Like what?" He still looked like he was having a hard time processing the news.

"Oh, he'd stand too close to me, or brush up against me while leaving a room, or lightly touch my lower back or arm. He would complement my clothes or my hair or make a remark about my perfume. He made it seem casual, like he was just being friendly, but it made me uncomfortable." Her face flushed. "Then he started asking me to his office at the end of the day, after his assistant had gone home. He'd sit too close, and our knees would touch."

She paused. Bill's face was unreadable. He leaned forward and fixed her with a Sphinx-like stare. "Go on."

"Remember when you were here two weeks ago? We had an argument. You left right after lunch."

"I remember."

She picked up her coffee mug, then set it back down without taking a sip. This was the first time she'd put her discomfort with Hicks into words with anyone other than Sally. Somehow, talking about it with Bill made it seem more real. "Soon after you left, I was doing my laundry, and Hicks called. He said he'd reviewed my presentation, and he wanted to talk. That he had some suggestions."

"On a Sunday? That's a little weird."

She nodded. "It gets weirder. He said he was working that afternoon and asked me to come to his university office."

"What!" He exclaimed, sitting bolt upright. "Did you go?"

"Of course not! I lied and told him you were still here, and he told me to bring you along. He said he wanted to meet you."

"What a sleazeball," he said with disgust.

"I think he knew I was lying. He kept pressuring me, and I finally hung up."

"Then what happened?"

"I called Sally and asked her to come over for some wine and cheese. I wanted someone to talk to. But she had too many things to do. Because I was really creeped out, I locked the door and turned on the TV. I didn't go down to get my laundry until hours later."

"Did he call back?"

"No. The next morning, his assistant called and asked me to come by his office before lunch."

"Did you go?"

"Of course. There wasn't any way I could refuse."

"How'd it go?"

"Fine, I guess. He acted very formal, made a big show of sitting behind his ostentatious desk. But he did give me several good suggestions and then posed some questions that might come up during the Q and A so I could think about how I might answer them."

"What kind of questions?"

Joyce pulled her robe more snugly around her waist, then stood up and began to pace. "The most disturbing one had to do with why McArthur funded the patient-assist program in the first place. He said not everyone thinks that public or private funding should be spent on IVF for poor couples. Then he said something really shocking. He said some people aren't meant to be parents."

"He's not wrong," Bill replied.

She stared, holding her breath as her mind spun trying to process his comment. "How can you possibly say that?" she demanded.

"I'm coming at it from a resource perspective. If there are only so many healthcare dollars to go around, maybe they should be spent on things like vaccinations or new cancer drugs or making sure everyone has insurance to pay for their prescriptions."

"I completely disagree," she retorted. "If two people want to be loving parents, we should do everything we can to help them conceive. IVF shouldn't just be for rich people with good insurance!"

He started to respond, then stopped. After a moment he said, "I don't want to fight about the healthcare policy implications of IVF for all. Let's go back. You were telling me about the Monday meeting with your handsy boss. So, did he say or do anything inappropriate?"

"Not really. I made it a point to keep my distance. He kept pushing me to have dinner with him on Sunday evening, but I told him Sally and I planned to eat in Atlanta on our layover, and he finally stopped asking."

"So, even if he's a jerk, this reception and breakfast sound pretty safe. There'll be lots of people around." Bill absently scratched his nose. "And Sally will be at the conference, so you'll have back-up."

"I hope you're right. That's a logical conclusion, but I can't shake my feeling that something bad is going to happen. And I don't know if I can rely on Sally."

He cocked an eyebrow. "Why not? Isn't she your friend?"

Indecision filled Joyce. She wanted to share Sally's revelations about Hicks but felt guilty about betraying her trust. Finally, she said, "Sally told me something in confidence. I can't share the details with you, but she said it's a known fact that Hicks is a womanizer who preys on graduate students and new faculty hires."

"Whoa." His eyes widened in surprise. "What are you saying? Could that really be true?"

She nodded. "I have confidence in her sources. When she described some of his past behaviors, a lot of it sounded exactly like what's been happening to me."

"But you aren't a new hire or a graduate student."

"I know." She shrugged unhappily. "Lucky me."

"How long has this been going on?" he asked, then clarified, "Not just with you—but within the department?"

"I don't know, but it sounded like there were at least two previous incidents, and maybe more. She only told me because I asked her point blank."

"Has anyone reported him?" His voice became indignant. "Surely this type of behavior wouldn't be tolerated. Has there been an investigation?"

"Not that I know of. Sally said no one would come forward because he's too powerful, and it would be their word against his. He's well respected, and he's a personal friend of the university's president."

"That doesn't give him a right to harass female faculty and staff!" he said angrily.

"What do you think I should do? I've really been looking forward to this conference. It's the first time I've been invited to be part of a national panel. I'm worried that somehow Hicks is going to ruin it."

"You need a plan."

"I know. But the best I've come up with so far is to avoid any situation where I'd be alone with him, though that's easier said than done. I've been hoping he'd get the point that I'm not interested and back off, but that's not happening." She hesitated before asking, "Is there any way you could come with me?"

Bill stood up and pulled Joyce into his arms. He felt warm and solid, and she inhaled his familiar scent. She felt a rush of love, and for the first time in weeks, she felt like they were a team. Confiding in him made her feel less anxious. She wondered why she'd waited so long.

"I'm sorry you're in this position," he said. "And I really wish I could come with you. I can't make that happen right now. But I have an idea."

She swallowed her disappointment as he continued, "Your boss is a world-class jerk who has no business harassing female subordinates. He has to be held responsible for his despicable behavior."

Joyce pushed back from his embrace. "Absolutely, *and* it needs to stop!"

Bill looked resolute. "I agree. But you'll need some kind of proof before you go to HR. So, here's what we're going to do."

Kumar, hunched over his microscope, looked up in surprise as Hicks appeared. He almost never came to the lab, and certainly not on a Saturday morning.

"Ajay, we need to talk."

"Certainly," came Kumar's quiet reply. "I'm almost finished. I can come to your office in half an hour."

Hicks pursed his lips and looked like he wanted to argue. Then he nodded curtly and left the room.

Exactly thirty minutes later, Ajay tapped softly on the partially open door leading to Hicks's inner sanctum. The outer office was like a tomb, cold and dark, and he'd had seen no one on his walk over.

"Come in," came the terse response.

Hicks was sitting at his desk with two large folders spread out before him. He motioned to the chair opposite the desk, and Kumar slowly lowered himself. He sat on the edge of the seat as if prepared to spring up at any moment and dash away.

"Did you know Richard Carnegie is applying to medical schools?" he asked unexpectedly. Kumar looked surprised at the question.

"Yes, I believe he mentioned it several months ago. He's on vacation this week, and one of the other techs told me he has some interviews scheduled. Did he apply here?"

Hicks brushed aside the question. "That's not important. Did he ever question you about using donor sperm for some of the IVF inseminations?"

"No, not really. I give him a list once a week when he's staffing the retrievals, so he'll know which eggs to inseminate with donor sperm."

"What do you call that list?"

Kumar looked confused. "I don't call it anything. It lists the date and the couples who are in cycle and need donor sperm."

"And is it recorded anywhere?"

"Not specifically. There is a place on the daily log where we place an 'A' next to the donor-inseminated eggs."

Hicks leaned forward and said in a low voice, "Well, our charming Frenchman spent time last weekend in the lab working with Mr. Carnegie, and now he and Joyce Porter are asking questions about an 'A' list."

Kumar sat stock still, his face impassive. For years, he'd dreaded this moment, and now that it was here, he felt oddly detached.

"What do you want me to do?" he asked calmly.

"I think we'd best stop the routine augmentations. Keep making your weekly list but only include couples with proper paperwork and consents. Our pregnancy rate may dip slightly, but hopefully your new technique will be ready soon."

Kumar massaged the crease between his eyebrows as if trying to stave off a headache. "That process is still very experimental, and I don't think it's going to increase fertilization rates all that much."

"It doesn't matter. It's only for a few weeks. I have another plan in mind."

CHAPTER 19

With the morning news playing in the background on the hotel room's wide-screen TV, Joyce multitasked, brushing her teeth while staring into the closet and perusing her wardrobe choices. The perky blond weather girl promised it would be "sunny and warm" in The Big Easy. The hurricane season had thankfully ended, and the temperature prediction was a pleasant seventy-eight degrees with moderate humidity.

Joyce chose a lightweight navy suit and a cream-colored silk blouse. She always wore trousers and long sleeves at conferences to combat the arctic temperatures of the vast ballroom meeting spaces. Last evening, she and Sally had checked in at the registration booth and received their name badges. Hers sported an extra green ribbon proclaiming her a "Presenter." Looking at it gave her a thrill of accomplishment along with a stab of anxiety. The name badge hung on a Mardi Gras-colored lanyard paid for by one of the pharmaceutical company sponsors. A competitor had gifted the participants with sharp-looking canvas bags emblazoned with their company's logo and filled with printed conference materials and other sales literature. The previous evening, Joyce had stashed her purse and room key in the bag in readiness for her early morning.

A glance at the clock showed she had fifteen minutes before meeting Hicks in the lobby. She did some relaxation breathing and practiced some tai chi poses, hoping it would quiet her "monkey mind."

Thinking about Hicks made her stomach tighten. *It's only breakfast, and there'll be plenty of people there,* she silently reassured herself. *Nothing bad's gonna happen in a room full of colleagues. It will be fine. It will be fine.* She mentally repeated this last phrase over and over, like a mantra, while slipping her phone into the pocket of the suit jacket. Taking a deep breath, she opened the door and headed toward the elevators.

When the doors parted on the main floor, she joined the crush of people flowing into the bustling lobby. She didn't immediately see Hicks, so she proceeded toward a wing-backed chair placed next to an ornate wrought-iron lamp in the window alcove. From this vantage point, she could see the elevators as well as the hotel's front entrance.

"Dr. Porter," a familiar slightly accented voice called out. She turned and saw Dominique. He looked very European in a navy-blue single-breasted suit with peak lapels, a small-collared pale-gray dress shirt, and slim blue patterned tie. She thought he must have a good tailor, as the suit fit like perfection. She was struck by the fact that he was a strikingly handsome man, albeit a little short by American standards. But his posture and confident stride made up for his stature. She felt a strong pull of attraction and immediately felt guilty.

She waved at him as he threaded his way through the lobby congestion. "Good morning," she called out as he approached her. "Pull up a chair."

He corralled a vacant seat and dragged it to the alcove, positioning it at right angles to her chair. "I wondered if I might run into you," he said. "My boss from my clinic in France sent me a message. His flight was delayed, and he's unable to attend this morning's breakfast, so he asked me to attend in his place. I thought I might join you and Dr. Hicks, if that's acceptable."

Bless you, there is a God, she thought. Out loud she said, "I'd love to have you join us, but we'll have to ask Dr. Hicks. I'm attending as his guest." Looking around for the absent Hicks, she continued, "He should be here any moment."

They chatted easily about their flights and room accommodations while watching the number of guests in the lobby steadily increase. Most were identifiable as conference attendees by their name badges fastened to the multicolored lanyards. Through a break in the crowd, Joyce saw Hicks standing and silently scanning the room. She hesitated for a second, then stood up and waved. Dominique got to his feet as well.

Hicks spotted her and made his way toward the alcove. Halfway there, his steps slowed as he noticed Dominique next to her. A brief scowl crossed his face but was quickly replaced by a neutral expression. As he reached them, he extended his right hand toward Dominique. "Dr. DuPage!" he said in a hearty voice at odds with his facial expression. "A pleasure to see you. When did you arrive?"

Dominique shook his outstretched hand. "Last evening. I believe you know my director, Dr. Henri Toussaint. He sends his regards. His flight was delayed, and he's requested I attend today's breakfast in his place. I was hoping I might join you and Dr. Porter."

A lightning flash of annoyance crossed Hicks's face before he resumed a neutral countenance. "Of course," he said evenly. He gestured toward one of the hallways where signs directed them to the smaller ballroom. "Shall we?"

The breakfast featured typical conference food, slightly rubbery scrambled eggs, overcooked bacon, and salty home-fried potatoes. The orange juice was tepid. The most flavorful part of the meal was the coffee, hot and fragrant with a hint of chicory, and oversized muffins in a variety of flavors. After a small bite of the eggs and potatoes, Joyce discreetly pushed her plate aside and decided to stick with a blueberry muffin, coffee, and juice. They were seated at a round table with colleagues from well-known IVF programs in Boston and San Francisco.

Joyce found herself sitting between Hicks and Dominique. They were each engaged in conversation with people on their opposite side, leaving her to gaze idly around the room. She was disappointed that Hicks's promise to introduce her to his colleagues hadn't panned out. Once they'd entered the breakfast salon, he'd excused himself and made a beeline for one of the conference organizers at the opposite end of the room. She and Dominique had introduced themselves to several other attendees, but most had ignored her in favor of engaging the charming Frenchman in conversation. Joyce had felt invisible as they flocked around their colleague from across the pond.

So much for expanding my professional network, she thought disgruntledly. The only person she'd really spoken with was a past mentor from medical school. Dr. Wiest had been quite friendly, inquiring about Joyce's position at McArthur and asking how she liked living in Richmond. She'd also promised to attend her panel discussion the next day.

Glancing at her watch, Joyce realized the Welcome Session was starting in fifteen minutes. The waiter had served another round of coffee, and no one seemed in any hurry to leave. She decided she'd had enough, tapping Dominique on the arm and whispering she was leaving. Then she did the same with Hicks who nodded brusquely and turned away. Pushing back, she accidentally bumped the table leg, which caused the freshly poured coffee to slop over onto the saucers and the ice cubes to clink in the water glasses. The table conversation ceased momentarily. Blushing, she made a hasty apology before fleeing the room.

She checked her watch and ducked into the women's room, where she finger-combed her hair, washed her hands, and freshened her lipstick. Stepping out of the room, she was surprised to find Hicks waiting for her. She glanced around, expecting to see Dominique, but he was nowhere in sight.

"Dr. Hicks, are you headed to the Welcome Session?"

"We didn't get to talk much at breakfast," he said in a waspish tone. Then he added slyly, "I thought we might sit together for the opening session."

"Ah, well," she said, momentarily nonplussed. "Okay."

"Did you connect with anyone at the breakfast?"

"Not really. Just one of my professors from medical school."

"Who?"

"Dr. Christine Wiest."

"Ah yes, Chrissy," he said in a slightly patronizing tone. "A good friend and colleague. She and I served together for years on the Society's Board of Directors."

"She asked about you, and how I liked McArthur."

"What did you tell her?"

"That I'm learning a lot and am very grateful to be working at such a highly respected institution."

Hicks snorted. "That's a very politically correct answer."

They presented their badges and were scanned into the main ballroom. The seats in the back of the room were almost completely full, and Joyce dreaded having to march down the center aisle trailing after Hicks. A movement at the periphery of her vision caught her attention. Turning quickly, she saw Sally and Dominque standing three rows ahead, gesticulating and pointing to a saved seat.

"Dr. Hicks," she said hurriedly. "I just remembered that I asked Sally to save me a seat, and she's waving at me from a few rows up. Thank you for the breakfast invitation. I'll see you this evening at the reception."

Hicks stopped and turned toward her, eying her steadily. "See that you're not late."

She desperately wanted to escape. Having Dominique join them at breakfast had been a reprieve of sorts, and she could tell it had angered Hicks. She inhaled sharply and replied, "Yes, sir. I'll see you tonight."

The evening cocktail reception was much better attended than the afternoon breakout sessions, and the room buzzed with a low hum of conversation. A small, raised dais, draped in the Mardi Gras colors of purple, green and gold and festooned with potted plants, supported a large podium displaying the Society's crest. Dual microphones sprouted from either side. Occasionally, a swell of laughter bubbled up from the casually dressed crowd. Joyce stood off to the side, beneath a curtained Palladian window, sipping a glass of pinot noir. She noticed the women appeared to be more formally attired than the men. White-shirted waitstaff circulated, offering plates of attractive but surprisingly tasteless hors d'oeuvres. A steady line formed at either end of the room around the amply stocked bars set up under Mardi Gras-themed signs proclaiming "Ovatech Welcomes You to The Big Easy." She'd arrived with Hicks thirty minutes before and couldn't wait to leave. Already her feet hurt, and the tag at the neckline of her sleeveless black dress was digging into her skin. Out of the chaos, Hicks appeared with a rotund bespeckled man in a tweed jacket, wrinkled white shirt, and a plaid bowtie.

"Ah, there you are," he said. He gestured toward his companion. "Dr. Jacob Goldberg, I'd like you to meet Dr. Joyce Porter. She's the director of Clinical Operations at McArthur."

"Pleased to meet you, Dr. Porter." Dr. Goldberg extended his pudgy hand.

She took it, finding the handshake surprisingly warm and firm. "Likewise."

"Dr. Goldberg and I knew each other back in medical school, but since then, we've gone our separate ways," Hicks said. "Where are you now, Jacob?"

"I'm in Oregon."

"Oh, yes, I remember now. Are you still doing research at the Primate Center?"

"Yes, about half time. The rest of the time I see patients, like you."

Hicks chuckled heartily. "Well, I don't have much time to see patients these days. I'm busy with my administrative duties and travel obligations. Somebody has to run the department! That's why I hire excellent staff, like Dr. Porter. She sees to the daily operations of our programs."

"How long have you been at McArthur, Dr. Porter?" Dr. Goldberg inquired solicitously. His face was open and friendly, and he vaguely reminded her of an eager puppy.

"About two years."

"Well, you've picked a prestigious place. My program is always striving for pregnancy rates like yours." He leaned closer, whispering in a conspiratorial fashion, "What's your secret?"

Just then, Hicks spied another colleague, excused himself, and darted into the crowd toward a tall thin man who looked like Ichabod Crane. "Charles," he called out in a hearty voice, "what a pleasure to see you!"

Joyce watched him for a moment, then turned back to her companion. "There's no secret."

Goldberg peered over the top of his horn-rimmed glasses. Though he smiled, his eyes revealed more than a hint of skepticism. "Now really, there must be *something* different. Nowhere else in the country comes even close to your numbers. I've heard rumors you have a new lab process that improves fertilization. Can you tell me anything about that?"

"Not really. Dr. Kumar runs our lab. We clinicians don't have much to do with what goes on there. I've only spent a little time with him. Mostly I'm too busy caring for patients."

Goldberg leaned closer, as if about to share a juicy secret. "Ajay running the lab," he said in a musing tone. "That's very interesting. He and Hicks were pals back in med school."

Furrowing her brow, Joyce asked, "Did you know both of them?"

"Not well. We attended the same school, but our class had over 300 students."

"I didn't know Dr. Kumar had a medical degree. I've always thought he had a Ph.D. in Embryology."

Goldberg shifted, his voice lowering. "He does. But something happened at the end of our second year."

Now Joyce stepped closer, having difficulty hearing him above the noise of the party. Goldberg took a long sip of an amber-colored liquid, then waved them both toward a tall table at the periphery of the room. It was slightly quieter. He set down his glass, cleared his throat and continued.

"One day, Ajay unexpectedly dropped out. Well, he didn't really drop out, he switched from med school to the Ph.D. program. It was all very hush-hush. No one seemed to know why, but it was rumored he'd been caught cheating, and the dean agreed to let him stay in the graduate program if he didn't contest the charge."

She took a slow sip of wine, trying to decide how best to respond. She didn't know if she should defend Dr. Kumar. After all, he was a colleague. But before she could summon a reply, Goldberg flagged a passing waiter and added two small prawn crostini to his plate. Joyce shook her head, declining the offer, and the waiter moved on.

As he chewed, Goldberg continued, "But that was a long time ago, and it really was all rumors. For all I know, maybe Ajay just didn't want to be a medical doctor. I understand he did quite well in graduate school, even winning a prize for most original thesis project."

Joyce placed her foot on the lower rung of the stool and tucked her skirt behind her knees before nodding and changing the subject. "What did you think about our keynote speaker this afternoon? I thought it quite interesting that someone from the FDA was speaking to a room full of reproductive endocrinologists. The FDA is all about regulation, which isn't something that's embraced by many of our colleagues."

Goldberg wiped the cocktail sauce from his mouth with a small napkin before answering. "You're right. It was an interesting choice. I'm not privy to the inner workings of the Society, but I think some of the board members are concerned that more oversight may be coming—either at the state or federal level. They're trying to position the Society to be out in front of such a push to either head it off or have substantial input into any regulations."

"Do you think that's necessary?"

"No one likes regulation, especially from the feds," Goldberg replied. "But you know those high-profile cases in the media recently describing fraudulent billing practices, quality assurance failures with culture media, and mixed-up embryos have got people asking questions, and that makes the Society nervous."

Just then, Hicks reappeared. He handed Joyce a fresh glass of wine. "Sorry to interrupt," he said to Goldberg, "I'm going to snag Dr. Porter." Turning to her he said, "Come with me. I'd like you to meet some people."

"Of course, of course." Once again, Goldberg sounded far too cheerful as he pushed back from the table and made a slight bow. "It was very nice meeting you, Dr. Porter. If you ever decide to leave McArthur, please think about joining us in the lovely Pacific Northwest."

Hicks put his hand beneath Joyce's elbow and steered her across the room. She followed along carefully, stopping to take several sips of wine to prevent it from spilling as she was jostled by the crowd. As they approached a small group, a deep male voice called out, "Good evening, Owen."

Hicks propelled Joyce toward the group. "Good evening, gentlemen," he paused, then added, "and lady." He nodded toward the lone female. "Allow me to introduce my esteemed colleague, Dr. Joyce Porter. Dr. Porter is the director of our IVF program."

Each member of the clique moved to shake Joyce's hand, murmuring various welcoming sentiments. Dr. Hicks continued, "Dr. Porter has been with us for two years, and we're expecting great things from her."

Joyce blushed and lowered her gaze as he continued to sing her praises. She noticed she was feeling slightly off, like a huge cloud of fluff had enveloped her brain. She also felt a slight headache beginning to throb at her temples. Absently rubbing her forehead, she looked up and realized all eyes were gazing expectantly at her. She struggled to remember what Hicks had been saying. As she floundered, he came to her rescue, "I was telling the group about your program for low-income clients and how successful it's been. I know you have a presentation tomorrow, but perhaps you'd like to give them a quick overview."

Joyce began speaking, and to her great surprise, she was having trouble forming the words. She couldn't imagine what was causing such mental haze. She'd only had one glass of wine, but she felt like she'd finished a whole bottle.

"I'm sorry," she said after giving a brief synopsis. She noticed increasing difficulty articulating her words. "I'm not feeling well. If you'll please excuse me. I hope to see you tomorrow at my presentation. It's at two p.m. in Ballroom C." Quickly, she turned, set down her glass on a nearby table, and headed for the door. As she walked, she found she had to concentrate on each step to remain erect. She thought about removing her high-heeled sandals but decided that might draw too much attention, and she wasn't sure she could remain upright. Hicks excused himself and followed her. He caught up with her as she entered the hallway.

"Joyce," he called as he reached out to take her arm. "What's wrong? You don't look well. Let me help you. Sit over here, and I'll bring you a glass of water." He ushered her to a group of chairs in a quiet hallway niche, and she gratefully sank into the plush cushioned seat. Then he disappeared back into the reception room, emerging a moment later with a glass of water.

"Here, drink this."

She complied, but the liquid failed to revive her. She took a few deep breaths, but the wave of stupor didn't clear. "I think I need to go back to my room. Perhaps I caught some kind of bug on the plane," she said, struggling to get up then stumbling slightly.

"Let me help you. What's your room number?"

"512, east tower," she mumbled. Leaning on Hicks, they made their way across the lobby toward the elevators. While waiting for the car, her headache and drowsiness worsened.

The ornate bronze doors opened, and several people stepped out. A female voice penetrated through the growing fog.

"Joyce, what's wrong? Are you okay?"

And seemingly from a great distance, Hicks replied, "She's feeling a little lightheaded. I'm taking her up to her room."

"That's not necessary. I'll go with her. I'm sure you have many engagements this evening."

After what seemed like a short tug of war and the distant sound of voices arguing, Hicks's hand was replaced by a much smaller one. Sally pushed her into the waiting elevator. As the doors closed, she leaned forward and hissed into Joyce's ear, "You look like death. What the hell happened?"

Joyce didn't reply, just slumped against Sally and passed out.

That evening, Dominique found himself at loose ends. He wished he'd arranged to have dinner with someone. New Orleans was filled with renowned eating establishments, and he hadn't eaten since breakfast. He suspected Sally would have jumped at the offer, but he didn't want to encourage her. He found her a pleasant companion, but she didn't appeal to him in a romantic sense.

Unbidden but not unexpected, Joyce came to mind. Since their first meeting, he'd thought about her frequently, probably more than appropriate since she'd told him she was married. She was witty, energetic, and sexy. One time, he'd found himself staring at her full lips, wondering what it would feel like to kiss them. If she hadn't been married, he'd definitely have pursued a closer relationship. As it was, he found himself fascinated by her. He knew if she gave him any encouragement, he would find it hard to remain professional.

Generally, he steered clear of office romances, but in this case, he'd have been tempted. After all, they weren't really working together. He was a visiting professor. Perhaps if they become involved, she'd consider coming to France for a few months, or even longer. He'd picked up on definite tension with her boss.

He wondered about her husband. He'd seen his picture in her office, and Sally had told him they lived in separate cities because of their jobs. He knew they saw each other on weekends, but every Monday, Joyce seemed stressed out rather than blissfully happy and in love. He'd kept things friendly and professional on his end, since he had a firm rule about not engaging in relationships with married women. His ex-wife had cheated on him, and he never wanted to be "the other man," but right now he was rethinking his stance.

He thought about calling his daughter, then realized it was seven hours earlier and she was sound asleep. He grabbed his jacket and decided to leave the hotel and wander. The French Quarter was only a few blocks away, so he'd explore and find somewhere to eat. He wondered if anyone in the French Quarter actually spoke French, and if he'd be able to understand Cajun French or Creole.

He moved with the stream of people on Bourbon Street, savoring the energy of the Quarter. He usually enjoyed his own company, but tonight he felt strangely alone. Turning onto a quiet residential street, he thought wistfully about Joyce and how much he was missing her. He wondered if she was enjoying the Ovatech reception. Earlier, she'd mentioned attending it with Hicks and asked if he'd be standing in for Dr. Toussaint. When he'd replied in the negative, she'd looked worried. She'd pursed her lips as if to reply, but then they'd been interrupted. He never learned what she was going to say.

He felt a vague unease and shook it off. She was a strong woman who knew how to take care of herself. They would see each other tomorrow, and he found himself looking forward to their dinner date.

No, not a date, he cautioned himself. They were just two colleagues having dinner. The fact that it happened to be in a romantic city was a happy coincidence and filled him with pleasant fantasies.

CHAPTER 20

Joyce awoke with a pounding headache and what felt like a wad of cotton in her mouth. The room was dimly lit by a desk lamp, and she was lying on a comfortable bed. Her brain was enveloped in a fog, and she felt completely disoriented. Panic overtook her as she tried to sit up. *Where was she? What time was it? Why did she feel so dehydrated and weak?* She attempted to maneuver off the bed, but the room began to rotate, and she was hit with a wave of nausea. With great care, she lowered herself back to a horizonal position and the nausea retreated. As some of the fuzziness cleared and the room once again became stationary, she realized she was alone in a spacious hotel room.

The desk lamp glowed softly, and the drapes were drawn. It was quiet, except for the soft hum of the air conditioner. She struggled to make sense of her situation and finally remembered she was at a conference in New Orleans. Glancing at the bedside table, she saw her purse, but she had no idea what time it was, or even what day. She lifted the soft blanket and saw with relief that, except for her shoes, she was fully dressed. She recognized her favorite little black dress and wondered why she was sleeping in it. *Where had she been?*

She strained to focus on the bedside clock. Squinting slightly, she read the bright blue digital numbers, 1:26 a.m. Then she heard a toilet flush and the sound of running water. *Someone was in the bathroom!*

Immediately, her heart rate doubled, and she broke out in a cold sweat. *Who is here? What happened? Am I in danger?* She shook her head, trying to clear it, but the movement made her head throb even more and the nausea returned. She closed her eyes and tried to think. The last thing she remembered was being at a cocktail reception and talking to a man in a bow tie from Oregon. *What was his name?* She couldn't recall. She remembered Dr. Hicks handing her a glass of red wine, but nothing after that. She doubted she'd gotten drunk and passed out, but why couldn't she remember how she'd gotten back to her room? *Was this her room?*

She realized she was too weak to run away, so she felt around for something to use as a weapon. Her fingers closed on her beaded purse. It wasn't much, but the jagged surface would probably hurt if it collided with someone's face or head.

The bathroom door clicked, and she saw a pool of light before it was switched off. Her heart pounded and she clutched her purse. With relief, she saw Sally step into the room. She was dressed casually in designer jeans and a teal long-sleeved shirt.

"Sally, what's happened to me?" Her voice sounded scratchy and faint.

"Oh good, you're awake," Sally said, peering down at her. "Why are you holding your purse?"

"I didn't know who was in the bathroom. I thought I might have to defend myself. Is that clock right?" She struggled to sit up and was finally successful.

"Yes, you've been out almost six hours."

"I'm really thirsty, and I feel like I have a hangover, but I only had one glass of wine. What happened?"

Sally grabbed a bottle of water from the mini fridge and slowly poured it into a tumbler. She handed it to Joyce, who guzzled the whole thing in one long gulp. She swiped her mouth with the back of her hand, then set the glass down and looked up expectantly.

"I have no idea. You tell me. I was in the elevator headed down to meet some friends. When the doors opened on the main level, there was Hicks holding you up. You looked terrible. He said you weren't feeling well, and he was taking you up to your room."

Panic set in like a wave crashing ashore. Joyce's hands began to tremble and her heart rate, which had just begun to settle, accelerated. "Oh my God. Did he?"

"No," Sally said decisively. "I ran him off. I told him we were rooming together, and that I'd take care of you. Reluctantly, he handed me your key and your purse, and I brought you back here. You've been sleeping ever since."

Joyce tried to stand but another wave of vertigo caused her to sway. Sally gently pushed her down and arranged the pillows behind her head. "Now, why don't you tell me what you remember. Didn't you go to the Ovatech reception?"

Joyce closed her eyes in an attempt to concentrate. Slowly, her memories began to trickle back. "Yes, that's right. I met Hicks there, and he introduced me to several people—first somebody from Oregon, someone he knew in med school, and then another whole group. I started feeling funny right after introductions. Hicks asked me to explain my presentation, and I could hardly form the words. It was like my mouth wouldn't work. I excused myself, but Hicks caught up with me as I was leaving. He made me sit down and then brought me a glass of water. I remember us walking toward the elevator, but nothing after that."

"Do you remember getting on the elevator?"

"No."

"How about giving Hicks your room number and key?"

"*No!* Oh God, did I really do that?"

"You must have. He knew where your room was, and he had your key."

Joyce put her face in her hands and moaned.

Sally gently asked, "Do you want more water?"

Joyce ignored her. Finally, she spoke in a muffled tone. "I wonder what else I can't remember. Sally, what happened to me? I only had one glass of wine. I've never gotten hammered on a single glass of wine."

"Did you get the wine yourself or did someone get it for you?"

Joyce thought back to the reception. Her thinking was still clouded, and she could almost feel the synapses in her brain firing at half speed. Her eyes flew open, and she glanced at Sally in shock. "Hicks. And I remember him bringing me another glass of wine while I was talking to someone."

A frown line appeared between Sally's eyes. "Hold on. I'm confused. I thought you said you only had one glass."

"I did, but then he brought me a second. It was very full, so I took several sips so it wouldn't spill as we headed across the crowded room toward his friends."

Joyce tried to sit up again, but Sally shook her head. She filled the tumbler with the remaining bottled water and set it on the bedside table.

"Don't try to get up yet. I think you might have been given some type of date-rape drug."

"What?" Joyce exclaimed in a horrified voice.

"Think about it. You barely had more than a single glass of wine, and yet you're acting like you drank the whole bottle. When I saw you, you could barely walk, and your speech was slurred." Sally got up and paced in front of the curtained window before continuing, "You slept for almost six hours, you can't remember anything beyond walking to the elevator with Hicks, and your memory before that is pretty sketchy. You had a blackout."

Joyce nodded slowly, her expression one of stunned misery. She reached for the water and took two careful sips. "I think you must be right. What should I do? Should I go to the hospital?"

"You could, and they might be able to do a tox screen and identify what you were given. But then what? At this point, you're awake, and your speech is normal. You look like crap, but I think the worst is over."

"Thanks for that optimistic assessment," Joyce muttered. "Who do you think did this?"

"Who do *you* think did it?"

"Well, the obvious suspect is Hicks, but why? I can't believe he'd be that vile."

"Joyce, this is what I tried to warn you about when I told you what happened to me. The man gets obsessed and stalks the unlucky target, in this case you, until he has sex with them. Then he moves on to someone else. No one ever reports him because who would believe them?"

"But why?"

"It's more about power than lust. He likes the chase, and he knows he can get away with it."

Joyce looked horrified. "Do you think he raped me?"

"Probably not. I'm so glad I happened to be on that elevator. Let's talk it through. What time did you go to the reception?"

"Around six, I think. I met Hicks there and he got us drinks. We milled around for a while, and then he introduced me to a man in a bow tie from Oregon."

"Do you remember what time that was?"

"No. But shortly before that, I remember looking at my watch and it was half past six. My feet hurt and I wondered how I was going to make it through the next hour."

"Okay. How long did you talk with the man from Oregon? Do you remember his name?"

"No, but you know I'm terrible with names. I think it was Jacob Something—like Goldleaf or Goldberg. Anyway, Hicks left for a time, and we sat down to talk."

"How long?"

"Maybe ten minutes or so. It turns out he knew both Hicks and Kumar from med school, and he told me that Kumar left med school and transferred to the Ph.D. program at the end of their second year."

"That's interesting, but let's get back to what happened to you. Do you think Dr. Bow Tie put something in your wine?"

"No. There was no chance. I already had the wine when we were introduced, and I never left it unattended."

"Then what happened?"

"Hicks came by with a fresh glass and told me he had some people for me to meet. I said good-bye to Dr. Bow Tie, and then we started across the room."

"Did you drink more than a few sips of the fresh wine?"

"No. Only enough so it wouldn't spill while we were jostling through the crowd."

"And then what?"

"We got to a circle of people, and Hicks introduced me."

"How were you feeling?"

"I was starting to feel odd. My vision was a little blurred. I was having trouble focusing and everything sounded muffled, like listening with cotton in my ears. Then someone asked me a question, and I realized I had no idea what they'd said. Hicks asked me to give a brief summary of my presentation, and I couldn't do it."

"Why not?"

"Because I couldn't make my mouth form the words."

"What happened then?"

"I excused myself and left the room. I tried to move quickly, but I was pretty wobbly. It was those damn heels. I hate wearing tall heels! Right as I left the room, Hicks caught up with me. He had me sit down and brought some water."

"Do you remember him asking you for your room number, or taking your key?"

"No. I vaguely remember him taking my arm and leading me toward the elevators. Then I woke up in this bed. By the way, is this my room or yours?"

"Yours. Now, do you remember meeting me in the elevator?"

"No."

"Well, it was a few minutes before seven. I think you must have ingested the drug fifteen or twenty minutes before. Since you didn't go anywhere between the reception and the elevator, it's unlikely Hicks had any chance to physically accost you. If you really want to make sure, we should go to the nearest ER so you can have an exam."

Joyce considered the suggestion. "Sally, help me stand up. I want to check my clothes."

Sally moved to her side and put her arm around Joyce's waist. This time the room didn't spin. They slowly made their way to the bathroom. Joyce shrugged off Sally's protective arm, entered, and closed the door. Looking in the mirror, she realized Sally had been right. She did look like crap. Her face was puffy, her hair was mussed, and she had large, blue-tinged circles under her eyes.

She reconsidered a trip to the ER but decided she could do her own exam. She'd done dozens of such exams when she'd been in training. She ran her tongue over her lips. They didn't feel bruised. She opened her mouth and looked carefully at her tongue, teeth, and mucous membranes. All looked normal. She examined her neck and didn't see any bruises or bite marks. Slowly, she lowered the side zipper and stepped out of her black dress. She removed her bra and noted with relief there were no bruises or other marks on her breasts. She held her breath as she carefully stripped off her pink bikini panties. No stain or discharge, and her genitalia didn't feel like she'd had sex. She blew out a breath and sat down on the toilet. After relieving herself, she slowly washed her hands while considering next steps.

She opened the door and called, "Sally, please hand me a robe."

A moment later, the bathroom door opened slightly, and the hotel's plush terry robe appeared. Joyce bundled herself into the soft robe and stepped into the main room.

"I think I'm fine," she told Sally, "Just very tired. My clothing seems okay and there are no marks on my body. I don't think anything happened."

Sally sat in the room's only armchair, and Joyce perched on the edge of the bed. She looked at Joyce expectantly. "So now what?"

"I'm not sure. Right now, I want to take a shower and go to sleep. When I wake up, I want to discover this has all been a bad dream."

"More like a nightmare. Do you think you'll stay for the rest of the conference?"

"Yes, of course!" she said. "I have my presentation and discussion panel tomorrow, I mean today. I can't miss that!"

"Are you sure you'll be up for it?"

Joyce straightened her spine, locked eyes with Sally, and stated firmly, "Absolutely. Hicks isn't going to take that away from me."

"Well, you'd better get some sleep then. Do you want me to stay with you?"

"No, I'll be fine."

Sally yawned and rose from the chair. Reaching the door, she turned back to Joyce, "Call me if you need anything. And remember to lock the door and use the deadbolt."

"Yes ma'am." Joyce gave a lopsided salute. She hesitated for a moment before adding softly, "Thanks for everything, Sally. You really saved me."

After Sally left, Joyce took a long hot shower, then sat in the armchair, wide-eyed. She didn't think she could sleep despite her exhaustion. With no thought of possible consequences, she reached for her phone. To her surprise, Dominique answered on the second ring.

Dominique frowned at his phone. Who would possibly be calling at this hour? To his surprise, Joyce's name flashed on the screen.

"Joyce?" he said, wide awake with alarm.

"I didn't think you'd be up."

"I never sleep well in hotels. Are you okay?"

"Not really," she said, a slight tremor in her voice. She sounded on the verge of panic.

"What happened?"

"I . . . I don't want to talk about it over the phone. Can I meet you?"

Oh, no, he thought. *Not a good idea.* Here he'd been having romantic thoughts and now she was asking to meet him in the dead of night.

"Where?" he asked cautiously. "It's very late, and I doubt anything is open."

"I'll come to your room. You said you're staying here, right?"

"Yes, but . . ." He stopped, unsure how to continue.

"Please, just for a few moments."

"I don't think . . ." but he was cut off.

"I think Hicks tried to drug me!" she said in a rush.

"Mon Dieu," he exclaimed. "Are you hurt? Do you need a doctor?"

"No. No. I don't think he assaulted me. Can I come see you, please?"

"All right," he said hesitantly and gave her his room number. After hanging up, he raked his hands through his hair. *Why had he agreed?* He glanced in the mirror and saw his tousled hair and unshaven face. He was dressed in sweatpants and a cotton T-shirt. He wondered if he should shave or change into street clothes. Filled with indecision, he hesitated. A few moments later, he heard a quick rap on the door.

Opening it cautiously, he saw Joyce dressed in pair of yoga pants, a hoodie, and sneakers. Her face wore a strained expression, and he noticed she was fingering a can of mace in the folds of her sweatshirt.

He looked at her with a mixture of sympathy and wariness. To his surprise, an emotional dam erupted. She threw herself into his arms and burst into tears. He'd never seen her show any emotion at this level of intensity. She was always cool and professional. His face registered surprise as he maneuvered her into the room and quietly closed the door.

"It's okay," he said sympathetically, stroking her hair. "You're okay."

They stood there rocking for a long moment before he gently tried to disengage and steer her toward the chair. But she tightened her arms.

"Please, just hold me. I need someone to hold me," she sobbed.

Reluctantly, he continued to hold her, rubbing her back. *Mon Dieu*, he thought. *What should I do next?*

CHAPTER 21

Bill clicked off his phone. He'd texted and called Joyce multiple times, but she hadn't responded. He looked at his watch. It was almost midnight. He was trying not to overreact, but given their last conversation, he couldn't help feeling concerned. He ran his hands through his hair in frustration. He still had trouble believing Joyce worked for a boss who was living in a pre-#MeToo time warp. How could the guy not know his behavior was way out of line? Or maybe he knew but didn't care, which was kind of the point of that movement.

For the hundredth time, Bill pondered if he should've dropped everything and gone to New Orleans when she'd first asked. Later, when he'd brought it up again, she'd said, "It's okay. I'm a big girl. This isn't the first time I've been hit on. I can take care of myself." That comment had come as a surprise, but they'd been so focused on Hicks that he hadn't asked for clarification. Now he wondered what else he didn't know about Joyce's life.

He needed to trust her, he thought, turning off the lights. The mattress sagged as Bill pulled up the covers and settled into bed. He realized much of his uneasiness resulted from the knowledge that she'd planned to attend an evening reception with Hicks.

And what about the Frenchman? He'd never been to a conference that didn't have its share of drama and boozy hookups, and that worried him. Where was she, and why hadn't she answered his texts or calls? It was not like her. He considered calling the hotel, then realized he didn't know exactly where she was staying. Because they both had cell phones, it hadn't seemed important to have a specific hotel name and phone. He wouldn't make that mistake again.

Restlessly, he turned over and punched the pillow, vainly searching for a sleep-inducing position. Once settled, he considered the pros and cons of living in Richmond. Maybe it wouldn't be such a hardship to commute to Baltimore for weekly seminars and meetings. They'd probably need a different apartment, one with an extra room that he could turn into a study. With Joyce gone all day, he imagined he'd get a lot of writing done. And they'd save on living expenses. On the downside, he wondered if Joyce would resume her campaign for them to start a family. That idea had really taken root, as evidenced by the fact she brought it up every time they were together.

It wasn't that he didn't want kids, but he couldn't imagine having them right now. Several of their medical school friends were parents, some of them on their second or third child. Most of them had some type of live-in nanny or they had nearby family who pitched in with childcare. Thinking about the myriad extra responsibilities strengthened his desire to wait until they were more settled.

One attraction with public health jobs was a tendency toward more predictable hours, and unless there was a pandemic, weekends were usually free. Bill thought this meant he would be able to shoulder at least half the childcare duties. He didn't know what that entailed, but he was sure Joyce had it all figured out and would hand him a list when the time came.

Giving up on sleep, he rolled over and clicked on the bedside lamp. Perhaps reading would quiet his mind enough to doze off. He picked up a medical statistics textbook. If it didn't put him to sleep, nothing would. Sure enough, two pages into the dense tome filled with charts and graphs, he began to feel drowsy. He struggled through two more pages. As his mind slowed, he switched off the light and finally sank into a troubled sleep.

Joyce awoke feeling sluggish and groggy as her phone alarm sounded. She silenced the annoyingly cheerful jingle and slowly sat up. She'd left Dominique's room a little after three a.m. and blushed at the memory. She couldn't believe she'd done that, thrown herself at him. She'd never done anything like it in her life! It was completely out of character. Then came the remorse. The drugs had clearly affected her judgment as much as her memory.

She viewed the phone's main screen and felt even more guilty when she saw three texts and two calls from Bill. She'd noticed them last night while setting the alarm but had decided not to wake him. From the tone of his last voicemail, he'd sounded concerned with a hint of anger. She needed to call, but what would she say? Should she tell him what had happened or what she thought might have happened? And then there was the reckless visit to Dominique's room.

Embarrassment turned into shame. This was the real reason she was stalling. What had she been thinking? It was completely out of character for her to do something so thoughtless and erratic. Before she made any phone calls, she needed to sort through her feelings. She was strongly attracted to Dominique, and he was present for her right now in ways that Bill wasn't— emotionally and physically. She'd been frustrated for the past six months with their marriage but helpless to change anything. Bill wasn't going to move to Virginia, and she wasn't going to quit her job. She'd read more than half of couples with long-distance marriages eventually divorced and wondered if they'd succumb to those statistics.

Her stomach growled so she splurged and ordered room service. She couldn't face a crush of people at the coffee kiosk in the hotel's lobby. Using the hotel's app, she ordered a yogurt, granola, and fruit parfait, orange juice and a pot of coffee. After completing the order, the app informed her breakfast would be delivered in thirty minutes. She figured she had time to shower and dress.

She felt much better with clean skin and hair. She donned her gray "power suit" and rose-colored blouse. She needed to bring her A game to the presentation and panel discussion this afternoon. She speculated about the people she'd met last night, and once again her face burned with humiliation as she remembered the difficulty she'd had forming her words when trying to describe her project. They'd probably wondered if she'd had too much to drink. Well, she'd just have to soldier on. If she saw any of them, she'd explain that she'd had a reaction to a new medication and leave it at that.

A few minutes later, a knock sounded on the door, followed by the words "Room service." She looked through the peephole and saw a uniformed waiter. She unlocked the deadbolt and slid off the security chain before opening the door. The waiter carried the tray into the room and set it on the coffee table.

"Is there anything else, miss?" he asked in a Cajun drawl.

"No, thank you," she replied as she handed him a generous tip.

He bowed slightly. "Thank you. Leave the tray outside the door when you're finished," he said before quietly letting himself out.

Joyce finished her second cup of coffee. It had been wonderfully rejuvenating, strong and hot. Reluctantly, she picked up the phone. She had no more excuses. It was time to call Bill.

As the connection formed and reformed somewhere in the

atmosphere where the communication satellites traversed their determined orbits, she bit her lip. For the umpteenth time, she pondered what to tell him. On the one hand, she wanted to dump the whole mess in his lap and hear him bluster on her behalf. And maybe he'd have some good ideas about what she should do next. But she didn't want him to overreact and go all caveman on her and rush to New Orleans to "save" the day. Right now, that was the last thing she needed. And then there was Dominique. She couldn't exactly tell her husband she had a crush on another man.

"Hello? Joyce, is that you?" Bill sounded slightly winded. "Thank God you finally called. I've been worried sick. Are you okay?" She closed her eyes and imagined him striding along with his messenger bag slung carelessly across his shoulder while he made his way toward the ivy-covered building that housed his grad school office.

"Hi, Bill. I'm fine. You sound out of breath. Did I catch you at a bad time?"

"No, it's fine. I overslept this morning, and I'm late for the department meeting. Is everything okay? Why didn't you call last night?"

Joyce wavered. He was running late and on his way to a meeting. It didn't seem like a good time to drop the whole story on him.

"Hello. Hello?" His voice was definitely tinged with annoyance. "Are you still there?"

"Yes, I'm here."

"Sorry, it was so quiet. I thought we'd lost the connection."

"No, the connection is good." Joyce fell silent, still paralyzed with indecision. The longer the silence stretched, the harder it became to start the conversation. She wondered why. When had she begun to withhold parts of her life from Bill? She recognized this whole episode crystallized the state of their marriage—separate lives with occasional shared interludes.

As she thought back to her original reluctance to share her

concerns about Hicks, she realized she hadn't been fair to Bill. When she'd finally read him in, he'd initially been skeptical but open to hearing her concerns. Eventually he'd understood the pattern of grooming behaviors, and then he'd been incensed on her behalf.

"Joyce?" Now Bill sounded concerned. "What's wrong? Did something happen last night at the reception?"

"The reception was fine. Dr. Hicks introduced me to several of his colleagues, but I left early. I wasn't feeling well."

"You were sick? That doesn't sound like you. What happened? How do you feel now?"

The strain of the previous night was still with her, and Joyce felt engulfed in a blanket of fatigue tinged with guilt. She didn't want to have this conversation right now. Their marriage might be shaky, but it wasn't going to end in the next hour. She wished she'd just texted and suggested they talk later.

"I'm much better this morning, thanks. I decided to skip the first few sessions and go over my presentation one last time."

"It must've been bad for you to leave early. Was it something you ate or drank?"

Joyce hesitated before saying, "I only had one glass of wine and a few appetizers, but I was feeling weird—dizzy and a little lightheaded. I met Sally on the elevator, and she walked me back to my room. I fell asleep as soon as we got there. I didn't wake up until the middle of the night. I saw your messages and decided to wait to call."

"That sounds very strange. Were you nauseated? Or feverish?"

"No, no. Nothing like that."

"Maybe you were dehydrated or had some type of arrythmia. Do you remember your heart pounding, or any fluttering or pain in your chest? Were you short of breath? Did you faint?"

"Whoa, slow down, doctor," she said with a slight laugh. "I'm not a patient for you to diagnose. Please don't worry. I don't have an arrythmia. Maybe I was a little hypoglycemic or dehydrated. I rushed around all day and skipped lunch. But I'm fine now. In fact, I finished a delicious room service breakfast."

"Room service, huh? You must have a great meal allowance."

"We get a per diem, but I haven't spent much on food so far."

She heard voices in the background, and then he said, "Hey, I just arrived at the meeting. Gotta go. I'm glad you called. Talk tonight?"

"Sure. I'll call you when I get back from dinner."

"Are you going with Sally?"

"No, Dominique."

There was a short pause before he said, "Have fun."

"Talk later."

"Right. Bye."

As she stepped off the elevator, Joyce's phone chimed. Bill had sent her a text wishing her good luck on her presentation. She was smiling when she bumped into a woman wearing tan slacks, a white scoop neck shirt, and a long black cardigan.

"Oh, sorry. Please excuse me," she said, looking up from her phone.

"No problem," the woman replied. Then she looked closely at Joyce. "Aren't you Joyce Porter?"

Joyce pivoted. Zeroing in on the woman's name tag, she tried to remember how she knew her. Suddenly, she flushed as a sick feeling accompanied the memory. This was one of the people she'd met last night right before she'd had to leave the reception. She reminded herself to stand tall and look the woman in the eye. She had nothing to be ashamed of. *Fake it 'til you make it,* she reminded herself.

"Oh, hello, Dr. Vaccare. I'm sorry I didn't recognize you."

"Please call me Caroline. You must be feeling better," she said with a smile.

"Yes, much," Joyce said gratefully. "I'm not sure what came

over me last evening. I think I may have reacted to a new medication."

"I'm glad you're well. Owen mentioned you have a presentation today."

"Yes, right after lunch."

"I'm looking forward to it. Good luck." She smiled, turned away, and joined the throng of attendees moving toward the exhibit hall.

Joyce drew in a long breath, counted to ten, and then slowly exhaled. In a way, she was glad she'd encountered someone from last night. From the woman's reaction, it appeared she hadn't done anything terribly embarrassing. Her brief explanation had been readily accepted. She squared her shoulders and moved toward the lobby.

Rounding the corner, she spied Sally and Dominique standing next to the registration table. She flushed slightly as she remembered her impetuous visit to his room the previous night. She'd have to blame her poor judgment on the lingering effects of whatever had been slipped into her drink.

They waved and she threaded her way through the crowd. She was glad it was just them and hoped Sally wouldn't pick up on any awkwardness with Dominique. She also prayed she didn't run into Hicks. She expected he'd attend her presentation to see how she "performed." From his grandiose comments, he seemed to think her career path depended completely on his goodwill. He'd made it abundantly clear he expected her to play along, and if she didn't, there would be consequences.

He doesn't know me very well, she thought, *if he thinks I'll buckle from last night's experience.* She squared her shoulders and walked confidently toward her friends.

CHAPTER 22

"I think we should tell your parents we're pregnant," Leon said to Evie while settling into the lounge chair facing the TV. He turned on the sports channel and found some college football reruns. He muted the sound.

She was lying on the sofa. Ignoring him, she wedged a pillow behind her back and began leafing through a pregnancy book. It promised "a week-by-week holistic nutrition guide for a healthy mother and baby." She thought it sounded like a lot of work, preparing all those weird smoothies and eating fruits and vegetables she wasn't even sure she would recognize. And what were chia seeds? Why couldn't she just eat peanut butter? She'd never eaten kale and didn't think she wanted to.

She had an appointment with a dietician in two weeks to talk about nutrition and weight gain since she was carrying twins. In the past month, she'd only gained a pound, probably due to her ongoing battle with morning sickness. Thankfully, it seemed to be improving. She hadn't thrown up in four days. The nausea had settled into a pattern and mostly occurred before she left for work. If she ate a piece of dry toast and drank a cup of ginger tea for breakfast, she got through the worst of it. She'd purchased a large box of ginger teabags and kept them in her desk at work.

She found having another cup or two of the tea mid-morning with some salty crackers seemed to stave off the queasy feelings for the rest of the day. A light lunch of soup, crackers and fruit stayed down, and by dinner, she was hungry enough to eat a normal meal. She wasn't wearing bigger clothes yet, but she did sometimes open the top button of her jeans. She also found herself wearing her shirts untucked because they were more comfortable that way. Soon, she'd have to start wearing the maternity clothes she'd borrowed from her sister.

"Did you hear what I said?" Leon repeated, a little louder this time.

She turned the page. "I heard. There's only a few weeks 'til Thanksgiving. What's the rush?"

"My parents and your sister already know, and I think your parents should know before we tell the whole family."

"My sister won't tell, and they don't really see your parents."

"Speaking of my parents, I'm so proud of my mom," he said. "I never thought she'd be able to keep a secret. And she hasn't bugged us with too many questions. I think Dad must remind her every day." The football clip ended, and he remoted it off.

He persisted, "Don't you think they'll feel bad if we don't tell them before everyone else?"

She sighed and closed the book, "You're probably right, but I don't want them grilling us, especially Mom. She's going to freak out when she hears we're having twins. And I'm not sure we can ever tell them we had IVF. You know how judgmental she can be."

"Let's keep it general, like we did with my mom and dad. We can call them. Keep the conversation short."

"But what if she starts pushing for details, like your mom did?"

Ever the optimist, Leon answered, "We'll say we don't want to talk about it until after our next ultrasound, and we'll ask them to keep it a secret. We don't have to tell her we've already had two scans—or about the twins."

"I think she's gonna be a lot more persistent than your mom. Dad will be happy for us, but he won't stand up to her like your dad did. He usually goes along with whatever Mom wants."

"Maybe we should do this in person. I'm not working this Saturday. We could ask them for dinner. I'll make my famous barbequed ribs and we'll tell them after dessert."

She made a face. "Okay," she relented. "I'll call Mom tomorrow and invite them."

He jumped up and gave her a hug. "I have a better idea. Let's call and invite them right now, before you change your mind."

Dominique and Joyce walked through the hushed lobby toward the guest elevators. It was after ten p.m., and a few hotel guests sat in the window alcove talking quietly. The conference registration desks were closed, and the bell captain looked up from his phone.

They had dined at Arnaud's, well known in the city for its local cuisine and impeccable service. After her embarrassing late-night visit to his room, Joyce had briefly considered cancelling, but in the end she decided to go because she knew how much he'd been looking forward to it. She'd tried to bring it up, but he'd brushed off her apology and said it was always a gentleman's duty to comfort a distressed woman. But for some reason, she couldn't stop thinking about how sweet and kind he'd been, and how much she'd enjoyed being cradled in his arms.

Dinner had been delightful. Dominique had been eager to try the Gulf shrimp appetizer in their famous Creole remoulade sauce. He'd also raved about the chicken-and- andouille gumbo and his entrée of redfish topped with Louisiana crabmeat. Her appetite fully restored, she'd eaten the redfish topped with an almond-lemon-butter sauce and a house salad. She'd passed on wine, the memory of last night's dizzy swoon still fresh. The tray of desserts had looked enticing and decadent, but they'd been too stuffed by the end of the meal to have anything other than coffee.

They'd lingered over the fragrant French press coffee and toasted Joyce's successful presentation. Her fellow panelists had been gracious and complimentary, and the following discussion had been lively. Afterward, several audience members remained and asked detailed questions. Before shaking her hand, two had requested business cards and one had invited her to lecture at his university.

Although Hicks had been present, he'd lurked in the back of the room and remained silent. He hadn't approached her, and when she looked up after the last participant departed, he'd vanished.

"Thank you for a lovely evening," Dominique said, turning and taking Joyce's hand loosely in his as they stood waiting for the elevator. "New Orleans cuisine has quite a reputation. Fresh seafood is one of my favorites and my meal was superb. I'm glad we had a chance to celebrate your success."

As he favored her with his dimpled smile, she felt her face flush. Looking into his warm brown eyes, she wondered what he was thinking and how to respond. Was he being a good friend and colleague, or was there something more?

"Thank you. It *was* a lovely dinner." She gave his hand a gentle squeeze then slowly withdrew hers. They stood in silence until the shiny doors emblazoned with the hotel's monogram opened. Dominique, ever the gentleman, motioned for her to enter and they stepped inside. The motor made a slight humming while they smoothly ascended. As they arrived at Dominique's floor, she smiled, suddenly feeling a bit shy, and bid him goodnight.

He hesitated for a beat before replying in French, *"Bien dormir,"* then added in his charmingly accented English, "Sleep well." Giving a jaunty salute, he stepped into the hallway.

As the doors whispered shut, Joyce leaned against the

polished brass rail and closed her eyes. That man was a temptation. He was so gracious, so charming, and for a moment, she'd longed to lean in for a kiss. He'd been so close, the confines of the elevator suddenly feeling intimate. It would have been so easy. She remembered the feeling of his strong embrace last night and found herself disappointed that he hadn't initiated a kiss. She imagined again the faint smell of the smooth skin of his neck and how it would feel to lean her head against his chest. The moment might have lasted long enough that the doors would have closed again as the elevator continued its stately ascent. Then what would have happened? Last night, she'd been a hot mess, and he'd gently rebuffed her efforts at anything more than a friendly hug. *But what if . . . ?*

The discreet ding of the elevator bell broke her reverie, and she hastily stepped out. Slowly walking toward her room, she chastised herself. *What was she thinking?* Dominique was her colleague and her friend. And she was married, for heaven's sake! She'd never cheated on Bill, had never even considered it. Then why was she thinking about Dominique's full warm lips? She felt confused and guilty for her traitorous thoughts. *Was it because their marriage was in a rough patch?* Or maybe she was still traumatized from last night, and Dominique had made her feel safe.

She deliberately turned her thoughts to Bill. Had it really been only two days since she'd seen him? Sharing her thoughts and concerns had reawakened hopeful feelings that they were still a team. It also made her remember what it felt like to be in sync with another person, to feel loved, respected and cherished. That feeling had been missing for at least a year, and she wondered if they'd ever get it back.

She looked at her phone and sighed at the multiple texts and voice messages from him. Why was he pestering her when she'd told him she'd call after dinner? Feeling embarrassed about last night and more recently her imagined elevator flirtation with Dominique, she fished the room key from her purse.

Double tasking, she pushed "Call" and held the phone to her ear.

She tapped the key on the sensor of her room's door and pushed it with her hip. As it swung open, something felt off, and she felt a tingle at the back of her neck. Absently she dropped her phone into her purse along with the room key. The door clicked closed as she stepped into the small foyer. From the foyer, the desk lamp emitted a soft glow. Had she left it on? She couldn't remember.

Moving into the room, she jerked to a stop at the sight of Hicks sitting in the winged chair next to the window, his legs casually crossed at the knee. She blinked several times in rapid succession, hoping she was having some kind of weird hallucination, maybe an after-effect of the stress of the past few days. The dim light cast his face in a partial shadow. His suit jacket lay neatly creased on the bed, and he'd loosened his tie. He slowly stood, taking in her shocked expression.

"Good evening," he said in a quiet voice that terrified Joyce. "Did you have a pleasant dinner with Monsieur DuPage?"

Bill decided he'd had enough. For the second night in a row, he paced his small apartment in a state of perturbation. Once again, his phone calls and text messages had gone unanswered. He'd asked Joyce the name of her hotel when they'd spoken earlier, and he'd even called the front desk and left a voice message on her room extension. Absently, he wondered if the little red light was blinking impatiently on the hotel phone next to the bed.

A nervous fear clenched his stomach. Although he had no proof, deep inside he felt something was wrong. He knew Joyce had been worried about Hicks, but she'd only mentioned leaving the reception early because she felt sick. Tonight, she was at dinner with Dominique. She'd texted him earlier, relieved the presentation had gone well, and said she'd call when she returned from dinner. Even allowing for the time difference, he should've heard from her by now. What was she doing with the Frenchman? Were they having an affair right under his nose?

He considered what he knew about the Frenchman. Joyce occasionally mentioned him, and he hadn't picked up on any particular vibe. When his name came up, it was always in reference to a patient or some weekend experience he'd had exploring the Richmond environs. He didn't know what he looked like, or how old he was. She'd mentioned he was divorced and had a school-aged daughter, but beyond that, she hadn't really talked about his personal life. He knew she admired his bedside manner, and she'd spoken gratefully about his ability to handle even the most anxious and demanding IVF couples. But wasn't it odd, just two of them having dinner? Where were Sally and Hicks?

Bill had never had any reason to doubt Joyce's fidelity. While they'd been in medical school and residency, they'd barely had time for eating and sleeping, let alone an affair. But things were different now. They were living separate lives in separate cities, focused on their careers. And did they still share the same priorities? He wasn't sure.

Reaching for his phone, he imagined the worst. Was she sick, injured, or maybe cheating on him with this mystery man? *Don't go down that rabbit hole,* he told himself. The phone vibrated with an incoming call. He saw it was Joyce and quickly hit "Answer."

"Hello," he said. Instead of her voice replying to his greeting, he thought he heard a conversation. The words ebbed and flowed, and one of the voices was definitely masculine. He listened for several seconds but couldn't discern specific words until, clear as a bell, Joyce said, "You need to leave. Right now."

His brain froze. Should he speak or remain silent? Should he be angry about a possible affair or concerned for her safety? Before he came to a decision, the voices abruptly ceased. He frantically tapped the screen, but the connection had dropped.

Hastily searching his call history, he found the number and pushed redial.

"Dr. Porter, it's rather late. You must be enjoying the charms of New Orleans. Or perhaps the charms of our visiting professor."

"Why are you here?" she demanded. "You have no right to be in my room! You need to leave. Right now."

Joyce dropped her purse onto the desk and stood, frozen with indecision. Lingering in a hotel room with a man who had possibly drugged her last night was beyond reckless, and she shuddered to think what might have occurred if Sally hadn't come along. But her boss was a powerful man. If she didn't play this right, he could ruin her reputation and her career. Joyce had no desire to compromise herself with a lecherous predator, and her mind whirled with possible ways out of the current situation. But damn it. Someone had to stand up to him.

"How did you get in?" she demanded.

"With a room key," he replied. A slight smile played about his lips, as if he found her uneasiness and confusion quaintly amusing.

"How did you get a key to my room?"

He laughed softly, "When you suffered that unfortunate dizzy spell, I offered to assist. You were quite indisposed, as I recall. You told me your room number, and I located *both* keys when you handed me your purse." He shook his head disapprovingly, as if chastising an errant child, and motioned toward the key sitting on the arm of his chair. "You shouldn't carry both keys with you, you know."

"Dr. Hicks, I'm still confused about why you're here," she said, her voice coming out in a rush. "Whatever it is can wait until morning. You need to leave. Right now! This isn't right, and you're making me very uncomfortable." She opened the door to the quiet hall and gestured. "Go! It's late and I need to call my husband."

"Ah yes, the absent husband.," he said, his lips curled into a sneer. "I've often wondered if he really exists. You seem pretty cozy this trip with *le docteur*. You have just returned from a romantic dinner, *oui*?"

She found his attempted French accent ridiculous.

As if on cue, her phone chimed. She walked back to the desk and fished it out of her purse. Bill's smiling face appeared. She turned the phone toward Hicks. "See, that's him—and he's already left several messages. He's expecting my call."

"Don't answer. We have something important to discuss."

Joyce swiped and tapped, then said, "You have one minute before I call hotel security."

He smiled, no longer looking amused. "Stop being so dramatic. I'm not going to attack you. I think you'll want to hear what I have to say, my dear, and it's going to take longer than a minute. Put that phone down and let's talk. I have a proposition for you."

She set the phone on the desk then positioned herself within reach of the heavy door. If she had to, she'd fling it open and shout for help.

"Okay. I'm listening."

A burly dark-haired man wearing a gold jacket with a patch proclaiming him "Hotel Security" quickly traversed the hotel lobby. Clarence Hebert was a former police detective and carried himself with authority and confidence. At this time of night, the lobby was devoid of inhabitants except for the fresh-faced night clerk who was running daily occupancy reports.

"Which manager is on tonight?" he barked.

The clerk, annoyed at being interrupted, took his time before drawling, "Ms. Landry."

"Is she in her office?"

"I'm not sure. Did you try calling her?"

Hebert glared down at him. "We may have a situation."

Glancing around the quiet lobby, the clerk raised his eyebrows skeptically. "A situation?"

"I just got a very odd call. The man identified himself as Dr. Bill Porter. He said his wife is staying here and he thinks she may be in trouble."

"Why does he think that?"

"He says he received a strange call from her."

The clerk's hands tapped the keyboard and brought up a screen. The cursor flashed over an empty field.

"What's her name?"

"Joyce Porter. She's attending the convention."

More tapping before he replied, "Yup, she's here. Room 512, East wing. I think her husband may have called earlier. He asked me to connect him to her room."

"He thinks she might be in trouble," Hebert repeated. "When he called, he said he heard muffled voices and then she told someone to leave."

"Did he ask her what was happening? Should we call the police?"

"He said the line went dead before he had the chance. Then when he called back, it went straight to voicemail."

"Why do you need a manager?"

"I want to give her a heads up. And I think we should investigate before calling the police."

The night clerk picked up the phone and dialed. "Sorry to bother you, Ms. Landry. Security is here about a possible situation."

He handed the phone to Hebert who quickly outlined his concerns. As soon as he hung up, a door discreetly labeled "Employees Only" on the far end of the lobby was flung open. Ms. Genevieve Landry, a statuesque Black woman who looked every inch of the Mardi Gras Queen she was, sailed out. She imperiously gestured to the two men, "Let's roll."

CHAPTER 23

"I'm listening," Joyce said and again wondered why she was allowing this man who had most likely drugged her to remain.

Hicks slowly uncrossed his legs. He tented his fingers thoughtfully then leaned back. He leisurely adjusted his posture and rested his hands on the arms of the chair. After what seemed like a lifetime to Joyce, he began to speak. "Your talk today was well received. I noticed you had quite the crowd."

She nodded.

"What would those admirers say if they suspected you didn't quite present the whole picture?"

She frowned. "What do you mean, the whole picture?"

"You have a problem, my dear, with the pregnancy rate." He paused before adding, "Those numbers you quoted for your charity patients are unusually high. They are above our average at McArthur and much higher than the national average."

"We've discussed this before. Most of the couples who qualified for the program were younger than our average couples and several had problems only with tubal blockage. It makes sense they conceived at a higher rate than older couples with male factor or unexplained infertility."

"Is it possible you may have boosted the fertilization rates in some way—say, by using sperm from a fertile donor?"

"That's absurd!" Joyce countered. "I would never do such a thing!"

"Hmm," Hicks said. "If I were to begin an investigation, I wonder if I might find several vials of our more 'successful' donors missing." He stared at her before continuing, "As is common with confidential internal investigations, you might be placed on administrative leave. Of course, we wouldn't tell your colleagues or patients the reason for the leave, but what do you think would happen to your reputation?"

She froze, stunned into silence.

"Maybe you would be forced to resign," he mused, before continuing in a conversational tone. "Do you think anyone would offer you a job if there was even a whisper about something like this?"

Joyce felt like she'd fallen into an alternate universe. She was numb with shock. She couldn't believe her boss, the man who was supposed to be her mentor, was making these accusations. It was beyond ridiculous. She would never do something so unethical, but she remained mute, unable to form a quick defense.

"You're awfully quiet." The silence pressed down on her, making it hard to breathe.

"People know me. And they know I would never do anything like that. No one will believe you," she finally said. Her voice sounded weak and timid.

"Maybe, or maybe not. Do you want to take that chance?" After a beat, he said, "But there is another option."

Joyce realized she was trembling, from anger or fear. Or both.

"What do you want?" she asked.

He smiled, but to her it looked more like a leer.

"I'd like to talk about our relationship," he said.

"Our relationship?" she said faintly.

"Yes, I believe I've made it clear. You and your career have much to gain from my goodwill."

"What did you have in mind?" she asked, dreading the answer.

"Smart girl. I knew you'd come around," he said with a self-satisfied smirk. "I would like us to have a closer, more *intimate* relationship. That's the way things work. Ask your friend Dr. Cohen."

Joyce felt a metallic taste in her mouth as bile rose and burned the back of her throat. Her skin flushed hot and then cold as her adrenalin surged. She fought to keep it together, to keep from throwing something at the arrogant bastard.

He stood up and moved toward her. Shaking off her torpor, she shimmied around him and grabbed his jacket from the bed. She shoved it at him, opened the door and pointed to the hall. He looked at her quizzically.

"Well?" he asked softly. She looked away.

"I'll think about it," she said after a moment.

"Smart girl," he said again while shrugging into his jacket. "I'd hate to see your reputation ruined." Without another word, he left.

Joyce closed the door with a thud, then engaged the deadbolt and secured the safety chain. Almost immediately, her arms and legs began to shake. She barely had time to sink down onto the bed before she heard an insistent knock on the door.

"Oh God," she muttered to herself, her heart pounding. "Is he back?"

Rather than taking the public elevators, Ms. Landry, Mr. Hebert, and the night clerk walked to a service elevator. It was off the beaten path and much less opulent than the ones facing the public. It allowed room service, bell captains, and the house-keeping staff to move between floors without disturbing guests. Ms. Landry used her ID badge to call the elevator and again when she pushed the button for the fifth floor. The three rode up in silence. After exiting into a small employee work area, they opened the door leading to the public corridor. Ahead of them, they glimpsed a gray-haired man wearing a dark suit moving quickly in the opposite direction. As they reached room 512, he disappeared from view.

Mr. Hebert raised his hand and rapped smartly on the door. After a few seconds, he knocked again, louder this time, and announced in a deep voice, "Hotel Security. Dr. Porter, may we come in?"

After a brief pause, they heard steps that stopped short of the door. A woman's voice called out, "Show me some ID."

Hebert raised his badge so it was visible through the peephole. The deadbolt disengaged, and the door opened a sliver to reveal a slice of a woman's pale face.

Ms. Landry stepped forward. "Dr. Porter," she said in a calm melodious voice, "my name is Genevieve Landry. I'm the hotel's evening manager. And this is Mr. Hebert and Charles Benet. We received a call this evening from Mr. Bill Porter. He identified himself as your husband. He said he was worried about you. May we please come in?"

Joyce closed the door, released the security chain, and opened the door to the trio. She gestured for them to enter. She walked to the armchair recently vacated by Hicks and sat on the edge.

Ms. Landry sat in the opposite chair, while the two men remained standing. "Is Bill Porter your husband?"

"Yes."

"Mr. Hebert received the call about twenty minutes ago. Mr. Porter sounded quite upset. He said you called and then abruptly disconnected, but he also thought he heard a man's voice and you telling someone to leave."

Joyce rocked from side to side before saying, "As you can see, there's no one here. I was at dinner earlier this evening. I haven't had a chance to call my husband."

Mr. Hebert looked at Ms. Landry, then stepped forward. "As

we approached your room, we saw a short gray-haired man walking in the opposite direction. Did he bother you?"

"That was my boss," she replied nervously. "I was surprised he showed up this late. But as you can see, he's gone now." She realized she was speaking too quickly and repeating herself. She needed to call Bill. *What was he thinking, calling hotel security?* She didn't know whether to be embarrassed or grateful.

They asked a few more questions before seeming satisfied that nothing untoward had occurred. For the second time that evening, Joyce found herself ushering unwanted visitors to the door. "It's late and I'm tired. I'm sure you have other things to do. I'll call my husband to let him know I'm fine. Thank you for checking on me."

She opened the door, and the men exited, followed by Ms. Landry. As she passed, she gave Joyce a searching look before carefully laying a business card on the foyer table. "We're sorry we've disturbed you. Please call if you need anything. Goodnight."

Once inside the service elevator, Hebert broke the silence. "I think there's more to the story."

Ms. Landry's left eyebrow raised as she looked at him. "How so?"

"Well, first off, she seemed surprised to see us."

Benet, who had a tendency to exaggerate, chimed in, "Well, it is almost midnight."

Hebert looked at his watch. "It's not even eleven yet." He continued, "And she was really nervous."

"Maybe she's having an affair with her boss and her husband is getting suspicious," Benet said.

"Maybe," Hebert replied. "But her husband sounded genuinely concerned about her safety. And last evening, as I was coming on shift, I saw a gray-haired man helping a woman who looked like she was either very sick or very drunk. They were coming from one of the reception ballrooms, and I swear it looked like the same woman we just spoke to."

"Did it look like the same man we saw a few minutes ago on the fifth floor?" Ms. Landry asked.

"I can't say for sure because I didn't see his face, but he was about the same height and had gray hair."

They exited the elevator and walked toward Ms. Landry's office. She thanked them, and all three returned to their routine tasks.

"Joyce, where have you been? It's almost midnight!" Bill said in a near shout.

"It isn't even eleven," she said wearily. "I told you I'd call when I got back."

"But that should have been hours ago."

"The restaurant was packed. All of the conventioneers must have read the same guidebook on 'Best Places to Dine in New Orleans.' It took a long time for us to get seated and then a long time before we were served. The food was excellent—fresh seafood and lots of good Cajun flavors. I think you would like the place."

"I don't really want to talk about your culinary experience, especially since you were there with another man." Bill sounded tightly wound. She figured it was partly her fault for not texting him earlier. And she had to admit, she and Dominique had lingered over their meal. But before she had a chance to apologize, he started in.

"What's going on with you?" he demanded. "You've been avoiding me and haven't been yourself for the past two days. Are you still sick? Did something happen with Hicks? And why were you out so late with that Frenchman?"

The enormity of the past two days slammed down on her, and she sagged with fatigue. Her head throbbed, her brain felt fuzzy, and her whole body ached. She wondered if she was getting the flu or if it was residual stress from last night. She wanted to share everything that had happened in the last twenty-four hours, but she knew he'd come unglued when he found out Hicks had stolen her room key and propositioned her. And she wasn't even sure how to explain the specious accusations. And then there were her confused feelings about Dominique, which she would never share. It was too much to process right now.

"Bill, I'm fine. Really, I am. But I'm exhausted. I didn't get much sleep last night and today was pretty stressful."

"Joyce, I've been worried sick," he said, some of the anger leaving his voice.

She cut him off, "I know, and I'm sorry I didn't call sooner. A lot has happened, but I don't want to talk about it. I'm tapped out. My talk went well, really well, and now Hicks is being an ass. Tonight, he accused me of juicing the pregnancy rates in my study." She rubbed her forehead trying to ease the ache and continued, "And he's threatening to start a rumor about me using donor sperm to enhance the pregnancy rates."

"What?" he shouted. "That's absurd. You'd never do that!"

"Of course not, but that's not the point."

"What about our plan? Did it work?"

"Maybe."

"What do you mean, maybe?"

"It's too much to get into tonight. I have to get some sleep and try to figure out why he mentioned donor sperm. I don't think it was an idle comment."

"Joyce, if he's threatening you, you've got to do something. You can't sit back and wait for his next move."

"I know," she said tiredly. "But I'm not going to do anything tonight except take some Tylenol and go to bed."

He started to argue with her, but she cut him off.

"Please, no more."

He fell silent.

"And thanks for sending in the cavalry," she said, her voice softening. "It alarmed me when hotel security banged on my door, but I appreciate your concern. You must have been very persuasive. Three people showed up."

"Well, I'm glad someone listened to me," he grumbled, sounding slightly mollified.

"And I'm really sorry for making you worry. I'll be back in Richmond Thursday night, and I promise I'll explain everything when we're together this weekend."

"Okay," he said. "And one more thing for us to talk about on Saturday—I've been invited to go to Peru for a month on a WHO project sometime in February or March. I have until next week to decide, so we have time to talk it through."

"If it's a good opportunity, you should go," she said reflexively. Inwardly she groaned, thinking the timing couldn't be worse. Then she wondered if she'd even still have a job in February.

"We'll talk about it. I don't have to go." This surprised her as it was the first time Bill hadn't been gung-ho to travel to some exotic location—the further off the beaten track the better.

He was still talking, "Please text me tomorrow if you're going to call later than ten. I don't think I could take another night of worry."

"Well, we can't have that," she teased, her mood a little lighter. After a quick "I love you," they said their goodnights.

She popped two Tylenol and an over-the-counter sleep aid then checked the door's deadbolt and safety chain. As she readied herself for bed, she wondered who she could talk to about the mess she was in. It wasn't bad enough that Hicks was harassing her, but now he seemed hell-bent on ruining her career as well. Lying in bed, a worry nagged at her regarding the pregnancy rates. She remembered the short-lived drop in fertilization rates and how evasive Kumar had been when questioned. One of her last thoughts before she entered a dreamless sleep was Dominique's question about an "A list."

What was the A list? And why didn't she know about it?

Just what they needed, another mystery involving the lab.

CHAPTER 24

Joyce awoke feeling rested. A beam of sunlight pierced the gap in the heavy curtains and snaked across the floor. Sunlight always elevated her mood and so did a good night's sleep. Almost immediately, memories of the past two days threatened to overwhelm—the reception and her blackout, Hicks's proposition, her attraction to Dominique, and guilt over keeping everything from her husband. Her brief flash of optimism disappeared, and she was gripped with a desire to keep the drapes drawn and hunker down in her room until it was time to fly home. Her eyes filled with tears.

Unbidden, she remembered an incident from middle school when one of the "mean girls" had accused her of cheating on a Social Studies test. That evening, she'd tearfully shared the incident with her father and told him she didn't want to go to school the next day. In her mind, she heard his bracing voice, "Joyce, you didn't cheat, and you can't let those girls get to you. You're going to school tomorrow. Talk to the teacher and tell him what happened. I'm right here, and if you need me, I'll talk to him too, but I think you can handle this on your own. You are strong and you are smart. If those girls are bullying you, they're probably doing it to others. You stand tall and do the right thing."

Her dad telling her to "stand tall" was their inside joke. She was the second shortest kid in her class. Her dad had high expectations, but he'd always loved her unconditionally and believed in her. She impatiently brushed away the tears and mentally prepared herself to "stand tall." The conference lasted another day and a half, and she was determined not to waste the opportunity to attend the events and network with colleagues. If she had to leave McArthur, it would be important to have friends in other places.

She swung her legs out of bed and resolutely stood up. Her first order of business was to open the drapes and take advantage of the mood-elevating sunshine and the expansive park view. The trees across from the hotel were mostly green, and she'd learned from a tourist pamphlet that they often didn't change color until late November or early December. She inserted the single-serving pod into the coffee maker, filled it with water, and pushed the brew button. The machine gurgled and hissed before a stream of hot fragrant liquid splashed into the waiting mug. Grabbing the coffee, she sauntered to the desk where a pad of paper and a pen emblazoned with the hotel's name and logo were arranged neatly next to the lamp.

Carefully sipping the hot beverage, she started a list. She began by concentrating on Hicks, both his accusations and his outrageous proposal for a more "intimate" relationship. From their first interview, she realized she'd never liked or trusted the man, but she'd ascertained the connections he could provide would be her ticket to an acclaimed career. She'd been so eager to curry favor that she'd ignored her misgivings and talked herself into the job because it was at a prestigious center.

Looking back on that experience, as well as their many encounters, Joyce wondered how she could've been so dense. A small internal voice, sounding suspiciously like her mother, pestered her and made her wonder if somehow she'd done something to encourage him. *Stop that!* she told herself. *You've done nothing wrong. You didn't drug yourself, steal a room key, and make a quid pro quo propo-*

sition. He's a scumbag and a predator. Sally said as much. So surely there are others at McArthur who've experienced his repulsive behavior.

Pulling the notepad toward her and picking up the pen, she wrote decisively,

1. *FIND OTHERS.* Underneath she wrote: *SALLY AND ?? HR*
2. *"A" LIST?* And underneath that, two bullets:
DOMINIQUE AND KUMAR

She absently clicked the top of the pen three times, then drew two lines through Kumar and penned Richard Carnegie.

Reaching for the coffee mug, she noticed it was empty. A brief look at the clock showed she needed to immediately shower and dress to make the morning's first event. She opened the bathroom door and turned on the shower. Her glance strayed to the small foyer table where she saw the night manager's business card. She picked it up, strode back to the desk and added one more item to her list.

3. *TALK TO MS. LANDRY*

The lobby was abuzz as Joyce dodged clusters of chatty conventioneers and crossed to the main desk. Only two clerks were on duty, and she joined the small queue of guests waiting patiently between the red velvet-roped posts. After a few minutes, a man with jet- black hair and a small goatee gestured to her from the farthest station. She approached, Ms. Landry's card in hand.

"Good morning, miss . . ." He paused, looking at her convention name badge. "Ah, Dr. Porter. How may I assist you today?"

"I'd like to speak with Ms. Genevieve Landry." She showed him the manager's card.

The clerk consulted his computer, stroked his goatee, then punched a number into his desk phone.

"Hello. Front desk calling. Is Ms. Landry in? A guest is inquiring." Joyce studied his face as he listened, then he looked up and shook his head. After another moment, he picked up a pen and jotted something on a nearby pad.

"Thanks, Claudia," he said. He replaced the receiver, tore off the top sheet of the pad, and pushed it toward her.

"Ms. Landry is our night manager, and she went home an hour ago. But she'll be back this evening at seven p.m. If you wish to speak with her, I suggest you stop by then."

"Is there a way I can leave a message?"

"I suggest you call the extension listed on her business card and leave a voicemail."

Joyce shook her head and said, "I'd prefer to send a written message. Is that possible?"

"Of course," he said, looking a bit annoyed. He opened a drawer, handed her a letter- sized sheet of hotel stationery and an envelope, and asked a bit snidely, "Do you need a pen?"

"No thanks," she said. "Do I give this back to you?"

"You can hand it to any of us at the front desk, and we'll see that she receives it."

"I appreciate your help," she said with a smile.

"You're welcome," he said more graciously, as if suddenly remembering she was a guest at a hotel that prided itself on Southern hospitality and gracious customer service. "Enjoy your stay and let us know if we can further assist you."

Joyce found a vacant chair in a quiet corner and extracted a pen from the bottom of her bag. She smoothed the piece of stationery against the back of the notebook balanced on her lap and began to write:

DEAR MS. LANDRY, THANK YOU FOR CHECKING IN LAST NIGHT. I APPRECIATE YOUR CONCERN FOR MY SAFETY. I

WOULD LIKE TO SPEAK TO YOU THIS EVENING IF POSSIBLE.
PLEASE CALL ME.

Joyce added her mobile number and signed her name. She sealed the envelope, walked back to the front desk and handed it to the same clerk who had previously assisted her. He gave a brief nod and promised he'd deliver it.

Joyce and Sally were seated at a high-top table in a window alcove at the hotel bar, sipping frosty gin and tonics while they made small talk. Beyond the window, a hot afternoon sun beat down on an indoor courtyard still filled with blooming hibiscus and other tropical shrubs. A few guests wandered among the lush greenery.

After a long swallow, Sally leaned forward. "Okay, now tell me everything."

"Where do I start?"

"How about last night's dinner with Dominique?"

A slight blush colored Joyce's fair skin. She glanced down, her finger absently wiping the condensation trickling down the side of the balloon glass. Finally, she said, "It was nice."

Sally threw back her head and laughed, an infectious deep-throated chuckle.

"You two go for an intimate dinner at one of the most iconic restaurants in New Orleans, and all you have to say is 'It was nice.' Come on Joyce, you can do better than that!"

"I'm not sure what to say," she said defensively. "The atmosphere was lovely, and the food was excellent. The place was crazy busy, so the service was extremely slow. I recognized a lot of folks from the convention."

"What did you talk about?"

"Just general stuff. Dominique told me a little about growing up in France, and I told him about my home in Maryland. We both have pushy mothers who make us crazy sometimes. And we both spent our teenage summers swimming—he in the Mediterranean and me in Deep Creek Lake."

"What else?"

"My presentation, our careers, where we plan to spend Christmas."

"Sounds like a first date. Does he know you're married?"

"Of course!" Joyce replied quickly, the blush creating twin spots on her pale cheeks. She pushed back the memories of her romantic fantasies and late-night visit, changing the topic before it veered into dangerous territory. "Let's talk about something else. How was your evening with friends?"

Sally stirred the drink with her straw, then pushed it away and grabbed a salted almond from the squat ceramic dish. She nibbled slowly.

"It was nice," she said and grinned.

Joyce rolled her eyes and laughed. "Now you're just messing with me."

"It was fine. They're all married, so I listened to a lot of talk about spouses and pets. *None* of them have kids, which I find fascinating. And in between, we talked about work, you know, how demanding some patients can be and how tired we all are of after-hour calls and working weekends. We visited for about an hour before we ran out of things to say and called it a night. I was back in my room for the ten o'clock news."

They both glanced out the tall windows at a toddler in a bright-green dinosaur T-shirt and matching shorts blowing bubbles while his mother sat on a nearby bench absorbed with her phone. The ambient noise of the bar swirled around them.

Joyce uncrossed her legs and shifted to a more comfortable position. "Hicks was in my room last night when I got back from dinner," she said abruptly.

"Holy shit," Sally exclaimed, knocking over the water glass. She quickly righted it and grabbed a napkin to mop up the spill. "What time was that? How did he get in?"

"It was sometime after ten. I said goodnight to Dominique at the elevator, and when I opened the door to my room, there he was."

"Did you scream and tell him to get the hell out?"

"No, I was too stunned to think clearly."

"Why was he there?"

"To proposition me."

"Oh God," Sally hissed. "What a snake. Did you tell him to go screw himself?"

"Not exactly."

"Joyce," she said in a horrified voice, "you didn't sleep with him, did you?"

"No! But that's clearly what he's after. He pointed out how much I could benefit from a more 'intimate' relationship.'"

Sally shook her head disgustedly. "What a lech."

"But that's not the worst of it," Joyce continued.

"What could be worse than that?" muttered Sally.

"He threatened me."

"In what way?"

"He accused me of artificially inflating the pregnancy rates of the couples in my study by surreptitiously using donor sperm."

Sally's eyes widened in disbelief. "What? That's ridiculous!"

"Of course it is. But he threatened to launch an investigation —said he wondered if he'd find vials of donor sperm missing. Said he might put me on paid leave and that my reputation would be ruined when news of the investigation leaked out. Then he threatened to fire me—or make it so I'd have to resign."

A waitress, noticing their empty glasses, stopped to inquire if they'd like another round. Both nodded affirmatively.

Once the waitress departed, Sally fumed, "That's beyond harassment. Joyce, you've got to do something! He's trying to blackmail you for something you haven't even done."

Joyce felt touched by her friend's fierce defense. Maybe this time Sally would be willing to get involved. She took a deep breath and thought, *"Stand tall."*

"You're right," she said firmly while looking her in the eye, "and I need your help."

Sally averted her eyes before replying, "Joyce, I told you before, I don't want to get involved."

"I know, but someone's got to stop him. And I think we can."

"I have to go to the ladies' room," Sally announced abruptly and slid off the stool. She grabbed her oversize handbag, wove through the crowd, and disappeared into a hallway next to the bar.

Joyce gazed at the ornate bar, admiring the skill of the bartenders as they filled one order after another while chatting amicably with the patrons. It looked like a well-choreographed dance. She rattled the ice against the side of her glass and drained the last of the clear liquid right before the waitress returned with fresh drinks.

"Do you need anything else?"

"Maybe some food. May we please see the menu?"

The waitress produced two menu cards from her apron pocket and whisked away.

Joyce studied their food choices. It was limited to traditional bar fare and a few salads. She thought she might order the Cajun shrimp skewers and a side salad. She pulled out her phone and checked her email. Most of it could wait until she returned to work on Friday. She smiled when she read that the Wolfs and the Lauderbacks were pregnant. Unfortunately, three of her other couples were not.

She looked up as Sally returned and hopped onto the stool. Joyce handed her a menu. "I'm hungry. Do you want to order something here or go somewhere else?"

Sally glanced at the laminated card and said, "Let's eat here. I'm ordering the Creole gumbo and Cajun fries. How about you?"

"You never eat fries!"

"I know, but tonight I'm splurging. After what you told me, I need sustenance."

She pushed the menu aside and looked at Joyce, "Now tell me how Hicks got into your room."

The waitress returned and they placed their orders. Joyce fortified herself with a long swallow of the fresh drink, then she related the details of the purloined room key and the late-night visit from the hotel's management.

"Oh my God!" Sally spat out. Lowering her voice but ramping up the intensity, she continued, "That's outrageous! On top of all his other lies and threats, Hicks stole your room key. Unbelievable! I don't know why, but somehow that makes the whole thing feel so much worse. And good for Bill, sending someone to make sure you were okay."

"I guess. At first, I was upset they came, but now I think it was probably a good idea. After dinner, I'm going to stop by the front desk to see if I can talk to that manager."

"Does Bill know?"

"Yes, I called him right after they left. He was pretty upset. I told him some of it, but I was too tired to go into the whole business."

"That makes sense. So now that you've had a chance to sleep on it, what's your plan?"

"I'm going to try to stop him, and I need your help."

Absently, Sally stirred her drink and looked toward the rowdy patrons at the next table. They were singing an off-key version of "Happy Birthday," raising their glasses to an embarrassed twenty-something man wearing horn-rimmed glasses and a sloppy grin.

After they finished, she looked back at Joyce and slowly nodded. "I'm in. Tell me what you need."

Genevieve Landry was waiting in the spacious lobby next to the front desk when Joyce arrived. As before, she was professionally attired in the hotel's blazer, pencil skirt, and block-heeled pumps, but today her stunning eyes grabbed Joyce's attention. Gold eye shadow shimmered discreetly, and a thick streak of eyeliner accentuated their almond shape. Her lashes looked impossibly think and long. She was tall and radiated an almost regal presence.

She welcomed Joyce with a quick handshake and escorted her to a small office. Joyce observed it was shockingly plain compared to the opulence of the public space. The manager offered her a glass of water which she politely declined. She seated herself and focused her amazing eyes on Joyce. "I was surprised to receive your message. How may I assist you?"

"First, thank you for your help last night."

"You are very welcome. We wanted to make sure you were safe and pass along your husband's message."

"Well, thanks again for following up." Joyce shifted in her seat and crossed her legs before saying, "I'd like to talk to you about what happened before you arrived."

Ms. Landry murmured her assent, and she continued, "I went to dinner last evening with a friend. When I returned to my room, someone was there." She grimaced. "It was my boss."

Ms. Landry's face remained impassive.

"He let himself in with my room key, a key that he'd taken the night before."

Ms. Landry raised her eyebrows quizzically, and Joyce rushed to clarify. "We both attended the Ovatech reception. I wasn't feeling well, and he offered to help me back to my room."

"Did you give him your key?"

A faint flush stained Joyce's cheeks. "I can't remember. I think someone slipped something in my drink because I don't remember much after leaving the reception. I must have had both keys in my purse. My friend Sally saw me in the elevator, and she said I looked really out of it. She told my boss she would take care of me. He gave her my purse and one room key, and she stayed with me until I woke up in the middle of the night."

"And you're sure you had both keys in your purse?"

"I'm not sure about anything," Joyce said in an exasperated tone, "but when I asked him how he got into my room, that's what he said."

"I see. I'm sorry for the interruption. Please go on."

Joyce glanced at Ms. Landry's face. She thought she detected a hint of sympathy in her warm brown eyes.

"I told him I was uncomfortable with him being in my room and asked him to leave." She stopped, indecision playing across her face as she debated how much additional information to share.

Ms. Landry leaned forward. "I can see this is difficult for you. May I ask a few questions? You don't have to share anything that makes you uncomfortable."

"Sure."

"Did your boss leave shortly before we arrived?"

"Yes."

"Is he on the short side with gray hair? Was he wearing a black or dark-gray suit?"

Joyce thought back. She remembered him picking up his suit jacket. "He has gray hair, but I don't remember the color of the suit. It could have been black or dark gray."

"I'm pretty sure we saw him walking down the hall toward the elevators before we knocked on your door. We have surveillance cameras in each hallway and at the elevators. If it's important, I can ask security to locate the footage for your floor."

Joyce nervously pushed back her hair as Ms. Landry gently prodded. "What else would you like me to do?"

"I don't know. I guess I'm here to ask your advice. I came back from dinner and a man was in my room, having stolen my room key the night before. What else can you do?"

"Let me begin by saying how sorry I am this happened. I can only imagine how frightening it must have been for you to return from dinner and find someone in your room. After he left, was anything stolen or missing? Anything out of place?"

"No, nothing."

"Did he threaten you in any way?"

Joyce looked away, then met Ms. Landry's gaze.

"Yes, he did, but not in the physical sense. He's trying to pressure me about something at work, but I'd rather not talk about that now. I'm mainly interested in what can be done since he broke into my room."

"I'd like to ask Mr. Hebert to speak with you. You met him last night. He's a retired detective from the New Orleans police. He'll know how best to proceed. Do you want to file a report with the police?"

Joyce looked worried. "I'm not sure about the police, but I do want to file a report. I want a record that he stole my key and used it to enter my room without my permission."

Mr. Hebert arrived, and Joyce recounted her story. He asked a few additional questions, including one about the conversation her husband had "overheard" before alerting them the previous evening. Joyce gave vague answers when pressed for details. Options were limited, he told her, since she didn't want to involve the police. He asked if Hicks was staying at their hotel, but she didn't know. He promised to check the guest list and also to review the security camera footage. He said he'd call her the next morning.

Joyce thanked them both, then headed back to the lobby. Ms. Landry watched her for a moment as she crossed to the elevators before closing the door.

"So, what do you think?" she asked Hebert.

"I think he's the man I saw with her the evening before, and that it probably happened exactly the way she said." He shook his head in disgust. "What a sleazeball. But you realize, there isn't a shred of proof. She didn't get evaluated at the hospital. And he can always say he was trying to help his sick friend and accidentally kept her key and that he stopped by to return it to her."

"At ten o'clock at night?" She lifted a brow and pressed her lips into a thin line.

He raised his hands in mock surrender. "I know, it's stupid. And I don't understand why she's being so evasive about what her husband said he heard on the aborted phone call. It didn't sound like a butt dial to me."

He jotted a note on a small pad. "I'll look at the camera footage and see if I can put together a timeline. We should be able to tell when he got to the floor, and we may even be able to see him entering her room before she got back."

"If he entered her room without authorization, that's a pretty big problem, key or no key."

"I agree. But it's his word against hers. Nothing went missing, and she says he didn't threaten her."

"Didn't physically threaten her," she clarified.

"Right," he paused, then asked, "So what do you think is going on?"

"I'm not sure, but there's definitely more to the story."

Hebert stood up, pocketed his pen and placed his notebook in the inside pocket of his blazer. "I'll write up a guest incident report after I review the security footage. And just in case, I'll save the footage from last night and the night before if I can find pictures of them leaving the Ovatech shindig."

"Sounds good. And thanks for your help. Keep me posted. I'm not sure what we can do, but I think she's in some kind of trouble."

"I think you're right."

CHAPTER 25

Joyce didn't see Hicks for the rest of the conference. She made a point of attending the remaining events with either Sally or Dominique because she feared running into him without backup. Bill texted her several times expressing his support and concern. She felt too distracted to attempt reassurance with anything other than brief comments like "I'm fine" or a thumbs up emoji. She couldn't wait to leave The Big Easy.

On the last morning of the conference, Hebert left a voicemail saying he had additional information and the final incident report for her to sign. She returned the call immediately.

"Dr. Porter, I know you're busy this morning, so I'll make it brief. I checked the hotel's security footage from Tuesday evening, and I can confirm Dr. Hicks entered your room about ten minutes before you returned from dinner. It appears he used an electronic keycard issued to you. I was also able to verify that he left your room shortly before Ms. Landry and I arrived. We saw him as he headed toward the elevators, and the cameras caught him again entering the elevator. He was registered at this hotel, and it appears he returned to his room after leaving yours. He didn't leave his room until the following morning when he checked out."

Joyce was surprised to hear Hicks had checked out. He hadn't mentioned leaving early. It explained why she hadn't run into him. "I see. Is there a way to prove he took the keycard and entered my room without permission?"

"Not really. I checked cameras from Monday evening, and I located some shots of you leaving the Ovatech reception together. You appeared unsteady, and Dr. Hicks had his arm around your waist supporting you as you headed toward the lobby. A separate camera showed both of you waiting at the lobby elevators, and then we saw you get off on the fifth floor with your friend Dr. Cohen."

"Did I have my purse while we were waiting for the elevator?"

"I couldn't say. We didn't see your purse in any of the shots until you exited the elevator with Dr. Cohen."

"So, what's the next step?" Joyce asked after a short silence.

"Have you changed your mind about involving the New Orleans police?" Hebert asked.

"No," she said firmly. "Is there anything else?"

"I spoke with Dr. Hicks before he left. I caught up with him as he was checking out."

Joyce hadn't expected Hebert to contact Hicks, and she felt a stab of worry. Would this make her current situation worse? Perhaps set her up for retaliation?

Hebert's voice continued, "He was in a hurry to catch his flight. He told me he'd discovered your spare room key while he was packing and had merely come by your room to return it. He was surprised to learn you were upset by his friendly visit." He emphasized the word "friendly."

Joyce grimaced. "You mentioned the report."

"Yes, I'd like you to stop by and sign it before you leave."

"Okay. What happens then?"

"Nothing. I'll give you a copy, and we'll keep the other on file. The information will be entered in an internal database where we track all reported incidents."

Joyce thought for a moment. "How long do you keep the report and the security footage?"

"Six months for the security footage and three years for the write-up. The abstracted data stays in an electronic archived file until someone decides to delete it."

"Has anything like this happened before?"

"Ma'am, I can't really talk to you about any incidents other than your own."

Joyce didn't like this reply, but it wasn't unexpected. "I understand. I can meet you in half an hour."

"I'm on my way home, but I'll alert the day officer. His name is Louis Benoit. Ask the front desk to page him. He'll meet you there."

"Thank you, Mr. Hebert. I appreciate the follow-up. And please pass along my thanks to Ms. Landry. You've both been very helpful."

"You're welcome, Dr. Porter. I'm very sorry this happened while you were our guest. Let me know if I can help in any other way. Safe travels."

Joyce and Sally discussed possible strategies on the way home. They were seated side by side in coach class, nibbling on pretzels and sipping white wine that was way too "buttery" for her taste.

After some brainstorming, Joyce decided to make an appointment with Human Resources, and Sally agreed to write a statement summarizing her experience two years before when Hicks pressured her into having sex. "Do you remember the name of the female grad student who left after six months?" Joyce asked.

"No, but Richard will. They dated for a short time." Sally relaxed against the faux-leather headrest. "Joyce, I said I would help, and I will, but what do you expect to happen? The two of us or even three if we can locate the grad student and she agrees to help—we're just lowly minions taking on a powerful department head. And don't forget, Hicks is a personal friend of President Cobain. I hear they both belong to The Commonwealth Club."

"Is that still an all-male bastion?"

"No. I think they let women in, but only on Mondays," Sally said with barely concealed sarcasm. "But you didn't really answer my question. What do you expect to gain?"

"I want to talk to HR about options. I'm hoping I can convince them there's a pattern of unacceptable behavior going back years and involving multiple women. If I say I'm being harassed, they at least have to look into it."

"Maybe," Sally said in a flat tone, "but what if they want you to go on some kind of leave—you know, to 'protect' you?"

"I'm not going on any leave! I have patients to care for. And besides, I don't think I'm in any physical danger. Hicks never comes to the clinic."

"But still," Sally said before Joyce cut her off.

"I have factual information to share about a university administrator engaged in harassment backed up with evidence. They owe it to me to check it out, especially if you and Ms. Grad Student file similar complaints."

Sally lurched forward. "I didn't agree to file a complaint! Let's be clear. What I'm doing is reporting a previous experience, and I'm doing it to support you. That's as far as I'm willing to go."

Joyce nodded. "I understand. And thank you for standing with me."

"Did the hotel give you a copy of their report? Is it enough to discredit a 'respected' member of the university administration?" Sally pantomimed air quotes for "respected."

"I have the report, which should be enough for them to take me seriously, and Mr. Hebert said he'll save the security footage for six months in case we need it."

"I'm sure you've thought about this, but why do you think

Hicks threatened to float a rumor about you using donor sperm to improve the pregnancy rates?"

Joyce looked pensive. "I've been asking myself that same question. And it made me remember an odd conversation. A few weeks back, Dominique asked me about an A list. Does that ring any bells?"

Sally's brow furrowed, and Joyce could almost see her analyzing past memories. Eventually, she spoke. "When I first started at McArthur, we had a weekend sign-out list. It was an actual printed sheet of paper showing all the couples who were in cycle. It also listed patients who recently had surgery and those being followed for possible tubal pregnancies. One weekend, I stopped by the lab to ask Dr. Kumar a question and saw a similar printed list on the work bench. The format was the same, and it looked like he had hand-written notations next to several names. It might have been the letter *A* or some other symbol. I really don't remember."

"Did you ever talk to him about it?" Joyce said.

"Nope, no reason to. When exactly did Dominique ask you about this list?"

"About three weeks ago. He was at loose ends one weekend and spent some time in the lab with Richard. He said all but one of the IVF couples that weekend used donor sperm for insemination. He thought that seemed high and asked him about it. That's when Richard mentioned a weekly list the lab received with all the couples who were in a current IVF cycle. If they had an *A* next to their name, donor sperm was used. If it said *A+*, he mixed donor with partner sperm."

Sally looked intrigued. "That does seem like a lot of donor couples. I maybe have one or two a month. Did you check into it?"

Joyce nodded. "Yes, the very next week. Both Richard and Kumar were out that day, and the assistant working said she'd never seen any A list, and she'd only used donor sperm for one couple that week. It was Jim's patient, and I looked at her chart.

His note clearly documented consent for donor sperm because her husband was azoospermic from chemotherapy treatment for cancer as a child. I also reviewed the sheet showing which donor they chose."

"Did they pick B007—you know, the super stud?"

Joyce laughed. "No, but they may have to retire B007 soon. His fertilization rate is off the charts! I think half the donor kids in Richmond have him as their bio father."

"We should ask Richard about the list."

"And leave Kumar out of it?" Joyce asked. "Why?"

"You told me Kumar seems secretive. If he's hiding something, he isn't going to talk to you. Let me ask Richard the name of the grad student. I'll make up some excuse. Then I'll casually ask how the lab tracks couples requesting a donor. I'll see if I can get our current donor list. I'll tell him I have an anxious patient who wants to know lots of details."

"If he gives you a list, it won't have any names, just demographic info," Joyce reminded her.

"I know, but it should show the number of vials still in storage, and also the number of documented pregnancies and live births."

Joyce ran her hand through her hair in a nervous gesture. "Okay, and I agree about keeping Kumar out of it. Something about him always seems a little off. He's super quiet and . . ." She hesitated before adding, "Sad."

"Will do. We can talk about it at our lunch next week. Let's eat in my office. That way we can shut the door if we need some privacy. Now let's relax and enjoy our plastic cup of cheap wine before we jump back into the chaos."

Sally opened the in-flight magazine and sipped the chardonnay. Joyce tried to do the crossword puzzle, but her mind kept wandering. Her schedule was packed the next day. She figured if she got there an hour early, she could stop by HR to make an appointment. Bill was coming this weekend, and they'd promised each other uninterrupted time, but maybe after he left on Sunday, she could poke around the lab and see what she could learn about donor inseminations. She began to devise a plan to obtain a key so she could investigate undisturbed.

Bright and early on Friday, Joyce entered the Human Resources offices located on the ground level of the Administration Building. The only other time she'd been there was to sign her employment paperwork. It had felt dark and unfriendly then, and it still felt that way in spite of several potted palms and a small water feature bubbling cheerfully on the receptionist's desk. A young man with ginger hair and a small mustache looked up from his computer. "May I help you?"

"Yes. My name is Joyce Porter. I'm the clinical director of the IVF Center. I'd like to make an appointment with Director Beck."

"I'm sorry. Mr. Beck is out for the next two weeks. What do you need? Perhaps I can assist you or direct you to another staff member."

"Who's in charge when Mr. Beck is away?"

The young man looked puzzled. "Why do you ask?"

Joyce's mind was spinning. She didn't want to wait two weeks, but she also didn't want to speak with anyone other than the director about such a sensitive matter. She needed someone she could rely on to keep the information private, talk through the situation and outline options.

"I have a confidential *time-sensitive* matter to discuss," she said.

"Does it involve an employee?"

Joyce hesitated before replying, "Yes."

"If it is a personnel matter, I suggest Janessa Bridges. She handles employee relations."

"Is she an attorney?"

The young man widened his eyes, opening and closing his

mouth several times before asking, "Why do you need an attorney?"

Joyce immediately regretted her word choice as well as coming in person to make the appointment. She debated whether to leave and simply call back or send an email request.

Ignoring his query, she replied, "As the clinic director, I need to speak with a senior staff member. I'm sure you understand."

"I see," he said, although his facial expression told a different story. "Janessa is your best option. Let me check her schedule." He clicked a few keys then frowned. "Oh dear. It looks like she doesn't have any appointment openings until next Friday."

Joyce pursed her lips, ready to argue, before saying, "Fine. What time?"

"How about one p.m.?"

Joyce tapped the appointment into her phone's calendar. "I'll be here. Thanks."

She looked at her phone as she traversed the gloomy hall and noticed she still had half an hour before her first patient. She climbed the stairs and entered the spacious lobby. It reeked of old money and power and was designed to impress. The marble floors were buffed to a sheen. Neoclassic columns rose to a domed ceiling decorated with an elaborately carved frieze. A pretentious sign with gold writing graced oversized wooden double doors on the far side and read *Office of the President.*

On a whim, Joyce walked over to the doors. *Stand tall,* she told herself as she squared her shoulders and tugged on the massive handle. The door felt like it weighed as much as she did, but it swung open easily. She half expected a gong to sound and a liveried butler in a white wig to appear. Instead, a middle-aged woman with an elaborate backcombed beehive of dark hair and too much eye shadow greeted her with a pleasant smile. She was seated at a desk in the corner of the anteroom. The name plate on the desk read, *Jill Hartwood, Executive Assistant to the President.*

"Good morning. May I help you?"

"Hello, I'm Dr. Joyce Porter. I'm the director of the IVF clinic. Is it possible to make an appointment to see President Cobain?"

"May I ask why you wish to meet with him?" The woman smiled pleasantly, but it was clear no one gained admittance to the inner sanctum without her permission. The awkward exchange with the HR receptionist still fresh in her mind, Joyce decided some discretion was in order.

"I just returned from a national conference where I presented McArthur's data on pregnancy rates in couples sponsored for treatment by the Foundation. It was very well received. Since President Cobain's support was vital in securing the funding, I wanted to personally thank him and discuss our program's results."

Joyce could tell from the woman's expression that her request was unlikely to make the cut for an in-person audience with the Big Man, but Jill Hartwood's smile remained cordial. "President Cobain is meeting with some donors today, and he's out of the office several days next week. Perhaps you could simply write a short thank-you note. Email it to this office, and I'll see he receives it."

Realizing her request for an in-person meeting was being denied in a none too subtle fashion, Joyce acquiesced. "That sounds like a good suggestion. Thank you for your time."

Back in the grandiose lobby, Joyce battled irritation. Today was turning into a bust. Now that she'd decided to act, she felt frustrated at the roadblocks and delays. She dragged out her phone, opened the staff directory and scrolled through until she found the office number for Mary Frances Welch. She hit *dial*. Maybe the Vice President and Director for Quality Affairs would be available.

"Hello, Office of Quality Affairs," a pleasant female voice chirped.

"Good morning. I'm Dr. Joyce Porter, and I'm the director of McArthur's IVF Clinic. I'm wondering if I could make an appointment to speak with Ms. Welch."

"She had a cancellation this afternoon at two. Can you come then?"

Joyce sighed, "Sorry, no. I have patients scheduled all afternoon."

"I see. How about eleven Monday morning?"

"I could make that work."

"May I inquire about the subject?"

Joyce thought quickly. "I'd like to get her opinion on some quality metrics we're following in our clinic."

"Very good. Do you have any info for her to review ahead of your meeting?"

"No. I'll bring everything with me."

"Very good. See you on Monday."

The phone went silent, and Joyce dropped it back into her purse. For the first time in several days, she felt a glimmer of hope. If she could find an ally, she might have a chance at calling Hicks's bluff.

CHAPTER 26

Saturday morning, Bill and Joyce sat at the small table in her kitchen cradling tall mugs of strong coffee and reading the morning news on their tablets. The clock read nine but it felt much later. Joyce absently pushed crumbs which had fallen from her toast into a small pile next to her plate. A single yellow rose, a gift from Bill reminiscent of their first date, nestled in a crystal bud vase. The previous evening, by mutual agreement, they hadn't discussed the conference or any of the week's events.

Bill had been surprisingly quiet since arriving, and she wondered if he was giving her space or holding back anger. Usually she could tell, but this morning his inscrutable expression only served to deepen her unease. Most Friday nights, after they'd been apart for the week, he wanted to make love immediately before settling into sleep. But last night when she'd turned to him, he'd gently rolled her over, gathered her next to his warm body in a spooning position, and murmured, "It's been a tough week. Let's just sleep."

Pushing her plate away, she captured his hand. He looked a bit surprised, then gave hers a gentle squeeze. They both knew it was time to address the elephant in the room and closed their tablets.

"I'm not sure where to start," she said quietly. "I know you have lots of questions, but it may be easier if you let me tell you the whole story before asking them."

"Fair enough," he said.

She withdrew her hand, stood up, and retrieved her phone from the nearby charging station.

"What are you doing?" he asked. She ignored his question and returned to the table, setting the phone between them.

"Let's start with what happened the night of the Ovatech reception. You already know some of it. I'm still not sure really about the details, but it felt like I'd been drugged. I had trouble concentrating and felt disconnected from my body. I've never felt like that before. Ever. On top of the weird feeling, I was dizzy and unsteady on my feet. Hicks was helping me back to my room when Sally saw us."

Bill's jaw tightened.

She rushed to continue, "She told Hicks in no uncertain terms that she would take me to my room and make sure I was okay. He handed her my purse and went on his way. That's when he took my room key."

"What?" Bill exclaimed, no longer able to remain silent. "You *think* you might have been drugged? *And* your sleazy boss took your room key? Why didn't you go to the nearest hospital—get evaluated? Or the police?" His face turned red. "Oh God, did anything else happen?"

Joyce held up her hand, hoping to stave off his ire. She feared he was going to lose it, and she was just getting started. "Please let me continue. I know you're upset . . ."

"Damn right I'm upset," he shouted, then his eyes narrowed. "How do you know he took your room key?"

"Because when I returned from dinner the next night, he was in my room."

Bill looked ready to explode, a vessel pulsing in his temple. Then his face relaxed and a look of understanding dawned.

"Was that the snippet of conversation I overheard when you told someone to leave?"

"Yes. I slipped the phone into my purse when I opened the door. It must have disconnected when I dropped the purse on the desk."

"I tried to call back, but you didn't answer. That's when I called security. Why on earth was Hicks there?"

Joyce handed him her phone. "I think it would be easiest if you listen to this. I used the app you loaded for me last weekend. I'm so glad we practiced. Some of it's a little faint, but it caught most of the conversation. See what you think."

Bill pressed *Play* and Joyce's recorded voice floated into the room. It sounded a bit muffled, and once or twice, Hicks's voice faded out, but the tone and the intent of the conversation were clear.

Several times during the next few minutes, Bill balled his fist on the table and looked like he wanted to punch something. Joyce found listening to the recording more traumatic than living through it the first time. That night she'd been protected by a haze of disbelief and a surge of adrenalin, but hearing the disembodied voices, one of which was her own, and seeing Bill's reaction, she knew it was useless to continue pretending the situation wasn't as bad as she'd imagined. It was worse, far worse. Listening to the recording stiffened her resolve to report his vile behavior, even if it meant losing her job. Her stomach in knots, she wondered what else she'd lose. Her career? Her marriage? She struggled to remain present and silently said a quick prayer.

Bill listened twice more, then sat back rubbing his temples. Joyce eyed him warily. Finally, he growled, "You are so. Damn. Lucky. That nothing happened! That night or the night before! That man is pure evil."

"I know," she agreed emphatically. "At first, I thought he was just a 'good old boy' hitting on the new hire, but it's worse. I think he's been doing this for years, and no one has been willing to call him out."

"He's not only pressuring you to have sex, he's threatening your reputation and your career!"

"I know. I know," she said again. "And I've been thinking about that. I'm not sure when this all shakes out that I'll be able to stay at McArthur."

Bill shook his head. "Don't get ahead of yourself. If anyone has to leave, it should be that dirtbag." Pointing to the phone he asked, "Are you taking this to HR?"

"Yes. The recording and the hotel's report." She handed him a manila envelope.

He removed Hebert's five-page typed report and studied it intently. It contained detailed information beginning with Bill's phone call to hotel security, notes from Hebert's interview with Joyce, the brief interview with Hicks, and information gleaned from the security camera's recordings. Hebert had run a background check on Hicks, which turned up blank. The report was very formal and contained a final paragraph stating, *Dr. Porter declined to report the incident to the police* and *All documentation, including security footage, will be retained for a minimum of six months.*

She grew restless watching him read and made another pot of coffee. While it was brewing, she contemplated eating something sweet and placed a mound of chocolate chip cookies on a small plate. She brought the cookies to the table, then returned with the pot and refilled their mugs.

He finally looked up, took a sip of coffee, then reached for a cookie. The silence was killing her.

"What are you thinking?" she finally asked.

He slowly chewed, then took another sip of coffee. "It's very factual and complete. Didn't you tell me he was a retired detective?"

"Yes, from New Orleans."

"It sounds like he did all he could do."

"I agree."

Bill looked troubled. "Then why didn't you follow his advice and file a police report?"

"Because I couldn't prove anything."

"Hicks was in your room, uninvited, when you came back from dinner! The hotel's security tapes confirmed it. Also, Hebert and the night manager saw him leave your room."

"I know, but nothing was taken."

"Joyce, he threatened you if you didn't go along with his *quid pro quo*! He harassed you *and* he questioned your academic integrity."

"Yes, but how would going to the police have helped? What was I supposed to do, have him arrested for being a sicko creep?"

Stubbornly, he continued to argue his point. "Going to the police would have established a written record and put him on notice that you weren't going to put up with his crap."

A quiet fury began to take hold. What she needed from her husband right now was unconditional support and a hug, and he wanted to nitpick the facts and question her decisions.

"That's your opinion," she said through clenched teeth, "but you weren't there."

"That's right, I wasn't," he bellowed, "and you deliberately kept most of this from me until now. You shut me out. How do you expect me to help if you insist on keeping me at arm's length?"

"You've kept me at arm's length since you arrived last night." She felt tears beginning to form.

"What's that supposed to mean?" he asked, genuinely confused.

"No conversation, no lovemaking, no anything!" She grabbed a Kleenex as tears welled up and spilled down her cheeks. "Last night, you were more affectionate to the cat. I hate it when you go all silent. It makes me feel . . ."

She stopped and swiped at her tears, feeling unloved, abandoned, and utterly alone. And if she was reduced to tears from Bill's questions, which weren't all that unreasonable, how was she going to get through the next few weeks? Suddenly her resolve to confront Hicks wobbled, then almost disappeared. Maybe Sally was right—she should let it go. Or maybe she should resign and start looking for another job. The bow-tied man from Oregon had told her his department was recruiting. That made her cry even harder. She and Bill were struggling with living two hours apart, and she feared they'd never make it separated by two thousand miles.

Bill looked worried as Joyce continued to quietly sob. He handed her a tissue, then got up and returned with a glass of water. He sat down and picked up her hand, lightly rubbing his thumb across her knuckles. After five minutes, she wiped her eyes and nose and finally looked up.

"Do you feel better?" he asked gently.

She tried to smile and ended up having to blow her nose again. "Not really. Now my eyes sting and my nose is running. I'm sorry I lost it. It's been a terrible week."

"Let's start over."

"Oh no, I don't want to—"

"I want to do my part differently."

She looked uncertain as he stood and raised her to her feet. He kissed her gently on the lips and pulled her into a warm embrace, cradling her head against his chest. They stood there for a moment breathing quietly as he gently stroked her back.

He cleared his throat and said gruffly, "I want to begin by saying that you are my wife and I love you, and I'm so sorry this is happening. The whole thing sucks, and you don't deserve any of it. You work hard and would never do anything to compromise the care of your patients. Your boss is a monster, and he deserves to be punished. And I'd like to punch him in the nose."

That made her smile, as she couldn't imagine easygoing Bill ever punching anyone. Feeling a little better, she extricated herself from his arms, and they both settled back on their chairs.

"You shouldn't feel pressured into reporting him," he continued. "Whatever you decide, I'll support you. One hundred percent. I'm sorry I acted like such a jerk."

"I might lose my job."

"Okay, then you'll find another one."

"What if no other IVF program will hire me?"

"Then we'll think of something else."

"I could end up being investigated, or worse, end up being hounded by the media if any of this gets out." That thought genuinely scared her. She didn't want to end up on the evening news. She always felt sorry for the poor souls who stepped out of their car and were swarmed by shouting media hounds carrying microphones and flashing cameras looking for the latest salacious story.

He chuckled. "Maybe, but probably not. Why don't you take one thing at a time? Who are you seeing on Monday?"

"Mary Frances Welch. She's the VP for Quality Affairs. I met her once at a reception. She's a no-nonsense type who's well respected. She's been at McArthur a long time. I think I can trust her to give me good advice."

"How much are you going to tell her?"

"I'm not sure. Maybe I'll share the most recent part about the conference. Oh, and one other thing. Sally agreed to submit a statement describing how Hicks pressured her into having sex a few years ago."

Bill looked surprised then nodded. "Was she the source when you told me about Hicks's pattern with female employees?"

"Yes, but you can't tell anyone. She wants to remain anonymous."

"What about looking into the donor situation? That's such an odd threat. What if something fishy is going on and Hicks wants to pin it on you?"

"We've got that covered. Sally thinks she can get a copy of the donor list. We'll also talk to the lab tech and see if he knows anything. Dominique might be able to help with that."

At the mention of Dominique's name, Bill's eyes turned cool, and he leaned his chair back slightly. Joyce blushed and felt guilty as she remembered her fantasies from the previous week. She took a deep breath and rushed to get the conversation back on track. "I should know more by the time I meet with HR on Friday."

"How is Dominique involved in any of this?" he asked in a voice tinged with jealousy.

Joyce shifted slightly in her seat. "He came to me a few weeks ago and asked about an A list. He'd spent a weekend working in the lab and wondered why so many of our couples undergoing IVF had eggs inseminated with donor sperm. But the day we went to talk to Richard, the lab tech Dominique worked with that weekend, he was out."

"Okay."

"Since I didn't know about a list, I asked Sally, but she didn't know anything either. She said she remembered a printed report when she first started at McArthur that tracked couples in cycle and other things the weekend doc might need to know, but she hadn't seen anything like that recently."

"As I said, I'm not going to tell you how to handle this, but you might want to limit the number of people involved. Dominique is an outsider who is only here *temporarily*." He emphasized the last sentence.

Joyce nodded. "I agree. The fewer people involved, the better. He's the one who brought up questions about our use of donor sperm, so in a way, he's already involved."

Bill opened his mouth to speak, then paused. Eventually he said, "I meant what I said before. I'm sorry you're in this mess, and I'll support you any way I can. But I can't help if you keep things from me."

She felt a rush of relief when he didn't continue to press her with questions about Dominique. "Thank you for listening today," she said. "I feel better. I didn't want to keep things from you, but I felt overwhelmed and couldn't go into all of it over the phone last week. I'll definitely let you know how my meeting with Mary Frances goes."

She looked outside and noticed the clear blue sky. "Let's go for a walk. I think we could both use some fresh air. You mentioned something about a possible project in Peru. I'd like to hear more."

"I have a better idea," he said, pulling her into an embrace and nuzzling her neck. "I'd like to make it up to you since you felt ignored last night. How about a redo, all the things we didn't do last night?"

They kissed deeply, and Joyce murmured, "An excellent idea."

An hour later, Bill asked teasingly, "Are you still up for that walk?"

"Absolutely," she said, standing up to stretch. "A walk sounds great."

They quickly dressed and headed down the street toward a nearby park that had several walking trails. They held hands as they ambled in companionable silence. Finally, Joyce said, "Tell me about the project in Peru."

"Are you sure you want to talk about Peru now?"

"I think we should. You mentioned it on the phone last week, but you didn't sound as enthusiastic as normal."

He laughed. "Who wouldn't want to go to the Amazon jungle during the rainy season?"

"But you're always Mr. Gung-ho. The rougher the environment, the better you like it. A rainy Amazon jungle sounds like it's right up your alley."

He stopped walking and said, "You're right, but it's not appealing like it used to be."

"Okay, now you're starting to worry me," she joked. "Who are you, and what did you do with my husband?"

"I feel like maybe now isn't a good time."

You've got that right, she thought to herself. Out loud she said, "Tell me about the project."

CHAPTER 27

It was a few minutes past eleven when Joyce stepped into the outer office of Vice President Mary Frances Welch. She was a little winded from her race-walk from the clinic. She clutched a legal pad and a manila folder containing a copy of Hebert's report. Her cell phone with its muffled recording of the conversation with Hicks rested in her blazer pocket. She hadn't decided whether to share it or not.

The administrative assistant looked up from her typing and gazed pointedly at the wall clock, which read 11:04.

She smiled weakly. "Good morning. I'm sorry I'm late. I got ambushed by a medical student."

"Please come in. Ms. Welch is ready for you," the assistant said with a curt nod. She rose and knocked twice on the inner office door, opened it and announced, "Your eleven o'clock is here. And the noon Cabinet meeting is in Admin conference 1." She gestured for Joyce to enter, then shut the door.

An attractive woman in her mid-fifties rose and extended her hand in greeting. Mary Frances Welch was tall with auburn hair containing liberal streaks of gray. Her face had smile lines and crinkles around the eyes like she'd spent a lot of time in the sun. Her attire was understated business professional except for an exquisite silver necklace studded with large turquoise stones.

"Hello, Dr. Porter. I believe we've met once before at a university function. It's nice to see you."

Joyce shifted the tablet and folder to her opposite arm and took the proffered hand, conscious that her own fingers were like blocks of ice. "Thank you for seeing me today."

Mary Frances gestured toward a round conference table. "Please sit down. Would you like some coffee or water?"

"No, thank you," Joyce fibbed, even though her mouth felt dry as cotton.

"I'm very interested to learn more about the IVF clinic. Since you've become director, the patient satisfaction scores have been excellent." Mary Frances pointed to the folder on the table. "I understand you have some quality metrics you'd like to discuss."

Joyce felt her heart pound and took a deep breath before diving in. "I do, but that's not why I'm here today."

Mary Frances looked puzzled. "Was the note on my schedule incorrect?"

Joyce shook her head. "At some point, I'd like to discuss our pregnancy rate data, but today I'm here to ask your advice on a personal matter."

Mary Frances sat back with a wary expression. "Go on."

Joyce leaned slightly forward, then began. "Since I came to McArthur, Dr. Hicks has taken an interest in my career. At first, I felt flattered. Over the past few years, he's overseen my research publications and helped me secure spots on speaker's panels and invitations to conference events. This year, he asked me to accompany him to conferences in Paris and New Orleans. I wasn't able to go to Paris, but I presented a paper at the American Society in New Orleans last week."

Mary Frances gazed at her steadily. Joyce swallowed and wished she'd asked for the glass of water.

"On Monday evening, one of the drug companies sponsored

a reception and Dr. Hicks invited me to accompany him. He said he wanted to introduce me to some of his colleagues."

Joyce felt beads of sweat break out under her arms and her foot began to jiggle. She uncrossed her legs and put both feet on the floor. "While I was at the event, I suddenly became quite ill, and Dr. Hicks offered to help me back to my room." Her voice became strained. "I don't remember much else, so I think it would be best if you read the report from the hotel's security officer before we continue." She flipped open the folder and pushed the pages across the table.

"I need my glasses," said Mary Frances. Before retrieving them from the nearby desk, she detoured to a small refrigerator and removed a bottle of water. She handed it to Joyce who immediately removed the cap and gratefully took several swallows. Mary Frances reseated herself, settled her glasses, and began reading.

Joyce slowly sipped the water and tried not to squirm. She looked at the clock and noticed it was half past the hour.

Eventually, Mary Frances removed her glasses and looked up. "This is a very detailed report. Is there anything else?"

Joyce's face felt hot but her hands were cold and clammy. *Decision time, to share or not share.* Slowly, she fished the phone from her pocket. "I'd like you to listen to a conversation. It's from the following night. I came back from dinner and discovered Dr. Hicks in my room."

Joyce hit *Play*, and Mary Francis listened, her face devoid of expression.

After the recording ended, Mary Frances toyed with her glasses. "Is Dr. Hicks aware you made this recording?"

"I don't think so."

"Have you spoken to HR?"

"I have an appointment this Friday. The director is out for two weeks, so I'm meeting with someone else."

Mary Francis brushed a miniscule piece of lint from her sleeve. She had on what Bill called "the administrator game face." "This is very serious," Mary Frances said with a small frown. "What would you like me to do?"

Joyce wasn't sure what reaction she'd expected, but this wasn't it. *Why was Mary Frances asking her what to do? Didn't she know? Of course she knew. Was it going to turn out as Sally had predicted, the institution closing ranks to protect their own?*

For a moment, she thought she might be sick. She took a deep breath. *Stand tall*, she told herself.

Sitting up straighter, she said, "I'm here for advice. We both know the university's policies about harassment. We've been to the same trainings. But we also know these situations don't usually turn out so well when a young nobody takes on a powerful university leader."

Mary Frances gazed at Joyce intently. With an almost imperceptible nod, she seemed to change gears. "You're right. As administrators, we both know the policies. Since you've obviously thought carefully about this, what do *you* think should happen?"

Joyce had rehearsed her answer to this question many times. But now those answers seemed inadequate, and she struggled to articulate her thoughts. She didn't want to sound whiney or appear like a helpless victim.

"I want him to stop using his position to prey upon women like me. We all depend on him for mentoring and guidance. Everyone who's anyone in our field knows Dr. Hicks. In the beginning, he came across as supportive, and I welcomed his help. But once I made it clear that I wasn't interested in anything other than a professional relationship, he began threatening me and questioning my work. On more than one occasion, he's told me my career will stall out if I don't have his support."

"I see. Ah, this *interest*, has it been going on for a while?"

"Unfortunately, yes. I didn't really see it, but it probably started right when I arrived two years ago."

"What's he talking about when he mentions donor sperm and high pregnancy rates in a study?"

"I'm not sure. A couple of weeks ago, Dr. DuPage, a visiting professor, asked me about our program's use of donor sperm augmentation for couples with certain types of infertility. I told him I thought it wasn't very common or different from other programs."

"Have you looked into it?" Mary Frances said. "I'm asking because as the Director of Quality Matters, I might be able to help with something like that."

"I've tried. The lab director is pretty closed-mouthed and the assistant who spoke to Dr. DuPage wasn't around when we went back to talk to him."

"And you're sure that none of your study participants used donor sperm?"

"Absolutely. I counseled all of them and supervised their cycles. None of them requested or consented to use of a donor."

"But is it possible that a donor was used without your knowledge? Maybe something changed at the last minute?"

"I guess it's possible. But we have pretty strict procedures and a rigorous informed consent process."

A knock sounded on the door and the assistant peeked in. "Your meeting starts in five minutes."

"Thanks," Mary Frances said. "Please call and tell them I'm running late." She turned and faced Joyce. "You requested my advice, and here it is. I admire your courage in coming forward and absolutely agree that HR should be made aware. But you must know if you file a complaint, it won't be easy. Dr. Hicks has many friends in high places. Your department brings in a lot of funding, and most folks credit that to Hicks. Additionally, the IVF program is one of the few patient care areas at McArthur that isn't in the red. If it turns out something is amiss, the fallout will be huge."

Joyce felt her shoulders slump. "Are you saying I should just let things go?" she asked in a faint voice.

"Not at all. I merely want you to understand that it's not going to be easy. I'll help as best I can. If you uncover anything at all that points to improper use of donor sperm, let me know right away and I'll begin an investigation."

Now Joyce felt frightened. "But that's what Hicks threatened to do! And he said I'd be placed on administrative leave."

"Not necessarily, especially if you're the one who comes forward with concerning evidence."

"What do you think I should tell HR?"

"Exactly what you told me. And might I ask, is Dr. Cohen somehow involved? Hicks mentioned her."

Joyce hesitated then said, "I don't feel comfortable discussing her situation, but it is possible at least two other women might be willing to share stories similar to mine."

"Oh dear God. That makes it worse!" Mary Frances quickly added, "Sorry. Please forgive me. I didn't mean your situation isn't serious. I meant that perhaps it's been an ongoing issue for others who haven't had your courage."

"I agree, and I think it probably *is* something that's been going on for a while."

"I need some time to think. Is it possible for us to speak again tomorrow?"

"It's my clinic day, so not much unscheduled time."

Mary Frances took a business card and scribbled on the back. "Here's my mobile number. Call me when you have a free moment, even if it's after hours."

As both women rose, Mary Frances put a hand lightly on Joyce's arm. "Are you okay? You're dealing with a lot right now. Do you have some support?"

Unexpectedly, tears welled up and Joyce felt a rush of gratitude that this woman got it. She understood her dilemma and was on her side. "Yes, thank you. I have a good support system."

After Joyce left, Mary Frances picked up the phone. She listened to the recorded message and left a voicemail, "Hi Warren. It's Mary Frances. I'm sorry to bother you on your vacation, but we have a huge problem. Please call me as soon as you get this message."

Joyce stopped by the lobby's coffee shop and grabbed a ready-made salad and a cookie. She wasn't really hungry but knew she'd be ravenous later if she didn't eat something. Her phone pinged and she saw a text from Sally: *Meet in my office ASAP*

On my way, she texted back.

Sally's door was open, and she waved Joyce in. "Shut the door," she said.

Joyce sat down and asked expectantly, "What's up?"

"I talked to Richard and got the name and phone number of the grad student. I called her and luckily she answered."

"Well?"

"Hicks did come onto her, and that's why she left. I won't go into all the details, but she finally got so uncomfortable with him constantly dropping by and his innuendos that she transferred. She's still in the program, but she's at a different campus."

"Did she tell anyone?"

"Her advisor." Sally said grimly, "And he recommended she switch labs and not talk about it."

Both women shook their heads, disgusted at the lame advice.

"Is she willing to talk to HR?" Joyce asked.

"Maybe. Her thesis is almost done, and she doesn't want to jeopardize her degree, but she's willing to write a statement *if* she can remain anonymous."

Joyce blew out a sigh. "Well, I guess that's something. I don't know how this stuff works, but I'll ask when I talk to HR on Friday. I'll tell them there are two other women at the Institute who have also been harassed but want to remain anonymous."

Sally looked at her watch. "Gotta go. Oh, I also asked Richard about the donor list. He's going to get it for me. I think we'll have better luck getting information about the other stuff if Dominique talks to him. It won't seem so suspicious."

"About that," Joyce said. "When Bill and I talked this week-end, he was concerned about involving Dominique. He pointed out that since he's a visiting professor, he probably shouldn't be privy to confidential university matters."

"What do you think?"

"That he'd be helpful."

"Do you trust him to keep it quiet?"

"Ah . . ." She hesitated, remembering her late-night trip to his hotel room, her tearful meltdown, and what had almost happened. "I think so."

"Then do it. Hey, how'd the meeting with Welch go?"

"Pretty well. I showed her the report and also played a recording from the night Hicks was in my room."

"What?" Sally exclaimed. "You didn't tell me you had a recording!"

"I know. I did it on my phone, but I was too wigged out to even listen to it until I got back. And I wasn't certain how much of our actual conversation it captured. But Bill and I played it on Saturday. It's muffled, but you can tell it's his voice."

"What did she say? Is she going to help?"

"I think she wants to help. She knows I have an appointment with HR, and she seemed shocked to learn he's been harassing other employees."

"You didn't tell her about me, did you?" Sally said quickly.

"No," Joyce said, deliberately omitting the fact that Mary Frances had specifically asked about her. "And she said if we get any type of evidence that donor sperm is being used improperly, she'll initiate an investigation."

"I'm glad you think she's on our side, because the minute Hicks gets wind of any of this, it's going to be Stress City around here."

"Yep."

"So, are you going to talk to Dominique?"

"Maybe. I think he'll help, but I don't want to put him in a tough spot. He's our guest, and he might be uncomfortable snooping around."

"Well, if it were me, I'd ask. He can always say no. Since he brought the question up in the first place, I'd think he'd want an answer."

At the end of the day, Joyce found Dominique in his temporary office. His back was to her as he rummaged through his messenger bag. She said hello.

"*Bonjour*," he replied, turning toward her.

"Do you have a second?"

"For you, always," he said gallantly.

Joyce felt her cheeks blush. "About that . . . night at the conference . . ."

"Joyce, please stop. We don't have to discuss it again. You were upset and I was happy to help. I hope you think of me as your friend, someone who can be trusted."

"I do. I want to apologize again for any behavior on my part that . . ." She stopped and felt the blush spread down her neck. "That might have seemed inappropriate."

He remembered her frantic phone call and nocturnal visit to his room. As much as he'd wanted to sweep her into his arms and make her forget the terror of the evening, he'd realized she was vulnerable and not in a place to consent to anything.

He stifled his regret at what might have been, then flashed his killer smile and the dimple appeared. "No Frenchman will ever turn away a damsel in distress, especially one as courageous as you."

"Well, that's good to know, because I could use some more help. This is a little awkward, and you can always say no. I don't want to put you in another uncomfortable position.

He looked intrigued, then nodded for her to continue.

"Remember that A list you asked me about?"

"Of course. Have you discovered something?"

"Not yet, but I'm wondering if something is going on since Hicks brought it up when he was threatening me. He said if he launched an investigation into my study, he might find that donor sperm samples are missing and that was why the pregnancy rate was so high."

"That's absurd. You don't have anything to do with the insemination process."

"I know, but it made me wonder if something is going on in the lab. I think we should talk to Richard."

He nodded.

"I wonder if you'd be willing to do it. If I start asking questions, it might get back to Hicks."

"What exactly do you want to know?"

"I want to see the A list. Sally remembers something similar when she first started at McArthur, but she hasn't seen one in years. If we can get a recent copy, I can check patient records and see if there's any indication of a discussion about use of donors. Sally talked to Richard and is getting a list of donors. And somehow, we need to get into that freezer and see if there are any 'missing' vials."

"Hmm." He ran his hand across his chin. "Of course I want to help, but I'm not sure it's my business. If something is going on, it would be awkward for me to be associated."

She nodded, feeling both disappointed and relieved. "I understand, but I thought I'd ask."

"Let me think about it. I want to help, just not in such a direct way."

"I know. One other favor then. Please don't tell anyone about our conversation today, or especially what I told you last week."

"You can count on me," he said with a slight bow. "A Frenchman is always discreet."

CHAPTER 28

Evie and Leon sat on the couch together enjoying a quiet Sunday evening. She hadn't had any bleeding for two weeks, and the morning sickness was manageable. The pregnancy had passed the three-month mark, and both babies were doing well. They celebrated by ordering a pizza and watching a rom-com. She wore loose sports pants and one of Leon's T-shirts because she'd gained five pounds and could no longer button her jeans. Although her sister had sent two cute maternity tops and a dress she'd found at an online sale, Evie wasn't quite ready to wear something "maternity." She figured she'd save the fancy clothing for the big family Thanksgiving dinner.

Leon's phone buzzed, and he opened a message. After reading for several minutes, he looked up, his face creased with a deep frown.

"What's wrong?" she asked.

"It's a text from my mom with a pregnancy-related news story link."

"Not another one! I wish she'd stop sending those articles. My OB has already hammered home all the risks associated with twin pregnancy."

'This article is different. It's about an IVF clinic in California where there was a lab mix up. Some embryos got switched and put into the wrong moms."

"What? That can't be right," she said, her voice rising in horror.

"It says that two couples went to the same IVF clinic and got pregnant the same week. One of the couples was Asian, and they had a red-haired baby who didn't look like either parent. Then the second couple delivered, and they had a baby with dark hair and . . ." he paused to read from his phone, ". . . half-moon shaped eyes with 'prominent epicanthal folds.' I don't even know what that means, do you? Anyway, the article describes the medical detective work, and after almost three months, the couples were told they had the wrong babies. Now they're suing the doctors and that clinic."

"That sounds awful. Those poor parents. Can you imagine taking care of your baby for all those months and then having to give him or her to complete strangers?"

"Nope," said Leon. "And even harder, seeing your real baby for the first time, and they're already three months old. You would have missed showing them their nursery and their first smile. You wouldn't understand their facial expressions or what calmed them down when they cried."

"And what about the babies? Will they think their parents have abandoned them to strangers? They could be traumatized for life. It's too terrible to even think about." Evie shuddered and protectively patted her baby mound.

"I hope that clinic gets shut down," he said, slapping his fist into his palm for emphasis.

"Me too. What if it happened to the clinic's other couples? Do you think they'll have to test all the babies—to see if they are with the right parents?"

"I don't want to even think about it," he said. "And I really wish my mother hadn't sent that stupid article. Now I'm going to have nightmares about taking the wrong babies home from the hospital."

"That won't happen," she said, taking his hand. "Dr. Porter is very careful, and don't you think we'll recognize our babies?"

"Of course we will. I hope they get your nose and not my big schnozz," he joked. He reached over and stroked her soft curls, "And your hair's a lot nicer than mine."

"Our babies are going to be beautiful no matter what! So stop worrying and get us some ice cream. I think we'd like butter pecan tonight."

The clock on the president's desk read seven a.m. Mary Frances Welch, HR Director Warren Beck and President Jackson Cobain greeted each other with forced smiles and no attempt at small talk. The mood was somber.

Cobain cleared his throat. "Thank you for coming in so early. This is a hell of a way to start out the week, but we have lots to discuss, so let's get to it. Mary Frances, please begin. I've asked the university's attorney, Kirsten Clarke, to join us. She'll be calling in shortly. It's three hours earlier on the West Coast, so she may be a little late."

Mary Frances opened a folder, removed some papers, and placed them before the president. She handed an identical set to Beck.

"I've assembled some information about potential irregular insemination practices in the IVF program," she said, gesturing toward the stack of papers. "The first page of my report lists the preliminary details of what we know so far."

President Cobain flapped his hand impatiently for her to speed up.

Mary Frances pretended not to notice and continued, "A week ago, Dr. Joyce Porter, the clinic's medical director, came to me about a different matter." She glanced at the HR director, who shook his head slightly.

She continued, "In the course of our conversation, she mentioned a possible misuse of donor sperm. She'd recently presented her data at a meeting in New Orleans. Afterward, privately, Dr. Hicks questioned her program's higher-than-expected pregnancy rates and implied she was illicitly using donor sperm. Dr. Porter denied this and said she had personally counseled and supervised every couple in the study and no donors were authorized. Later that week, she provided me with a copy of a so-called 'A list.' It's an off-the-books list given weekly to the lab techs showing which IVF couples are using donor sperm for insemination."

She flipped to the last page and pointed to an image of the list.

"Dr. Porter reviewed the medical records of all the women on the list and found that two identified as needing donor insemination did not have proper consent forms, nor was there a record of any discussion about use of donors with the couple."

Both men looked alarmed. "Has this already taken place?"

"No, thank heaven. The list is for IVF retrievals scheduled this week, but without further investigation, we have no way of knowing if this is an aberration or an ongoing issue. A big question is whether this plays any part in the outstanding pregnancy success rates McArthur boasts, especially with male-factor clients. I think we need to consider pausing the program for a time to launch a full investigation."

The president pinched his lips together before annoyance turned to anger. "I have a hard time believing this is happening in Owen's program. It must be some kind of documentation error, which is concerning but not the end of the world." His voice became antagonistic as he turned his ire toward Mary Frances. "And no one is shutting down any program!"

He stood up and paced the room. "I've known Owen for a

long time, and he has a sterling reputation! I brought him specifically to this university to start what has been and will continue to be an outstanding program. People come from all over the world for treatment *and* to study with his team. Let's call him and hear what he has to say. Surely if there was a problem, he'd be aware of it. And if he brought it up with Dr. Porter, then perhaps he has some suspicions about her. This can't get out! This program is too important. We've got to clear this up immediately."

He returned to his desk. "I'll get him on the phone, and we'll straighten this mess out."

The HR director, who'd remained silent during the previous exchange, put up his hand. "Ah, sir," he said, "please wait. There's something more to discuss before you make that call."

The desk phone chimed. The president snatched the receiver and lifted it to his ear, "Hello."

After a brief pause, he said, "Good morning. We've just started. Let me put you on speaker."

He turned to the group. "I've asked Kirsten Clarke, the university's attorney, to join us." He pushed a button and said, "Go ahead, Kirsten, you're on speaker. Our HR Director Warren Beck and our VP of Quality Mary Frances Welch are with me."

A woman's voice, faintly adenoidal, emerged from the phone. "Good morning. I'm sorry to be late. It's four a.m. here on the West coast. Dr. Cobain tells me there may be a problem with the IVF clinic."

Cobain nodded to Mary Frances, who quickly summarized the situation.

The group waited for the attorney to comment but heard nothing but a faint buzz.

"Kirsten, are you still with us?" Cobain asked in a loud voice.

"Yes, I'm here," said the attorney. "I'm trying to decide what to say. This situation is quite concerning, and I'd like to review the written report before giving a full opinion."

"I was telling the group I have complete confidence in Owen

Hicks," said Cobain heartily. "He and I have known each other for a long time. I can't believe anything unethical would be going on in his lab."

"If a donor insemination was performed without the patient's consent, it's beyond unethical. It's illegal," the attorney stated with a flat tone.

Everyone in the room winced.

"State laws vary, and the only national standards are some unenforceable professional guidelines, but 'insemination fraud' is a big deal. Much of the recent case law is around fertility doctors inseminating patients with their own sperm, which was more common than anyone thought back in the '70s and '80s when fresh semen was used and the world wasn't worried yet about HIV. It seems to fall through some existing gaps in both criminal and civil law because those women knew they were being inseminated. But using donor sperm, without proper informed consent, is much clearer. It can be classified as medical malpractice, misrepresenting a medical procedure, or even as a form of sexual assault. And depending on the charges, it can have civil penalties, criminal penalties, or both."

The three administrators stared at the phone in consternation.

"And furthermore," the attorney continued, her voice getting stronger, "if it's happened more than once, the university will have to inform every single couple who've ever become pregnant and potentially offer counseling and genetic testing to determine if the children are biologically related to their parents. There'll be a string of lawsuits, and the university will be on the hook for massive legal fees and compensation to victims. It could drag on for years."

President Cobain's face grew ashen. Eventually, he summoned the strength to speak. "What a nightmare! How much of this would the university be on the hook for? If one of the doctors or lab technicians is at fault, wouldn't it be on that individual?"

"Maybe. But aren't all the doctors and staff your employees?"

Cobain looked at Warren Beck, who affirmed, "Yes. Yes, they are."

"The university, as the employer, is the deep pocket. You need to contact your insurance carrier immediately."

Cobain looked at Mary Frances and Warren Beck who both nodded grimly. "Let's not assume the worst," he sighed. "Let's all take a pause before we get too far along this path. Do we really need to talk to our insurer right now, before we have any other proof?"

"I would say yes," the attorney replied. "Any discussions with them are confidential, and they will have ideas about investigations and patient notifications if that is necessary. If we get to that point, my office will also want to be involved to protect other university interests."

"Okay, we'll follow through on our end," Cobain said. "But for now, this stays contained to our group. I'm not at all convinced it isn't just some miscommunication or an isolated irregularity. Right before you called, we were getting ready to call Dr. Hicks. I'm sure he can address our concerns and clear this whole mess up."

"Ah, Dr. Cobain," Warren Beck interrupted. "As I said before, there is something else to discuss before calling Dr. Hicks."

Cobain looked pained. "What else, Beck? Make it quick. I have to be on the road soon for a meeting, and you know how beastly traffic is on a Monday."

Beck and Mary Frances exchanged glances, then Beck reached into his briefcase and took out a folder stamped *CONFIDENTIAL* in large red letters.

"This is about the personal matter Mary Frances referred to at the beginning of our meeting." He nodded to Mary Frances.

"The reason Dr. Porter came to see me originally had nothing to do with potential misuse of donor sperm," she said. "It had to do with harassing behavior toward her by Dr. Hicks."

"Good God!" Cobain blurted. "You've got to be kidding me. What is this, some kind of witch hunt?"

The attorney cut in. "Can you repeat that? I thought I heard something about a harassment complaint."

Beck consulted the file and summarized the original complaint, including the recorded conversation from Joyce's hotel room and the hotel's report. "Mary Frances and I have both spoken with Dr. Porter and reviewed the recording. We feel it's genuine. We also followed up with two other employees, both of whom wish to remain anonymous. They've submitted written statements alleging harassing behavior by Dr. Hicks that has taken place within the past three years. They didn't speak up sooner because they feared retaliation. Apparently, he has something of a reputation among female employees, but this is the first time it's been brought to our attention."

"Do you have a copy of the recording and those other employee statements?" asked the attorney in a no-nonsense voice. She sounded wide awake and in full-on containment mode.

"Yes," he replied, "I'll send you a written transcript of the hotel recording and copies of their statements when we're done with this call. Should I messenger them?"

"No, send them to our confidential electronic drop box." She rattled off advice in a rapid sequence. "Speaking as the university's attorney, you must communicate with Dr. Hicks today. He should be placed on administrative leave ASAP. You also need to have an attorney present at that meeting. Since I'm out of town, I'll call the office and arrange for one of my partners to stand in. And you must block all his access to the university's buildings, email, and records so he doesn't have any opportunity to change things. This is very important. Do it soon! And finally, you must complete your investigations into both matters as quickly as possible. Make certain there are no other previous complaints against Hicks and figure out how to solve the question about use of donor sperm. Do you feel you can trust Dr. Porter?"

Mary Frances spoke up. "Yes, I do. It took a lot of courage for her to come to me—both with her complaint about Dr. Hicks and her concerns about possible harm to her patients. I think it will be much easier to do a timely and thorough investigation if she is involved."

"Kirsten, do we have to close the IVF clinic?" Cobain asked with a baleful stare at Mary Frances. She gazed back unperturbed.

"That's your call. It really depends on the extent of the problem. How many patients are seen each week?"

"I'm not really sure," said Mary Frances. "But I can find out. And not all the patients who come to McArthur are referred for infertility. Some have other hormonal or surgical issues."

"How many patients each week actually have the in vitro procedure?"

Mary Frances hesitated before she spoke, "Again, I'm not sure of exact numbers, but I think it's around nine or so."

"Obviously, the university has to do everything in its power to prevent any possible harm. And from a patient's point of view, especially if they're already taking hormones and expecting to have IVF this month, there would be some harm to shutting everything down immediately. But if it were me, I'd look carefully at that list and make sure donor sperm is only used with documented consent. And someone is going to have to get into that lab and find out what's happening there and who's authorizing it."

A heavy silence descended.

"All right, folks," said Cobain. "We have a lot of work ahead of us. Kirsten, thanks for joining us. When did you say you were back?"

"At the end of the week. I'll update my partners and make sure you have someone immediately available this week."

"Thanks, we'll be in touch. Goodbye."

Cobain disconnected the call and looked at his watch. "Forget that DC meeting. Traffic will be terrible. Is there anything else you need from me?"

Mary Frances shook her head.

"No sir," said Beck. "But I do have a request. I know you are personal friends with Dr. Hicks, but it's important that you *not* reach out to him."

"I'd never do that!" blustered Cobain.

"Of course not, but I wouldn't be doing my job if I didn't remind you that we're dealing with two very sensitive matters here, both involving Hicks. We need to do everything by the book."

Cobain sat down heavily behind his desk and rubbed his chin. "Yes, yes. I know. It's just that I've known Owen for a long time, and I'm finding it hard to believe any of this. But you're right. I'll keep out of the way. I trust both of you to see that we protect our patients and our employees. Keep me updated. And let's meet this afternoon at four for a recap."

Owen Hicks exited the Starbucks drive-thru with a grande black coffee and a pumpkin scone, careful to protect the interior of his luxury sedan. As he drove toward the university, he brooded about the Joyce Porter situation. The brief interaction with the security officer at the New Orleans hotel over a week ago had unnerved him. He couldn't believe she'd turned him in to hotel security! He knew his story had been flimsy, but the man hadn't pushed much after his brief explanation about returning her room key. He figured since they'd been away from campus, and it was her word against his, he was probably safe from any university complaints. Oh, they might slap his wrist and make him do some type of sissy HR training if she said anything, but nothing else would come of it.

His phone vibrated. Pressing the answer button on the steering console, he said, "Hello."

"There's a problem. Where are you?" asked a familiar voice.

"In my car. About five minutes from campus. What's up?"

"Meet me at the food court on the first floor of the Whittier building."

"That's nowhere near campus!"

"Exactly. See you there."

"But why? What's the problem?"

No one answered. The caller had disconnected.

CHAPTER 29

It was late morning when Hicks entered his office. His lips were pinched, and he looked pale.

"Dr. Hicks, are you okay?" Esmeralda inquired.

"Fine," he muttered. "Any messages?"

"Yes, two. They're both from Warren Beck. He'd like to meet with you this afternoon around three in his office. You don't have anything else scheduled. Would you like me to call and confirm?"

"I may have something else at that time." At her puzzled look, he continued, "An off- campus appointment. I must have forgotten to put it on the calendar."

"Shall I mark you out for the whole afternoon? Or just from three p.m. on?"

"Fine," he said, striding into his office and closing the door with a resounding thud. He dropped his briefcase and massaged his temples, trying to stave off a migraine. His desk phone chimed. He let it ring so Esmeralda would answer. A minute later, a soft knock sounded, and her head popped in.

"It's Warren Beck. Again. Maybe you'd better talk to him. It sounds urgent."

Hicks sat down heavily in his chair and signaled for her to

shut the door. After a long minute, he picked up the phone and barked, "Hello."

"Dr. Hicks, Warren Beck here. Something's come up, and I need to speak with you today."

"Well, it will have to wait! I'm extremely busy and am off campus all afternoon. How about next week?"

"No sir. It can't wait. It's about a potentially serious issue in the IVF program, and our legal counsel feels we need to get on top of it. I'm sorry for the inconvenience, but is there any way you can reschedule your afternoon? We can meet earlier, or even at noon if that's more convenient."

"Why are *you* calling me?" Hicks asked suspiciously. "What's this about? And since when is IVF an HR issue?"

Beck didn't miss a beat. "The issue is very sensitive, and it involves employees."

"So tell me now and let's skip the afternoon meeting!" Hicks blustered. "Why do you HR folks make such a big deal of everything? Which employees? I'm not really responsible for direct supervision of anyone, you know."

"Dr. Hicks, I really can't say anything more over the phone. Will you be there at three?"

"Make it four," he snapped. "I'll see what I can do."

He hung up the desk phone. Paranoia kicked in, and he decided to use his mobile to contact his personal attorney. A pleasant female voice answered on the third ring, "Fanning, Saunders, and Associates. How may I direct your call?"

"This is Owen Hicks. I need to speak with Paul immediately."

"No problem, Dr. Hicks. I'll put you right through."

Hicks rocked back and forth in his chair and rubbed his forehead.

"This is Paul Saunders," said a man with a warm Southern drawl.

"Hello, Paul. Thanks for taking my call."

"Hey, old friend, I haven't seen you around the club lately. How've you been?"

"Not great, which is why I'm calling my attorney."

"Sorry to hear that. What's up?"

"Too much to go into on the phone. I've got one, or maybe two problems," he replied testily. "Are you free for lunch today?"

"I think so, let me check." While on hold, Hicks rummaged through his desk for a bottle of over-the-counter pain relievers. He'd left his prescription medication at home.

"Owen, are you still there?"

"I'm here."

"I can meet you at one. How about the Fireside Lounge at the club?"

"Sure."

"One question—is this business or personal?"

"Maybe both. We'll talk more. If you get there first, order me a dirty martini."

"Will do." Saunders clicked off.

A few minutes past noon, Ajay Kumar sat at his desk ruminating. In many ways, it felt like a typical Monday, with leftover work from the weekend bleeding into the new week. But in one very big way, this Monday was what he'd dreaded for years.

From the beginning, Hicks had insisted that McArthur achieve top-decile pregnancy rates. He had overridden Kumar's preference for taking a year or two to refine their processes and work their way into that elite group. In those early years, Kumar felt he had no choice but to go along with the shady practice of "augmenting" some patient samples with potent donor sperm to improve the rates. His justification had been that it was a *temporary* measure to achieve a desirable outcome. However, Hicks had kept up the pressure, and after a few months, the "temporary" fix had become more or less the de facto practice for certain couples undergoing IVF. And it had worked, leading the clinic to national and international fame.

As their reputation increased, so did the workload. The past few weeks had been intense, and he and the two assistants were working ten-hour days. On top of that, the sperm bank was running low on samples, and he was responsible for managing it since the director position he'd requested twice hadn't been filled due to university-wide budget cuts. A week ago, Dr. DuPage offered to assist with the donor program as part of his visiting professor assignment, and it had seemed like a godsend.

Thanks to the efforts of DuPage and Richard Carnegie, the bank recruited five new donors and the inventory was up to date. While this alleviated much of his workload, Kumar now wondered if this decision had somehow triggered the current investigation.

His stomach rumbled even though he didn't feel hungry. He grabbed his lunch and carefully locked both his office and the outer lab door, grimly smiling at the irony. *"Locking the barn door after the horse has escaped."* Stepping into the bright autumn day, he zipped his jacket and headed toward the park. In spite of the warm sun, he shivered. He had some tough decisions to make.

He ambled slowly, lost in thought, oblivious to the riot of fall colors surrounding him. He carefully reviewed the morning's events, starting with his arrival. He'd been an hour later than usual because he'd wanted to accompany his wife and Riya to an early morning appointment. Although Richard hadn't been at his work bench, he'd merely noted this as unusual but not alarming. He'd felt a warning tremor when he read a note from Richard saying he was at an audit with Vice President Welch. His concern escalated when Richard returned in an agitated state.

Waving his arms and pacing the length of the lab, Richard described answering several questions about the use of donor sperm during IVF. Kumar had winced when he mentioned giving Welch a copy of patients in cycle for the past four weeks containing notations about donor sperm. The young man was indignant because Welch had inferred some patients were being inseminated erroneously, and he'd admitted to her he didn't know why two patients on the current week's list were missing written consents for use of donor sperm. He'd defensively reminded Kumar that he wasn't responsible for the consent forms.

Kumar had ushered him into his office and tried to calm him, but Richard, sitting on the edge of the chair, remained tense. "You don't get it," he'd shouted. "I didn't do anything wrong. You know I follow instructions! I'm always careful. I know how important our work is. We're talking about people's lives, their families."

Abruptly, he'd changed topics. "I have no idea how those lists are generated, do you? I've always assumed they came from the clinic. I'm just the lab guy. I don't look into patient records. Jeez, I'm applying to medical school. No one will admit me if they think I did something illegal."

Kumar deliberately ignored the question about the lists. If there was a problem, he assured Richard, he would tell Ms. Welch that Richard wasn't at fault. As he entered the park, he hoped he could keep that promise. He felt sorry for Richard's distress, but he needed to focus on his own part in the rapidly unraveling situation. The more he thought about it, the more convinced he became that he'd be left holding the bag. Once again, Hicks would get away scot-free.

Kumar plopped onto an empty park bench. He absently munched some naan while sorting through options. Finally, he extracted a family photo from his wallet, taken last summer on a vacation in Myrtle Beach. He looked at it sadly and wondered how he was going to face his wife and daughter. Their lives would be ruined, and it was all his fault. As guilt assailed him, he rued the day he'd met Owen Hicks.

Sitting in the warm sun, he closed his eyes and repeated his favorite mantra. Although not a practicing Hindu, Kumar still remembered the prayers he'd learned as a child. In a few moments, his face relaxed and he leaned into the calm. His path forward was clear. After stuffing the remains of the uneaten lunch in the bag, he looked at his watch and calculated the time difference between Richmond, Virginia, and Chennai, India. He dialed, hoping his brother was awake.

"Hello. Ajay is that you?" a resonant voice said in Tamil.

"Sanjay, I'm so glad to hear your voice," Ajay answered in Tamil. Then he switched to English, "Are you alone?"

"I'm in my study. I think everyone else is in bed."

"Good. Listen, brother, I'm in trouble, big trouble. I may need to send my wife and daughter to stay with you for a while."

"Of course, Nita and Riya are always welcome. But what's happening?" Sanjay asked in alarm. "Are you ill?"

"No, much worse. I may go to jail. My lab has been involved in some shady practices for a while, and it's about to blow up."

"Surely it can't be that bad."

"I think it might be," Ajay said wearily. "And I've decided to come clean. I'm through with lies and deceit. I only hope I haven't hurt too many people, and that, someday, they may find it in their hearts to forgive me."

"You're scaring me," Sanjay said. "Please don't do anything rash. Whatever it is, get a good lawyer and talk it through."

"I know what I did. I want to blame my boss who is a pig and a bully. But in the end, I went along because I wanted to stay in America. I needed a steady job to support my family." Sounding ashamed, he added, "And I wanted to share in his fame."

"This is not like you," Sanjay said. "You have always been a good and honorable man. What does this boss have over you?"

"Something happened a long time ago, in medical school. It's too long to explain, but he's held it over me ever since. But no more, I'm done doing his dirty work and covering it up."

"Ajay, please slow down and think this through" Sanjay

implored. "Do you need money for a lawyer? I can arrange a bank transfer tomorrow."

"I don't think money can fix this. Right now, it's enough to know my family will have a home. I have to go. There is much to do. I'll be in touch. And thanks for being such a good brother."

"You know I'm always here for you. And I'll take good care of your family and find Riya good doctors. Be safe."

Kumar stood up and walked toward his office. A couple emerged from the imposing entrance clutching an ultrasound picture and talking excitedly about their pregnancy. Witnessing their happiness, Kumar allowed himself to feel a small measure of pride. He prayed he'd done more good than harm during his time at McArthur. Then he resolutely turned his back on the Institute and headed toward a new destination.

***

"Come on, Joyce. Pick up, pick up!" Bill swore softly as her cheerful voice directed him to leave a message for the third time in an hour. He rarely called her at work because she usually didn't answer, but after reading her earlier text referencing "fecal matter hitting the oscillating unit," he'd decided to make an exception. Details had been minimal, other than reference to an investigation and heads rolling. Bill sincerely hoped her boss was the first to get the ax.

He turned to his office mate. "Hey, Jake. Would you cover for me this afternoon? I'm supposed to staff a Stats tutoring session at three. Only about eight kids usually show, so it shouldn't take more than an hour."

Jake swiveled his chair. "What's up?"

Bill hastily shoveled research notes into his bag. "I'm going to Richmond."

"Weren't you just there?"

"Yeah, but something's come up. My wife's in the middle of

an ugly work situation. I got a text from her about an hour ago. They've started an investigation."

"What kind of situation? Is she being sued?"

"Not sure. I don't have time to go into it. All I know is she's worried she might lose her job."

"Whoa, that sounds serious. Sure, I'll cover, but you owe me a beer."

"No problemo, I'll buy you two." Bill grabbed his stuff and bolted for the door. "Thanks, man. I owe you."

Owen Hicks emerged from Warren Beck's office, his face contorted with rage. He could hardly believe it. They'd put him on administrative leave. The whole idea was preposterous. He was a world-renowned figure, a pioneer in his field.

In a rational corner of his mind, he congratulated himself for maintaining his cool. Paul Saunders had been adamant it was best for him to appear without legal representation and act dumbfounded by any accusation.

In the end, it hadn't been difficult. He wasn't surprised to learn about Joyce Porter's complaint, but he'd been truly shocked when Beck and some fresh-faced attorney had played a recording of their hotel room conversation while Welch drilled him with an icy stare. He'd never liked that woman.

In spite of the recording, he felt he'd skillfully denied any wrongdoing and expressed only heartfelt concern for Dr. Porter's wellbeing. Fortunately, parts of the recording were muffled. In response to an inquiry about possible misuse of donor sperm, he'd spun a tale about her desperate quest for success at any cost, then clammed up, insisting he'd answer no further questions without his attorney.

Warren Beck walked silently at his side. When they reached his office, he noted with relief that Esmeralda was gone for the day. Under Beck's watchful eye, he surrendered his laptop and keys. When Beck tried to take his cell phone, he refused, claiming it was his personal property. Shrugging, Beck took his time searching Hicks's briefcase. With this ritual complete, the duo strode somberly to the building exit.

Hicks glared at him. "My lawyer will be in touch," he growled. Without a backward glance, he walked to his car.

Sinking into the luxurious leather, his mind whirred as he considered next steps. Finally, he called his longtime friend and colleague, Jackson Cobain.

"Hello?"

"Jackson, it's me. What the hell is going on? That wimp Beck and some smartass attorney put me on administrative leave!"

Silence.

"Are you still there?" Hicks said in a near shout.

"Yes."

"What do you know about this? That business in New Orleans was a misunderstanding. Porter was really ill, and I was just trying to help."

More silence.

"Call them and tell them I didn't have anything to do with unauthorized use of donors. That was Porter wanting to make a name for herself. She's a nasty piece of work."

"Owen, there's proof," Cobain said.

"What proof?" Hicks sputtered. "You mean that barely audible fake recording? That could be anyone."

"I shouldn't be talking to you, but I have one thing to say."

"What's that?"

"Get a good lawyer."

As the line went silent, Hicks sat in stunned disbelief. He was in deep trouble. Because of their friendship, he'd always enjoyed a privileged status at the university, but it seemed friendship had its limits. It was almost five p.m., and he supposed he should go home, pour a double scotch, and call Saunders. But he couldn't face home where he'd have to engage in pointless chatter with his wife about her volunteer work or latest fitness fad.

How dare they humiliate me? he thought as his jaw clenched. *Joyce Porter is to blame and, by God, if I'm going down, so is she!*

He drove his car to the public lot in the park across from the Institute. It offered a good vantage point of the employee lot where his luxury vehicle would have looked out of place among the employees' more modest sedans and trucks. Over the next half hour, a steady stream of workers hustled to their rides and headed home. Finally, only a few vehicles remained. He felt no surprise Joyce wasn't part of the exodus, as she often worked late.

Lacking a key to enter through the Employee Only door, he climbed from his car and headed to the main entrance. The public entrances of university buildings didn't automatically lock until six p.m. He strolled through the luxurious lobby, noting the fountain, the modern wall sculpture, and the well-tended greenery. As always, its style and grandeur filled him with pride. He'd built this program and its reputation from scratch, and no one was going to take it away from him.

"Damn you, Joyce Porter," he cursed, mildly surprised that he'd spoken aloud. He spun around, relieved to find himself alone in the cavernous space.

He heard a rattling sound, and the IVF clinic door inched open. He instinctively stepped behind one of the large potted palms and watched as a bulky cleaning cart emerged, followed by the evening custodian, earbuds in place, head bobbing rhythmically. The door swung closed as he stooped to pick up a fallen rag. Stuffing it into a bag swinging from the cart, he slowly made his way across the lobby and entered the hallway leading to the labs.

When the man was out of sight, Hicks approached the clinic door cautiously. He hadn't really planned how he was going to get in without a key. He had a penknife but wasn't ready to stoop to breaking and entering. He gently tugged on the door, and to his amazement, it popped open. He entered the darkened waiting area, then pulled the door closed, listening for the click.

Satisfied it was secure, he crossed the room in five large strides. The door to the back office was propped open, and he continued uninterrupted. He walked quietly past several closed doors toward the end office and a pool of light.

Peering inside, he saw Joyce bent over a lower desk drawer. After retrieving her purse, she swiveled and carefully lifted her head. She started, dropping her purse, as Owen Hicks stepped into her office and closed the door with an ominous click.

CHAPTER 30

Joyce swallowed reflexively as she took in the menacing sight of Hicks. He vibrated with anger, and she found his flushed cheeks, disheveled clothing, and clenched fists particularly unnerving. The can of pepper spray in the bottom of her purse was too far away. She considered shouting for help but wondered if anyone would hear her given the late hour.

"Dr. Hicks, why are you here?" she asked in a hoarse whisper.

His eyes glittered with rage as he hissed, "I'm here to ask what the hell you think you're doing—lodging a baseless HR complaint against me. On top of that, you're blaming *me* for questioning *your* use of donor sperm to inflate the pregnancy rates of *your* patients. All specious accusations, and stupid too. You have a lot to lose if any of this comes out."

She couldn't believe Hicks was threatening her again. In the logical part of her brain, she wasn't surprised he'd turned the whole situation back at her. He'd promised as much in New Orleans. Her primitive brain, however, was fully engaged in the "fight or flight" response. Although she'd feared his wrath, she'd never imagined a physical confrontation. Less than an hour ago,

Beck had informed her that Hicks was on administrative leave and barred from the campus.

Yet here he was, and she was utterly alone. She had no evening plans, and no one knew she was in her office. She couldn't depend on Landry and Hebert to save the day. Her primitive brain screamed at her to flee, and she briefly wondered if she could skirt the desk fast enough to kick him in the balls and escape.

Hicks, intuiting her thoughts, gave a harsh laugh. "You can't escape, and there's no one here if you call for help. They've all left for the evening."

"The evening custodian usually comes in about now," she lied.

"Nice try," he scoffed. "I just saw him leave. And I doubt he'd hear you anyway. He was listening to music, off in his own little world."

"What do you want?"

He ignored the question and glared at her. Something in his arrogant stance ignited her own fury. She'd had enough. No more pandering to this sociopath. She wasn't going to run, she was going to fight. It was time someone stood up and held him accountable. She recognized the danger in poking the bear, but she was done tiptoeing around.

She shoved her chair back and stood. Hicks was not a tall man, but he still had at least four inches on her, so she tilted her head and looked him square in the eye. "I didn't go to Welch and ask her to start an investigation. I went because you threatened to tell lies about my work and my patients if I didn't sleep with you."

"So you say," he sneered. "It's your word against mine. The way I remember it, you came onto me. You aren't the first ambitious woman to try and sleep her way to the top. The president and trustees know that. And nice try deflecting the blame for your donor sperm swindle on me. You won't be able to make that stick either."

"I know I'm not the first woman you've treated this way," she shot back. "There are others who've been afraid to talk, but they've come forward. It's time it stopped. It's time *you* stopped. And I'd *never* use donor sperm without consent!"

"Prove it," he taunted. "I have a lot more pull around here than you ever will. Everyone knows you are a ruthless career-climbing bitch who's desperate to make a name for herself. Your schemes and lies will destroy your career and hurt your patients."

"That's not true—"

"Save your breath. How many lives do you think will be ruined if patients worry their husband might not be the father of their baby? How many marriages will sour, and how many kids will grow up wondering who their 'real' dad is, and if they have siblings?"

Time stopped as she processed Hicks's words. She felt a flicker of shame because she hadn't fully considered the impact of this scandal on her patients. She'd been too focused on calling out Hicks, forcing him to be accountable, and saving her own neck. She pictured Evie and Leon, faces beaming as they viewed the sonogram of their twins, followed by a mental slide show of other couples who'd conceived against all odds. How many of those pregnancies were the result of unconsented donor treatment? The sheer volume of potential heartache threatened to overwhelm her. Who was she to unleash such a torrent of pain and chaos?

The parade of faces was replaced by an image of her father, his deep voice telling her how proud he was at the time she'd stood up to the mean girls. "Never be afraid to do the right thing," he'd said. And then she knew. The best way she could help her patients was to stand up and fight.

"You are an evil man," she said, fists clenched. "And if our patients' lives are ruined, it's on you and the people you suckered into your vile scheme. How long did you think you could get away with it? *You* betrayed our patients, not me! Kumar's come clean, you know, and he's been very clear that you were the mastermind. I may get dragged into it, but I will do everything in my power to provide our patients with the support they need to move forward and reclaim their lives."

"Brave words but meaningless," he mocked.

She seized the desk phone receiver and shook it like a police baton. "Screw you! Leave now or I'm calling the police."

"I think not." Hicks snatched the receiver from her hand and threw it to the floor. She moved from behind the protection of the desk and lunged for the door, but in the small confines of the office, Hicks got there first. He was so close she could see the large pores on his bulbous nose and smell the cloying scent of his aftershave. As he grabbed her sweater, her tai chi training kicked in and she unexpectantly yielded toward him while twisting sideways. She swung her hands out and then down to dislodge his grip on her clothes. She quickly followed with a head butt and a knee to his groin combined with a two-handed backward shove. The desk lamp crashed to the floor, and Hicks lay sprawled across the desk, nose bloodied, and eyes dazed.

In class, Master Chan always made his students practice the movements slowly, deliberately tracing the energy flow from their thoughts to their actions, yin into yang, defense into offense, but he'd also shown them the martial arts applications for each traditional move. It was that training that had taken over her thoughts and actions when Hicks grabbed her. Unexpectedly, she smiled. She'd added the head butt on her own, but she thought Master Chan would approve.

Bill pulled open the plate glass doors leading into McArthur's pretentious lobby and rushed in. He'd driven ten miles over the speed limit the entire trip but got bogged down in rush-hour traffic outside the city. He'd spotted Joyce's car in the parking lot and felt relieved she was still here. En route, he'd received a text saying she was fine, but he couldn't shake the feeling he was reliving the New Orleans nightmare. On the drive down, he'd considered alerting the campus police, then dismissed that idea. They'd think he was nuts.

He frowned as he faced the locked door to the clinic reception area. He turned the knob and rattled the door slightly.

"The clinic's closed for the evening," called a voice with a slight European accent from the opposite side of the lobby.

A handsome dark-haired man in a trench coat with a well-worn messenger bag slung over his shoulder crossed toward him. Bill didn't see an ID badge, but the man appeared to be an employee.

"Perhaps you can help me. I'm supposed to meet my wife, Dr. Joyce Porter, but she isn't answering her phone. I saw her car in the lot, so I'm assuming she's still here."

The dark-haired man studied him for a moment, then stuck out his hand. "You must be Bill. I'm Dominique DuPage, a colleague of your wife. I thought you were in Baltimore."

Bill immediately stiffened. *So, this is the mysterious Dr. DuPage,* he thought. This was the man she'd dined with in New Orleans. He appeared polished, urbane and professional, and Bill felt a searing jolt of jealousy. Maybe his marriage was in worse shape than he'd imagined. He returned the handshake, trying to make his grip a bit firmer.

"At lunch, she texted me about an investigation. She sounded upset. I know she's had some trouble with her boss."

Dominique's face remained impassive.

Bill added defensively, "I was worried and decided to come. Would you please unlock this door?"

Dominique slowly withdrew a key from an inside pocket. "Let's walk down to her office together." As they entered the back corridor, a loud crash followed by the sound of breaking glass pierced the quiet, and both men sprinted toward the noise. Bill got there first and shoved the door.

As it exploded inward, Joyce barely had time to step back. Her steely eyes met the worried gazes of Bill and Dominique.

"Are you okay?" they said simultaneously. Then they took in the moaning figure on the desk, his bloodied nose and the broken lamp.

"What happened?" Bill asked.

"Dr. Hicks showed up and threatened me, so I decided to practice my tai chi. I think his nose may be broken. I was about to call the campus police. He may need medical care."

CHAPTER 31

Over the next two weeks, a swarm of lawyers huddled behind closed doors with university leadership and the Board of Trustees. They'd managed to keep a lid on the story of the after-hours encounter between Drs. Hicks and Porter, but word quickly spread that both Hicks and Kumar were on leave. Neither answered their phone, and email queries resulted in automated "out of office" messages.

Dr. DuPage was temporarily assigned to oversee the lab, and all the techs except Richard Carnegie were suddenly given two weeks' paid vacation. When questioned about the unexpected changes, Dr. Porter said she couldn't confirm or deny any details. The rumor mill zoomed into overdrive when new patient visits were suspended, and all future IVF cycles placed on hold due to vague "safety" concerns. People spoke in hushed tones, and the atmosphere was grim. The phone chimed constantly. Patient calls were answered by confused nurses with a generic message and a promise to return their call when they knew more.

The internet exploded once McArthur posted a message on Facebook and Twitter stating, "All fertility services, including in vitro fertilization, are temporarily suspended pending an investigation into possible inconsistencies regarding use of donor sperm." More than one hundred patients who had become pregnant simultaneously received registered letters referencing the "possible inconsistencies" and were directed to call and arrange counseling and/or genetic testing as appropriate.

In a separate internal announcement, Human Resources Director Beck informed staff that Dr. Hicks and Dr. Kumar had resigned, and Dr. Alan Meijer had been appointed temporary department chair. Until further notice, Dr. Joyce Porter was overseeing all operations at the McArthur Institute.

Leon tucked into a ham-and-cheese sandwich and checked his phone. It was midafternoon, and he had the lunchroom to himself. He almost ignored a text from his mother until he noticed it mentioned McArthur. He clicked on the link and read a brief item quoting a statement posted by the university on Twitter. It mentioned safety concerns at the IVF clinic and something about donor sperm. He decided it didn't really concern them since they hadn't used donor sperm. He switched to a news item about the Tennessee Titans and finished his lunch. As he was throwing away his trash and preparing to head back to the shop, his phone rang. It was Evie. He felt a stab of concern. She usually texted when he was at work. He prayed there wasn't a problem.

"Hey, what's up? Are you okay?"

"I'm fine, and the babies are fine," she said in a rush. "When I got home from work, there was a note in the mailbox about a registered letter. Someone has to sign for it. Can you get off a little early and swing by the post office to pick it up since you have the car?"

"I guess I can do that. We're almost done for the day. But why are you home from work?"

"Remember, I've cut down my hours and today is one of my early days."

"Oh, that's right. Okay, I'll talk to the boss. I don't think he'll have a problem with me leaving a few minutes early."

"Who do you think would send us a registered letter?"

"No idea. I guess we'll find out. See you soon."

After hanging up, Leon returned to the text message and reread the article about McArthur and frowned. Could the registered letter have something to do with the article he'd just read? He'd never received a registered letter, but he remembered one of the shop guys getting one from a collection agency because he was three months behind on his car payment. He didn't think they were behind on any bills, but the IVF treatment had sapped most of their savings. He entered the garage and hurried over to ask the manager if he could leave a few minutes early.

Leon sat in the car, hands trembling, and reread the letter. His heart thudded and he noticed his hands were sweating. He and Evie hadn't used donor sperm, so why had they gotten this letter? Had someone made a mistake? Suddenly, he remembered that terrible article his mother had sent about the embryo mix-up in California. "Oh no," he prayed. "Please Dear Lord, not us."

He finally started the car and took the long way home to give himself time to think. Evie would know something was wrong the minute he walked through the door. About thirty seconds later, his phone chirped. At the next stoplight, he looked down and noticed she'd texted, *???* He ignored it.

She pounced on him the moment he stepped inside. "Don't make me wait. Who was it from?"

"McArthur."

"Why would they send us a letter?"

"Maybe you'd better read it."

He led her to the sofa and sat silently while she read.

Finally, she looked up. "I don't understand."

"Me neither. We didn't use donor sperm."

"Do you think somehow they might have accidently used some?"

His face wore a deep frown, and his Adam's apple bobbed as he swallowed. "Maybe."

"Is this like the mixed-up embryos from that California clinic?"

"Absolutely not! Those people had the wrong babies."

She slowly folded the letter and put it back into the envelope. "So, what do we do next?"

"I guess we call that number." He glanced at the clock. "It's too late now. Maybe first thing tomorrow."

"I wish we could talk to Dr. Porter."

"Do you still have her number from when she called us that weekend you had the bleeding?"

"I think so."

"Then let's call her now."

They placed the call and were disappointed when it went to voicemail. Evie left a short message saying they'd received a registered letter and asked Dr. Porter to call back as soon as possible.

Dinner was a quiet affair. They'd both received worried calls from their families, who'd heard about McArthur's problems on the news, and cut the conversations short. After washing and drying the dishes, Leon cleared his throat. "What if they didn't use my sperm?" he said quietly. "What if they used a donor? I might not be the father."

"Leon, we don't know that," Evie said as she rushed to embrace him.

He stood stiffly in her arms.

He stepped back, took out his phone, and pulled up the story from earlier in the day. The item had been updated with news of Hicks and Kumar's resignations. The comment section had over a hundred remarks, many from men with the same concerns as

Leon. Evie pulled him into a fierce embrace. He rested his head against her hair while they slowly rocked back and forth.

Bill watched as Joyce listened to a voicemail and frowned. She had deep circles under her eyes and had lost weight. The barrage of phone calls from patients and colleagues had been continuous. On top of that, she'd been working ten-hour days and was even going in on weekends, which didn't make any sense to him since the IVF program was suspended. When he'd asked, she'd repeated some legal mumbo jumbo about an ongoing investigation. He'd pressed for details, and she'd told him she was reviewing hundreds of patient and lab records going back to the beginning of the clinic. She said she had daily meetings with Mary Francis and the hospital attorneys that sometimes lasted hours. It appeared that use of donor sperm without consent wasn't just a recent "lapse in protocol." He didn't think physically or emotionally she could keep up the pace.

Ever since Hicks had attacked her two weeks ago, he'd stayed in Richmond, and he planned on staying at least through December. He'd received permission to work remotely and was grateful he hadn't had to choose between his marriage and his graduate program. Dr. Smythe had been disappointed when he'd turned down the spot on the WHO team, but he'd assured her he'd stay on top of his research and writing. He'd taken on another assignment for his "free time" and promised to check in weekly.

"That call was from another one of my patients," she said. "She and her husband got one of those letters from the university's risk management team. I really want to call her back, but I'm exhausted. And they'll ask for reassurance I can't give them."

He handed her a glass of red wine. "It can wait until tomorrow. Come and eat dinner—your favorite, minestrone soup, caprese salad, and fresh bread."

"What's the latest the internet is saying about this mess?" she asked while they ate. "I haven't had time to check out today's stories, but one of the clinic nurses said she heard a news item on NPR while she was driving to work today, so I guess we've made national news."

"The usual mud fest. Don't waste your time. They really don't know anything, so they're making stuff up and filling the space with 'expert' opinions that are purely speculative."

"It figures. As if the patients aren't already terrified."

Her shoulders slumped. "I hate this, and I don't know when it will end."

He took her hand. "Probably not for a while. Now it's someone else's problem to manage. You've been burning the candle at both ends, and I'm worried about you. Can you take a few days off to sleep, maybe get a massage? Do tai chi?"

"Not really. The news outlets call daily. We have a PR person, but she calls me to help craft replies to technical questions. And even though new-patient visits and fertility procedures are suspended, we're still seeing patients with other endocrine problems like polycystic ovary disease or premature menopause. Starting tomorrow, we're counseling couples who may have conceived from donor sperm they didn't request. I'm dreading those conversations, but it has to be done as soon as possible."

"What will they do?"

"We'll offer them genetic testing and counseling. Beyond that, I guess it all depends on the lawsuits."

"Have any been filed?"

"Not yet," she said wearily. "But the university was contacted by a big New York law firm that specializes in class action cases, and it's almost certain something is coming. There could also be individual suits for neglect and distress. It will take years."

"How about Hicks and Kumar?"

"Rumor has it that Kumar's family is back in India. I don't think he's allowed to leave the country. Hicks lost his national committee assignments and all his speaking invitations. He may lose his medical license."

"Sounds like he got off easy."

"Oh, it's not done. The malpractice insurance may not cover him if he's personally sued, so he'll be ruined financially as well. And someone said his wife and daughters left him and moved to Minnesota."

Bill sighed. "It sounds like there is no end in sight anytime soon. What about Sally? And DuPage?"

"Dominique only ever planned to be here for six months, so he'll go back to France in a few months. He's been wonderful to have around, so supportive and helpful in dealing with the distraught patients and the lab issues."

Bill felt a recurring pang of jealousy but realized he should be grateful to DuPage for lightening Joyce's workload. He also knew he'd be fooling himself if he didn't acknowledge that meeting DuPage had caused him to realize he needed to be in Richmond to support his wife—Ph.D. or no Ph.D.

"Sally and I haven't talked much. There's been no time for our weekly lunches. I know she's happy Hicks is gone, but she's worried. She hasn't said so, but one of our nurses told me she's applying for positions in Texas and on the West Coast."

"What will happen to McArthur, long term?"

"I guess the university will keep going. They've got deep pockets and this is an isolated problem in our department. I expect they'll shut down the IVF program or maybe close the whole Institute, at least for a time. There are other IVF programs in our region." A sad smile graced her dejected expression. "They'll probably want me to stay around until the bitter end. I'll be the one who turns out the lights."

"I know this isn't the right time to make plans, but then what? Will you look for another job?"

She rubbed her eyes, slightly bloodshot from lack of sleep. "I can't even think about that. I might not be able to get another job. Hicks said my career would be finished if any of this became public, and he may be right. No one will want me while McArthur is still radioactive. And to be honest, I'm not even sure I want to stay in the field, too many unanswered ethical questions that no one wants to talk about. Just because we have the technology to do something, does that mean we should?"

They moved to the living room and sat on the couch. He put his arm around her shoulders and pulled her close.

"I'm so sorry you're stuck in the middle of this," he said gently, kissing the top of her head. "I admire you so much for standing up to Hicks and being there for your patients. They'll be grateful for you as they sort through their concerns and emotions."

"It's so hard. Risk Management thinks everyone should get genetic testing, so they know for sure if they received a donor, but I'm not sure. Some people might not want to know. Would you?"

Bill hugged her, then turned her face to his and tenderly kissed her lips. "I pray we never find ourselves in this situation. But when the time comes, I think we're going to be great parents, and I'll love our baby no matter what."

She sat up and searched his face, "Does that mean . . . ?"

"Yes."

"It may take a while, you know. We're both older and . . ."

Bill chuckled and cut her off with a deeper longer kiss. Pulling her onto his lap, they made out like teenagers. When they came up for air, he said, "You think too much. I'm staying in Richmond until all this is sorted, so we have plenty of time to enjoy the process."

Joyce smiled her first real smile in days.

Evie and Leon Coleman entered the lobby of the McArthur Fertility Institute and stood closely together. She absently rubbed a barely visible baby bump. The water feature splashed gently but failed to induce any sense of calm. They barely glanced at the opulent surroundings as they slowly approached the mahogany door with the discreet nameplate.

"Should we throw a coin in the fountain for good luck?" he asked.

She paused, remembering the last time they'd tossed in a coin, then took his hand. "We don't need luck." As he reached to open the door into the empty waiting room, she stopped him gently and whispered, "Leon, I love you, and I love our babies. No matter what."

He gently squeezed back, "Me too. Now let's get this over with. I bet our kiddos are hungry for ice cream."

EPILOGUE

On an unseasonably warm December day, Joyce discovered two envelopes with U.S. postmarks in the afternoon post. She rarely got mail from the States since most of their family and friends communicated via email or video chat. She smiled at the return address on the first. It was a Christmas card from Evie and Leon Coleman. Her stomach clenched and she felt a wave of nausea when she looked at the second. It was from McArthur.

She fanned herself with the envelopes and brushed back a strand of long blond hair. As she walked the short distance to their bungalow, she savored her rare day off. Three-year-old Max had gone down for a nap, and Bill was off with the Cholera Response Team. He was due back tonight. She had a few hours to herself and was looking forward to a nap. She was eight weeks pregnant with their second child and afternoon fatigue was a daily occurrence. Morning sickness had been minimal, so the nausea was probably from the unexpected McArthur communication. *What could they possibly want?*

Tapping the envelope nervously, she realized she hardly ever thought about McArthur. Five years had done a lot to dull the painful memories. She'd heard Hicks had been stripped of his medical license and was in prison. No one seemed to know what had happened to Kumar. She bet some of her previous patients, like the Goldschmidts, were no longer together. She felt a pang of sadness mixed with guilt as she wondered how the couples who'd unwittingly received donor sperm were doing. She worried she could have done more.

In her current job at Doctors Without Borders Women's Clinic, her patients were women, and sometimes very young girls, who were all too often victims of sexual violence. She provided basic obstetric and gynecologic care and a safe space to talk about their concerns and challenges. It was demanding work and immensely rewarding and had almost nothing to do with her previous life.

As she opened the Colemans' holiday card, a picture fluttered to the floor. She retrieved it and examined it closely. The twins, Avery and Asha Rose, were dressed in matching elf costumes and sitting on Santa's lap. A brief note told her Leon had been promoted to lead mechanic, and they had recently moved into a small three-bedroom house near his parents. When the twins started preschool in September, Evie went back to work at the insurance company. They were all healthy and happy and wished the Porter family a joyful holiday season.

She grabbed a bottle of water and sat at her small desk before ripping open the McArthur letter. She scanned it and let out a short laugh. They were restarting their IVF Clinic and wanted her to come back. *As if . . .* she thought ruefully. Suddenly, she was filled with memories and a longing to go home. Home, where she could ask for ice water without worry. Home, where there was no threat of becoming ill from a tsetse fly. Home, where she could live in a two-story colonial with maple trees that turned russet and gold each fall.

She pondered her current life in Kenya. It was so much different than she'd ever imagined growing up in western Maryland. Bill was in heaven, doing work he found both interesting and meaningful. They had an international cadre of friends and a comfortable home. They went back to the U.S. for a month each year for R and R and to visit their families. After their last visit, Joyce had feigned excitement about returning to Nairobi, but deep inside she wished they didn't have to go.

She flipped through a string of pictures on her phone that had been taken on a recent weekend trip to a family-friendly resort on the coast of the Indian Ocean. Max, wearing a pool shirt and a floppy hat, was splashing on the steps of the kiddie pool. Bill was making a goofy face holding an umbrella drink, and fair-skinned Joyce was reading a romance novel on a chaise under a thatched cabana. Her family was thriving. Would they want to leave?

An hour later, the door flew open, and Bill bounded in. He tossed his duffle beside the couch just as Joyce emerged from the hall with a sleepy-looking Max on her hip. He kissed them both enthusiastically, then went to the refrigerator and grabbed a bottle of water.

"You're back early," she said. "Max and I just woke up from our naps."

"We got done sooner than expected," he said as he shuffled through the mail.

"Hey, who sent the Christmas card?"

"Evie and Leon. Their twins are in preschool now."

He frowned as he looked at the one from McArthur. "What do they want?"

She gave a short laugh. "For me to come back."

"You're kidding."

"Nope."

He shook his head then surprised her by saying, "I got a letter too. Well, an email really. A week ago, from one of my grad school pals. There's a job opening at the National Institute of Health, and he thinks I'd have a good shot. The City of Baltimore is also looking for a director of public health."

She put Max down next to his toy box and looked at Bill in

amazement. "Wow! Would you consider moving back? I thought you loved it here."

"I do, but I can tell you're ready to leave. I wasn't sure you were going to get on the plane after our last trip home."

"Why didn't you say anything?"

"Well, for one, you're pregnant."

"What does that have to do with it?"

He embraced her and kissed her forehead. "You can be a little emotional sometimes, especially during the first trimester. I know better than to rock the boat."

She laughed and snuggled closer. "That's kind of a sexist thing to say, but it's probably true. I haven't had any crying jags today, so let's talk."

"I've read the job postings, and I'm definitely qualified for both positions. It will take me a while to update my resume. And what about you—would you look for another IVF job or something else?"

"I have no desire to go back to work at McArthur or any other IVF clinic. Too much stress. I'd like to deliver our baby in a U.S. hospital and then take at least three months off. I'll look for work after that. Maybe in family planning or public health. Or maybe I'll go back to school."

"Really?" he said, looking intrigued. "And study what?"

"Maybe psychiatry . . . or law."

"Wow. That's quite a switch, and not at all related." He paused, "Well, kinda related. Some of those lawyers you worked with during that whole mess were a little crazy."

"I don't have to figure it out today, but it's something I've been thinking about."

"You know I'll support you one hundred percent, but I do have one request."

She cocked her head and looked at him quizzically. "What's that?"

"Whatever we do next, we both have to be in the same city."

AUTHOR'S NOTE

Although this story is a work of fiction, I drew on my experience and knowledge of medical situations and themes to help bring the characters and their struggles to life. While the descriptions of certain procedures and scenarios are based in fact, some details have been fictionalized. The focus of this work is on human experiences—courage, resilience, connection, and hope—not absolute medical facts.

If you are seeking information or guidance about infertility, I encourage you to consult a qualified healthcare professional or trusted resource, such as The Society for Assisted Reproductive Technologies (sart.org), the American College of Obstetricians and Gynecologists (acog.org), or RESOLVE: The National Infertility Association (resolve.org).

ACKNOWLEDGMENTS

Many thanks to my first readers, especially Carolyn Tate, Kathy Walsh, Diana Glenn, Mary Catherine Schumacher, Jan Knoll, and Beth Habian. I appreciate your insights, wisdom, and encouragement. And to my mentor and friend, Kathryn Mattingly, you've given me more than words can capture.

And finally, a special thank you to Marci Clark, Jessica Hammett, and all the talented professionals at Acorn Publishing for your patience and guidance during the "birthing" of this novel.

ABOUT THE AUTHOR

M.J. Kuhar worked in private practice as an OB-GYN for over a decade before shifting to a career in higher education, first as an assistant professor, then as a college dean, and finally as a vice president.

Her dedication to helping patients and students left her little time to write, but the idea for a novel stuck with her. Inspired by deeply moving stories of couples undergoing IVF, she developed her first novel, *In Vitro*.

Now retired, M.J. lives in the Pacific Northwest with her husband and a spicy cat named Simon. She volunteers at a local elementary school, where she reads with kindergartners to foster a love of books. Tai chi, crafting, and wine tasting are a few of her favorite hobbies.